*Leav

Leave No Trace:

FestiFell

Jordan McMahon

Copyright © Jordan McMahon, 2024

The rights of Jordan McMahon to be identified as the author of this work has been asserted in accordance with the Copyright, Designs and Patents Act, 1988

This is a work of fiction. Names, characters, places and incidents either are products of the author's imagination or are used fictitiously. Any resemblance to actual events or locales or persons, living or dead, is entirely coincidental.

Jordan McMahon

Thank you for choosing to read this book, by doing so you are supporting a dad buy his son a new Hot Wheels car, his wife a bunch of flowers, and himself a sandwich. If enough of you read it, I may be able to replace the old and battered sofa I am currently sat typing on, or even redecorate my sitting room.

One small favour if you enjoy this book: Pass on the word, give a nice review online, Instagram or tweet (or X or whatever you call it now), a nice message and share it with your following, gift someone a copy for Christmas or a birthday. Do what you can to help. It would be greatly appreciated. You are supporting a man pursue his long held dream. Be fully aware I appreciate it.

Big Love x

Leave No Trace

For M.G.M. you are my everything.

For L.M. the love of my life, always. x

'Someone passed some bliss among the crowd.' David Bowie

'...how everything turns away
Quite leisurely from the disaster; the ploughman may
Have heard the splash, the forsaken cry,
But for him it was not an important failure; the sun shone
As it had to on the white legs disappearing into the green
Water, and the expensive delicate ship that must have seen
Something amazing, a boy falling out of the sky,
Had somewhere to get to and sailed calmly on.' W.H Auden

Wednesday

Wednesday
Seb

So here we are - Battering along the dual carriageway with tarmac groan. Westbound and very nearly festival bound. Making brilliant time except for that inevitable dawdling tractor for the first ten miles of the journey. Spitting yellow hay into the verges. The air-con is howling at full blast, it's absolutely sweltering outside. Car's MPG rating is drastically reduced. Midday sun almost vertical above, boring through the sunroof and heating up the black plastic interior. It smells of stale air, like an old VHS after a thorough rewinding. Some old film taped off the telly by Dad. Save the money. Fast forward adverts like watching them in double speed through Venetian blinds. Radiated dashboard heat making my forehead salty and damp, armpits not fairing much better. I was already feeling moist from lugging all the camping gear from the loft into the car. Several back and forths. Cursing myself that I hadn't done that particular job earlier, roped Mia into helping out last night even. Lactic acid still aching away at my arms and shoulders as I steer roundabouts, junctions, and slip roads. The schools are striking today meaning I've had to juggle car loading with two separate kids' breakfasts, two packed lunches prepared, three sets of teeth brushed, two kids dressed, and shoes on with maximum resistance from the younger of the two. My own gear thrown on in haste. Then two kids packed up and delivered to their grandad's house. Not an easy task when already chock full of cortisol and fuelled with only strong coffee, all hot and bothered.

'I don't want to go! He's naughty!' Reuben running up the stairs for the seventh time. Hiding under the spare bed.

'Where do polar bears sleep?' Emily all coy grins followed by a great succession of, 'why?' questions. Shoes deliberately put on the wrong feet. Backwards beeping like a truck, retreating into the recesses of the dining room. Brash grins on defiant infant cheeks flushed with energy, wrestled from under the dining table. Dragged across woollen carpet leaving tramlines from pointy elbows.

'I'm hungry!' rummaging through the festival snack Sports Direct bag, Pringle crumbs strewn everywhere.

'I need Pushka!' a toy dinosaur which required several kitchen implements and a pulled shoulder muscle to reach and retrieve from behind a radiator. Luckily, it has not been on for a few months. The youngest one's sleeping companion squirrelled down as a sacrificial attempt to wind down the clock. A ploy that worked. I was dealt with a series of unwelcome roadblocks to the morning. They were running rings around me. I swear they can smell vulnerability. Get me to those bloody fields.

The packed lunches were consumed en-route to their grandad's house meaning they'll probably succumb to his awful idea of food after all. Some dreadful screechy nursery rhyme playlist kept them subdued as I mentally built myself up for the dread of an interaction with my old man. Upon arrival they feet drag up the driveway, reluctantly shuffling into his house as I exchange a few phatic pleasantries whilst handing over a satchel of their stuff. I try not to feel too enraged at the sly thinly veiled digs at how I'm parenting:

'His hair needs a cut,' as the youngest passes with a head scrub.

'Where's your jacket at?' as the older dips away from his pendulum hand and disappears inside in search of the Sky TV remote. A luxury treat they're not afforded at home, then again not quite the status symbol it was when I was a youngster.

'Dad man, it's like 30 degrees or something, they don't need a coat,' I snap, turning the latter part slightly musical, and therefore more jokey as I realise it's futile arguing. A well-worn tactic. I am, after all, in need of his assistance today. A debt that pains me.

'Aye wey,' he dismisses, Geordie accent more pronounced. I'll bottle up my anger as per usual, save that for another time. Probably at 3am one random sleepless night when the circus starts in my head. All the arguments I never had battle it out for attention.

'Say goodbye to your dad,' booms Grandad, knowing fine well I'm Daddy to the little critters. A subdued noise returns back, all final syllable 'iiiiii's.' They've no doubt already fallen under the dazzling spell combination of Grandad's telly and a battered, but admittedly, extremely comfortable sofa.

'Terrah... and thanks,' I part with. The door clashes behind me before I've even fastened my seatbelt or started the engine. Then I'm off with a car empty of kids, but a perfectly executed Tetris packed boot. It's remarkable how it's packed, no spare air gaps and no recoil when you whack the boot closed. One slight pull then, thunk, closed. Perfection. Almost feels a shame that in a few hours, I'll be spoiling that. There are a few things in the back seats of the car, something that annoys the perfectionist in me. It did consume a few minutes trying to fit them in. Can't win them all I suppose. A couple of camping chairs and the food bag. I'll be amazed if there wasn't some gnaw marks in the bag of sweet stuff after having those two locusts in the back before. They did seem too quiet for my liking. I switch the screechy nursery rhymes off and stick on Radio 2. The news is part way through, and I deliberately pay little attention as I head home to drop off the kids' seats.

As predicted, the space revealed upon removal of the seats shows a great snack graveyard. Having no time to hoover, I chuck a spare picnic blanket over the mess. Hiding the potato and corn-based evidence before I pick everyone up. Having no time to shower, I chuck a Greenpeace-angering amount of deodorant on, an ecological disaster under my armpits. I figure I'm going to smell at some point this weekend, but perhaps best not to do so quite so soon. Regardless of my sympathetic opinion on the climate, today the ozone can get stuffed.

I get to Jasmine's about 12:07, a bit late, which is an annoyance, but that's more down to the fact she sent me the wrong postcode. I've dropped her off at hers a thousand times after work, but never approached it from the other side of town. The postcode she shared takes you to the centre of a rather sizeable street. I had to do several laps of the road, which is littered with estate agents, kebab shops, a vape shop, barbers, and a few derelict pubs until I finally recognised Akbar's corner shop. A few doors down is 140B. I drive, squinting out the window reflections of the sun, moving at a snail's pace to count down the even door numbers. I look like some shite Northern England drive-by shooter. By the time I reach hers, I've received a few car horns in my direction and a definite wanker hand gesture from a rented white van driver. Why is it always the white vans? Honestly, lads, just take a break from it.

A small red wooden door I've parked outside of many times before is on the other side of the road today. The sun is unforgiving in showing that it is in dire need of a good sanding down and a good lick of paint, appearing almost brown in the light of the midday sun. Door number all oxidised and dull with toothpaste blue flakes. After a few minutes and a text message, her head appears at the upstairs window, she gestures with an open hand and exaggerated mouth mime meaning five minutes. I see this same gesture all the time at graft. Usually in response to me asking if she's coming for her lunch break. Mouthed 'five', she'll gesture whilst grappling with a telephone handset and computer mouse. Chin pinning phone to her clavicle, curly brown hair obscuring the phone.

I'm parked on double yellows, hawk-eyeing everyone as a potential parking attendant. Engine switches into CO_2 saving mode. Tinnitus replaces pistons. I turn off the air-con to concentrate. Another sweeping glance looking for anyone official in appearance and with no yellow hi-vis in sight I check my emails. There's quite a lengthy follow-up one from a recruiter who, just a few weeks ago, had seen my CV online, offering a 'great opportunity', for 'progression and uncapped earning potential', at a 'dynamic and ambitious business'. Corporate bullshit I know, but I went along with the first interview, mainly due to my wife's encouragement, only to become more and more intrigued by the job on offer. They seemed keen and I began to wonder, picturing a bright new future. Maybe it was a great sales pitch by them, or maybe, despite my protestations that I'm not totally money-driven, I am indeed driven by the potential of an upgrade to this car, getting that extra bedroom and bathroom in a house in the catchment area of an OFSTED 'Outstanding' secondary school, the Barker and Stonehouse sofa and matching snuggle seat, and to add another star on the hotel that we holiday in as a family. I skim-read the email, it's interview feedback, I've had two interviews so far. They'd tried to call me before, but I hadn't answered. Aye, I was too busy wrestling with the bairns, shoving toothbrushes towards scrunched-up faces. Upon glance it's complimentary. 'Enjoyed our conversation', blah blah, 'would like to explore further.' The recruiter has a little summary for me to read, says he has spoken to the MD, and thinks they're pretty certain to offer me a position next week unless anything crazy happens over the weekend. They want to talk numbers. Okay, well

I'm interested, my increased heartbeat confirms this. Shallow ego massaged sufficiently by corporate speak. The recruiter wants to set up a final chat with the top brass very soon, just to iron everything out. The haste due to the nature of the project that the company is working on. A mixture of emotions hit me, the excitement of something new 'a change is as good as a rest', as my dad often would apply to absolutely everything except anything that would directly impact him. Easily spoken words from a man who worked at the same firm for forty-two years. There's also an overwhelming anxiety that hits me over the prospect of change. Thirteen years in the same company is quite some time, I'm comfortable. Bored yes, but also very comfortable. Institutionalised even. I don't want to wind up like my dad, though I would however take his final salary pension, but never mind. My current role doesn't really impact my day-to-day home life. Clock in, do, go home. That's all there is to it. Get a reasonable enough wage every four weeks. Rinse and repeat. Maybe I'm complacent. An underachiever. No, it's been a decent enough job, mainly because of the people I work with, I'd call them colleagues mainly, not friends. But nevertheless, I'd be leaving some pretty solid people. Mainly Jasmine.

Just as I begin typing up my reply there is a rap on the window. Fuck, Traffic Officer? No, it's Jasmine pulling an exaggerated daft kid's TV presenter face, wide-mouthed and wide-eyed. I open the window. Asphalt stench from the melting road wafts in. Diesel fumes and the sound of everyday life becomes sharper. Like it does when you surface from underwater at the local pool. Been a while since I've had that though, what with the council closing our nearest.

'Alreet? In you come.' I say, as she skips around onto the pavement and into the passenger side, chucking herself into the seat.

'Morning,' she says. Deeply exhaling.

'Afternoon actually,' I correct, 'one rucksack? I'm well impressed.'

'Yes, and my handbag. I'm very proud of myself on that one, only brought the essentials,' she beams as I spot earplugs, a pocket poncho, and what I'd hazard a guess is an eye mask in the mesh side pocket of the bag. Good shout that.

'I'm surprised at that like. You ready?'

'Absolutely,' seatbelt stretch sounds like a vinyl record scratch. With that, we set off leaving the enormous street which she lives on, down the familiar slip road which I use five times a week, and along the dual carriageway. We debrief on our respective mornings as the motorway turns into a rural A-road as we head to

Shaun's flat. It's been quite some time since I've been around these parts and every so often, I get that stomach anxiety churn that I may have taken a wrong turn. Jasmine's patter is distracting my full concentration, but no sooner does that notion cross my mind then I spot a point of interest that I recognise. It's usually a pub truth be told. I'm thinking of the reply to the recruiter and how I'll have to slide off to a motorway service station toilets to type up my response. A mental flick of my diary tries to visualise the best day to arrange a chat with my prospective new employer. Definitely not at the beginning of next week, no way. I'm no youngster anymore and based on previous experience I'll need to write off at least up till Wednesday, or even Thursday. My brain will be a foggy mess, thoughts wading through sludge as my liver works overtime breaking down all the awful chemicals that will enter my body over the next few days. The pack of six big Lucozade bottles and the high fat, high sugar, and high salt order that I have planned to arrive on Monday afternoon upon my return. The closer to Friday the better. Not back till the following week so wouldn't even need to find an excuse to leave the office for a few hours.

'You mind?' Jas asks as she rummages in another side pocket of her rucksack and brings out an ancient relic of an MP3 player.

'Go ahead,' I nod as we drive past the Rose and Crown, five minutes from Shaun's gaff. Shaun a regular there, or at least he used to be. I hear my Samsung message alert whistle and vibration drone coming from the door pocket of the car just as Jasmine plugs in her relic and starts playing some high-energy dance music I'm familiar with. A favourite of late-night Radio 1, a tune by Misca & Venus, a dance duo that are playing The Dance Tent this weekend. Can't say I've listened to much of their other stuff, then again can't say I've listened to much of any of this weekend's line-up to be fair. Don't think the ankle-biters would appreciate kids' audiobooks and their sing-along song replaced with 150 bpm rave tunes blasting out of the Passat's speakers. Little milk teeth vibrating with the bass. I don't have a drastic amount of idle time these days, what with raising and entertaining kids, a Henry Ford-prescribed working week, and generally trying to stay afloat occupying the majority of my time. Every spare second is backloaded into the end of the day. A precious few hours when kids are asleep and me and Mia can switch to being grown-ups. This usually entails scrolling listlessly through Netflix, desperate for something to pique a collective interest. All 'Nah', and 'I don't fancy that.' Remote chucked at one another in frustration. Choosing a film that has that magical elusive facet of fewer than 120 minutes run time. Don't want to be biting into our 10pm weekday bedtime. Sleep is king these days. One of us nodding off in front of chosen film more often than not, much to the annoyance of the other party.

Shaun bought me tickets for this weekend. They're a 40th birthday present, despite the small matter of the fact that I was only 36. Bless him, never been great with numbers. It's a bit of an inconvenience to be honest, I'm a bit out of touch with music these days. We used to do gigs, festivals, and whatnot pretty often, at least once a month back when we were younger. They were great times; we saw some absolute class acts. We also saw some absolute shite, but that was just an excuse to get peeved up even more and have a laugh. This kind of fizzled away when the kids started coming along. Mine, not his. He's yet to gift the planet with his offspring. Maybe for the best at the moment. My responsibility kind of killed off any form of gigs and festivals. Well, responsibility and finances. Hard to justify spunking a load of money on a festival when there's a gas bill to be paid. I can ill afford to pay for this weekend with the trident combination of recent mortgage repayment interest hike, the cost of utilities going mental and the overzealous spending of my darling wife skewering me and leading me to look for higher paid work. There's a long-haul holiday next year to pay off too. I'm even doing overtime on the occasional weekend. That's totally unlike me. Needs must. Speaking of the wife, Mia, that'll be her text that just came through asking how the kid's drop off went, knowing what my dad is like. Probably will be followed by an idea she's had for the kitchen. Something that I personally didn't think we need, nor can we really afford. But if it makes her happy. Plus, I can't really say anything, I'll do a couple hundred quid in this weekend easily. I've got a hundred quid float to start me off. That's what she's slipped me in an envelope on the kitchen worktop this morning. Biro scrawl on the back of a bin cleaning service flyer. 'Seb's Beer Fund. Don't forget to eat! Love M x'. Nice one darling. She's all for this weekend to be fair to her.

'Have some lad's time. It'll be good for you's two to catch up,' she said before remembering Jasmine's attendance, 'and look out for Jasmine, she's had a shitty time, keep an eye on her, okay?' before remembering Shaun's ability to cause himself a bit of bother. '...and him!' she finished with.

I pull into a dreary looking cul-de-sac. All OSB boarded garages and double story grey bricked and painted white pine panelling clad flats. It looks like a George

Shaw painting. It's bin day and there's a lot of bottles in the glass boxes on the curb. A neighbour must be getting a new sofa, the old one on its back on the path waiting for the council. Stuffing bursting out the armrests. Shaun is already outside standing between the sofa and his blue IKEA bag. He has a fat looking rucksack slung over his shoulder. Judging by his gait as he lifts the IKEA bag, it's heavy. A semi smile and an eyebrow raise from him. His sheepish greeting. God, he looks pale. His dark hair looks darker with a pale complexion. He waddles over swinging the bag as he shuffles. Backdoor opens.

'Alreet?' emphasis on the 'e'. Smell of spearmint and the sound of clacking as he wrangles himself into the backseat. Still sticking with the Lynx Africa deodorant, I notice.

'Hi, you okay?' an enthusiastic greeting from Jas.

'Shaun, this is Jasmine.'

'Nice to meet you,' their eyes meet as she screws herself around to see in the back. The click of a seatbelt as he rocks into the chair. 'You looking forward to it?' Big toothy greeting, chewing gum wedged between teeth. I reverse back out of the cul-de-sac almost wiping out a glass box. Then we're off on the road again. Finally, fest Bound.

Wednesday
Shaun

Fucking hell man, it's like a budgie cage in the back of here. So far, I've batted out crisp crumbs, sand and a Hot Wheels car from the arse of my 501's arse crack. I think it was a Dodge Viper. There's no end to the shite bursting out of the little pocket on the back of the front passenger seat, a seat I'm obviously not worthy of. Torn magazines, colouring in pages from chain pubs, folded tourist flyers for places I know for a fine fact he'll never go. Tell you what, Dad never let us leave his car like this. Some things don't pass down the family tree, I suppose. There was no eating in the back of the maroon Escort when we were bairns. Radio 2, no scran, no complaining or fighting. Especially during Popmaster or Sunday Love Songs. Choking in the back as him and me mam used the little push button cigarette lighter under the dash, a proper orange glowing thing to light their Regal King size. 'FUMAR MATA', tabs brought back from someone's holiday. Smoking and dissecting the trip we'd just embarked on, complaining about the cost of entry somewhere, or the queue for the café. Me winding down the windows with my infant muscles, face like a fucking fish at the gap sucking in fresh air. Tell you what though, can't help but think a bit carcinogenic smoke would improve the state of this interior a little. Tell you another thing, speaking of Levi's, bad fucking choice man, absolute swamp arse, should have lumped for my shorts but the rucksack is full as a bull's arse. The air-con of his lipstick red Passat not reaching the second-class carriage of the back seats. I feel sorry for his bairns when they're holed up in here on one of their camping trips, car sick city. Must remember to notify Childline of this gross negligence, allowing children to sit inside the last working blast furnace in the North East. Good job I've dusted that sand away, I'd be making glass in the back seats with my derrière before long.

I know I shouldn't be, but I'm a little jealous of the lass in the front. Her name I can't for the life of me remember, pretty sure it's something plant related. Might be Primrose, something like that anyway. Don't want to risk saying it in case I make a Class-A arse of myself quite so soon. Plenty of time for her to discover that particular part of me. I'll have to listen intently for clues to her name, hard graft for me like, or just fess up when we're mollied out of our nut, if that's her scene. Yeah, I am fucking jealous but it's not even about the unbearable heat, nor is it even about the ample legroom she has at her disposal or the nice unobstructed window, mine clad in a safari themed sunshade, smiling lions and giraffes look down on the back seat dwellers. It's proper bad animation, shitey Chinese clip art, trippier than any fucking sight I'll see this weekend I imagine. Well actually, I doubt that very much. But no wonder they're smiling, residing in conditions akin to the African savannah. I've got a cool box wedged between my legs and three camp chairs spearing me like a fork every time we turn right. So far, I think we must have used every right turn in the north of this fair country. I'm beginning to really dislike these Asda chairs, wankers. Tesco wouldn't do this to me. I try again to crack open the window a tadge using the little flicky button just in case I was too stupid to work it last time, I can only assume the child lock is on. He's too deep in conversation with the plant named girl to interrupt. Fingers crossed we don't crash into a lake; I'd have absolutely no chance. Water would be cooling though.

Bet he wouldn't dare drive like this with Mia in the car, she wouldn't let him, what with her incessant tuts and 'What speed are you doing?' Looking down her gegs knowing fine fucking well how fast the fella is doing, her head practically in front of his, ogling the speedo all meerkat-like. He doesn't have to worry about that today though, no, not Colin McRae here. I'm sure there is a more present, alive, driver I could compare him to, but my knowledge extends as far as PlayStation 2 games I played with Seb back when we were young'uns. Another spear from the Asda trident as we whip around a roundabout on what feels like the outer rims of the driver side wheels. You know, you wouldn't think this knacker worked in insurance based on today's escapades. I look at him and his Gant rugby polo top, one of Mia's birthday gifts if I remember correctly, looks suitably Tory like, I can't wait to see that caked in mud and puke. Probably be about four hours time.

She's got her music on the AUX cable, a little iPod thing from years ago, metallic pink. Doesn't seem to have a proper phone with her. Says she doesn't trust herself with technology, thinks she'll lose it down a long drop. What is it with these insurance people? Absolute liabilities. Suppose we're all charlatans in our jobs really though. Chancers. There's probably brain surgeons who go home and struggle to work the Sky remote, or pharmacists who can't knock up a decent Margarita. Anyway, the music is really decent to be fair. Seb's invited her along with us as her pal or someone dropped out, at least I think that's what he said. Actually, she might have been on a bit of a downer and needed a decent laugh. Something like that. Good luck with Gant boy in the front like. A laugh a year that fucker nowadays. You know, listening isn't quite my strongest point, well I can listen well, but retaining information is where the process falls down. I told him it was 'Sound', absolutely fine that she came along, not a problem whatsoever. I suppose it's not really like; they say three's a crowd but then again who are they? It was meant to be a birthday gift, a bit of a lad's catch up, because truth be told I haven't seen him properly for an age. Like properly seeing him, not with the bairns and Mia and life vying for a split of his attention. That's the reason why I'm jealous of her being in the front. A constant tug of war to see those I care about. Never mind, eh.

I bet Mia is spitting feathers at Mr. Generous offering his company to Plant Lass, that's if she knows. Ah nah, he best not be knocking her off. I can't be dealing with a family breaking down, not again. I also can't be dealing with the squelching sex noises coming through the tent fabric when I'm trying to sleep. Grim come noises and slurping kisses. Thought broken with the next track up on the iPod, well aye an absolute banger bursts out the poor abused VW. Plant Lass turns up the volume a fair decent whack. Seb looks, registers, hesitates, then smiles. Aye, not one of the bairns to bollock. His window is cracked open slightly as is hers, there's a wud wud wud air blast sonic boom that bashes about the car playing in tandem with a big beat banger. Proper fucking slutty bass, a psychotic donkey shriek, all beeps and bloops. Imagine this at 2am in a field. Pangs of excitement. Her hair catches in the cracked window vortex sending strands into my face, it smells feminine and floral. My head residing in the middle propped towards the centre console, back muscles straining so as to not miss anything. Look at that man,

86mph. Calm it down Mr. Very Nearly Back to the Future. Someone is eager to get there, or anxious.

Wednesday
Jasmine

Sorted for E's and Wizz - Well, not quite. Never even experienced the latter, I'm not entirely sure what it is. Speed, I think. Why would I possibly want to be even more skittish and restless than I already am, doesn't appeal to me in the slightest. But Mr. Cocker crooning out the song on the speakers raises a few smiles from the lads in the car. Enthusiastic chorus sing-along before it collapses into a stuttering crash of random hummed vowels, then silence as they evidently fail to know the verses. The black tagliatelle cable from the dashboard meets an old iPod mini I found in my bedroom drawer, alongside all sorts of forgotten trinkets and vignettes from my past. I've got to hold the AUX cable between thumb and forefinger, holding it steady in a semi-fold so that the sound is heard in stereo. The first few tracks of this driving DJ set spent bouncing between left speaker output, whole car output then a static doom vibration as I twist and skew the cable, wrestling with the cheap crap wire to prevent my misophonia from going into overdrive. I feel an enormous sense of responsibility for everyone's audio sanity. I fear judgement if I fail, the constant concern of letting someone down.

Turns out, the iPod is unlikely to last the car journey, old electronics battery decay letting the team down. Bummer. I've taken the boldest of choices by leaving my phone at home in the self-same drawer the iPod found itself released from, instead opting for an old Nokia. A polyphonic thing that I'm yet to hear ring since switching it on, orange backlight and hard-wearing plastic composition from god knows how many phone contracts ago. I might have even still been at school. Dear me. Got myself a SIM and £10 credit for it the other night as well as a bottle of

Californian white and a Bounty bar from the local corner shop. Not even necessary to my weekend, the Nokia serves as more of a comfort blanket. In case of losing the lads and any emergencies that might unfold. I hope £10 credit is enough, I genuinely have no idea what that gets you nowadays. Would be a hundred smutty messages to a boyfriend back in my younger days, simpler times. Finding a hundred different ways to sext is actually easier than it sounds, lads have simple imaginations and appetites, genitalia also having triple figure pseudonyms helps. If memory serves me correctly, the replies would slow after four or five. Presumably, the texting hand was busy elsewhere. Ribbons of spunk lashing into socks. How smartphones changed all that.

The reason for such a rash move of leaving my phone at home is a simple one: Ellis. Fucking Ellis. Six years of Ellis, six years a slave. My attempt to block him out, save myself from him, and him from me. Five days and nights away to detox, to cleanse myself of him. The iPod in my hand older than our relationship, save for a few scratches and bashes I'd say both me and the tech are physically unchanged, classic design. Sleek even. But much like my retro MP3 loaded icon, our batteries are depleted, internals battered and exhausted. In many ways, both of us have spent the better part of the last decade in the dark, in a drawer. Things got pretty bad at the turn of the year. Things got pretty nuclear bad last month.

Seb seems a bit tense behind the wheel, revving and late braking, not his usual calm and controlled behaviour that he portrays in the office and on the drive home. I hope that's not just a work personality. The calm controlled and irreverent attitude which has always endeared me to him. He's a friend, like actually only a friend. Nothing like that. A friendship which was proven when he noticed me bug eyed and blotchy after reading some vicious Ellis-Mail some idle afternoon in the work kitchen area. Coffee smell like a teacher's staff room. He lent a paternal hug. They are proper warming, assuring. As warm as the two mugs that steamed behind us. Everyone knows someone who can dish out them proper hugs, it's quite the skill. The kind of hug a man gives without the ultimate aim of graduating to a shag. He subsequently helped me with my workload during a period in which my head was battered from night after anxious night spent overthinking and under sleeping. Thrashing in a crocodile roll with my duvet. Imagining worst case scenarios to hypothetical situations. Mine and Seb's friendship communicated without words when he glanced at my arm bruises as he stood up to loudly stretch from his desk, mouth like a seal, me opposite him slyly checking the aftermath of post-football loss Ellis under my oversized citrus woolly jumper. More recently addressing the self-inflicted straight forearm crimson hieroglyphics from a bread knife and wine Thursday night combo. Playing sad violin with the Ikea kitchen implements, my weeping flesh the strings.

A tall man, but not athletic, nor fat. Just normal. A token gesture of hair sticking around on the top of his head like a treasure island. His work shirts baggy around the midriff, work pants seeming tight around the thighs. He approached me one day when I felt particularly vulnerable with a suggestion, maybe out of pity. I feel a bit bad, no doubt he didn't offer in seriousness, maybe more of an empty suggestion. But I was pretty low that day. Really low actually. It was Thursday, vodka replaced wine in the fridge today and the bread knife was in the dishwasher waiting to be emptied. Another string of sheer abuse had filled my phone notifications for the best part of the morning from the stagnant bus trip all the way through till the pre-lunch conference call, paused for a few hours as the sender must have been sleeping, then resumed again for my afternoon and all through the Seb provided lift home. The phone switched off and chucked onto the unmade bed when I got home. A long shower. Tears mingled with lather and a stare into the mildew clag in the grout, the hairline fractures of old white tiles. Then I perched on the end of the bed, towel wrapped around hair, another around my body. Staring. Ear tuned expecting the banging of a door at any time. Then, rather than reaching for my normal paraphernalia of misery and pain, I instead reached for my laptop, credit card details, expiry, and CVC. 3rd, 4th and 7th character. Please do not refresh. Then: 'See you in the fields'. My screen adorned with green foliage and a spectrum of colourful flags, deer, butterflies, and tent imagery. The website banner displayed a triangle of band names, most of who I've never heard of except The Red Eyes, and maybe a couple of others. Never mind, I could learn. Hope and colour radiated out into my grey and bare rented flat. I took his offer. Phone back on and a message sent in childlike glee. 'I'm coming too, got a ticket. So excited x'.

Wednesday
Shaun

We pull into the services. Seb parking as far away as possible from the entrance, right up next to the trucks full of wanking drivers eating Pot Noodles. Still can't park for shit I see. Just as well we're here as I'm feeling last night's kebab and Guinness combo churning away in my stomach like a bastard. Plus, I'm bursting for a lag. I climb out of the dirt infested backseats and feel the ache in my lower back, my arse numb with sitting, brushing crumbs off as I stretch and exhale. I'm getting old, I fear.

'I'll see you's in there,' as I head across the car park, hot as fuck tarmac, feel it sticking to my trainers. Pits and crevices feeling damp with sweat, they're not going to air off out here. The ripping sounds of rubber on the motorway off in the distance, geet big artics and tankers tear arsing along, probably doing that annoying thing where they overtake each other for about seven miles just to gain ten metres advantage over the other.

Near the entrance there's two coppers sitting in a patrol car supping down Costa coffees with their windows wound down, the cough medicine yellow stab vests bright as fuck in this sun. I've left my sunglasses in the car, so basically, I'm screwing my face at them as I gawp. They're oblivious to the fact I have a chunky wrap of coke in my pocket alongside four high strength ecstasy pills I have nestled in that little pocket in a pocket on the right-hand side of my jeans. Levi Strauss repping the fans of molly. The warm air farts out of Greggs, queues of Greggasaurus' out of the door, fidgeting with phones and fingers awaiting their beige buffet. Snotty nosed brats squabble. Business blokes look flustered. Seagulls waiting eagerly for a dropped bit of puff pastry or better still, a whole sausage roll. Beady eyed fat cunts nowhere near the sea like, they know where their bread is buttered nowadays. I head down the slope, that little sad bit of grass on the left, a token patch of greenery that's used primarily by dogs to do their piss on after being cooped up in the back of a car en-route to Scotland.

Through the double doors, a magazine shop flogging some very reasonably priced camping chairs in an array of colours and some screen wash, available in blue and red. A plump flower stand looks joyful with pinks and yellows beside a shelf of boxed chocolates, it makes me think it's for the guilty businessmen who have been knocking off some little mistress in the hotel across the car park, poor wife back at home looking after the kids and house whilst he gets his balls drained. The Burger King belches out greasy obese fumes into the foyer of the service station mixing with the bitter roast of coffee from the warm looking café over in the corner, I'm fucking salivating man. Fruit machines glowing behind a little barrier, fat bloke slumped in a creaking stool feeding in coin after coin, he's waiting for his tachograph approval to move on. Bad receding hairline and sweaty neck glistening. Looks a couple of Ginsters away from death. Hi-vis under fluorescent lights. Like Salvador Dali's take on the police officers outside. Like what would happen if you microwaved a copper. Imagine the tabloid headlines. Then there it is, the little blue rooms, the shitters. Could have found my way here blindfolded on account of the smell. Big convenience food shites, rancid. Bacon, sausage, and egg based cack. My body knows it's nearly safe as I pick up the pace past bloke after bloke in the narrow corridor. Proper walk of shame, avoiding eyes. Bet half these lads haven't even washed their digits. A sign on two hooks reads 'Female Attendant in Operation', poor lass. Deserves a medal the poor hin. Doubt she's English inall, our lot too proud to scrub away their own piss and shit. Leave that for the people who supposedly steal our jobs. I get deeper into the cave of fume, there's a cubicle free. Great. Pants are scarcely down, and I've dropped my bait in no time. One big log. Relief. Utter fucking relief.

I sit for a moment with waves of solace and the acute knowledge that this will most likely be my most hygienic and pleasant shit for the next five days. Fuck me, imagine that. This stench infested room of grunts and groans, hand dryers screaming like jet engines, and the hockle of spit into a urinal being the height of luxury compared to tomorrow morning's dump. My guts regular, no matter what the situation. The porcelain here already decorated with an unknown number of previous occupant's gut contents; seat was still warm from the previous brute's arse. Graffiti on the back of the door, how retro. 'Add me on Snapchat @fuckmeforfourtynights'. What a handle. Religious too. Niche. Lower down is a pretty impressive anatomical drawing of a vagina, hairless. Must have taken quite some time to draw, someone escaping reality perhaps. My eyes fixed on the labia, reminds me of someone from the past. Some lass in my uni days, remarkable shag actually. Spoke with an Aussie accent despite being from Derby and only ever leaving her hometown that weekend she met me. Wouldn't surprise me if it was a drawing of her actually, she's worth celebrating. Beside the canny fanny is a blue permanent marker scrawl of 'Wanna play toilet tennis? Look left...' Instinctively I look left only to be greeted with the same handwriting and same blue ink, 'Look right' and, as predicted on the opposite wall I snigger as I spot 'Look left'. Impressive lads, some 7/10 toilet vandalism going on here. I'm not one who can think up such witty stuff on the hoof.

    Sitting there, I begin to fiddle into the little jean pocket, the one on the right, slightly bulging with payload. A few finger twirls and I've got the baggy of coke, I look at it all crystalline and white clagged into a thin clear film bag. Under the unnatural lighting of the spotlight above me, I wonder whether these are the ones that stop smackheads from finding veins. I fancy a little key for the journey, start of me holidays and all that. Just a little bump to keep the conversation flowing. Truth be told, I'm feeling a little shy in front of this lass. She seems decent patter, but this brain fog I'm suffering from last night's sessioning isn't shifting. The heat is affecting my craic. Being consigned to the back has relegated my chat. Aye, a little key will unlock it, the necessary social lubricant I need. So, I fish out a little key worth on my flat's front door key and honk it down. Pause. Sting in the back of the nose, acidic stink of it overwhelmed the shite reek of this place. Couple of secondary sniffs and hocks to get the remnants down, then I'm sorted. Couple of scrunches of shit-roll nettle sandpapers my hoop, contactless flush, the water violent as it sends my shit seaward. Then I'm out of the cubicle. Pudgy short arse with Harry Potter geps waiting for his turn. Good luck there mate. A grim smile from his spotty face. Bet he'll love that Biro fanny. Wouldn't put it past a young lad to pull his plonker in there over it. I did my fair share of plonker pulling over the thought of the Aussie fanny for months after the shag like. I wash my hands, water is way too hot, 'Do not drink' sign. Aye, I don't plan to. Don't bother with the twenty seconds of washing, those days are behind us, and besides, I'm anxious to get out of here. Shake my fingers, drag them down the front of my Levi's to dry. In this heat, it'll take no time at all. Down the shuffler's passage, then back into the foyer faster than I went in, the coke has got me fevered now. Seb stood there texting away, waiting next to the Peppa Pig ride on car. The state of that Gant top man, it's embarrassing. He looks up all shifty, forcing a welcoming grin, sheepish, almost shy.

'Alright?'

'Aye sound, where's she at?' I ask, following a loud sniff.

Wednesday
Jasmine

The scratched, sprayed, and burnt Perspex held in place by spider house rafters, peeling paint, and webs. A bridge between southbound and northbound. A thin veil is all that separates me from a ten metre drop on to the three carriageways southbound. Scania, Volvo, DAF, or Iveco flat fronts decimating my flesh, shattering my bones, and sending me into the eternal darkness. Nothingness. Quiet. Peace. I wonder whether I would register the pain, whether it would be instant, or would I lay sprawled breathing bloody chokes into gravel specks, my last thought a one of regret. Or relief. Hopefully, my life wouldn't flash before my eyes, that would be utterly boring viewing. What if it went wrong? A shattered spine and a few broken leg bones, years of rehab and consultants' efforts. A huge burden on the already struggling NHS as well as everyone else. The result as we feared. Unable to move anything but my mouth and eyes, witnessing the pitiful glances of family and friends as I'm wheeled into a room. Paper decorations and sugar icing cake. Someone's 60th in a social club, I'm taken in the side door as it has a ramp. Pushed around by some minimum wage carer reluctantly provided by the state, a small table in the corner near the fruit machines, my brakes applied. A J2O fed to me whilst people do their duty and humour me with trivialities for five minutes before they can scurry off and discuss 'How sad' it is how I ended up in a fate maybe worse than the worst-case scenario. Trapped in the forever, merely a witness as the years disappear before me, as sheets, calendars and carers change. My mind hardened with the emotion, the longing for escape and the wish for something beyond TV and retail parks to occupy me. The memory of an orgasm, of dancing, and ambition, one getting more and more difficult to recall. What about the driver, traumatised to the extent he himself led into a despair that I so eagerly and, as some people say, cowardly ran away from. Unable to love his wife, to care for his kids, or get behind the wheel as he did before. Crippled with emotional scars that no amount of therapy can clear. Unable to hear loud sounds without being transported back to that fateful day, when he was driving southbound in the sun with Madonna's 'Immaculate Collection' playing at full pelt, drumming the steering wheel singing along with - *holiday, celebrate* - His last shift until Lanzarote, then bam, a girl falling out of the sky.

My eyes trace the Perspex and read the graffiti adorned: various people are slags, a few fucks and cunts and a couple of football team stickers, some peeled dotted here and there. I wonder what a football ultra does when there's no football on. Then recall the recent riots, and shudder. It's a stifling heat in this tube. I rummage in my bag and pull out a water bottle. Carbonated fizz. Liquid relief cascades down my throat. I screw the lid back on and replace it in the bag. My Louis Vuitton bag, an outlandish choice to take to a festival, but, honestly, it is one I have no emotional connection to. A purchase that still angers me to this day. I felt obliged to buy it to fit in with what Ellis thought of us. His football mates' girlfriends and wives all pouty lips, fake eyelashes, and designer gear, they were canny girls. Really sweet to me actually, but a few thousand miles away from where I see myself. I'm not one to stick on two hours' worth of makeup. My wardrobe is a couple of years old and anything new is usually bought from a charity shop if I'm feeling skint, Zara if I'm feeling flush, and my vocabulary extends beyond 'eeee' when expressing surprise. My forehead actually moves when I am surprised. That bag took the whole sum and some more of a performance-based bonus at work. I'd worked really hard and been rewarded. Unable to think for myself as to what I wanted to do with it, I found myself in Selfridge's during a weekend trip to Manchester. His treat. Newcastle were playing Man United away. Ellis's arm tight around my waist. 'You should get it hun', not an encouragement but an order. Who was I to argue? Then there it was. A beacon of how far we'd come, we'd made it. A contrast to everything I owned and everything I stood for. Leather too, despite me being a vegetarian. A bag. For carrying things. Like empty purses and bills maybe. Tear sodden tissues. The anger building up like bile in my throat, I picture myself throwing it down onto the tarmac below and watching it get ripped and smashed by the traffic. See the stitching explode and leather tear under rubber and metal, patterned linings streaking across the lanes and copper buckles burst into different directions, skittering over windscreens. If I lose this bag at the festival, I wouldn't care a jot. In some ways, it might free me of the emotion it evokes in me. Should it survive, I'll sell it, save the money and have another go at thinking of how I'd like to reward myself for my own hard work. Even giving it to charity would be better.

I look back once more at the hypnotic cars disappearing under my feet. Rubber vibrations and metal punching holes in air, people going about their lives, some will be no doubt FestiFell bound. The ones with loud music - *you won't fool the children of the revolution* - fading in, then quickly out of earshot. Car boots piled high with camping gear are shoe-ins for it. I should head back to the lads, they'll be wondering where I am, maybe. One final Scania truck passes and so with it subsides the fantasy of its radiator grille meeting my face. Windscreen wipers spreading a rainbow of my blood and organs. I turn heel and head through the tube. At the end is a fence already claimed by the labyrinth arms of a hawthorn bush, jagged spines and foliage growing around and through the painted wood. A dunnock skits between the branches. Nature claiming its domain back, slowly. When we're all gone, I imagine football stadiums reclaimed with thirty metre sycamores and oaks growing on the pitch, wild deer stalk the terraces and waterfalls gush down the concourse. One day none of us will exist.

The lads are in the distance, milling at right angles of one another by a bright green AED bolted to a wall. Shaun squinting out the sun looking fidgety alternating his weight on one leg and then the other. Seb's arms crossed, nodding, and appearing to look dead ahead through sunglasses. They don't seem to be talking much. A nervous pang in my chest spreads as I approach them, feeling like an intruder for a moment. As I approach, both turn to face me. Expressions soften, welcoming. Shaun is saying something about someone Spanish sounding, I assume it's a football player. A lot of their common interests that I've observed so far are on the safe subject of a mutual appreciation of football. Transfer rumours and pre-season friendlies, predictions for next year and who they need to get rid of. All foreign to me, I zoned out of all that talk years ago. We trudge quite a distance to the top of the car park where Seb's car sits alone, cooking on the black tarmac. Feels like my bright white trainers will melt into the ground. Heat that I can't remember from previous years pounds us. No breeze to provide relief. We contort ourselves into the car. Shaun with more difficulty than us two. Stale hot air means the food bag already smells like it's on the turn. I scroll through the trusty iPod to find something up tempo, something that'll blast away the rest of the dark thoughts that clutter my mind, and leave them at the last stop before the fields. AUX hums as I finger it into the sweet spot. Engine starts. Music follows. 'Pjanoo' plays.

Wednesday
Seb

That accident has knocked our schedule. Took nearly two hours of stop start clutch control, only to see that the accident wasn't even on our side of the road. Four miles of tailbacks and frustration, just to gawp at the rear-ended Vauxhall and battered front end of an unrecognisable car on the other side of the dual carriageway. Some other cars are scattered about at right angles looking naughty. Looks like Reuben's car mat at bedtime. Everything mashed and warped to varying degrees. Helicopters were heard. Plenty hard shoulder blue lights went past and the airbags in each car were deployed. Must have been a bad one. Fire engine foam and a car roof decorate the road. Police cars still in attendance, helmet headed and boot clad men brushing glass to the central reservation. My eyes fix on a family huddled under a foil blanket on the grass verge. Pale stony expressions pulsing reflections of strobe blue light flash. As soon as we're past the scene, the speed increases and we are knocking off minute miles again. On our right is an endless line of frustrated drivers stifling in their cars, wishing they'd packed a bottle of water as the wreckages are scooped away, and normal life can resume. The music volume turns back up as enthusiasm returns for the rest of the journey, and we can forget about what we've seen. The frustration of the accident being so near our turn-off yields. Hunger mediated with some snack samosas from the food bag. They're sweaty. Expertly eaten without a drop of pastry, all whilst steering towards the third exit on the roundabout, past a packed ESSO garage and a brown direction sign for some old stately home I've been to with the Mrs. For a moment, during a lull, I think for a split second, as if by instinct, about leaning towards the passenger seat and squeezing the knee of Mia. It's something I do. A silent, 'I love you', issued on car journeys. Just for a moment, until I realise that it is not my wife in the passenger seat, but my colleague.

'Reckon we could get the windows open again?' Shaun's face wedged between the front seats asks, his flushed face looking damp, his eyes looking tired. I silently oblige with the two fingered flick of the right hand. He then rummages in the snack bag himself and brings out a tube of Pringles. As he opens the tube, my sideways glance into the rear-view mirror reveals he isn't having the same success as myself with crumbs. He's shovelling in two crisps at a time. Greedy git. I find myself keep watching, in morbid fascination. Like watching an animal eat. Much like the car crash from before, there will be a lengthy clean-up operation needed after this, then I remember the state of it after removing the kids' seats. The crackle of a water bottle and violent glugging as the salt hits his bloodstream and demands moisture. His tongue tracing his teeth, as the clag of crisp is removed with moist probing and polishing. I try to focus on the road ahead. Enjoy the curving corners and changing horizon, as jagged mountains grow in size with every mile that passes. Thinking I'm Jeremy Clarkson test driving a new supercar. A fork in the road and I slow right down, pull the visor down to block out the sun as I process the directions. Indicator right. More of the same.

The car in front of me is littered with war nostalgia. An upsetting amount of tat. All blue, red, and white. Bulldogs in military helmets, spitfires spraying bullets into the bumper, and an English knight with a gauntlet proudly held aloft. We're a nation that is obsessed with the armed forces. It can't be healthy. Not me, I grimace at the Facebook shares of people I used to go to school with. Consider defriending them. The ones who, once upon a time declared soldiers should be paid footballers' wages. Aye, no bother, let's give a trained killer half a mill a week for scrapping over in the Middle East. Not a bad idea at all. They've now evolved to using soldiers as a vehicle for their racism, sharing and liking obvious lies about immigrants taking veterans' housing. Sharing posts that claim to be repeatedly taken down by the supposed Facebook police. My dad has fallen victim to this hogwash on many an occasion. As I approach closer to the tailgate of the car, I read 'If you can't stand behind our troops, you can stand in front of them'. A crouched figure points a gun alongside this slogan. I pause for a moment, fixated on the back of the car, eyes darting between spitfires and poppies. I ruminate on how ridiculous this statement is. I picture the Chinese factory churning out this bumper sticker, the fractions of the lowest denomination of the currency the worker got, if even a worker was involved. I picture the Norwegian container, loaded onto a Philippine flagged shipping vessel in which it lived in a box for a fortnight after dispatch from Guangzhou, alongside the plastic shit you get in kids' party bags and fake Paris SG jerseys. Alongside all the tat Mia floods our house with after a cheeky night on Wish, when she isn't really feeling the box set we've settled on after hours of scrolling. I picture the shop this individual walked into one day, the rack which they span until such a sticker captivated him. It's presumably a him, it struck such a deep chord with him and compelled him to part with his money. I picture the pride with which he placed it on the bumper of his Japanese made Nissan Juke, the pals he told about it in the pub whilst supping down Danish beer. I then focus a little closer and realise that the soldier crouched alongside the text is, in fact, an American GI. Vietnam era, if the rifle is a M16, as I think it is. I very much doubt the driver is a Yank, not likely considering the Union jack tat stuck to the rear glass of his car. How bizarre.

We're now approaching Lochtdale. The roads have been winding and rural for a fair few miles now. Bushy hedgerows and drystone walling flanking either side like crash barriers for about ten minutes or so of national speed driving. There's very little to note, except for the odd stone-built barn or farmhouse to break the repetition. The beginning of one dance track and the end of another seamless, so there's no audible markers of time. Conversation has stunted as the sonic boom of open windows and Jasmine's dance playlist drowns out all other sound, including Shaun chewing gum loudly in the back, dog like head bobbing and turning to everything of interest we pass. We're in a trance like state of anticipation, on the watch out for the temporary yellow road signs to direct us to the relevant entrance gate. We're watching countryside unravel itself before us. It really is quite beautiful on a day like today.

'YOU ARE NOW ENTERING LOCHTDALE: PLEASE DRIVE CAREFULLY'. Followed shortly after with 'twenty's plenty' signs. They're accompanied by a child's cheerful drawing of four fingered families and square wheeled cars waving at one another on a zebra crossing. Crayon rub wiry hair and thick lipped smiles. A dog that looks like a shit with eyes on the end of a fat red leash. Innocence and happiness. Cute, but a cynical and twee attempt to pull at the heartstrings. Funny, the children in this rural hamlet deep inside a UNESCO World Heritage site are considered far more worthy of protection than your average scallywag around our way. No such signage exists where the house prices are lower than anywhere else in this country. Reuben and Emily will have to make do with a speed bump some 100 metres away down the road to protect them from the local joyriders and twats on trail bikes. 30 maybe not enough for some of the ones around our neck of the woods. A stretch of green lawns, circles of joyful primary coloured bedding plants arranged in symmetrical patterns. Tree lined main street and stone built terraced houses offset from the road. Wooden sash windows and engraved slate door numbers. Some of the houses don't even have numbers but, rather names like 'Granny Cottage' and 'Strawberry House'. A butchers and farm shop are the rustic touches I notice, as I slow to 20 and amble along the road.

'Well, this is nice,' utters Jasmine, as she turns down the music to a respectable level so as to not invite glances of disdain from the country folk that are plotted in their setting, like characters in an old kid's story book. Old ladies are shuffling down cobbled side streets, couples push prams up to shop windows and peer in at the trinkets on display. White overalled decorators queue for hot beef sandwiches from Ye Olde Tearoom, before getting back to refitting an old vicarage with top of the range paints. Sea shale grey and towellen blue. The cost of living crisis doesn't seem to have washed upon these particular shores.

Lochtdale looks like the sort of place where men are men and always have been. Callous hands set onto a battered wooden table. Knife and fork in hand at 6pm ready to tackle meat and veg. The wife had been working over a stove all day. They'd mutter in a dialect only understood by those very local locallers, never divulging feelings. Gossip about the neighbour's affairs, their new hanging baskets, whether the husband is 'an uphill gardener.' Long and hard workdays, the weather today betraying the cold and wet winters out in the fields and in the fells on a mud splattered quad. Drink hard at the Rose and Crown, none of that continental shite. Proper beers. English ale. Gods drink. Eight cask ales, if the gilded gold on black sign is to be true. Leer at the barmaid. Appreciate her big fat tits, and tell her exactly that after one too many social ones. Drink drive home, no one ever gets stopped. Stumble through the door, chuck flat cap and waxed jacket onto the mahogany coat stand, boots kicked off by the door then hunt down the wife for a little romance, before collapsing into a throaty sleep. Rough hands wrestling the blankets, ale breath stinging her nostrils. Wake up early with the morning light and be back to task.

My wandering ITV fuelled fantasising is broken with the sight of a phone box, a seldom seen sight. The one en-route, up near Shaun's was kicked in, the glass still strewn on the floor, probably been there weeks. Next up is a beautiful vegetable garden in front of a chocolate box cottage. Abundances of leafy green veg in neat rows protected with netting draped over blue half-moon piping. A few metres later there's a national speed limit sign beside a raised stone-built planter, filled with the same bedding plants that hung from hanging baskets and filled the grass lawn circles. 'Lochtdale. Britain in Bloom Shortlisted'. This is the place they project in Hollywood films. A far cry from the everyday reality of normality. My foot whacks down and the sound of fresh hot air wafting back into the car returns. A few barns later, the yellow A-frame held in place by a sad looking sandbag stating: 'Festival Parking Green Zone' and an arrow right shows we are near. The indicator ticks and we're heading up a narrow farm track.

Wednesday
Jasmine

The engine stops. The keys rattle in Seb's hand, then into his pocket. A moment of quiet, birdsong and voices. A yellow jacketed man with wraparound sunglasses has marshalled us alongside an SUV cram packed with plastic boxes and bedding. A couple get out and fish out their young child, probably three or four years of age. Pink cheeks and curly hair from the heat. Amazing the little thing didn't suffocate under the landslide of stuff they've brought. I get a slight fear that I've travelled too light, then remember that I don't have a kid to keep alive all weekend. I thought I'd be a mam by now. Always imagined I'd be a proper mamma, like my own at this point in my life. Don't know whether I'd be taking it to a festival though. Seems like a recipe for disaster in my opinion, but then again who am I to judge anyone on anything? Makes sense now why there is a Junior Monopoly and Snakes and Ladders game packed amidst the tubs and bags. Teaching the little thing early doors how life works. A true metaphor for life. It wasn't until I was in my thirties, that I realised the free parking tile is probably the best space on the board. Also, there's far more snakes than ladders in the world.

Shaun's already clambered out of the car and he's stretching with an exaggerated groan. Dusting himself down of crisp crumbs, he surveys the scene. I climb out as well and am greeted immediately with a jet of heat. Feels like when you get off the plane on your holidays, a stifling sauna blast of hot air. These clothes will be getting changed at the first opportunity. I can feel the sweat saturate the cotton already. Then again, I'm on a strict ration of clothing. I look around. We're in a field and cars go on as far as I can see, right up beside a drystone wall. We're sloped slightly downwards, cars parked sideways on a scattering of reds, greys and blacks unnatural against the hues and dappled greens and browns. Beyond the wall, it descends suddenly after a tree line, down to the valley. A brown snake sidewinds through asymmetric fields. Look like jagged blocks gridded out by ancient hands. Bucolic beauty. Hedgerows and trees, moss covered walls, stiles, and wooden gates as far as the eye can see. A palette of greens stood over by one dominant shade of brilliant blue.

Closer to us there's movement everywhere. Trollies, sledges, and arms are loaded up with camping gear and beer crates. A whole supermarket's beers, wines and spirits department is slowly dragged up the slope towards the entrance gazebo with straining arms and aching backs. The woman to my right loads her kid into a child carrier on her back. I appreciate how at ease she performs the task, one fluid movement. She's all blonde hair, hi-top shoes and bronze legs. Flawless. Her stubbly husband on the other side unloading, what surely is one of several trips into a pull along trolley. They look like one of those units of a family who have their shit together. We on the other hand appear not to have such a solution to carrying our gear. Pure endurance and brute force it'll have to be. Seb's frenziedly unloading bag after bag after box onto the long waves of grass by the car boot. Consciously throwing it over a sizeable pile of animal manure. It looks fresh. Shaun is slinging several bags over his shoulder; he reaches towards mine with a gesture.

'No, I'll manage, thank you,' I find myself saying. Kind of him to offer, but I expect no help with my pitiful amount of luggage. I sling it over my shoulder and look around for what else I can carry. I want to show him I'm a helpful person to have around.

'You going to be alright with this?' asks Seb. It's a shopping crate you get from your online food shopping. He's obviously pinched it after getting a delivery. The cheeky scamp. It is cram packed with disposable barbecues, little tarpaulin bags and polyester drapes. Looks heavy, but I'll surely manage that. Going to get them guns working.

'Aye,' I say, leaning over and picking it up. I hear a metallic movement inside the box, tent pegs or something, but it's bloody heavy. 'Don't show weakness,' I tell myself, 'make a good first impression.'

'Lift with your knees, not your back,' I chortle. Something Papa used to insist as I bring it upright. The car is emptied with speed, then the lights flash orange as it locks. Wing mirrors retract automatically with a robotic whir. Seb's looking anxious yet satisfied he's got everything he needs. Scanning the gear and patting down pockets, muttering 'Right,' and 'okay,' to himself repeatedly to confirm his mental checklist that everything is there and accounted for. Me and Shaun look at one another, laden like pack horses grinning in strain. My arms already wobbling as sinews and fibres in my arms stretch and rip. Shaun hunchbacked with three different bags slung over his shoulders. On one hand is the tent bag and a cool box in the other. I'm impressed by his strength. Biceps seem to be stretching the sleeves of his T-shirt. He's definitely more athletic than his brother. I reckon he's a builder or something, maybe even a fireman. He's got the look of that sort of thing. Then again, Seb would have surely mentioned something like that. Dewey sweat beads are already forming on his forehead, understandably, but a firefighter would be able to cope a bit better in this heat. His forearms twitching, blue veins swelled and pronounced. Skin appears bright white with the sun's reflection. Won't stay that colour for long at this rate, he obviously doesn't work outside.

'Tickets,' Seb mutters to himself. I'm unsure whether it's a question. I've given mine to him. He's got a printer at home and is one of those people who still likes to print out tickets even though everything is digital these days. I soon realise it's still part of him checking his internal checklist again looking like the stressy dad he can be at times. His eyes are sort of pointed up and right, as if he's not looking anywhere in particular except the parts of his own brain where plans are kept. 'Tent, bag... Right, I think that's everything,' he states towards us, marking the fact he is satisfied, and we can head off. He leans over and slings two bags over his own shoulders, then manoeuvring in a way that allows him to lift both a laden Sports Direct bag and three crates of alcohol. 'Bloody hell.' He groans as he gets himself upright and finds his balance. Hissing out the strain pain through clenched teeth.

'Howay then,' says Shaun. His voice already seems like the weight of all this gear is getting to him. We set off up the hill, a great triangle of people is forming towards the entrance gate at the top. At least it doesn't seem too far to walk. In this heat we'd surely perish if it was any longer. As we walk, every so often one of the lads has to utter a 'Hang on a minute,' plea, as they shake and shuffle to allow for a bag to get put back on a shoulder, muttering an insult towards the inanimate object that's slid off their person. An opportunity for sunglasses to be pushed back up the sweaty ramp of a nose. The whole thing probably only takes ten minutes or so until we're in the switchback queue separated by little metal fencing, but still, it feels pretty brutal. The tray of whatever the hell it is I'm carrying is heavy as anything, but I don't want to complain. Aware of my own getting off lightly with only one bag and tray, and the fact that I'm the guest in this whole thing, I don't want to appear anything other than compliant. The backs of my legs are feeling achy, the hill tougher than it looked from the car. I very rarely walk anywhere other than for the bus, to the corner shop, or to the kitchen area at work these days. At least the metal fence is waist height, so I can use it to take the weight of this tray as we shuffle forward in the queue. It's like a Disneyland queue for a ride. One which we'll be riding for five nights. There is a weird silence as we approach the entrance. People knackered from carrying all their shite, breathing heavily and glint with perspiration. Worried about how far it is to the camping pitches. Inside the gazebo, you can see people getting their bags searched. Whole bags of carefully packed and curated items are scattered across the tables by man mountains in yellow polo shirts. Clothes and toiletries strewn in a heap, raked through by blue latex gloves. Radios squawk and screech. Nerves set in. The people they select seems indiscriminate. Every tenth person or so, seems to be mainly the men though. Mentally counting the people ahead of me, hoping it's not me. Not that I've got anything to hide unless this box is laden with contraband. I just don't fancy my greying knickers on view for everyone. I wasn't going to bring my good underwear here, was I? The contents of my bag probably too sad and boring for anyone to actually note or care. Charity shop clobber and supermarket own brand toiletries. A dog is wandering about on the far right side of the trestle tables. A cute spaniel thing that reminds me of my childhood dog. He was called Alan. I loved him. He's the only bloke who never let me down, until he died. But, I can't hold that over him, he was riddled with cancer. I want to go over there and make a fuss of the little thing, scuffle its ears and rub its belly. I'm a proper moose when it comes to dogs, but cats fill my life now. I hope it comes over this way, wonder whether it can smell the cat on me. Look at its little police jacket man. Tongue hanging out as he excitedly sniffs the piles of boxers, socks, and T-shirts. Bet I've never looked that happy at work.

Shaun seems to be nervous, fidgeting about checking his phone and the straps of one of the many bags on his shoulder as we wait in the scorching heat.

Lifting up his payload and dropping it with every metre we get closer to the ticket inspection. At least everyone I can see is a sweaty mess. Solidarity in that sense. Beyond the table searches, there is another line of yellow polo wearing people, this time pat searching random folk in the queue. The women selected patted by women only, by the looks of it. I feel shame in the fact that I hope to get pat searched. I eye the line and care not whether it be man, woman or dog who touches me, just wanting one of these marshals to firmly stroke me up and down. They'll find nothing other than someone who can then say that Ellis wasn't the last person to touch me all over. It'll be the next stage of freeing myself of him. We shuffle further forward. Shade from the gazebo now cast across the tops of our heads. Seb has the tickets poking out of the arse pocket of his shorts. I worry someone might snatch them. Shaun is looking red faced, pissing sweat from his hair, his T-shirt showing patches under pits. I dread to think what it's like inside them jeans of his. This airport security vibe makes me feel irrationally guilty. I'm feeling nervous about getting through, coupled up with the fact I haven't a clue what's inside this big green tray. Could be ten kilos of heroin for all I know.

'Move forward, please.' We're ushered along, through the lanes, past the tables. Doesn't look like our bags will be searched after all. Shaun close behind me, Seb in front. We walk past the friskers. Looks like I'm in the clear. Shame. That shaven headed younger bloke is a bit of alright, a bit like a young Mike Skinner. He's fit, but he knows it. Shaun is selected though. A great groan as he takes off all the bags and drops down his cargo for hopefully the last time before we've set up camp. We turn back and see a grey-haired pot-bellied man's hands firmly manoeuvre around him. Shaun jabbering away, looking like he's cracking some jokes or something. The guy is concentrating on the job at hand. I almost imagine a squelch as he frisks around his jean area, his hands half threaten to give it a pat down, but think otherwise, instead giving a half arsed light touch pat on the arse. Bloke nods after his moves are done and Shaun can then load himself back up.

'Move forward please,' he bellows again to the next in the queue. Shaun parts with a 'Cheers mate,' and rejoins me and Seb, practically skipping towards us. Tickets are passed over to a braced teen girl clad in green tabard, red laser light and satisfying beep. Arms are laid, then tickets are exchanged with a metallic clunk of a wristband. Embroidered with floral pattern like the website background. Before we know it, we hear a 'Have a good festival, guys,' lisped by the girl as we're

Leave No Trace

back out of the gazebo and back in the heat. Now inside the site of FestiFell, our home for the next five nights. We stand for a moment and drink in the scene. Shaun is a few paces behind, putting his wallet back in his back pocket and lifting all the gear once again. He's bought himself a lanyard with stage times on it from the braced girl. Handy, I'll have to study it to seem knowledgeable about who is playing, because I'm really none the wiser.

'How much was that like?' Seb asks him.

'Tenner.'

'Bloody hell.'

I feel a flood of excitement, as the site reveals itself whilst we descend down the other side of the slope. Elation being a sensation I haven't felt in quite some time.

Wednesday
Seb

'This'll do?' I hear myself rhetorically say, breathing in great gulps of stuffy air as my cargo falls to the ground. That was gruelling. Gritting teeth through searing muscular failure and ears ringing with the exertion of carrying all that gear up that bloody hill and down again. Like the Grand Old Duke of York. Could have done with two thousand, or ten thousand, or however many men he took up and down again. What on earth is that crackpot doing that for anyway? Can only guess he was looking for a Pizza Express at the top of that hill. I, unlike him, have a great ability to sweat. Kid's songs are crackers when you actually think about them now as a grown up. 'What shall we do with a drunken sailor?' Well, 'Put him in bed with the Captain's daughter,' obviously. Bet that went down like a lead balloon. Did the Captain's daughter have a say in any of this?

I'm wondering whether this wristband is too tight, or whether my wrists are swollen with the heat. It's a nice little design. I'll be cutting that annoying flappy bit as soon as this lot is put away though. *Thump thump thump* - the bags drop to the ground from Shaun and Jas. Just as the intro thumps of - *waiting for the gift of sound and vision* - can be picked out, through all the other hubbub in the distance. – *Blue, blue electric blue* - Well, our room where we will live is green. The Green Goblin, as the bairns call it. It sits squashed up inside its bag, waiting to get wrestled out and erected. Turf is prickly dry, and soil seems baked hard. Good job I've packed that mallet, otherwise I'd be struggling to get the tent pegs in. It'll take a fair whack to drive them in. Just think of Matt from the team at work as I bash them in, that'll do the trick nicely. Remembered to take the mallet after that trip to Normandy with the family, mentally scarred from scanning beaches for rocks or old D-day rifle butts, anything to welly in the already bent and mangled pegs into the ground. Picturing the kids flying into the English Channel if I didn't tether our holiday home down sufficiently. The winds can be tasty around there. Ended up using the surprisingly resilient bottle of cheap wine we'd picked up en-route. One of a few Calais specials, picked out whilst Mia took the young'uns for wees and poos, scoping out the standard of the facilities. Celebrating the miraculous erection of The Green Goblin by consuming said wine, watching the kids consume the Pringles and car sweets for their evening meal. Got twatted and gave Mia oral that night, after much persuasion, if I remember correctly. She had to shove a hoody over her head to muffle her moan. Kids slept just across the way, dreaming innocent dreams of sandcastles and treasure hunts. We must have been drunk.

'Shit myself there like,' Shaun says after catching his breath, hands on hips, leaning over bags he's jettisoned, 'see that bloke pat searching me? Fucking hell man.'

'I'm jealous, I wouldn't have minded a little pat down,' jokes Jasmine. Shaun too busy huffing to say anything in return. He grins as the adrenaline begins to wear off.

'Fucking hell. There was a dog there inall! A fucking Fido!' He exhales as he puts himself upright. Hands on hips looking as if he's ran a marathon or something. Then begins scanning the pile of bags on the floor. His eyes fix on the cool box. 'Anyone want a cold one?' He's pulling out a can, heavily wrapped in condensation. Looks delicious actually. Ring-pull hiss, then three great gulps. Satisfied exhale. He's mended. Easily rescued from the trauma.

'I'll have one in a minute,' I say, knowing I'll be occupied with this tent and unpacking everything how I like for quite some time to come. 'I'll get this up first,' I say. It then occurs to me why he was so concerned about getting searched. He's carrying more than just phone, wallet and keys. He's carrying not-so-legal party enhancers. He never said for certain, but knowing him he wouldn't be doing without. Based on his face now, I guess he's not buried them in a wash bag or in a sock bundle like previous times, but rather has them close to hand. Hopefully not wedged anywhere too intimate. Arse crack drugs never do shift that bummy odour.

'Yes, go on then, chuck one over please,' nods Jasmine, the least sweaty looking of the lot of us. Having done a decent chunk of festivals in my life, this is always the toughest bit. Lugging tonnes of gear from your car, through the entrance and then picking a camping spot. Always worried you've picked a dodgy pitch, don't want to have a load of knackers as neighbours. Don't want anyone too young, or too old. Don't want any shaggers, but you don't want prudes either. Don't want any smackheads or dealers, but you don't want anyone who's going to grass on you to the nearest campsite marshall if they smell anything slightly herbal. Or hear a prolonged sniff, but no nose blow. Strictly no children nearby. That's a must. Got stung with that once before which made for some spectacularly psychedelic experiences, rushing hard on some dodgy substance in a tent as a mother streamed Teletubbies to her infant less than a metre away. - *Time for tubby bye bye* - as I try and stop my fiery fingers from laughing at me. It'll be some years until I even consider bringing the spawn here. Experience has taught me though, that ultimately it doesn't matter, it's up to the festival gods. As long as you're not too near the shitters, not too near the dance area, or on the path of a main thoroughfare, you're halfway towards success. Break that rule and smell, noise and filth will destroy you. The distance between entrance and my pitch choice is getting shorter every year that passes, age doing its best to destroy my stamina. I picture the graph it would make, and wonder what Excel formula I'd need. Might do that one day. I know I won't. Just like I never made that epic food plan.

A quick check of this spot showed no red flags prior to picking. No neighbours present at the scattered tents, but no hints of anything sinister. Looks standard enough. A couple of tents away there's a bloke sitting staunch with white vest, cargo shorts and a straw hat on his mush. He's drinking a deep brown drink. Cans of real ale lined up next to his legs. Staring about looking suspicious of what's going on. Looks like a bloke who booked it thinking it was Camping and Caravanning Club and accidentally ended up doing it in a festival field, but is too stubborn to move or accept his mistake. Looks moody but nothing ropey. There's no MAGA hats or swastika tattoos that I can see.

'Wanker with a guitar,' Shaun announces. Pointing subtly with his can grasping hand. I look in the direction he's gesturing, it's behind me. Sure enough, there's someone with an acoustic guitar sitting cross legged on the grass, plucking away with his fingers as a couple sits watching holding hands, girl's head on boy's shoulder. Falsetto singing of something I don't recognise. All plinky and slow. Wrong mood for this time of day, we need something energetic and bouncing. His eyes are closed as if he's doing the most important gig of his life. To me, it's just an annoyance muddying and tarnishing the far superior tunes of Bowie I can hear over yonder. Guitarist is a handsome bastard admittedly, but with awful clothing choice. Some pink and yellow number shirt, he looks like a deflated beach ball that stands out through the waves of blue and green tents in that direction. Bet he doesn't go short of a shag this weekend though.

'There's always one isn't there?' Shaun says, 'There's always a wanker who brings their own guitar to a festival,' he rants to Jasmine, who smiles and laughs back. Her eyes drawn to the pink and yellow plucker. 'I mean why? Honestly. Line-up not good enough for you like?' he continues haranguing into his can.

'I see that. Mustn't have thought there was enough music scheduled,' she whispers. Along with steel string ring, there's an ambient din of laughter, chatter and phone music playing, all treble. Percussion of tent pegs getting driven into solid soil. An old woman a few tents in Jasmine's direction is sitting playing Candy Crush loudly. I'd recognise that sound anywhere, owing to the months I lost Mia's attention on an evening. A period when sex drives were low, and Netflix's output was uninspiring. We even considered cancelling our subscription, never too convincing in our threats. Somewhere over in the distance I hear Lee Perry talking about Sunscreen. - *If I could offer you one tip for the future, sunscreen would be it* - That would be a tremendous idea to heed that advice actually, I will as soon as I get this tent up. I lean down and start unzipping the bag, remembering how much of a git it was to fold up and cram back in the bag last time we used it. Scotland, I think it was. Midges everywhere. Half expect to get attacked by the offspring of the ones that terrorised us at Loch Lomond last summer. I remember the frustration of getting bitten every five seconds as I jostled and wrestled with the tent, crushing out every cubic centimetre of air to try and get it back in its carry bag. Hating the unknown person who packs the bloody things at the factory, jealous of their effortless ability to pack things into their carry bags with such ease. 'It'll be a machine you knacker,' said Mia, but until Greg Wallace shows me that factory and proves my darling dear wife correct, then I'll firmly believe it's some smug arse person. Someone with pneumatic thumbs.

'How can I help you?' Jasmine leans down as the innards of the tent bag start spilling out like some prolapsed intimate body part. The smell of year-old log fire smoke still strong in there.

'Erm, start with these please,' I hand her the fibreglass poles. Clinking and swishing as I pull them out the wound. I'm a restless surgeon. A job I'd be shit at, but at least the theatre would be spotless.

'Shaun, stick that somewhere,' I point to his beer, 'and give me a hand with this.' He instead upturns the can and takes several massive gulps. Silent belch muted by hand, and he's crouched grabbing the other end of the tent fabric. The grass is prickly on my legs, bristly on my skin. It's browned a bit in patches, toughened by the unrelenting heat of the last few months. Starved by the unusually long period of dryness. Hosepipes are banned down south apparently. Not up here yet.

Before long, we're all deep in task laying the groundsheet and sliding in poles, the boys taking the slack whilst Jasmine bites her tongue in concentration threading the poles. Doesn't take a great deal of time until it's up, and ready to be hammered into place.

'Stick the door in that direction,' points Jas.

'Aye, good shout,' agrees Shaun. We take the weight and shuffle foot our home for the weekend into its final resting place, pointing towards the mountains in the distance. Pulling it taut on our respective sides, Shaun trying to take two corners. I'm then hunched down with mallet and tent pegs, tethering in neon green guy ropes. Knuckles take a few bashes, forearms feel brittle with the brute force, but then it's in. No fear of the wind blowing these two anywhere. They're chucking the strewn bags inside our abode now. The smell of plastic fabric and stale air heated in the sun hits me and sparks off such a litany of nostalgic memories. Amazing it still holds that Chinese factory new smell too. Shaun scurries into the left hand pod inside, unrolling sleeping mat and then bag. Jasmine waits back.

'Which one you want?' she asks.

'That one at the back,' I say without hesitation. The one I always share with Mia. The one between the two kids. Our little chrysalis. The only one I can guarantee is clean enough for me. I set about unrolling, unpacking, and arranging my home for the next five nights, manic in my movements. Then, then I can have that cold beer.

Wednesday
Shaun

The longest shadows of the day stretch and yawn across the site as we all gawp at the passers-by. I'm baffled by the clobber these lot are wearing. There are some absolute weapons walking about, but there's some epic Adidas on display to balance it out. Our disposable barbecue sits on two stones that Seb spent a good few minutes combing the ground for like a lunatic. Inviting looks of 'Who's this cunt like?' from the audience of camp chair dwellers and tent erectors. The coals are turning cocaine white as we dish out another round of cold cans from the cool box. A nearby food vendor is playing David Bowie. I guess it's the greatest hits, based on the back-to-back banger. - *John, I'm only dancing, it turns me on* - Fucking love the guy, it all went to shit when he shuffled off this planet as far as I'm concerned. We're embraced by our camp chairs, wrapped in high tension fabric letting mesh cupholders do all the heavy lifting of our drinks. The comfort allows me to forgive and almost forget the battering my ribs and arse received on the way here. I'm like a domestic abuse victim, thinking Monday's journey will be different. Jasmine is mouthing along to Jean Genie. Tapping her hands onto the lid of the can that sits wedged between her thighs. Her name I picked up with hawk like ear when Seb asked, 'Jasmine can you pass the mallet out of that green bag please?' Knew it was something floral. Wouldn't make a very good detective me, funny that I was in line to join the police at one point too. What a joke. Couldn't swan through the entrance of this place with a bag of pills and several grammes of decent quality coke in my pocket if that was my career path. Pure madness.

Seb has whacked a whole eight pack of plant-based sausages onto the barbecue. She's apparently a vegetarian. Seb is, I shudder at the thought of the word, flexitarian. Bowk. Good for blood pressure he says. Consciously cutting down red meat, in an attempt to not resemble it in middle age. Some fad that no doubt has come from Mumsnet, through the conduit of Mia and into Seb's repertoire. Comes to something when your brother is minding his blood pressure, that's the march of age right fucking there.

'Suppose it doesn't matter if they're a little undercooked?'

'Yeah, fine,' smiles Jasmine pleasantly, 'no one has died from an undercooked pea before'. Her teeth as white as her ribbed white T-shirt with capped arms. Sunglasses like John Lennon in that famous picture of him, and patterned blue and white yoga pants complete her evening attire. Looks canny like. Changing clothes so soon into this marathon may be something she comes to regret further down the line. Judging by the size of her bag, there won't be much on the subs bench for her.

'I'll grab the buns,' I say as I dive into the plastic reek of our tent, which is already getting stiflingly hot inside despite only being up for about an hour. 'Phwoar, hope it cools off in there tonight like.' I re-emerge with a six pack of white buns in hand. I can't imagine sleeping well in there if it's anything like that heat. Going to have to ensure I'm totally fucked.

'Long days around this time of year inall,' pipes up Seb, over the sizzle and steam of his little barbecue which he is crouched over attentively. Prodding and poking in intrigue at the browning sausages, 'going to be well hot in the mornings too. The weather app says anyway,' he concludes. Him and the weather.

'We all sleeping in our birthday suits then, is it?' blurts Jasmine. Me and Seb both look at one another with a mix of amusement and embarrassment. We scrunch our familial schoolboy grins, lost for words. Jasmine looks betrayed by the effects of alcohol and quickly retracts, 'I am of course only joking.' She then changes the subject entirely, 'who we got on tonight?' she nods towards me, noticing the line-up lanyard draped over my lap. Well, my crotch to be precise, as I reach to grab it.

'Err...' I punctuate the wait as I rifle through the pages. A map, a review section, interview with a local band. '...ah here!' I elongate as I arrive on

Wednesday's page, 'tonight, we have a few people on. There's The Flying Squad on later on, for fans of that one good song.'

'Hmm, not too bothered by that.'

'Could be fun though,' I continue, 'then there is someone called H.P. Milton at The Plantation stage. 10pm, it says.'

'Great, he's amazing, plenty of time to get them sausages rammed down,' she replies, dimpled cheeks as she turns her head to the low sun and necks the remnants of her cider can before cracking open another. Far less hiss from those fruity ciders like. She looks noticeably at ease. The artificial smell of her drink hitting my nostrils.

'Don't know him, what does he sing?' I ask. Seb's too fixated on ensuring the pea protein sausages do not burn and receive an all-round tan.

'You'll know loads of his stuff. Used to be in The Echoes, got some epic songs actually. He's got that new song too. It's everywhere at the minute,' she struggles through a sipful of cider, 'duh duh duhhh doooo,' she begins, before collapsing into giggles at the sheer futility of her attempt. My expression a one of confusion, I'm sure.

'Fucking hell!' I laugh sounding like a young kid's attempt at a machine gun.

'You'll know it Shaun, you've got to man, he is good like,' offers Seb, 'and The Echoes were class inall. He's got some bangers man, honestly. It's one of the performances I'm looking forward to... and know,' he adds.

'Not sure like.'

'Call yourself a music fan?'

'No, not anymore I don't, maybe ten years ago.'

'You'll know the new one, I swear down. Duh duh duhhhhh,' she offers again, mouthing the same notes, but with more emphasis. Like an Englishman does when ordering a beer abroad. 'Two beers por favor!' I reply with an exaggerated accent, all tonguey. I grin, as she fruitlessly tries to twig a tune in me. Ain't gonna happen. No way.

'Shaun, you'll know it,' she protests.

'Not like that you won't.'

'I don't man. Try and sing another one.'

'Please don't,' Seb pipes up deadpan. Sunglasses still yet to steer from the sausages, probing with a spork which, to my uneducated mind will melt like a bastard if he lets it linger there any longer. Then again, these sausages are surely nowt but plastic anyway. It doesn't look like Jasmine's going to be serenading me anymore to this bloke's back catalogue as she's giggling again, an infectious laugh, childlike almost. But not annoying, yet. Her shoulders twitching with the laugh. 'Just wait and see,' she states as the giggle subsides. She looks bonny when she smiles. Mind, I've noticed some scars running up her left arm like a train track after a landslide, mostly healed and white but some looking recent and fresh. Looks like the logo for Monster energy drinks. Three great gouges. Must be self-inflicted. I understand and avoid looking too much. She just wears her pain on the outside, that's all.

After a brief pause, Seb offers, 'I think these are done,' he scoops the sausages with spork individually and flicks them onto a paper plate. He switches to using his fingers after the first two, both near misses, and winces each time the hot plant-based fat meets his fingertips. Do plants even get fat?

'Lovely,' with an extended 'o' from Jasmine as Seb hands her the plate, she fingers two into a bap, before squirting a liberal amount of ketchup on top. Lid flapped shut she smiles.

'Cheers bro,' I say as I fish two sausages off the now saggy plate into my own bun, 'ahh ya bastard,' I hiss as the hot fat burns my own fingertips.

'Careful they're hot!' Seb smiles. Sarcastic bastard, just like Mam used to say. I eye up the third sausage that I really fancy, but lump against that. Must be courteous, don't be a pig, early days with the new company. Ketchup squirt. Ignore the farting noises, we're all adults here.

'Have another, man,' he gnarls as he thrusts the sausage plate back towards me, 'not like you to be polite!' he says before continuing, 'Shaun used to pride himself on his eating abilities.' Here we fucking go. 'Yeah, his particularly impressive achievement in life was how many Yorkshire puddings he could eat at our grandma's. He used to scran as many as possible before any of the other grandchildren got a chance.' Jasmine is smiling, slowly chewing her bap, little inhales of fresh air to cool the fake meat getting mashed up by those lovely white teeth.

'Yes, Grandma's dinners are always the best!' she agrees with great big nods in between inhales, 'My nonna, my grandma even, made the best pizza, like epic how good it was.'

'Pizza? She was cool!'

'Italian,' she states through chews, 'though she spoke like a Geordie. Was quite the blend. Fully embraced the British ways, except the food of course.'

'Oh aye? Good old grannies, to be fair ours' Yorkshire puddings were class. Yet to have tasted better since,' I defend.

'I wouldn't know, never had one with a gannet like you around,' Seb jibes.

'Har har,' I mock laugh, unable to think of anything witty to say in the moment, 'trust me, they were. But...' I pause for dramatic effect, 'Mam's were a close second in the rankings like.'

'Yes. You're not wrong there,' I sink, just for a moment. Drift into a different time, mind wanders to the Sunday dinner dining table, windows steamed up with all four gas hobs boiling away gravy and green veg. Brown scorches on the oven glove from a hundred Sunday roasts gone by. Mam there in her pink pinstripe pinny whipping up a dinner of epic proportions. Well, at least they seemed to our infant eyes. Mountains of peppery swede, potatoes crispy on the outside dripping in vegetable oil, green veg of every variety, and of course, the Yorkshire puddings. Then there was the chicken, roasted to perfection. The hum of the electric oven a bass melody alongside the Top 40 charts playing over a massive FM radio. Black plastic sound system claggy with kitchen grease from eight years of home cooking, speaker holes filled with unidentified matter. Me and Seb aching from booting a flat peeling football about all morning on the local school field back before they put up that green metal fence and anti-vandal paint. Arms stinging from nettles after the constant need to fish it back from the hedgerow, my job as I was the youngest. Throat horse from shouting 'Shearer!' or 'Asprilla!' when booting it goal bound, imagining we were playing to a packed St. James' Park in the FA Cup final. The prospect of one day doing so being something other than a ridiculous notion. Dad would be dozing on the sofa as Formula One cars screamed around Hockenheim. Michael Schumacher claiming yet another victory. The allure of the red Marlboro car. Mam would pour the pan juices into the gravy. Then pour that into a cloudy plastic jug. Through sheer alchemy she'd create the best gravy I have ever tasted. 'Dinner's up!' she'd bellow, 'Someone wake your father up please,' playing rock, paper scissors as to which poor bastard got that risky job. We'd all scurry from our little settings to gather around a table. My knees still mucky from celebrating goals with a knee slide, telling everyone about my overhead kick whilst the salt and pepper is passed around. Dollops of carmine cranberry sauce spooned onto white chicken breast. The smell of grass seeping out of my fake Newcastle top that Mam got from the Quayside Market. I snap back into this field, smell the present-day grass, and take a bite out of my very first vegan sausage sarnie. The sweet acidity of the ketchup hits first, followed by the pepper and herbiness of the sausage, tastes exactly the same as a normal one. I have to purse my lips in order to inhale some cool air.

'You know what?' I say, as I exhale steam and mouth soft white bread, 'That's a decent sausage sandwich that,' I'm not even lying to them out of politeness.

'And no dead piggies suffered either,' jabs Jasmine, as the jagged guitars of Bowie's – *fame puts you there where things are hollow* - plays from the nearby food stall. Jangly disco chords and feedback drones. Not one of his best, but still class like.

'So, who are we all buzzing to see?' Jasmine asks. Truth be told, I've given very little thought about who I'm arsed about seeing beyond Origins of Sound and Everest 1922. I tend to care more about the lawlessness and spontaneity of these places. The opportunity to take drugs and lose myself to repetitive beats.

'It's all about The Red Eyes for me,' she chirps. I've heard their stuff and it's pretty good, should be a good closer to the weekend.

'Yeah, they should be good, so will Origins of Sound... obviously,' says Seb, 'but to be honest, I've kind of lost touch with music in recent years, I hope we discover some new bands.' Aye, that would be good.

'Same for me,' I offer, 'it's more than just about the music these things,' then again, it would be nice to get excited about something new.

'Ah, makes me feel less conscious about not knowing much of the line-up then,' she says, easing a little into her chair.

People are emerging from tents and the light is getting older with every passing minute. People are still flowing in from the main gates at the top of the hill. Pausing to rest their arms, they observe their surroundings and the imposing slab of rock beyond the site. Bodies ache and voices say, 'This'll do,' to the patch of grass they gasp for breath on. They drop down their gear in a heap. We were like this a few hours ago. Feeling smug as fuck it isn't us now, drinking and resting. My biceps feel like they're finally feeling normal again. The earlier settlers are wandering around their home for the weekend. Flip-flops replace trainers, and shorts replace jeans. Tin drum sound of toilet doors slamming in the distance, bashing constantly along to Bowie as beer and wine are excreted to make way for more and more.

Wednesday
Jasmine

'I'll finish this, get to the ladies' room, and then we'll go explore yeah?' I say to the lads when the conversation between them falters. We've already covered off our top five bands ever seen live, mine shockingly bad versus those two. Bless them though, they didn't laugh too hard when I said 'Westlife' when I was eight years old. The sun has moved from burning necks to noses since we pitched up. Sensing no urgency from them two to move on, I decided to take the lead.

'Yeah, sound.'

'Aye.' So, I whip back my drink and stand up from the fabric hug of my chair, instantly feeling the giddy-leggedness. Deviating from wine crying for a change is doing wonders. Pause for a moment to gauge how to walk. Look to the toilet area, grimace at the thought. Can almost see the air go wavy with fumes above it. Imagine the smell. Like Sicily 1999. That café by the beach, where my parents gave one another the silent treatment. Bad memories. Can still remember the smell. Takes me to a sad place. Put on your big girl pants Jasmine, this is the way this weekend. I set off on the slalom through the tent shanty town that's growing with every passing minute. Flagpoles, gazebos, and awnings punctuate the scattering of polyester homes. As I walk past pockets of people sitting, chatting, and drinking, they all seem to turn and smile. 'You alright there?' and 'Hi,' they say. Seeming more at ease than anyone in the normal world you'd come across. My drunken grin smiling back a giddy 'Hiya,' socialising was never my strong point, I was never the first to strike up conversations, find it increasingly hard to make friends, but something that bizarrely doesn't fill me with dread here. There is an air of feel good. Soon enough I'm on the flattened grass walkway, a wide strip that resembles the brushed hair of a horse, almost tan colour with the straw dryness. Animals on my mind as the sight and smell of the long drops, I've long since heard about, get closer with each tipsy step. A row of twenty or so metal framed PVC doors adorned with spray painted whimsical designs slam shut as people skitter in and out. Is this artwork here to distract you? To take your mind off what is about to happen? It's like a game of Guess Who, where the tiles fight back. There's a small queue formed beside a little shiny metal standpipe that has an octagon of faucets and hand towels. Not many of those who leave the little PVC cells use the wash facilities. Some leave pulling hand sanitiser bottles from pockets, others light cigarettes or hold beer cans in defiance, almost celebratory. Like war veterans sent mad by the experience. Looks like we could be at the epicentre of the next pandemic if we're not careful. I join the queue behind a girl in a bucket hat, super straightened hair and a military jacket over baggy cargo pants and Converse. Must be in her early 50s, but still looks like she's clinging on to her youth, well too. Can't help but worry she might be a tad warm in them, dressed for battle though. We exchange a knowing look, a gimpy smile of best wishes for what we're about to witness. Paradise is about to be lost. It feels weird not being able to fill this idle time with checking my phone. Scrolling and fidgeting until it's my turn. Numbing my mind with triviality and bullshit. It occurs to me how unbelievably uncomfortable it has become to just be. We have lost the ability to be bored. Or not even be bored, but just to be. I find myself studying the floor, shuffling feet. The jazz rhythm of the long drop doors crashing closed gets louder as the queue edges forward. A bemusing sight as I see blokes leaving the cubicles with toilet rolls or baby wipe packets in their hands. Apparently not phased that everyone knows they've been dropping their effluence into a great communal pool. I suppose this will all become very normal as the weekend goes on. At least as a girl it's not totally clear. Bucket hat lass goes into the fray. Good luck sister. I see you. She's replacing a leggy girl, early 20s or something sporting an Adidas tracksuit and blue WKD. Looking pale and unwell from what she has encountered. She'll need something stronger to drink now.

A door on the far left opens and slams behind, heavy set bearded bloke with The Levellers T-shirt, which he probably bought on their first tour, leaves grasping a pink packet of sensitive baby wipes. I can only imagine what he's left me. Our eyes meet. A split second. I don't know whether that's the decorum, or whether that's his silent apology. Here goes. I canter up the three galvanised steel steps and enter my cell for the next minute. Push the fabric door. Colourful heart design with legs and big husky eyes and eyelashes. Like a children's hospital ward decoration, a distraction from the sad purpose of being there. Spring loaded door slams behind. A muting of the outside sounds. Push the cold metal bolt in. Impregnated with endless amounts of awful matter no doubt. God, imagine the germs on that thing. How many fingers have touched that so far today? How many of those fingers have touched dirty willies, dirty fannies, and dirty bums? I'll just have to make my body as inhospitable as possible for any germs through alcohol. I'm alone. First thing I notice is the heat in here. A little hotbox.

    Then, the smell.

    Wow.

    Quite literally breathtaking. Baking in the heat of the day is the excretion of hell hounds. There is no God, and if there is, this would make him cry in shame. The gates have only been open for single digit hours and this is how they smell. Christ. Going to have to prepare myself for Sunday's squalor. Perfume under the nose maybe? Going to have to get myself some Vicks from somewhere. Wonder whether I can keep in a number two for how many days? Five. No chance. I'll give it a good try though. Wow. Best get this over with, Jasmine. Knickers and yoga pants down in one combined movement. Don't look down. Don't think about the seat, try and hover. Clear your mind. Breathe in and out through the mouth. Imagine the waste matter in my lungs. Urgh. Picture something else. A far off place. Feel the relief. Must have had four cans of fluid to get rid of. Taking forever. Minimising breaths. I feel a strange draught hitting the backs of my thighs. Cooler than the ambient air. Unsure how I feel about that knowing what lies beneath. To think of that horror story from Leeds Festival, where some poor lass ended up taking a plodge in there getting her handbag back. I'd welcome that cursed bag of mine to fall into there. A fitting end to it, I'd say.

Done. Wipe. Knickers and pants back up. Touch the dirty bolt and down the three steps to hell. Back into the bright, hot, and clean air. Now I know why people are dodging the wash facilities. They want to get away as quick as possible. Away from Saigon. Away from the reminder that we're all just filthy, dirty animals. I'll dig out some sanitiser back at the tent and cover myself in it.

Slalom back towards the yellow smiley flag a neighbour has erected; I recognise faces of people I greeted on the way before. I look at them now with a slight sense of shame, but feel more mature. Now at the ripe age of 33, I've experienced a festival toilet. There's no going back now. It's part of me. I am rock and roll. Practically Courtney Love now.

I see the lads standing with their backs to me, they look like they're laughing. Shaun's shoulder shaking like a diesel generator. Right elbows point sideways on both of them as they stand in can holding positions. As I get closer, the sound of an acoustic guitar gets clearer. They're watching the pink clad bloke playing.

'Alright, lads?' I say, slapping Seb on the shoulder.

'How was that?'

'Fucking horrible mate,' I spit. I grimace at my use of the word, 'mate'. A term I very rarely use, usually in an ironic way, when I'm backed in a corner or as a way of showing I'm fucked off and trying to project aggression. Used it quite a lot in aggression towards Ellis when I felt brave enough. Babe more often used, as a way of trying to stop the blows.

'Let's go wandering then,' Shaun hands me another cool can as we begin a sauntering meander in the opposite direction as we set off exploring. Willing for the night to take us away from ourselves. Willing for the next toilet to be nicer.

Wednesday
Shaun

I'm stood in the riptide of the bar queue, minimum wage kids in black T-shirts 2nd gear speed pouring bad looking pints into fucking plastic cups. A sea of straw hats, bucket hats and sweaty foreheads edge forward begging for their order to be heard. Fellas left and right have been served before me despite arriving later. Keep it calm Shaun. Peace and love and all of that shite this weekend, remember? But I do feel a great bastard strain suppressing the anger that arises from both bad bar service and bad queue etiquette. How hard can it be man? Fuck me, I'm so English. The fat curly haired kid who was serving in front of me is now nowhere to be seen, and I'm standing in a dead zone. Fucking fantastic. Bank card perched in my hand like a limp cock. The volume of the chatter is deafening, bouncing off the plastic roofing in here, it's proper disorientating. I'm hot and bothered and all I want is a proper fucking pint. I managed to navigate past Checkpoint Charlie, the right good frisk you get when you enter the arena to ensure you're not smuggling any drink in beyond the campsites. Don't want to be making any financial losses on punters keeping their own wallets in order by bringing their own peeve, do you? Lest we forget the shareholders. Doesn't seem like they're arsed by the movement of Class-As though. Guess that's not really something that can compete with the stuff they're selling. Not like the days of legal high tents that were around when Seb was just getting started on the festival scene, remember him telling me about them. Quite a radge thing to have if you think about it. I'll make it my mission this weekend to get some peeve past these jobsworths at the checkpoint though. I like a challenge. Imagining whether I could fit a 440ml can up my arse. It probably would eventually fit with a great deal of effort, but wouldn't be ideal like, probably need a fuck load of lube, or a bit Lurpak if the budget stretched that far. Never know though, I might like it. Never been that way inclined thus far mind, well except for that lass who slipped a pinkie up my hoop during a blowie that time. Blasted my beans quite quick after that to be fair to her. Dirtying a perfectly good retro Oasis T-shirt of hers as she wiped her chin and finger on it. Ah, memories. A gaggle of girls jabber behind me, cackling away proper loudly at something that won't be that funny.

'Sorry mate,' one says as she elbows my back whilst rummaging in her bag for something. Maybe a flare would be handy. A whistle and a torch would also be useful to alert these casual grafters of our thirst plight over here. Makes a mockery of the job this like, I'm ashamed on behalf of the profession. 'Sorry about your wait,' one says to a heavy-set lad at the front, could quite have easily been, 'Sorry about your weight.' Contactless doesn't work, 'try popping it in the bottom,' she says. Jesus.

'No worries,' I say as I turn and see a lass surely no older than 16 and her pals queueing. A waft of perfume and cosmetics hits me hard. Nearly choking I'm transported back to GCSE maths and sitting next to Tasha, me hiding the groin aching pain of adolescence under a compass scratched melamine table. Barely able to concentrate on Pythagoras and all that shite when all I wanted to do was spurt me load. Ideally on or in Tasha, but at that time I wasn't choosy. The maths teacher would probably do if chance allowed. Those years were punctuated with masturbation and Rocky chocolate bars, reverse sleep patterns and more masturbation.

The lasses are all in white T's, denim shorts and checking reflections in cracked and scratched phone screens. Pouting and giggling at Snapchats from boys back home. Fake nails all pointy and primary colours. Couldn't be receiving a finger up the arse from one of these lassies, would be shitting blood for a week. One sucks in a red plastic vape, a scent of strawberry mingles with the Impulse deodorant and Boots 3 for 2 gift set smells. I look up above one's daisy chain headband and see Seb and Jasmine chatting away. Seb looks animated with radge arm gestures, all vertical and horizontal. Showy prick. Jasmine looks like she's laughing at everything he's saying, hand covering mouth. Look back at the bar and curly haired kid is sauntering back from behind the run of pasting tables. Past the two litre bottles of Coke and little cranberry, orange, and tonic bottles. Hurley from lost, that's who he reminds me of. He's fiddling with his lanyard swinging and twisting it on the end of his sausage fingers. Walking with an arrogance that makes me think he's been for a shite. The bastard better have washed his chubby hands like. Lanyard swinging around his finger as he surveys what his fellow colleagues are doing. Working slowly, that's what. I want to wrap that lanyard around his pock marked neck and make him eat the till card it holds. He looks like he smells. Looks like he's only existed on cans of Monster and microwave pizza, fuelled by the light given off from a TV screen as he's switched from wanking to playing on his games console. Bet his mam wangled him this job all, 'There's jobs going at that festival, I think it'll do you good to get out there. Will be good for your CV.' All bar work is good for on a CV is more bar work, let me tell you. Hotel fucking California.

Finally, his fat arse and greasy beard reappear in front of me, and naturally, the lad in front is ordering drinks for what I can only assume is the entire weekend's line-up. Combination of slow poured pints and drinks with mixers, as well as soft drinks. Thank fuck they don't serve hot drinks here; he'd be all over them inall given the chance I bet. Skinny flapaccinos with oat milk and hazelnut fucking syrup. An uncomfortable feeling as a drop of sweat runs from my armpit down my oblique. Don't know whether I'm muscular enough to describe it as an oblique mind. Maybe love handle is more appropriate, if only it saw the occasional bit of love. The pink and black glowing light of Pornhub probably doesn't count. There's not much love in some of the things I've seen on there either like. The big ball of bastard in the sky is still beating down on my already tender neck. That's the problem with long days, more time to burn. It's chucking out some serious heat today, even now at this early evening hour.

As curly finishes pouring the last of the soft drinks, I lock eyes on the fucker. Like a fish on a hungry man's hook, I ain't letting this bastard get away. Pre-empting the bloke in front's predicament of too many drinks to carry at once, I dip and squeeze as he turns to a figure on the periphery and hands them the squidgy cups.

'Two lagers, one cider, and three bombs,' I say in the split second my hand touches the sticky bar. I'm not giving this fella the courtesy of a please. No smile or expression from him, he's a man lobotomised. Synapses too clogged with spunk and cheesy chip grease to form a thought. I'm kind of perched on one leg next to the too many drinks man, desperate not to topple over, as he fucks about dispatching an endless stream of drinks to the shadowy figure behind. Must be an octopus with the number of things they will have to hold for him. Being just 50cm closer to the bar has afforded me some shade and the movement of the slow workers is even providing the slightest of breezes. It's ever so slightly cooling. Imagine how chilled I'd be if they worked like proper bar workers. Punters would be ice cold with my top grafting work rate. Would be frozen solid when I'm full of gear on a Friday night shift.

'£42,' he says, not even a please from him. Ah, the bastard is cleverer than I predicted. I try to stifle my shock at the price, no doubt it's obvious on my face, not that he'd care. Probably revelling in it, might even be taking a cut to buy himself another energy drink. The contactless beeps. I bury my fingers in the cups, remembering they haven't been washed since the services. I've done a few wees since and clarted about putting a tent up in a field that is normally home to deer and sheep. Let's hope the sterilising properties of alcohol are all they're cracked up to be. I turn and head back towards the clearing, back into the big ball of bastard's dying rays. Past the white-T Snapchatters. The back of my sweaty head now probably being sent to their thousands of followers as a background to their pouting faces. I'm heading out of the rhubarb rhubarb rhubarb hubbub of noise of heightened folk jabbering nonsense.

'Fucking queue,' I say, as soon as I thrust the drinks towards Jasmine and Seb. I chin the bomb in record speed not even waiting for a cheers. The sickly-sweet burn extinguished with three enormous gulps of the most expensive beer I've ever purchased.

Wednesday
Seb

We've each bought a round from that bar and now I'm feeling a tad drunk, could even be sunstroke. We were meant to be exploring the bits of the site that are open. But each get distracted and pulled in by whatever shiny object catches our attention. I'm laughing at the hats they're selling in this stall. Mexican wrestling masks. Kermit the Frog heads. Big stupid wigs. Massive knitted cock and bollock hats available in all popular skin tones. Pulling them onto my head and posing for those two grinning idiots. Finding myself craving their obliging laughter. It feels nice.

'That looks mint man...' Shaun's choking as I arrange a blonde mullet wig on my head. Checking myself in the mirror. Acknowledging my own reflection, a more relaxed version of my usual self greets me, albeit one with a fabulous new hairstyle, '...like a sexy Pat Sharpe.'

'Pat who?'

'Never mind.'

'Seb, get it,' Jas is urging through laughs and breaths. I've parted with forty odd quid on a round of drinks before. What's another fifteen on a wig? The pints and the bombs fuelling my fingers to pull out my bank card as I approach the till.

'Card okay?' I ask. Of course it is. Everyone takes card nowadays, except the Turkish barbers around the corner from me. A fact I keep forgetting, testing the proprietor's patience and trust as I jog to the local cashpoint hoping it's working.

'Of course. £15 quid please,' a bemused look back, dark eyes raised momentarily from a phone screen. Purple and black streaked hair.

'You sell, erm, room odorisers in here?' I ask. Strangely craving the head rush and headache of poppers. The drunkenness and newfound freedom's ability to remove any inhibitions clear to see. I have the moral fibre of a wet sponge.

'Nah mate, they all got banned a few years back now,' they pause, then continue with a smirk, 'no odorising of rooms for you.'

'Really? Fucking Tories!' I bark, 'oh well, cheers anyway,' I shout as I head back out to the waiting Jasmine and Shaun, who again fall about at the sight of my mullet.

'Can't believe you bought that!'

'Fifteen quid!' the punch of the expense already nipping my conscience. That's nearly five meal deals, that.

'Looks ridiculous man,' scoffs Shaun.

'You said I looked class a second ago man, you dick.'

'It's a good look. It suits you. Sexy,' says Jasmine, 'sexy Matt Sharpe.'

'Pat Sharpe,' I correct, indignantly. Almost immediately I feel the itch of the cheap material on my scalp. Defiant, I leave it on. It's not just Mia who can splurge her money on cheap Chinese tat. It'll come in handy one day. Some work charity do, or something, hope they don't do all that nonsense in my new place.

We head out into the emerging night riding a wave of intoxication and childlike excitedness. Christmas Eve vibes all sugared up and giddy with anticipation. Jasmine glint with innocent amazement like a child seeing the paper decorations and balloons of their own birthday party for the first time. I'm feeling light and nimble, bursting with energy. Maybe it's just the chemicals from the wig seeping into my skull. Wasn't it a mercury laced hat that sent the Mad Hatter mad? We amble in no direction in particular, sharing observations of the visual and audio onslaught we're surrounded by. Rainbow flags everywhere. People free to be themselves. A spectrum of colour and love. - *there goes the fear* – Ah, great songs litter the place. There's a constant smell of grass. Like the long summer evenings of childhood. Six weeks holiday a thing that never ended, choc-ices and bruised shins. There's a neon glow about the place. Vapes are like party streamers in mouths of shuffling explorers. Dance music is bursting out of the waltzer speakers nearby. High pitched shrieks of G-force and cider combining. A small Ferris wheel. Dangly legs hanging above make me feel woozy. We walk past a gigantic sculpture; it's surrounded by people taking photos. Couples taking selfies, arms outstretched.

Hoover lips kissing. Slurping noises. It spells '#Love' and is painted in a Pollock-esque splatted fashion. - *that I won't disappear, in this city, I've got nothing to fear* - We walk by pulling bemused faces. Scoffing at the cheesiness, it's Instagram bowkiness. We're far too old and cynical for such nonsense. But secretly I wish I had Mia with me to pose beside it. Would love to be kissing her here and now. To share this excitement with her, this moment. I wonder if my grinning companions have mixed feelings about it. Horns play - *I will be your light, I will be your light, I will be your light* – from an Oxfam vintage clothes tent. The place is a vibrant expanse of excitement joined by great ranges of flattened fields. It feels airy but intimate at the same time. The night brings everyone closer together. The tightening of a rope.

As we delve further around the site, a quick glance at the VIP section is worse than I feared. Caricatures of festival goers spilling glasses of hipster swill performing hi-jinks in expensive suits ill-suited to the Northern fields. Looking more like a wedding, one of them faux-farm ones done to make interesting photos. The guests look like characters crafted in the minds of London centric press and corporate guests speaking at one another, one-upmanship and cocaine fuelled nonsense. Like the London Stock Exchange. All blowjobs and ladder climbing. KPIs and PDPs shat into the craft beer sponsored petri dish of middle class wankery. All neatly separated by a purple rope. I turn away from the depressing sight. My mood sucked by it temporarily. Turn to the trees, and the fields of normal folk. Get chatting with some lad who claims to play for Stoke City youth team. He's hoofing pinecones across the grass with pinpoint accuracy as we chat whilst waiting for Jasmine and Shaun to return from 'The posh looking toilets,' as Jasmine put it. A queue far larger than your standard long drop. But then again, we have nothing but time. Tonight is ours. Save for an engagement with The Flying Squad at 9.15pm. More for novelty value than anything else, just to see that one song. A friendly chatter about nothing in particular, sports nutrition and physiotherapy then: 'See you later mate,' the alleged footballer says as he departs, clicking on a lighter and sucking down a great inhale of a cigarette. Smoke cloud rises into the ever deepening of the dark blue summer evening sky. -*come together as one* -

There's a young lad on his back over near the bins, he's peaky looking. Alone. Eyes wide open, staring up into the void. I approach him with Jack Sparrow like legs, wobbly with hitting the drink hard. 'You alright mate?' I slur. No response. His eyes glazed and distant. But he's smiling. Maybe even muttering something, can't hear him over the sound of - *then I swore when you were the last. When you were the last high* - Churros van pumping tremendous tracks and sticky smells out into the cooling air. Generator chugging away. It's like I'm looking at a younger version of myself. The first night casualty floored by exuberance. Icarus of the drink and drugs. Brought down with a bang. He stirs. Grunts. Then a great smile erupts. A crescent moon. Eyes widen and trace my face. Wherever his mind is, it's far from here. Maybe surfing on the surface of the sun that's sinking somewhere over the horizon.

'No wonder he's smiling with that fucking stupid mullet on your dish,' Shaun has returned, walking like Liam Gallagher, as he does when he's sufficiently peeved up. A heavy hand on my head. Ah yes, the one hour's wages head adornment. I'd almost forgotten.

'Alreet Matt Sharpe?' he taunts, with a smirk on his face.

Wednesday
Jasmine

Well, that Portaloo wasn't much better than before, but the chemical blue foot pump and sanitiser bottle at least made me feel slightly cleaner when having my wee. The illusion of sanitation. There wasn't a draught up my crack too, which I've decided will cause a bladder infection should enough faecal matter get carried in the winds of the long drops. That would be a nightmare here. Already dodged the bullet of a period by a matter of days. Being a girl can be quite a pain at times.

We've been wandering the site, laughing and jesting about things I can scarcely remember now. But I'm having fun. I'm actively enjoying the small talk with random strangers who pop up like moles in the fields. Folk are equally energised to be outdoors and engaged, able to chat at leisure, not needing to dart off to do an email, take a quick call or see to their kids. Being in the moment almost. It has been textbook first night of holiday feels.

I've come out of the toilet area and found the lads stood over some kid looking off his nut. Despite my first worry, they don't seem overly concerned for his welfare. 'We've all been there,' and 'first night innit?' they both say. I hope I don't befall a similar fate tonight. Those bombs from the bar before caused my heart to do some serious beats. - *We make hits* - There's a carousel of sounds around. All genres and decades. I feel like moving. A feeling I haven't felt in some time. Tonight, I have people instead of cats to share my moves with. This is what I've been practising for. Lock up your sons, or daughters.

'Let's head to the stage,' I say. The lads oblige, so we're strolling again in the direction of the only area for live music tonight. Before long we reach our destination. A few dodgy stop and studies of the lanyard by a wobbling Shaun, head scratches, and scans of scenery delaying our arrival only slightly. But we're here. Place is buzzing with bodies. A semi-circle stage with a modest rig of blue and red lights pointing at the stage. There's some 80s band on, a minor deal back then, but produced a song successful enough to fill enough festival slots to pay the bills. They're probably halfway through their set. Bald singer crouched behind a synthesiser flanked with two younger lads on bass and guitar. The stage stood over by pines some ten metres tall. West facing, so the sun's final descent over the horizon is behind backs, the sunburn sting numbed by a cooling air and alcohol's anaesthetic ability. I'll be feeling that tomorrow. Bright spots of reflection dotted around the crowd of bald-headed men; the ones who look more animated than others with this band.

'Not the original members, just the singer,' a random yellow Patagonia T-shirted man with a face like an old leather armchair stood next to us offers. He's stood with, what I imagine are his wife and two daughters. Late teens. A proud looking unit. Sharing a plastic Tupperware box of sausage rolls, he offers me one, but I refuse.

'How have they been?' we ask.

'Alright. I mean, everyone's just waiting for their hit, in't it?' he replies. The teens nod in agreement. The crowd seem to be rippling with occasional foot taps and applause at the end of each synth heavy pop track. The overzealous bassist evidently a generation younger than the band that he's representing, desperate to inject more energy onto the stage. He looks high on the fact that he hasn't a great deal to do. Three or four notes he's alternating between. Getting above his station with his holiday feels too. Jumping and overhead clapping, making crests to the crowd. Big spindly arms sticking out of an oversized vest. The 60 odd year-old singer looks like he just wants to get paid, and then retire to a Premier Inn bed. Mumbling introductions and explanations of songs into his microphone, trying his best, bless him. The crowd humouring by listening with one ear. The other ear occupied with cider sniggers and catch ups, 'Who-you're looking-forward-to-seeing,' and, 'So-tell-me-about-your-love-life,' whilst patiently waiting for the hit. The lads start naming other one hit wonders, the odd contention of 'No way, they had loads of good songs,' punctuating a brain fogged list. Junior Senior 'Move your feet', and Len 'Steal my sunshine,' both bounce out together from the duelling brothers. My own contribution stunted by the cider swishing around my cranium.

'T'Pau,' the best I can muster. 'Ah yes!' they say to that, 'Bit old mind.' The gap between each hit named grows a longer pause. Plenty 'errs,' and 'ermmms.' Pine trees stood tall in judgement; branches crossed. Before long, the mumbling singer announces it's the last song and we all begin paying attention. A great hearty cheer, then a pulse of energy as the first droning chord of the well-known track reverberates with a single finger on the synthesiser. Bassist concentrates on his big moment, lining up his fingers on a not so complicated progression. No showboating now that it's game time. The drums and guitar crash in with stabbing hooks and glossy chords rich with nostalgic tone, one unmistakably 80s. The bald-headed men in the crowd twisting and turning severely to an aged tune that takes them to their youth, when hair was slicked in the style of the singer that's sat crouched before him, when the future was a one of hope and opportunity. The ripples are now undulating waves of expression. Pent up energy and excitement released by bodies clapping and moving in instinctive intoxicated ways, as music pulses into their ears. Bombastic chords unapologetic in their brashness. It's infectious and joyful. The mutual appreciation lifting my limbs like a puppet. I'm drawing shapes with jutting arms. Ball of my foot pressing down, heel raised, lifting my vision a few notches higher to the love that's being expressed in front of me. Is it love? The lads are shoulder to shoulder, arms draped over one another chanting the lyrics into each other's faces. A scene replicated around the crowd. Togetherness. The Patagonia man is hugging his wife one armed around the lower back. His kids doing their own modern retelling of the song with their own dance moves, not fazed by the aged crowd. A great scene. It's feel good. I get a slight pang of sadness that I have no one to embrace me, no one to put their arm around me or to scream the lyrics alongside without fear. Ellis would never have done anything remotely like this. But, as soon as that thought arrives, it's kicked aside with a mass sing-along of the chorus. Blue and white sweeping stage lights. A sound that splits the night. Shaun swivels to me, puts his hands on my shoulders and chants with me. I erupt with a peal of nervous laughter, looks like my emotion was premature. His pink face looks infant like, like a sweaty child all curly haired from running around too much at a soft play, fuelled by sugar and a late night. No sense of bravado or affection as he reaches the high notes, all oooooo's, pursing his lips, eyebrows arched. Seb joins him by his side, arms intermingle almost of their own volition, both lads now stood in front of me, serenading me to an 80s classic. One with a ridiculous wig perched upon his head. In my peripheral vision, the small bouncing dot of a bassist jumping around the stage as the song ends and the bald men clap like seals full of fish.

*

During the break, we had another round. The lads opting for spirit and mixers, their gassy belching getting too much. I've already learned to hold off my inhales when I see them tense their chests up. Another sticky-acid cider for me. I'm not one for mixing drinks. I'm feeling really quite drunk. Feel less tense than I can remember. A softening of my vision around the edges, the darkness of night now fully here. The stage lighting rig more powerful. The backlighting of the bar area more pronounced. Little black polo wearing robots dispensing party fuel for the revellers. - *raise the pitch up, smack my bitch up* – follows - 'Little Fluffy Clouds' and 'I Think I'm In Love', notable songs played whilst the roadies swept and set up the stage. Taking me back to headphone nights as a kid, cross legged on my bed listening to my brother's minidisc player. Exceeding my bedtime in favour of escaping into the music. Imagining myself in a vast crowd of people, bathed in light and sound. I would be listening intently to see if I could notice the better sound quality that he insisted existed. He was much older and had discovered the escape of clubbing. Not the early 90s farmer's field rave stuff, but the post-criminal justice bill city centre nightclub stuff. Queues and stamps. An ill-fated lad's holiday to Ibiza when he was 19 which saw him spend three days in a Spanish hospital with a combination of sunstroke, dehydration and alcohol poisoning. Apparently, it was pretty serious. His mates posed as my parents on the phone to the doctors so as to not worry them back home. Putting on ridiculous accents in character apparently. 'No, no we won't be able to fly over, but if you please keep us informed as to how he is please.' He somehow managed to hide that from my parents for years until he came out with it one Christmas Day after sharing a bottle of port with Papa. Thinking his age exempted him from any parental disapproval or worry. At hearing the revelation, described in every detail through boastful expression, they looked shocked and aghast. Not at the fact he was hospitalised, but the fact he didn't trust to tell them. Sensing the story didn't have its desired effect of a, 'You cheeky scamp,' and an ear pull he went on the defensive. He tried to laugh it off, but the mood around the table shifted at that moment. After a few minutes, Mamma excused herself by taking the cheese board into the kitchen, Papa did shortly after with the box of crackers. 'What?' my brother protested with a guilty expression as my eyes bored into his. Head unconsciously moving side to side. Through the closed kitchen door, we could hear the hushed whispers of a husband consoling a wife.

'Do you remember minidisc players?' I slur to the lads.

'Mini what?' Shaun asks, 'them daft music things?' And with that, we're onto our next topic. The sensible dads of the earlier gig have shuffled off in search of the real ale tent and its comfortable seating. The night belongs to the younger lot now. Perhaps we're at the top end of that age bracket, but we'll keep going. 'Papua New Guinea' plays whilst I hop to the Portaloo by the bar when I spot a break in the queue, already getting acclimatised to the toilet situation. A few fleeces are unpacked from bags and a few bodies start swaying that bit more as I head back to meet the lads. My own stagger is clear. Probably drank more today than I would have in the depths of my Ellis misery. Then again, the stumble from bedroom to bathroom is a well-trod path. Here there are tree roots, resting legs and grassy knolls to navigate. We wait for H.P. Milton, voices are louder and more drawn out in speech, laughter is more violent. Chat is more physical now, hand gestures more animated, a dig in the ribs after a cheeky remark, a hand on the forearm in understanding. There's a false start where the music stops and leaves a gap. Everyone looks around only to be confronted with the introduction of another tune. Build up resumes. Then, after 'Voodoo Ray' fades out, the lights signal the arrival of the next performer. Lighting rig fades to black and a red spotlight follows a pork-pie hatted man with an acoustic guitar heads from left to right centre. The loud cheers and claps everyone seems to take him aback as he stands behind the microphone, spare hand holding palm flat against his chest, gently patting where his heart belongs. 'Thank you, wow, thank you!' then his sunburst guitar finds itself slung around his shoulders with a rainbow strap. 'Lochtdale! Thank you!' he shouts into the microphone before strumming the opening chords of the song I was humming to Shaun before. He better know that bloody tune.

Wednesday
Shaun

As soon as the music starts, I feel a jab in my rib. Takes a few seconds to notice like, because I'm feeling canny pissed. I'm proper struggling to see the fella on the stage making the music. Eyes doing that thing when the peeve saturates them, and they fancy going for a wander in different directions. I turn and squint; it's Jasmine, her nose is all scrunched up like a sniffing bunny rabbit or something. She's going, 'I told you. This is the song!' and poking me over and over. I can tell she's canny pissed up herself like. Her blinks are slow. Proper swooshy. 'That's the song I was on about!' she keeps repeating. That finger of hers hurts.

'I don't know it, man!' I protest to her, hands in surrender pose. But she's still prodding. 'Stop prodding me man, you radge.'

'Listen to it, you'll know it!' then she's singing along to this H.P. bloke as is half the crowd. Must be one of his popular ones, because there is a fair volume coming from them, sort of like when people sing along to 'Sex on Fire' or 'Mr. Brightside' in nightclubs, all screechy and out of sync and key. Do my fucking head in them songs mind. Overplayed nonsense. Shite. Not this, seems canny. Proper old school indie sort of stuff. There's a faint familiarity to it, but then again could be any song. There are only so many chords a man can play. Just ask that ginger cunt Ed Sheeran and his massive legal team. Someone down near the front is on their mates' shoulders, next thing I know they have a flare going and the whole crowd has a green shade about it. Fucking pyro man. Barmy as owt, it's only a Wednesday night. Chemical smell of the flare. Smoke drifting straight up, barely any wind to move it anywhere. Singer smiles as he sings at the reaction he's receiving. Bet he's loving it. Feels like a foreign football match, somewhere over in Poland or something like that, pyro and party.

'Listen, the chorus you'll know, I tell you.' She's prodding me again, desperate for me to recognise this song. Crowd volume ratchets up a notch.

'Howay then,' I say, leaning in intently as the guitar and lyrics start to lunge towards some sort of uplift. Then, the big bastard penny drops. The chorus. 'Ahhhh, fucking hell man, it's this song? I fucking do know it!'

'Yes!' she screams in total relief. Hands on her cheeks, 'Oh my god, you are so frustrating! Thank god for that!' Seb's behind us laughing behind a cigarette he's pilfered from someone nearby that we chatted to about Sony Walkmans and taping music off the radio. He's semi singing along, smoke erupting from his nose and mouth as he sings. Looks well fucked, great to see. There's a certain level of pissedness that Seb needs to reach before he'll consider a cigarette. Think he was a smoker when he was younger, for like minutes, because he thought it would make him look interesting and edgy. He said smokers' terraces were a good place to meet lasses. Wouldn't have met Mia on a smokers' terrace mind, she'd shove it up his arse lit end first if she ever saw him with a tab. It smells manky like, but then again, the pyro over the way doesn't smell much better. I chin the rest of my JD and coke, wince as it goes down, then turn to the stage again. Ice slams back into the bottom of the cup. Fucking hell, the crowd loves this bloke, there's arms all over the place. The flare is going strong, blokes in hi-vis jackets struggling to get to the area where it's burning. Crowd protecting their own. What are they going to do when they get there anyway? The things burn at like 1000 degrees Celsius, can't really wrestle over it, can you? The singer's voice can barely be heard over the crowd belting his songs back at him. Bet that feels immense like, one minute you're some daft cunt scribbling down lyrics in the back of a sketchpad, next thing you have a thousand pissed and coked up young'uns screaming your own words back at you, and you're getting paid for it. All done with an acoustic guitar and words. A good looking acoustic too. Bet it's a grand's worth of kit at least that like. This is mental, great to see. It's only day one inall. Think what the main days will be like. Back home I'd be working the pub quiz crowd. Plenty of Think 25 to be done on quiz nights like. Lime and sodas, a few lagers here and there, bottle of wine to share. Ed fucking Sheeran playing on the speakers during the break. Now I'm surrounded by people loving life, being serenaded by some bloke in a hat. I feel another prod.

'Fucking told you,' Jasmine's eyes linger, a proper wry smile across her face. Her nose scrunching up again all cute like. She's proper bonny. Buzzing that she's decent craic like. Was a bit cynical to begin with, but she seems proper decent, feels like I've known her donkeys inall. Needs to stop it with these jabs like, Connor McGregor over there. I'll have bruised ribs at this rate. Not minding the attention though.

'Aye well done you,' I tell her all ironic voiced and that. We smile at one another that little bit longer until this Milton bloke launches into his next tune, and the salvo begins again. My disco fingers are now free of a drink to join in with the pointing and punching of the smoke-filled air. It's like the trees are smouldering. Let's fucking have it.

Wednesday
Seb

Mia would be loving this. It is brilliant, pure fun. Like a proper knees up in an Irish bar that you see on the TV. Everyone pissed up and slapping their thighs and punching the sky. First night of giddiness. Smiles and voices wide and high. Like the drunk dancing we would dish out on a Greek dance floor, on the first night of our holidays, our very first holiday actually. Back before we were parents and could stay up till whenever we wished. Staggering out at last orders, French kissing in the street propped up by a lamppost. Then watching the sun rise and our eyelids sink on the balcony as we chatted that deep talk that's reserved solely for them early morning hours. No time for idle chatter then, it's for revelations and plan making. Massaging her feet slowly as she looks into the distance telling me of her childhood, letting me in. The highs and lows that made her who she is. Things she never told anyone else before. Saying we would never be like that. Eyes reddening with the sunrise.

The singer on stage has been cranking up the energy with every sing-along and witticism dished out to the crowd. Cockney slang and bar-room banter. Shaun is bouncing around like Tigger, chucking his arms around me and Jasmine, seems he's getting wrapped up in the collective buzz over the music. Jasmine is singing along with gusto, massive plumped up cheeks with smiling. I laugh at the obvious wrong attempts by Shaun to sing along. Getting key words wrong. Shifting meanings. I keep having to waft away hair strands from my wig, feels quite nice to do mind. 'Jas, I want you to paint me wearing this. Wearing only this!' She's howling with drunken laughter, turning between me and the stage.

Between songs, there's a bleed of sound from the rest of the site. Despite not officially starting until Friday, there's activity and noise all around. A distant track from a burger van wafts through the trees. Breeze smells like a B&Q car park on a Sunday. The pine trees smell like a B&Q wood yard. I love B&Q me. I look around as the singer swaps acoustic guitars, from sunburst to ebony. Day to night. There's a bloke a few metres away with his back to the stage, leaning into cupped hands into the ear of another fella. One bald, one with a ponytail. Bald guy looks like William Hague. For a second, I think it is. Can't be. This wouldn't be his scene. Plus, the bastard looks like 90s to 00s Hague. Not the modern meeker and milder version. I feel conflicted. Roll back a few years and the teenage me would be giving daggers. Digging nails into the palm of my hand. Stifling the curse of 'Scum!' at him. Irrational, or maybe even not irrational, but inbuilt hatred of his kind. I used to despise the bastard. Was always told to dislike his kind by Dad. Parroting for approval. Nowadays though, he would be a welcome face compared to the shit-show bastard circus performers who call themselves politicians. My sentiment has softened, not on the Tories, but of the elder leaders. Such a shame Blair was a war mongering shit. All went a bit wrong after that. It's a new dawn on that front, I suppose. Let's see how that goes. Then, I realise, I am an old grumpy bastard harking back to the days politicians had integrity. - *There's a girl lives up the block, back in school she could turn all the boy's heads* - The distant burger van plays, there's an ambient buzz of a collective anticipation, mingled with the single string ring of this Milton guy tuning up his guitar in prep for the next track. Intrusive thoughts still managing to permeate through the alcohol infused blood.

'Lochtdale, please welcome to the stage my good friend Michael Winters!' Enthusiastic applause and a collective look of 'Who?' Fella comes onto the stage from the left hand side and plugs in an electric guitar. A nice cherry coloured thing, glossy as anything. It reflects the stage lights and leaves little micro scars on my vision. A few blinks and they're gone. Nearby Scottish voice proudly states 'He's from The Magees!' I'm none the wiser. Sounds great to hear in a jock accent mind.

Two lasses are sitting cross legged a few people in front of us. They're using the break in play to dig into a bag of powder and are in a world of their own, scraping two lines of whatever it is onto one of the lasses' compact mirrors. Looks just like the one Mia carries about in her handbag, on the very rare occasion we go out. The default bag these days is a Karrimor rucksack with toys, change of clothes and pac-a-mac, tuna sarnies and a bruised apple in. The lassies look young, not like underage young, but uni young. Then again, I suppose there is no age limit for insufflation. They're a bit slapdash with scraping these lines out. I've decided it's cocaine, based on the fact it seems these days everyone and their dog is on it. Wednesday night and people are on the powder. That's gutsy. Flick of wrist left and right with a green bank card. Drunken shakes. Frustrating to watch. Terrible technique. I feel agitated watching. Want to show them how it's done, but that wouldn't be appropriate. Then I hear it, the muted string slap of H.P.'s most famous song, one he performed with his old band. An indie championship classic, as me and Shaun would describe its type. I look around and there's a recognition of the intro flicking into a thousand heads. H.P. starts it slower than usual, but it's definitely it. A song title that evades me in my pissed up haze, but is instantly recognisable. I look down at the two girls, still oblivious to what's about to happen. Still struggling with the mirror and the bag. Legs twitch all around them. Sinews stretch and joints lumber up. All ready for the drop. Like the starting line of a sprint. Like me at the bairn's sports day when the teachers usher the parents up to have a race. H.P. speeds up incrementally, the three chords: G to Cm to D. Even I know that and I'm not a guitarist. Shaun taught me some simple chords on that bloody Fender Jaguar that still makes me angry. Never mind, it's surely a piece of piss of a song to play, but it's all in the build-up. This Winters' guitar starts plucking out the lead part of the song, a feel-good progression. Uplifting and energetic. Sound that cuts through the crowd and the bullshit. A tone you cannot hide from. The pace increases and people legs twitch more. My own included. Chords struck with more force. Piercing lead follows. The lassies are readying a fiver note, one leans down, and then it happens. The plectrum drags down the big fat string, gives a droning ripping sound, then H.P. belts out the chorus chords. Lead joins in with a violent burst of sound and the crowd are up in the air jumping in unison, trying to keep up with the machine gun guitars. A great mangle and mash of bodies. Then I see it, the unmistakable cloud of 40 odd quid's worth of cocaine, poof up into the low air as the mirror and girls get caught up in the bouncing legs of a possessed crowd. Columbian powder pressed into English soil by springing Nikes, Toms and Converse. I feel a sprig of sympathy for the split-est of seconds. Knocked and bashed away to a soundtrack of nostalgia and feel good. A thousand bodies bounce to a song they bounced to some fifteen or so years ago, in every indie night they ever had in this land. I danced to this at club nights when I had money in my pocket, and down at the local rec grounds when I was skint. My pals with their cars pointing to one another, yellow headlights creating an arena. Hazards making a strobe. Dav's speakers were louder than mine, his engine idling so to not wear down the battery. His windows wound down to bleed into the great outdoors. Coke cans and a stack of CD-RWs vibrating in the door pocket. I had a lower hairline back then. Highlighted and straightened as was the fashion. Looking swell as you like, looking back it was quite androgynous, actually. The same old dance moves make a comeback. Jutting and jagged dancing, like Ian Curtis meets Bez. Legs ache far sooner from the pogoing, but who cares, this is class. I imagine Mia next to me right now, probably laughing into her palm at the misfortune of the lassies who now stand upright, 'Karma', she'd say. The only two faces in the crowd not having a good time. Shuffling towards the back looking defeated, chucking blame at one another. The night claims two more casualties. My two companions are arm in arm bouncing as one in the melee. As the dualling guitars come to a stop there is a deafening cheer from the crowd. Pure emotion. I shout so much my throat stings and my ears tickle. I don't care. A release of energy. Pent up over months from sitting behind a shitty desk answering shitty calls and dealing with shitty people for thirty-six and a half shitty hours a week. Shaun was right, this is just what I need. Jesus Christ. A collective deep breath that is absorbed by the bowing bodies of the performers. The cheers ebb and flow with each bow they make.

'Right, right listen, they're saying it's too late to do another song, y'know?' A huge roar of boos from the crowd. Riled up and ready to die for more stimulation. '...but listen, yeah, it's to do with the music license. There's a curfew today. It's only Wednesday innit? These speakers have to go off right. Just for tonight. The locallers have got work to do tomorrow, farms to tend and all that you know,' his Cockney voice cracks over the microphone, 'no farmers, no food.' Crowd respond with another wave of boos.

'Right, I have an idea yeah? You with me?'

Collective cheer.

'I need you all to be really quiet, yeah?'

Another joint roar.

'Let's try it yeah, not a peep right? Can you do it?' Just as he says that the yellow polo shirted man, who has been standing looking pensive at side stage for the last five minutes, takes his microphone off him. Desperate to not look at the crowd. Protecting himself from the pantomime villain role he's been assigned. He quickly disappears into the warren he's come from as H.P. holds his finger to his lips. Like a supply teacher. His pal takes his ebony acoustic guitar. H.P. waggles his finger to his lips, shifting his face towards all corners of the arena, a shushing noise hisses out from pockets of the crowd. Everyone obliges. They quickly descend into an eerie silence. Like a minute's silence at a football match. Volatile silence. The rest of the site must have also had the same message, as you can't hear any burger van speakers anymore. No screaming waltzers. Nothing. Just the high-pitched squeal of ringing ears that have been battered for the last few hours. A few coughs and shuffling noises, then the jangling guitar begins to play. This Winter bloke hitting the strings as hard as possible, so the sound reaches as near to the back as possible. Steel string ring metallic. The song is recognisable by its chords alone, it's a cover. Then H.P. with chin lifted and chest pointing proud to the sky begins. - *Everybody's gotta live, and everybody's gonna die. Everybody's gotta live, I think you know the reason why.* - Just for a split second I feel I'm in the centre of the universe, basking in the moment. In the now. I love this song. Stunned into stillness by the sheer beauty of standing here, lead footed, as to not make a noise with a crunched leaf or scuffed stone underfoot that will puncture this delicate place. H.P.'s voice now tender and full of emotion and passion, despite it being so far away. Soul like. As the thousand stood before him in silence contemplate. Churning over the lyrics. Drunken minds sobered up by the simple meditation. The choice of song seems almost fatalistic as he blares out - *everybody tryna have a, a good time.* - It seems to me so perfect for this moment, in this place in space and time. Four chords go round and round. Shaun and Jasmine are propping one another up, her head tilted slightly toward him. I long for Mia. Melancholic at the - *everybody's gonna die.* - I think about my brood at home and hope it's me that goes first. I couldn't deal with any more loss. I shake my head to flick the thought away. - *I was surrounded by fifty million strong-* I look at the still heads of those I am sharing this moment with. Still. Not a glowing phone screen in sight. Everything makes sense. As the song finishes with the Cockney drawl lingering on – *whyyyyy* - The crowd pauses for a beat, as though to afford one final moment of contemplation, before the ripple, then tsunami of cheers, woos and trills erupts. Mass applause, as H.P. and his pal head off the stage arm in arm tossing plectrums and his pork-pie hat into the grateful crowd. A tussle ensues. They make a heart symbol with one another's hands and point it to the crowd. Then they disappear into the rear of the stage, and it is done.

'Well, that concludes proceedings for today,' I declare in my official sounding voice to Shaun and Jasmine uncoupling from arm and arm as they turn to me, almost apologetically. We walk in a mutual silence, three abreast as the adrenaline wears off and thoughts turn to sleep. Not a silence of awkwardness, but one of community. Words not needed. Like a married couple learns. Communicating without conversing. I think of Mia. Fatigue mixed with stimulation battling for supremacy as we walk with the great crowd out of the arena over soft bark chippings and trodden flat grass. String lighting rigs waymark the way back to the campsite. We walk past food vendors that smell like school dinners all greasy and sickly. We have no need to eat, not with sleep on the horizon. The crowd dissipates into various directions. There's a murmur, a hushed chatter between people now. Not fighting with a hundred thousand different speakers to be heard. A consciousness of others trying to sleep as we wander through the camping fields. The perimeter lighting twinkling like distant stars. A cold white luminescence like outdoor Christmas lights. I pause for a moment and take in the scene. My eyes foggy with intoxication and tiredness. We go to the long drops for a bedtime piss and meet back around the nearest light. Jasmine is the last to come back, eyes baggy looking with tiredness. We walk back along the pathway, then I spot the path to our tent, I lead the way. Stepping over guy ropes and discarded bottles and cans. Zig-zagging towards our home for the weekend. I see it there. Enveloped in darkness now, but definitely ours. I unzip the door and climb into the main communal bit, kicking off my shoes and emptying out my pockets into the room I'm sleeping in tonight. Sitting on my knees. Wallet and phone placed in the little pocket by the head. Then I climb in and wrap myself in my sleeping bag. Not planning on sleeping yet, but just resting my aching body. I suppose it's early-ish by festival standards, but today's been knackering.

'I'm going to hit the hay,' I hear Shaun say as he disappears into his own room. All zips and fabric shuffles as he clambers into his own.

'Goodnight,' I hear from a sleepy sounding Jasmine, as I hear her wrestle with the zip on the front door of the tent. Good lass. The mutual shuffle and hiss of three tired bodies preparing for bed subsides after a few minutes. I roll over to check my phone and see I have a message. It reads, 'Goodnight darling. Have you heard from the recruiter yet? X,' sent two hours ago. I won't reply tonight. I click on the contact photo of Mia and look at her smiling into my lens. A memory of a trip to Switzerland, my eyes close to the imagined sounds of waterfalls and cowbells. Blurring with the actual sounds of whispers, polyester rub, a more subdued Bowie CD, and a chorus of snoring. A long tumbling fart is emitted from nearby, I presume it's Shaun. Giggling from a nearby tent, the sort of laugh that hurts when you try and stifle it. And, with that, I close my eyes on the first day here.

Thursday

Thursday
Jasmine

Deep brown and red bark wood, warm forest tones and intoxicating earthy fragrance emanate from underfoot. A calmness in the morning air, early birds are whispering utterances. I'm in a great green expanse of a field. A saunter. In the distance in front of me is a hedgerow, white spray blossoms attracting bees, scrawling in movement like yellow calligraphy. Beyond are flagpoles, a row of ten or twelve. Ropes jockey whipping the aluminium pole at half speed, cheered on lazily by the prevailing breeze. The tinny bell chime, like buoys on a serene sea, warning idly of their presence. The flags are proud, they hoist a kaleidoscope of colours and iconography in contrasting patterns, like a nursery art session that's got out of hand. The shapes are rippling and nodding like an elderly loved one drifting off in a wing-back chair, afternoon naps in convalescence care. A great wumph of a rare gust, the crisp white duvet cover whipped up as the fresh bedding descends onto the bed.

A metallic clunk to my left reveals a young child filling a plastic water bladder from the silver trough standpipe. They're finding the technique to hold the heavy container and tap in tandem a challenge. Tongue wedged between left canine and lip in concentration, eyes focused on the flow. Several generations stand, mouths foaming with fluoride bubbles removing last night's yeast and potato starch film. The morning sun is reflecting off the aluminium basin and faucets leaving a yellow and green strobe scar in my vision. The grass nearby is greener, but specked with mud. Beyond, the meadow has a hue of yellow, straw like. Behind is a century old dry-stone wall, moss, and lichen green cling.

Leave No Trace

As I get closer to the hedgerow, a gap reveals itself, an unassuming arch of foliage and trellis. A colour chart assortment of greens and leaf shapes wrap around and jostle for the sky, the sign atop reads: 'The Allotment', the wellness fields, as the lanyard in my hand describes it. I've borrowed it from the floor of the tent to help navigate my morning stroll. It describes a place for 'peace, harmony and escape'. Escapism, my word, I could do with some of that in my life. Peace, yes please. Harmony, come at me babe. I stroll in the direction of the entrance. It's early morning, before anything kicks off, I've been awake early after a deep breath and gasp awakening. Alcohol infused sleep. A bad dream I do not remember properly, something about a deer and a car. Dozing for a while, but never getting back to slumber as the tent began heating up with every passing moment. A thin dark green coloured hot box, our tent. Normally I'd be sleeping with windows open in my flat, letting the carbon monoxide and diesel fume belch of the bus route cool me on a summer morning, but the tent does not afford me such luxuries. The stagnant air of two lads baking and perspiring in sleeping bags is my morning breeze. As I lay there, my mind wandered somewhere dark, that's what time can do for you. Fuck it, I'll explore, I thought. So, I am. Coffee is the poison of choice for the smattering of early risers up at this hour, I suspect a few people may have only just settled down to sleep, based on the seemingly constant din of conversation going on 360-degrees last night. Dreams merging with reality, both too confusing to differentiate.

The sun is restorative, it's caressing my face, my vision is still awash with greeny blue smears, those new sunglasses are still buried in a side pocket of my living quarters, make a mental note to retrieve. A slow woodpecker hammering reveals tool-belt and boots crouched readjusting a teepee peg to my right, a fellow hi-vis stands beside, supervising with coffee and cigarette. 'Do it at more of an angle. Yeah, like that.' They encourage, as their colleague drives in the wooden stake with ferocity. It's a tent selling hippie fashion items of all sorts of rich saffron yellows, jungle greens and spirulina blues, blood reds. Natural fibres, Aztec patterns. Scratchy looking gear, warm and comfortable, but irritating to the skin. Tie dye and beads hang from a carousel rack, incense smoke punctuating the morning's profile. For a second, I'm back in Bali. Three paces ahead of Ellis in paradise.

I'm crunching through a pathway of bark that snakes through the field, towards the ancient trees beyond the line of shop teepees. Oaks resemble King's Guard bearskins. Colourful uplighters and speaker monitors ratchet strapped to their trunks, black cables weaving down to sealed boxes like ECG machines ready for the evening's display. A street sign sunk into the turf is topped with a dizzying array of directions all around the site. From my view I see The Main Stage and various camping areas shown, pointing in asymmetric fashion.

Once I've passed through The Allotment entrance, the woody air and dappled shade embrace me like an old loved one. Calmness. Calmness illustrated with birds speed dating between the branches of the oaks, singing their individual songs, and showing themselves off with pride as they go. Bang, bang, bang, another last-minute tent support is driven into the grass, penetrating the earth, tension required. Not here though, no tension as I stride through this scene. I feel something I haven't in a while, restfulness. I'm in the present.

Thursday
Shaun

Jolt awake. Violent inhale. A whimper. The sound of zips and voices. Voices all around. Zips in stereo. Takes a second to work out where I am. Heart battering like it usually does in the morning. Peeve ache in my head. Right at the front. It's fucking hot in here like. I'm bursting for a piss. Been needing it all night. Waking up all hours confused as fuck. A constant presence of sound. When the voices finally died down, I was woken by the sound of crows. Or whatever bird that is. Pecking over the remnants of the first night. Chip and burger bun brekkie. Human corpses maybe. I drifted off again and again to some disjointed and disturbing dreams. There was a rustle of movement before. Fuck knows who it was. No idea if they've returned again. I flip over onto my front and pull a jumper from my rucksack and drape it over the back of my head. Trying to block out the light of whatever hour this is. I need more sleep. Just another hour. Please. Give my liver time to do its thing. Settle down my heart. It's so fucking hot in here man. It's awful. This jumper won't help matters. A thirst. Baffled hand scurries and dances across the tarp floor in search. Like a desert elephant blindly searching for a discarded bottle. It comes in the shape of an Oasis bottle. Fuck it, that'll do. Elbow into the airbed, I'm at a 45-degree angle chugging down the orange sweetness. Soothing the thirst. Hungrily gulping. Little streams dribble down my chin dripping onto the sleeping bag. They'll evaporate in no time. Bottle empty, my sandy eyes fix upon the empty vessel. It takes a second, but amidst the brain ache an idea is hatched. The wide neck of the bottle offers an opportunity. I sit upright at 90-degrees now. Quick gander around. Scrunching myself up in a prayer position. Wrestling with the zip of the sleeping back so it's down to my waist. Welcoming ventilation. I pull out my chap and place it into the rim of the Oasis bottle. A decent fit. But a sad as fuck sight. A depressing fish hanging on the edge. The sticky moisture of the lip feels weird on my bellend, but fuck it, the relief of pissing is immense. I don't care if the waterfall crashing sounds are heard by anyone. I don't care if my silhouette is visible from outside. I've been dying for this all night. Excreting the liquid poison I filled myself with last night. A slight panic eased as the pissy stream slows before it reaches the top. Relief. Ensure the lid is screwed back on tightly. Double check. Bottle warm. Ribbed lip hurting my palm's grip, then placed tucked upright into the mesh by the side of my head. I flop back onto my front and take a deep exhale. Close my eyes and hope for that extra hour of sleep.

Thursday
Jasmine

'The energy treatment?' the man confirms with sonorous yet hushed tones, calming and assuring. He reminds me of the Samaritans voice I spoke to a few months back when I really hit a low ebb. The blood and the tears combined on the laminate floor that night. Blink and headshake that intrusive memory away. He looks like the cross between a geography teacher and a caricature of a monk. He looks familiar as he comes into view, but I can't quite put my finger on it. Hopefully not a police mugshot in the local paper, I think, half-jokingly. He has a balding head, his stainless-steel NHS spectacles perched on a Roman nose. He's clad in white drapes, his smile is minimal, but not in a grumpy or hostile way, a genuine caring countenance, listening and nodding slowly. Stood imposing above me as I lay prone and feeling vulnerable. He wears a reassuring expression from this angle. One of a priest perhaps. Hope one of the good ones. Shake away again the thought of a sexual assault. Brain in constant overdrive in these situations, stuck in 6th gear, no brakes. Feel my quickened heartbeat through the linen, bouncing off the bed. My fingernails press into my palm, the uncomfortable sensation to divert my darting mind as I lay on my back enveloped in fluffy towels and white sheets breathing in through my nose and out through my mouth.

My morning directionless wander has led me here in the heart of The Allotment. A quiet shady spot in the dappled light of the ancient trees. It smells of my childhood, Germoline smeared grazed knees and nettle stings combined with the mossy forest scent of peat and pine. Amidst the positive affirmation signs hand-painted and hung at jaunty angles from the branches of the oaks and sycamores, there's a scattering of blackboards and adjacent domed white tents of varying sizes. Blackboards advertise in chalky colourful cursive writing reiki, crystal therapy and morning yoga. The yoga piquing my interest, however, I'm in no mood for company, the confidence I feel is internal. I don't want to make small talk with others, only to instantly compare myself to them and feel immediately shitty about myself again, especially not whilst sober. I'm not unattractive, I don't think, but I get intimidated by these natural beauties who glide through life with smiles and elegance, as though not challenged in any way shape or form by their own demonic minds, not like me. I don't want to struggle with a downward looking dog as Lycra clad experts flop down with ease. As I ambled by the large yoga tent I spotted my monk. There he was, hands on lap, straight backed. Almost statuesque, or maybe garden gnome. Perched on a tree stump his eyes pointing straight forward, seemingly content by just being there, not rustling for something to occupy an idle mind. Beside him, a hessian banner, black type: 'Massage and Energy Treatments'.

'Fuck it,' I mouthed, barely audible to myself as a pep talk, gaining the confidence to head towards the awaiting man. When was the last time I did something for me? When was the last time I truly spoilt myself? I thought, as I pensively approached. Money exchanged hands, ailments were discussed, then clothes were whipped off and chucked over a wooden stool, hastened by the fear the monk waiting outside the tent drapes might come in quicker than I could unrobe. Clattering onto the bed and under the covers I lay waiting, willing my heartbeat to slow down, focussing on the shadows and shapes projected onto the roof of the tent. Now I'm here and ready to be energised.

The tent smells of menthol and incense. It's not overpowering, just enough to notice a pleasant aroma. Just right. Ambient.

'Please lay onto your front.' Of course, silly me, I oblige, as he looks in the other direction, like shop workers do when you enter your pin, as I wrestle myself around and get myself comfortable, fearful of a stray boob or fallen towel. From somewhere I can't pinpoint is a speaker emitting a soothing blend of running water and lazy chimes. The towel is teased down over my bottom half whilst an occasional waft of the tent fabric gives a slight roll of cool air across my exposed skin.

'Are you settled?' geography monk asks.

'Hmmmph,' I muffle into the massage table. Jaw obstructed by the little hole my face fits in and the towellen gag sheet. A large sniff in case gravity brings any snot into the little basket of pot pourri. The scent of Indonesian streets a younger me walked. I close my eyes.

He chimes a bell once.

Twice.

A cooling menthol oil meets my skin, steadfast hands spreading it across my lower back, upper body, shoulder then neck. Firm pressure, confident. Circular motions up and down. Figure of eights, pirouettes. Round and round the garden like a teddy bear. I feel the gravelly knots in my back, the strains from carrying all the tent gear yesterday. Muscles starved of nourishment in favour of cider and burger. Tension from unaddressed emotional strain, a dripping tap. I feel the menthol hands trail as I begin melting into the towellen table, the hole moulding around my face. Years of tension addressed, thumbs and menthol painful and wonderful. Tackling clicks and lumps confidently. A flash of pain, grimace, then relief. Awareness of breath.

It occurs, as I keep melting into the table and my own psyche, that this is the first physical touch from a man since Ellis. My naked flesh remaining under cotton, hiding healing bruises and fading scars. The thought of physical contact, more often than not, one received with revulsion. Always blown hot and cold with that sort of thing actually. I struggle to let people in, for fear of being hurt, or something. Turns out, that's a legitimate worry, as Ellis has shown. This is totally different though. Yin and yang. I don't feel the cold clam of fear, the nauseating Houdini stomach tension. The doomed acceptance of indignity and intrusion. I feel the opposite, at ease. Was it always like that? When did I learn to accept that as normal, or anything other than downright abuse? When did I cease to love me?

The hands find a particularly tense spot on my upper back and gravitate towards that. Pain is good, restorative. Reminds me I exist. Puts me in the present. I picture the fibres of my muscles straightening, unfurling, stretching, and thriving like the ferns that litter the woods around me. Hands rhythmically sending tension away, back into the past, where the darkness is. Sending good blood to cells, filling them with white light and life.

After an unknown amount of time slowly melting further and deeper into the fibres of the towel, time is a triviality, he asks me to lay on my back. He works away the tensions of my front. I feel no vulnerability, eyes closed and groin to breast covered by warm tucked sheet. The cool rolls of the morning breeze remind me of my location. After a period of relieving knots from limbs and extremities, he finally lays his hands on my head.

Gentle.

Reassuring.

Parental.

'Everything is going to be okay,' and as he utters such a simple statement, I feel the back of my throat sting with the genesis of a cry. A building ache, as I fight back the urge to burst, a release of emotions desperate to manifest and escape my limp body. My tear ducts are the first to get their own way, eyes closed pools of saline begin to flood my eyelids. Deep breath. Shaky exhale. Compose yourself, Jasmine. Hands warm on my forehead and hairline. Unmoving.

I feel myself getting lighter. As if transcending this place. I'm a bug skittering in the trees outside the white drapes. I'm a fish in a nearby pond, beyond the chain link fence, basking under the shade of 9ft bulrushes. I'm sheltering under a water lily; I'm laying my eggs away from the eyes of a soaring bird. I'm a bee tasting the sweet nectar of a sunflower that adorns The Allotment arch. I feel because I am. I see hues of yellow in my vision. Then, I think no more. In and out, the cool air on my rising and falling chest, menthol trails evaporate.

Yellow. Breeze on my leg.

Breathe. Hands warm.

Blood oxygenated from the trees all around me, filling my muscles with life.

Yellow.

Breathe.

Unfurl.

'Open your eyes. Feel alive,' he whispers, my eyelids slowly blink in the light of this beautiful new morning.

Thursday
Seb

Deeply disturbing dreams. Kids' faces talking, but no voices. Shouting and no one hearing me. Dishwasher spitting out dishes like a Vegas fruit machine hitting the jackpot. Mia with her back to me, walking away. The sound of high heels slopping down a travertine corridor. An old shopping centre from my childhood where all the shop units are still occupied. Must have been just past midnight when I hit the hay, shutters came down big time. Think I drifted off reasonably quick enough, all things considered, but was awoken by the noise of life occurring for 20,000 happy campers beyond the fly sheet and green polyester. Life occurring and Shaun snoring. I assume it was him. A blocked drain gurgle sound like the one giving me jip back at home, vomiting wastewater from sinks all over the patio, creating a sludge trail. The snoring raised a few comments from the deep voiced real ale beard fella from the tent nearby. A few 'Fuck's sakes, listen to that' to his mute wife, but before long he's joined the throaty choir himself. Hypocrite.

    Sticky hot inside my mummy sleeping bag. I rolled over on one of the many wake ups and whacked the nearby hoody over my head, burrowing one ear into the floor and balancing a decent chunk of fabric over the other. A vain attempt to drown out the cacophony. Trying to stifle the noise of a couple of night owls discussing geography and the former names of African nations. To my annoyance, I found myself playing along with the rally, muffled through Hackett hoody. Admittedly, I found myself impressed by their extensive knowledge on the subject. There were a thousand different voices swirling around, they were all having enthusiastic conversations. Excited by life and everything in it, they had no agenda for sleep. Gossiping, complimenting, sharing embarrassing tales, and wondering where the vodka was. The last time I recall my Fitbit lighting up in my mummy bag, squinting at the brightness, it was 2.14am, around the time I zipped open my pod door to grab water, it remains limp now.

It's 10:37am. No wife by my side. No kids waking me up early demanding sugary cereal, CBeebies and the construction of an epic wooden train set. Weirdly, it is quieter at this hour than it was from most of my observed evening. The alcohol hitting the spot and stifling out the chat about pervy window cleaners and the girl from the bakery having genital warts. I have no idea where the other two are or whether they are up or not. I have very little desire to find out anytime soon either, the warm cocoon and the near silence too indulgent to give away cheaply. I heard the zip go what could have been 2 hours or 20 minutes ago. I scroll through my phone for a bit, looking at the usual drivel. I do this out of habit, but convince myself it's a means to maintain some level of normality. I look around my surroundings for a bit, feeling slightly worried for my family tent; one normally adorned with toys, Fruit Shoots, and board games. One which would normally be organised immaculately with stackable trays liberated from a series of Tesco.com orders over the years, sweeping brush following chocolate digestive wielding child, shoes lined up in a box at the door. Order. Now, the tent is littered with beer and detritus of two messy guests. Shaun farting into the early hours, gurgling away in the pod Emily usually fills with her Care Bears and colourful bunting for imaginary tea parties. Jasmine stumbling about, scratching about taking out contact lenses in Reuben's. Don't be precious about the stuff, I tell myself. It'll clean up, it'll air out, you'll find that missing tent peg. Mentally scheduling the afternoon Sunday next week, to put it up in the garden to sweep and wipe down. Pack it away properly. Find myself checking the Met Office app to see if Sunday next week's weather is up yet. No. Looks like the forecast for this weekend has changed for the worse though. Can't see it changing too drastically myself though. I look at my Fitbit. 25,612 steps yesterday, plenty of time in the fat burn zone. Great, I'll burn off those cheese toastie crusts and leftovers the kids left on their plates, as they scrambled upstairs to harvest the last drop of playtime before the dreaded toothbrush and bed. Those cheese toasties have been clinging to my midriff more and more since I hit 30.

Suddenly, I hear the ruffle and rip of a zip, must be our front door. Zip one. Zip two. Fabric rummage.

'Good morning campers!' It's Jas, she looks alive. Glowing and smiling with ease, letting in the morning air and sun stinging my eyes, with her face poking through the tent door flap. She looks radiant, but best of all, she's clutching two takeaway drinks cups.

'Coffee's up,' she smiles, as Shaun's head pops through his pod's zip like a mole, his hair all over and sallow looking.

'You beautiful legend,' he husks like a postman's boots on a gravel drive. Reaching towards the liquid elixir.

Thursday
Shaun

'The first of the day,' I say, with a cool beverage poised in my hand. Aloft in the morning air. We're all up now and we're sat around in a circle banging on about what the first thing you'd do if you won the lottery. The sun is lush and I'm comfortable. Getting out of the tent was a struggle like. A coffee and a less than gracious roll and groan to get up. There's barely any space and my body is fucked from lugging the shite up that hill yesterday. Can tell I'm getting soft. Used to be able to do that no bother. This drink will help soothe the aches and pains.

'I'd go to the airport and get the first plane out of this country. Go somewhere hot and green,' Seb offers.

'But it's hot and green here?' Jasmine challenges, spinning her head around our surroundings, 'What more could you ask for? It's beautiful.'

'Not usually though.'

'What about the kids?' I ask.

'They'd be coming with me. Obviously.' Not my idea of a good time like.

'You know, I'd get that bottle of Lanson out the back of the kitchen cabinet. I'd dust it down. Then I'd pop that little madam. Wouldn't even wait to chill it. I'd sit calmly drinking the lot. Raising a cheers to my cats. Figuring out what the fuck I'd want to do with my life,' Jasmine says.

'Reckon I'd got travelling around the world. Would spend a good year or two travelling wherever took my fancy. South America, Asia, that sort of thing. Then, when I got back, get myself a nice house. Find a nice wife...'

'Ha, I guess that's not Sara then?' Seb scoffs. I ignore.

'...get a nice car. Maybe buy an old pub and run that. Just to keep me busy y'know.' I picture a stone-built pub out in the countryside. Frequented by decent folk. Drinking nice single scotches and tucking into game pies cooked by my chef. A hothead rogue who has a mean skill of conjuring up culinary delights. People would travel for miles to sample our Sunday dinner too. Best Yorkshires in the county.

'Travelling sounds good. There's so much to see out there. Money would give you the freedom to do that,' Jasmine nods contemplatively, 'I'd take a masseuse everywhere with me.'

'Harder to do all that with the kids like,' states Seb.

'Aye, you could just pay the fines they send with the massive pile of money you'd have,' I joke, 'or you know, homeschool.'

'Bollocks to that. Had enough of that during Covid!' he spits bitterly.

'You had fuck all else to do, getting paid 90% to sit and wank all day,' I say, inviting a nibble.

'I wasn't on furlough man! It wasn't quite the privilege to sit on my arse at the dining table chained to the laptop and phone for nine hours a day. Insurance still needed dealing with and people were angry. Kids needed teaching and entertaining whilst Doris rang up about her roof leak, and all my staff were sick. Shareholders still needed appeasing,' he bites.

'You bit big time there, brother,' I say cooly. Mission accomplished.

'Aye ha. Nah, I know,' he smooths down a bit, settles back, more relaxed knowing I'm just winding him up. Seems a raw nerve to touch that one. Can see it still affects him, all that. He continues, 'I'd build a home, designed myself and everything. Out in nature. One that had like a fantastic play area outside. I'm talking tree houses. Rope swings. Water slides. All sorts, you know.'

'And a little pad for your brother too?' I say, affecting a sweet smile and fluttering my eyelids. Don't think he can see them behind these sunglasses like.

'Of course, of course,' he says almost too enthusiastically, like people do when they're flogging you a lie, 'I see you in a city centre pad actually. A penthouse suite even.'

'Oh, aye that'll do.' It fucking would do inall. I drift off and picture a hypothetical wife. Brunette. Tall. Dark features. Maybe Spanish or Italian. Exotic looking. Padding around in her tights and cocktail dress. High heels kicked off by the Persian rug. Reflection in the floor to ceiling glass. Dark wood furniture and deep red textured artwork on canvases adorn the grey moody walls. We've just returned from a meal in town. Taster menu with wine pairing. No big deal for us. She pours a glass of wine. Deep red. Blood red. Slinks over to me slowly. Catlike. Handing me the glass. A subtle cheers. Lipstick meets glass. Eyes locked, tracing the contours of one another's lustful faces. Fingers grip the stem of the glass. Her eyes dark brown, shrouded in eyeshadow. Glinting with the soft lamp light. Knowing that once these glasses are drained, we'll be fucking like mad, sweating and gasping in pleasure, ripped tights doggy style looking out over the orange glow of the cityscape of Newcastle's bridges at night. Our reflections visible in the bedroom glass, leather headboard reflected behind. Loud orgasms that never end. A dream version of myself. More muscular. More confident. Better dressed. Richer. Someone fucking else. I break that thought. Look at Jasmine who is drinking from her water bottle. A pink plastic thing with 'Jas' in a scrolly handwriting. Might even be one of them Love Island bottles. I can't be sure.

'Not drinking?' I ask.

'No, not yet, today is long. Don't want to peak too soon.'

'Sensible,' offers Seb who is now standing up and scanning the scene around us. Looking left, right then spinning on himself, and scanning the other side. Watching people go about their morning. Doing life.

'Much going on?' I ask him after a while. Sensing the conversation stagnate.

'Nah. Just taking it all in,' he remains there for quite some time, 'just soaking it all up.'

Thursday
Seb

We're walking adjacent to a row of white tarp gazebos on top of a slope which is blinding me in the sun, despite the expensive Ray-Bans perched on my perspiring nose. We've been up an hour or so now, maybe more, it's almost gone lunchtime. We've been slowly rousing ourselves for the day ahead. Sharing patter and morning beverages as the sun blared down its morning rays. Reeling off names of bands and songs who belong to the indie championship, inspired by H.P. Milton last night. It swiftly moved on to naming top songs about school shootings. Not your normal breakfast patter, but one that occupied us for a beer. Shaun reeled off 'Pumped Up Kicks' and 'Jeremy', almost too enthusiastically, whilst Jasmine told us of Kelly Rowland's 'Stole'. Even giving us a cheeky rendition of the chorus. I'm none the wiser. The best I could come up with was 'I Don't Like Mondays'.

It has been a contrast to the usual morning routine of chasing kids out of the house. Clock-watching. Gulping down a shake as I slam the front door behind me. Going back to check if I locked it. We had crumpets and jam from a nearby stall. A 'Thank you for having me', from Jasmine. Dread to think how much she paid for something that costs about a quid for six from Tesco. Not my first choice of breakfast. Nice touch though. Thoughtful of her. And, the coffee was essential.

On our right, there are queues of varying lengths snaking out from the doorways of the gazebos, like a bar chart graph. On the left downslope there's a scattering of people cross-legged and content on the grass chowing down whatever food they've opted for. We meander through the flow of gastronomic pilgrims, gawping at the paper trays growing greasy and floppy, adorned with cuisines from around the globe. Korean, Brazilian and Thai. There's a coffee stand, vegan curry, Greek flatbreads, tapas, macaroni cheese, Cuban, fried chicken and a Yorkshire pudding stall. We casually glance at the menus as we half pace past. Great gulps of the wondrous smells. Cinnamon, cardamom and clove, a waft of winter and the festive season contrasts with the summer scene before us. Coconut, a memory of the expensive sun cream Mam used to buy for our annual Spanish jaunt. Bay, coriander, and fennel mix with the earthy notes released from the rapidly crisping grass underfoot. Sticky soy belch, cumin nose pinching. The homely reassurance of a Bisto bassline. Garlic and citrus are the high notes. A whistle stop of the globe and its olfactory vignettes. Each gazebo plays its own playlist over tinny speakers, the treble making up for what the bass is lacking. Each song vying for dominance, like a Monday meeting at work. Everyone all shouting on top of one another, not listening or considering each other. Silo. Sounds fizz and pop, fat on grills, moisture screaming to escape from burger patties. Milk frothers dish out their torture indiscriminately on cow, soy, and oat. I make a mental note of what looks like the best value for money based on the weightiness of the trays of those who have been served and slink away down the slope to consume. The hunger pangs will arrive soon enough, I must be prepared.

As we walk there's an occasional meet of all three pairs of eyes. A nod and an 'mmmmm', in mutual agreement that something looks or smells particularly appealing. The louder the hum, the greater the appeal of the food.

'That looks epic,' towards a colourful bowl of rice and curry topped with an assortment of fruits, nuts, and unidentifiable delights.

'That doesn't,' as me and Shaun grimace in mutual assessment at the attire, or rather lack of attire, on some lass walking towards us. Gusset and side-boob on display for all to see. I often find myself, much to my own anger at myself, shocked by the evolution of fashion. I try not to sound like my father, but the slow diminution from jeans to leggings is something I can understand. I can even appreciate it, depending on the physique. But the one from leggings to near nakedness is one I'm yet to get on board with. I find myself wondering whether they feel cold wearing such little clothing. The cold is one of the more favourable things they might be subjected to. Perhaps the father in me brings with it a certain prudish protectiveness for the younger generation of women, these places can be ropey.

'Go on lass!' bellows Jasmine in encouragement, the ambient din too much for there to be any risk of the lass knowing it's directed towards her. In such a way the lass won't hear but me and a red-faced Shaun do. I'm unsure whether it's encouragement for the lass, a dig at me and Shaun's judgmentalness, or actually sarcasm. Acres of white flesh reflect the sun on the barely adult lass. Her outfit all strings and straps. She walks with her pals holding a plastic wine bottle like a dinner bell in the school yard that she presumably has bunked off from to be here. I resist the urge to encourage her to stick some sun cream on. Shudder, as I again realise, I am such a stale old dad now. The group of lasses laugh hysterically as they pass around the wine bottle between one another, throwing the other arm up into the air in dancing delight. Could murder a nice glass of red now, come to think of it.

Everyone seems at total ease this morning. Me included. Well, more than normal anyway. Buoyed by the possibility of the day and the knowledge of what I'd be doing currently at work if I were not here. Rotting in a meeting, clutching a coffee close to my face as I try my best to hide my exasperation when some sycophant spouts utter drivel, much to the pleasure of my overpaid and under skilled manager. I'm picturing Matt here in this scenario. Backstabbing wanker. Boss replying with whatever bullshit jargon he's absorbed from the podcast he's listened to that morning, in his tailgating, fast lane drive to work. I'd be kicking Jasmine under the table as she looks to be losing concentration. Eyes buggy from white wine Wednesdays, we call it. Still need to tell her about the new job. I've made it a thing now, should have just told her straight away all casual. I'll miss her if and when I go. Can't tell her now though. Not now. Back to the meeting, we'd be getting the whole 'teamwork' speech from the senior managers crouched over an A4 agenda. 'We all want the best guys.' Aye, easy for you to say, when you're on a 45% bonus structure, shares and final salary pension. Arseholes. But not today, today I'm being marinated in the sun and the sensations of the surrounding smells, sights, sounds and the taste of a frosty cider, a nice change from beer. One of the last from the cool box. Amazing it still held its chill. A bargain off Amazon. Mia has Prime, of course.

Another thing that feels weird is not having the kids to have a constant eye on. As we walk past a spit roast spewing charcoal and crackling scent into the area, music playing explicit version of - *Straight outta Compton, crazy motherfucker named ice cube* - I lapse and look around me to see if the kids are nearby. The thought of them not being there for that microsecond sent a hefty dump of dopamine into my bloodstream. Irrationally forgetting my situation, I shake my head and laugh to myself. I've often found myself thinking I've lost the rucksack which contains spare outfits, kids' water and snacks even when I'm out and about without them. My brain is hardwired nowadays to default care mode. It's exhausting. Old habits die hard, they say. I take another mouthful of sweet sticky cider to aid me on my journey to forgetting for a bit. I can even crack jokes about spit-roasts and cumin in food. Pronouncing it 'cum in.' Then pulling a disgusted face. All 'eww that's manky.' Mild ripples of laughter return. Not really my best. Then, I look at the two alternate kids I'm with this weekend and wonder whether I'll have to utter the usual:

'Do you need a wee?', 'Have you drank enough water?', Stop squabbling!' and 'Keep your hands off her.' Time will tell. I look at them as they survey the scene of feel-good slogan T-shirts and denim shorts. Straw hats bob by like sailing boats on a calm sea. The sun an ever presence, giving light and life to the watercolour vista before us.

Through the great expanse of grass dead ahead of us we see the great tower majestically straddling the outer edge of the site, just beyond it is the chain link perimeter fence, obscured in places by wooden boards sprayed with graffiti images of things like rock stars, animals and spacecraft, all colours bleeding into one another. Very impressive artwork. Rainbow colours of the ribbons from the great tower glisten and ripple in the lazy breeze. The tower looks even taller with the downward slope to the left, which leads all the way to a natural amphitheatre dotted with a few defiant oaks, where people are already sheltering on camp chairs and tartan blankets sharing picnics and drinks. At the bottom is The Main Stage, scaffolding still up to the lighting rigs as little worker ants in hi-vis jackets are scrutting about making final preparations. A white noise buzz of great speakers warming up in readiness for the official beginning of this year's FestiFell tomorrow. We make it to the bottom of the colourful tower and are greeted by a spiral staircase of galvanised steel steps. It hurts my neck to look to see if I can see the top. Strides above waltz overhead with a percussive tap. I know Shaun isn't good with heights, I look at him and he gives a silent knowing nod of, 'I'll be alright,' I don't want to show him up in front of Jas.

'We good?' I ask in general.

'We're good,' comes back.

'You lads go first, I don't want you's to be greeted with a sight of my arse in these shorts.'

We make the ascent.

Thursday
Jasmine

As my eyes wander into a sort of unblinking daze, my imagination begins to roam from some twenty metres or so that we are in the air. My subconscious given Carte Blanche, takes over as I picture what lies beyond the steel link fence, beyond the flags, the camper vans, the parked cars, and shuttle buses. What lies beyond?

Beyond the fence behind me is the majesty of a Southern Hemisphere seabed from 155 million years ago, it now stands imposing on the landscape. Time and power too great for my mind to understand. The Lochtdale Fells, fading from dark to light grey into the horizon. In the foreground is its jewel, a grey and black face of rock. Bowman Crag. A thing of beauty, its jagged edges I've found myself tracing in the drunken haze in my camp chair since we've arrived. It inspires awe, the climbers who I imagine hike and rope up it as I stand here make me feel insignificant. The steel spiral staircase to get me to the top of this tower nearly put me on my arse. I'm pathetic and weak. Instead, I focus on the other side and let my imagination fly like the kittiwakes above.

On the horizon, the town of Barlow-on-Sands. Miles and miles of sands which go on as far as one might dare look when the tide is out. Beaches where children pick bottle caps in lieu of shells, for there are few of them remaining. Ropes and gloves, Xbox 360 fronts, and picnic food packaging washes up into a great heap. Satanic stacks of a decommissioned power station dominate the skyline, still radioactive for just another hundred million years or so. Shade from sporadic clouds cast upon it and the community which sits in the shade of the cooling towers. A clutter of pipes and sheds, corrugated metal rusting into cracked slabs.

Prefab buildings, breeze block canteens. Concrete pores and peeling mint green paint in long empty canteens that emit 50 years of onion reek to the occasional security contractor's, or urban explorer's nasal passage. Mould spores and stagnant air fester. Linoleum flooring scratched and faded with age; rats scurry about undisturbed.

Nearby a community centre foisting with rot and mildew, council too impoverished and bogged down with bureaucracy to tear it down. Too busy dealing with compensation claims against them. Slips and trips from the uneven high street paving slabs. Grey bricks stand firm and green, shutters kicked off kilter, names of long since fallen out lovers etched in the paint or Sharpie scribbled on bare aluminium. A phallus and tits fingered in the dust of damaged windows. Cracks shaped like spider webs. The asbestos in the roof one for a future generation to discover. No leek shows, kids' clubs or line dancing nights are hosted there anymore. The A4 print out of a clairvoyant night still blu-tacked onto the door's safety glass. The edges curled with moisture; the paper bleached with the sun. The medium long since dead of bowel cancer. She didn't see that coming. The kitchen kettle long since boiled, the beer pumps long since pulled. Best One pint cans and games consoles fill the void now.

Rows upon rows of locked doors and post-war housing have surpassed their life expectancy, 'Not like the good old days when you could leave your door wide open,' the elderly mutter through counterfeit cigarette butts. Did anyone actually live like this? Perhaps they have a point, as county lines gangs capitalise on the streets and those who gather on them, those who crave relief from the monotony and the pointlessness of it all. Decaled cars with Sparco seats rev and intimidate sleepers, as lifelong dependencies are dealt through tinted glass. A gram of whatever, taking any last semblance of mobility and opportunity away from the latest generation who dared to hope, who were unfortunate enough to be born in a place that should have long since been torn down. A depleted police force of one full timer and one CSO depressed from the abuse and the stones thrown by 'those little scumbags'. A term uttered by the rake thin girl who wears sliders and socks, wrestling with pram and autism spectrum pre-schooler. Arm wrenching back from traffic, wondering if it would be easier to just let go. Kid fuelled by unburnt energy and e-numbers. 'There's not much to do for the young'uns nowadays,' she says, as she passes the William Hill and Vape King shops on the sunnier side of the high street. Visiting rights for Daddy in 10 days time, not too far as the crow flies actually, beyond the stacks and over the horizon. Still, two buses and a good few hours round trip though. That's if they turn up. Bus stop roofless and no doubt it'll rain on that day. Meanwhile, early retirement, final salary expats sizzle in record temperatures that their frequent flights have fuelled. 'Too hot to do anything but drink cocktails,' they toast as they clamber out of pools, glittering bronze in evaporating chlorine.

The sepsis artery of a dual carriageway to the east muted by the ambient buzz and bass of the vibrant field some 20 metres below me. A road that rolls past Barlow-on-Sands without even a turn-off, ignoring it as an unfortunate relic of the past. The place where time stood still, even if the church clock still moves. A couple of blue lights strobe up the black road, flashing off the drudgery en-route to another tragedy. The cars in front slow, fearful for a second they'd been caught speeding. Praying for the speed awareness course, rather than the points. Can't afford for insurance to go up again, overdraft fees already slaughtering them for the last fine they paid. A split-second scenario relieved the moment the blue lights zoom past. Radios can get turned back up and play whatever the stations that do have signal around here play. Another teen sensation touted for greatness on account of a plinky plink melancholic piano version of an old classic song used on a supermarket Christmas advert. Abused and fleeced by the aged white men of the boardroom, stealing away rights and dignity, chucking the scraps of the royalties to trickle down. Solidarity sister, I hear you, I see you. Change comes to everything eventually. I look back at the power station for case and point. Shame it's leaving its poisons for the younger generation to deal with.

Scorched earth meets green fields. Pinpricks of cattle. Children ripped away from mothers for milk and meat. Hedgerows upon hedgerows, centuries of toil and graft and dry-stone walling. Flanking trees approaching a millennium old perhaps. The things that they have seen. They're keeping schtum. Best way sometimes. A meandering river runs parallel to the motorway, taking evasive action and bearing a hard right before Barlow-on-Sands. It knows. The River Oz, if my pre festival Google Maps search is to be correct. A smudge of brown winding water heading out to the horizon and the grey sands. My mind is snapped back to the present, as someone on the platform squeak screws on the lid of a metallic water bottle embossed with FestiFell logo. A freebie supplied by the local water company. I find great irony in such a thing, considering the well-publicised fact that this company has dumped tonne upon tonne of human waste into the Oz. The brown colour is more understandable now that the press has revealed the contempt with which the company has treated its community. Ancient sewers remain crumbling, there are complimentary bottles to provide and shareholders who need paid. Holiday homes need tiling, the Porsche needs a service, and the kids need their maintenance. Litre after litre of untreated shite released, the fish reply by flipping onto their backs and playing dead, forever. The Oz leads to a church spire some 20 metres high itself, like a modern-day equivalent of the tower I'm currently standing on. As my eyes zigzag down, heading back towards the festival site, I spot undulating landscapes, smears of browns and greens. Stone wall lines and flecks of foliage. Silver tree trunks in the sun. Stone built houses and greenhouses. Outbuildings and pubs. People pottering, busying themselves, gossiping, drinking, shagging, escaping, dreaming, imagining, dying, entertaining themselves to death. Elsewhere there are a billion other stories all wandering about their lives. Unknown tales of heartache and happiness, and everything in between.

Thursday
Shaun

We're sitting cross legged on the grass. It's a proper cliché look like. Under the partial shade of an oak tree. A knobbly tree root runs right through my arse crack like a woody bike saddle. We look like something out of a university prospectus, one of the good ones anyway. We've done some exploring of the site and now seek some rest. Been up that massive tower, which was terrifying as owt, but I didn't want to flake out in front of Jasmine. My legs have finally stopped shaking, thank fuck.

We've been and poked our noses into a few different tents where we could hear some music coming from, but with it being Thursday and early, the quality of performer wasn't that great. There was a decent enough acoustic set in a charity tent though. A handful of people obviously sheltering from the radge heat, sitting with their backs to the tent material, legs crossed like they are big kids. Two blokes doing comedy songs. Slagging off the Tories and making jokes about Vladimir Putin. Easy enough listening like, raised a chuckle. Then some lassie came onto stage with a puppet of a snake and a piano, and right then we knew it was time to get out. There was a moment when we headed into the cinema tent and caught the tail end of Forrest Gump. Couldn't quite believe it when Jasmine said she'd never seen it before. Haven't got a clue how that is even possible. Shame we missed the bit where Jenny gets Forrest to feel up her tits. Got things stirring as a young'un, that scene did like.

'I love you Jen-aaayy,' I kept on saying every five seconds, her turn to be mocked for not knowing something. I feel comfortable enough taking the piss out of her now, she seems fair game. I enjoy her annoyed reactions.

'My name's Gump... Forrest Gump!' I kept on repeating to Seb as well as reeling off all different ways to cook shrimp, as we stood side by side at the pissers. Him desperate not to indulge me, fighting back an annoyed laugh. 'Shut up man,' he'd bat back.

We stopped and watched a few songs from some lads at The Plantation Stage, where we'd been yesterday. Weird seeing it in daylight like, weird to think it's the same location of last night's brilliance. The lads on stage today looked and sounded like a Sixth Form band from a local comp. Bit too shit to waste time sitting through. We wandered a bit then succumbed to the temptation of wine, Jasmine raising the prospect when Seb was whinging on about beer being so gassy, and cider giving him heartburn.

She's now twirling dandelions between thumb and forefinger. Crushing the stem with each roll. The sticky yellow sap she wipes onto the blades of grass that tickle our legs. She's kicked her shoes off and tucked her feet under her arse. I'm fiddling with the damp ingredients label from the silver bladder of wine we're passing around to one another. Peeling off the pulpy bits and flicking them off in Seb's direction. I've landed a few head shots without him noticing. The wine is rosé and nasty, but refreshing at least. We couldn't settle on which colour to go for, so opted for one that disappointed all of us. Jasmine bought it. She seems to be keen to pay more than her way today. Mentioned something over breakfast about being really grateful for having her along. Something about us not having to have been so obliging, blatantly a hangover reflection. Peevers fear. A feeling I know all too well. Saying she wouldn't be offended if we wanted some time alone. As if we'd do that. To be fair to the lass, she's got better patter than my brother and looks a hell of a lot better. Can't help but cop the odd look at her as she potters about in her own little world. The big test will be when I broach the subject of narcotics mind. Friday is rapidly approaching, not that I've not had a few cheeky tasters so far like. I've had lasses spooked at the sight of a baggy. Gone cold on me when I've started offering around the pills. Sliding away off into the night. I don't expect anyone to feel like they need to partake in it like, just would be nice to share the moment all as one. Nowt worse being the only one on another planet, whilst someone stands in front of you flat footed sipping down mineral water asking, 'Are you okay?' Can kill a vibe that like.

She's paused fiddling with dandelions to apply a ChapStick to her lips. Borrowed the shining phone screen of Seb to observe her reflection. Top lip then bottom lip. Rub against one another then ChapStick back into her bag. I find myself hypnotised by the rhythm and fluency at which she does this. Her nude lips looking plump and appealing. She looks like Scarlet Johanssen in Lost in Translation. Lush. I mustn't think that way. She's Seb's mate. Must be the heat and the peeve getting me horned up a bit. Always feel more groin strain in summer. She sets about adding to the daisy chain she started earlier. Digging a nail into the thin stems to make a little opening. She started it sometime between the chat about shittest jobs we've had and the shittest partners we've had. Her contribution was a bit cryptic. A topic Seb jogged along quite quickly. I struggled for shittest job; the options too plentiful. But, that food packaging factory up on the Valley was the most fucking mind-numbing. Can still hear the whir and clunk of the machines. The dystopian nightmare I found myself in. I don't even know if half a day at Amazon can be counted. I was barely out of the induction, riding an awful comedown, when I realised there was no way I'd be putting up with that shite. Fuck two buses to get to some grey monolith of misery out in the sticks, where no one can hear you scream. Seb's was some clothes shop when he was still in school. Said he was that bloke who handed out the little coloured bits of plastic in the changing rooms of some old man shop. Never copped a sneaky look of anything other than aged men's arse cracks, apparently. Rotten that like.

'You know when we went to bed last night?' Seb asks.

'Aye?' I say all curious.

'Almost straight away, you let out this massive guff. A proper satisfying sounding fart, you know. I could hear the neighbours howling. They were pissing themselves!' he says laughing into his cup.

'As if? It took me ages to get to kip.'

'Just reporting what I heard. Sounded like yours. And your pod smelt a bit on the turn this morning.' He's scoffing away like a fucking anteater, eyes tight shut in case they fall out his stupid cunt head, all 'hur hur hur'. Why the fuck is this cunt accusing me of guffing? He loves doing it, the prick. Trying to knock me down in company, belittle me. He's more like Dad than he fucking knows. So, fuck if I did, even though I'm pretty certain it wasn't. It took me donkeys to fall asleep. I should know. I spent probably half an hour contemplating going for a piss. Switched my phone back on, chucked some music on. Had no messages waiting for me. Had my headphones on playing some of that H.P. Milton's top songs on Spotify. Really liking it. Took me straight back to being there, was nice to know the words. I was occupying my wired mind with imagining myself scoring for Newcastle in the FA Cup final. My go to non-sexual fantasy. Swatting away my go to sexual fantasy successfully. Picturing catching a 40-yard volley so sweetly from some South American's pinpoint cross, that I bury the ball top bin in the dying seconds of extra time. Queue a pitch invasion and chaotic scenes. Getting lifted up by all the euphoric Geordies and tossed in the air. I'd be given freedom of the city. Never have to pay for a drink again. Dad would be proud. Marvellous. In fact, I know for certain it wasn't me, because I went to bed nipping in a fart because I didn't want Jasmine to think I was a dirty pig. Woke up with a pain because of it. I'd made a huge effort yesterday to come across like a normal, fully functioning member of the human race. I think I did a pretty good job. Why is this prick now coming at me with accusations? I'll do what I always do though and laugh it off, avoid the aggro. I hope she doesn't think it was me like. I look at her, but her head is lower, turned a few degrees further away from us. She's deep in concentration threading daisies together. Mustn't be listening. Just as well.

'Fucking wasn't me like,' I say after a little while, still furious he's trying this one on me. Turning my head across the field. I see a pocket of movement and sound. The Kidzfieldz is over in the distance. Sponsored by Capri-Sun. That's a blast from the past. A sore memory like. Our household more ASDA Smartprice cartons of juice than premium exotic brands. Only got Capri-Sun at other kids' parties. As a treat. It's a fenced off little area. Good idea, keep the little critters in there. Don't want any escaping out and ruining the adults' fun. They're all hedged in with plastic bamboo and flowers with big butterflies on and that. They're doing a baby rave. Fucking baby rave man. I only know from checking the line-up lanyard; after wondering why the fuck they're playing Darude 'Sandstorm' in the kid's area. Turns out, it's a thing. Parents and kids dancing to rave classics. Strobe lights and loud music into little faces. Definitely a path to ADHD or something. Saying that, the bairns looking to be having more of a dance than the old fucks on the other side of the hedge. There is a scattering of little people who have managed to escape the

Orwellian nightmare of a tent and are pottering about pushing over huge stacks of foamy blocks and twirling about colourful ribbons. Little boys popping bubbles and little girls doing handstands. Sad looking parents wondering what the fuck they've let themselves into. Staring into the middle distance, looking full of regret and tiredness. Wishing they'd booked Tenerife and that kids' club they saw. Or pulled out and spaffed elsewhere.

'My childhood was never like that,' I say in an attempt to change the subject from flatulence, 'most I ever had was a box of cars and that toy garage. Remember that garage Seb?'

'The one with the windy handle and the little bell?'

'That's the one. I fucking loved that garage.'

'I remember the day Mam and you came home with it. Was the car boot sale down Blaydon, you remember?'

'Was it? Ha, did I ever get anything new?'

'Way aye,' he pauses and thinks, 'that car wash. Remember that?'

'Fuck yes, had little squirters didn't it?'

'And them sponge rolls.'

'Ah, god yes!' I can almost picture it in my mind. White plastic with blue trim. Driving cars up and down the ramp for hours and hours. Little Matchbox cars. 'Pocket money cars' we called them. Background soundtrack of Robbie Williams first album coming from the kitchen. - *I hope I'm old, before I die* - A leftover chicken turned into a korma for tea. Water leaking from the little reservoir under the toy. Frantically wiping it from the wooden coffee table with my sleeve before anyone saw. Before it soaked into the grain. Before it left a mark. 'Tea's ready.' Seb would thump down the stairs. Blinking away games console glare. Megadrive, none of that PlayStation nonsense back then. We'd sit around the table and shovel down spoonfuls of curry and tear at naans whilst my mother sat back and asked with an anxious, 'Is it nice?' It always was.

'Remember when it broke?' I ask, after a while.

'No?' replies Seb.

'Me and you were wrestling on like usual. You chased me around the house trying to stick a snot on my face. Big green bastard you'd picked out and come to show me.'

'Ha, no? That's manky!' his turn to look a bit embarrassed.

'Yeah, I remember being fucking petrified you'd make me eat it or something. I ran up and down the stairs away from you, and then I trod on the thing when I was trying to hide behind the sofa. It made this awful snapping noise.'

'Really? Oh.'

'I was devastated. Properly devoed. Couldn't stop crying. I remember Mam thought the snapping sound was my leg coz of the crying. Went out screaming for Dad to call an ambulance.'

'Actually, that rings a bell.'

'Dad looked worried as owt when he came boshing in covered in soil, up until he twigged what it was all about.'

'Bet he was sympathetic,' says Seb sarcastically, 'what did he do like? Bollock you?'

'No, he actually was,' I protest, 'took me into his arms and told me he'd try and fix it.'

'And did he? I guess not.'

'Nah, he did try like. But it ended up in the bin the next week. Took me weeks to get over it.' I imagine it now, buried hundreds of metres into the ground. Like that bloke who chucked out his old computer with millions of quid's worth of bitcoin on it. Silly bastard. I picture my car wash crushed and compacted alongside twenty odd year old plastic packaging. Findus pancake boxes, choc bar wrappers, carrier bags. Like a time capsule. Buried in a great mass of shite we've all forgotten about. It'll still exist. In some form. Somewhere. Then I think of my mother. Her ashes. Scattered a hundred or so miles from here by the sea and spread quickly back to the land with the winds. Maybe some part of her is here in this field. In the blade of the grass that tickles the backs of my knees. Or in the wine that Seb is knocking back. Maybe she's in the white petal of the daisy that Jasmine is picking between her fingers. Daisies were her favourite flower actually. That's what she used to tell me anyway. When I picked them for her on picnics in Wylam, that place by the river where you could hear the trains scuttle past. Closest thing to paradise I've ever seen that. Threading them into her buttonholes on her mustard coloured cardy. I called my guitar Daisy because of that. Not that I'd ever tell anyone that. Ever. A white Fender Jaguar. Fucking stunning thing. Always wanted one but could never afford the thing. When she died, I got a little bit of money. Was some dosh she'd squirrelled away whilst she was ill and made my dad swear he'd give us it when she died. Told him to make sure we bought ourselves something nice with it. Wrote it in a letter that I've always found too painful to bring myself to read. We were never flush with money as a family, and she wanted us to spoil ourselves with it. I did. On the Fender Jaguar I used to gawp at through the Jimmy Chandler Music window on High Bridge Street up in town. Wondering what I'd have to do to be able to afford it. Turns out all I'd have to do was lose the most important person in the world to me to get it. I remember Seb berating me for buying it. Bollocking, proper shouting at me saying I was a stupid bastard wasting my money on a 'fucking guitar'. I understand now he was angry. He'd lost someone too. I didn't see his point. We argued like fuck. I'd done what she said. Treated myself. Just because he saved his up to put down on his first house. He was always a saver. I look at him now. Face pointed towards the Capri-Sun kids raving away to Ibiza anthems. Freaky sights. Smoke machine. Glow-sticks.

'Ah Shaun, I've been meaning to say, H.P. Milton is coming to Newcastle in winter. I saw this morning, we could go?' Seb says. I'm taken aback a bit.

'Yeah, what date?' I ask, trying not to sound so surprised.

'Not sure, but if it works out you fancy it?'

'Yeah, sounds good.'

'Sweet, I'll get some tickets when we're back.' We'll see if that actually happens like, I'm dubious about it.

'You're welcome to join us inall Jasmine.'

'Thanks, I'll have a think.' Another handful of grass ripped out and patted into a pile by her side.

I scan the surrounding faces. Others sharing the shade of the tree. I've been earwigging on some Southerners nearby. Typical poshos. Describing these made-up jobs, they tend to come out with. Like the people you get on Location, Location, Location. Still spotty faced, but full of confidence. Massive budgets. 'Oh, yahh I'm a sports nutrition consultant and my budget is tops £750,000.' Yeah, mate? I call bullshit. I reckon your mam and dad are fucking loaded, but well done for trying to justify your own wealth. 'Yeah, it's part of a start-up. I usually work in this really inspiring open office.' I hear from the Southerners behind me. Wish Dad could hear this nonsense. Would be good entertainment watching the blue veins in his head twitch. Would be a hoot seeing him make sense of baby rave over yonder inall. Poor bastard is stuck in a different time, then again, I'm increasingly feeling like that.

My eye catches onto some other fucker in the field, stood up all animated. Arms moving like one of them robots in a car factory. He's wearing wellies, top hat and a hoody. He mustn't have seen the weather. Mustn't have looked up when he shuffled out of his tent. Too busy psyching himself up to tell this story by the looks of it. He seems to be the one enjoying the story the most. Guffawing like a fucking donkey when he gets to a loud bit. His properly dressed friends sitting down squinting every time his head moves and unblocks the sun from behind his daft hat. They're nodding along, chuckling on queue. Beyond him and a few metres to the right is some shifty looking fucker who looks like he's won big at the bingo, or stowed a dead body into a freezer. He's with some lass who carries the face of someone who has scranned all the chicken skin off a Sunday roast before the meal has been served. All greasy faced satisfaction and shame. A scruffy lass is walking alone without shoes on heading in the other direction. Hippie looking. Quite fit actually. There are some lads huddled over a box of pizza. Stringy cheese like elastic as they tear at it. Looks immense. There's a family; mam and dad walking swinging their kid. His face pink with joy. He's got a mushroom haircut like I did. Sweet looking thing like. I feel a churn in my stomach unsure whether it's the kid or the pizza that caused it.

'I love cheese me, that's my weakness,' Jasmine notices the epic looking pizza too.

'I love my women like I love my cheese. Smelly and covered in mould.'

'Aged six months,' she adds with a coy grin.

*

Much of the afternoon continued in this way as early evening threatened to arrive. We've foregone food in favour of liquid nourishment. Ripping up handfuls of grass in idleness, people watching and chatting shite in a circle under the shade of the oak tree. Shielding from the big ball of bastard up high. Laughing and feeling freaked out in equal measures as a human sized fruit took to The Kidzfieldz and started singing 'Mango Number 5' followed by 'Mango Italiano'. Worried for a second I'd been spiked earlier. Vivid hallucinations turn out to be reality. Then taking it in turns to make the cramp legged walk down to the bar area whenever a gap looked to have appeared. The wine bladder consumption paused in favour of something a little less minging. Watching little kids collect discarded plastic glasses from the grass, dragging huge stacks to the return point and swapping it for 10p per return. Quite the money maker for them, bet it's not long until they can buy some football boots by doing the graft us adults can't be arsed to do.

We've been conjuring up meaningless patter about 'Would you rather?' and 'What would be worse?'. As the peeve made its way into my system, the beauty of Jasmine became more and more clear to see. She has that skin, tight like a drum, almost airbrushed it's so flawless. She looks like she drinks a lot of water. Like the amount that they say you should actually drink on the telly. Them TV doctors. To be fair to the girl, she can handle her peeve inall based on this afternoon's showing. Despite being under this tree for several hours it looks like she's still caught the sun. Seb's just come back from a piss and is telling us about some lads from Burnley who have told him about a secret set that's happening soon. He's flicking through the lanyard on the floor all excited to confirm a gap in the schedule. Nodding in confirmation. It's marked TBC.

'Top secret, they told me. There, to be confirmed it says.'

'Aye, top secret for you and a hundred of others in the pissers.'

'Nah they were sound. Quite insistent inall. They noticed my T-shirt,' he says pointing at his band T-shirt, 'said "Hey lad we've got something you might like" told me Cassady Way are doing a set soon.' I feel confused, as the T-shirt bears no mention of that band.

'Aw, that sounds great, I love them! We should go,' chirps Jasmine. She's right like. They have some decent tunes and I suppose we are here for music after all.

'That'll be you prodding me for an hour then?' I quip, 'Sounds good, aye. We really should move away from this tree like. Maybe get something to line our stomach or something?'

'Yeah, good shout. It's been nice though,' Jasmine says, pulling up her daisy chain, showing Seb her handiwork.

'Lovely,' he offers, like he says to the kids when they've done a shite picture destined for the fridge, then quite quickly the bin, 'Aye, we'll head that way. Lost track of time here.' She puts the chain around her neck and stands up dusting down the grass and bugs off her legs. Slipping her shell toe Adidas trainers back on. We head instinctively towards the wood-fired pizza stall, working out of a greeny blue horsebox. The smell of molten cheese, oregano and plump tomato is enough to make me part with fifteen quid for a ten incher.

'I love my men like I love my pizza,' giggles Jasmine into her wrist. Blue latex gloves get to work kneading and rolling up my sustenance. Seb quietly huffs as his card makes the contactless beep. Tight bastard.

Thursday
Jasmine

The natural light changes, the sunburn on my neck soothed by the cooling air, the onslaught of the 'big ball of bastard', as Shaun has been calling it, relents. Vinegar tang in the back of my nose and throat, a symptom of today's acidic drinking. It nips each time I drink down from the wine bladder dregs. I shudder as I decant it into the coffee cup, and then into my stomach. Hues and smears of orange and red on the horizon. Like the tapas restaurant I went to as a kid, for a treat. El Cabanas, I think I remember it being called. Patatas bravas, calamari and a Diet Coke. Parents sharing a bottle of white to the sound of flamenco music playing, all whilst sitting quietly watching the passing people of the shopping centre slink by. I thought it was a different world.

We're sauntering now towards a 'secret set', which doesn't seem to be very secret. Wafts of neroli and foliage underfoot as we mosey to its location. We meander, ebb and flow through the early evening crowds by the bracken, oaks, and sycamores. The uplighters have flicked on, casting dapples of greens and reds on the ragged bark of the ancient gents. They're ready to pull an all nighter. There's a palpable energy present. Vibrating anticipation. Bodies are dancing around a random solitary speaker pole, bursting out drum and bass in the middle of a clearing to our right. Euphoric screams from nearby waltzers and slingshots, all neon lit and strobes, can be heard through the trees. Intoxication is everywhere. Confident swaggers and step overs of roots, divots, and prone legs as we head through the trees down a bark covered path. The fragrance is woody and warm. A monolith of rainbow flags marks the entrance, shrouded by pines and conifers. Foliage deep green and firm. The sound bath of food van soundtracks and all major chords hushed the further we tread into the wooded area. The sun trails of the sinking sun cast behind Bowman Crag and its smaller companions shatter and displace before us, lasers from a distant dance scene shiver momentarily over the treetops, the bass can be felt through the ground with every step that lingers. Nature and human-caused spectacles intermingle. Day is preparing to pass on the baton to the night once again. And the night is for us. It may be drunkenness, but there seems to be a constant chorus of laughter, smiling faces, and positivity flick booking in the crowd. Reflecting in me too, my chin is higher, gait more confident. The lads are chattering freely, bouncing into one another like dodgem cars as they walk, unsteady with booze. They're naming 90s footballers, bathing in nostalgia, 'I had him as a shiny as a kid, Martin did a swap for Ian Rush and Nigel Winterburn,' before ape like beer drinking motions with big swinging arms, then resuming the rally about best left backs of 97 to 99. We get closer to the pines, the background soundtrack of the waltzers is still loud enough to pick out a - *Love it if we beat them, love it!* - The lads cheer and sway. It decays into the bassy groan of what appears, if the painted way markers are to be correct, The Rabbit Hole. Location of the secret of the century. Grass becomes mud soft on our soles with decomposing pine needles, a beautiful rotting smell, pungent and poignant. Pathways are pockmarked and flanked by trees, felled presumably in last winter's brutal storms. A prosperous time for the roofers in our area. A busy time for the insurance companies, I can tell you. Climate change. The gaffa's desperate to look for an 'act of god' reason to attribute to it, so as to not pay a penny out. There was a fair few animated conversations following that. Ethics and morality never winning the shouting match.

The lighting rig comes into view showing the rainbow bunting flagged arena in its full majesty. A clearing no bigger than a couple of tennis courts. A beautiful, ramshackle rudimentary log-built stage, which looks like it would struggle to house a four piece comfortably, sits at the end of the area. There's a smattering of bodies milling around and chatting, laughing and dancing in the comfort of the wooded haven. No one is playing on the stage yet, but the PA system is playing old 90s R&B tunes. - *You know eye love you better* - The volume is one that allows conversation and not shouting. Feeling like a granny as I see this and point it out to the lads. They break away from conversations about Darren Anderton and Jamie

Redknapp as we form a circle in the middle of the clearing, encircled by trees ourselves.

'Special this isn't it?' we nod and look around in awe, expectation, and bellies nervous at the prospect of seeing Cassady Way play here. Does look like a well-kept secret actually, considering we'll be sharing it with a very select few, based on the people around us. A well-kept secret indeed. Suppose there is still time though. Shaun is off towards the little wooden built stand that resembles an Englishman's take on a tiki bar. Thicker wood, more screws, and straighter angles. Rifling for his bank card in the several different pockets of his shorts, before exchanging a beep for three bottles of luminous yellow alcopop. Seb's eyes meet mine with a smiling roll.

'Chin, chin!' Shaun returns with gusto, buzzing there was no queue no doubt, based on his earlier gripes I've witnessed so far when it's his round. As we chatter and shuffle, I notice just how red the lads' faces are from today's sunny onslaught. Shaun has his sunglasses on, unfashionably reflective, I hold his gaze during an anecdote about one of his mate's trips to Ayia Napa and someone pinching all of his clothes off a beach when he was skinny dipping, just long enough to inspect my own reflection. Self-diagnosis, sunburn across pretty much all of my face. - *With a little bit of luck, we will make it through the night* - Sledgehammer sounds out of the woodland speakers strapped high into the pine trees with torque straps. I look up and see the two-stroke blink of a jet plane leaving a trail of etch a sketch jet-streams in the ever-darkening sky. A tube of expats and cheap drink pilgrims head off to a record-breaking scorching destination. 'It's hot, it's just too bloody hot,' they'll say. - *With a little bit of luck, we will make it through the night* -

'Alessandro Pistone. That's his name!' Seb barks with a celebratory punch to the air.

'Yes!!!' celebrates Shaun, 'Thank god for that.' Then they're back on to the football duelling for airtime as they rally with nostalgia from childhood. It's nice to see, but I turn and survey the crowd to occupy myself. See people in the same predicament seek solace in their phones, hiding themselves from the loneliness. Focus in on a bloke who looks like the cocaine-era Robbie Williams, eyes like microwave dials, showing his son the ropes, hoping he will follow in his footsteps of gigging and drinking. Reciting stories from his youth and how it wasn't like it is now, back then. Lad in 'Nine Inch Nails' T-shirt looks nervous with his nose ringed girlfriend wearing Fleur De Lis tights. She reminds me of someone, but I can't quite place her. I watch a blonde permed bloke in painter overalls and a denim jacketed girl lead one another to the front of the crowd, much to the dismay of a camel jacketed third wheel left standing smiling whilst wounded inside. New lovers bouncing with excitement into the unknown.

Thursday
Seb

Phone screens light up the moment the Cassady Way bandmates take to stage. Like an old switchboard. Like how I imagine the control room of a nuclear power plant is. There's an old one nearby here, actually. We're stood a fair distance back, but you can tell the band are young, skinny, and beautiful. Exploded onto the music scene, captivating young and old, then collapsing in on themselves like these things often go. The tabloid tales of the guitarist and her relationship with another celebrity helped elevate their status. They announced via social media earlier in the year they were recording new stuff together. Tours and festival dates are rumoured, but yet to be confirmed.

A higher pitched sound of cheers welcomes them on stage, the screams of a younger generation. A flood of youngsters plagued The Rabbit Hole area some ten minutes ago, shuffling and occupying every available space. The rumour must have hit the socials. A blonde-haired singer in a tartan dress, Doc Martin boots and bouncing energy as she bounds towards the microphone. She's flanked by shirt and waist-coated bloke looking a bit like the Madri fella, he straps on a bass guitar. A pony-tailed guitarist with an oversized Ramones style leather jacket and stonewashed jeans, knees torn, saunters onto the stage swigging a Red Stripe. The dregs splashing the crowd as she launches it into the crowd, expressionless. Peace symbol fingers follow. The drummer with a retro Argentina football top and Umbro sweatpants on fiddles with her stool, draping a towel onto the stand behind her. I find myself watching their entrance on the x2 zoom of the screen in front of me. Held aloft by an excited teen in snakeskin boots and neon bag.

'1.2.3.4!' The drummer clinks sticks and the band launches into a cacophonous raging song full of angst and energy. The sort that can only be authentically and unapologetically be done by the young. We were the generation who grew up during reasonable stability, these lot have had no such pleasure. I don't recognise it, but it's full-on in-your-face stuff. Bobbed singer is gripping microphone, dangling from it almost and grappling with all her strength, screaming her lyrics into it with a pained expression. - *I exist, we exist* - The sound is loud, the guitars blaring and bleeding over the vocals. Madri man's head sweeps from side to side as the verses and choruses crash and distort. I can barely make out what she's screaming, eyes closed, but I know she feels those lyrics. The expression is one of pent-up relief, as she confesses to the crowd through her art form. Spilling out her traumas and experiences through words and music into the phone cameras of a crowd of gawpers. The drummer's hair is whipping across cymbals as she battles with her kit. An angry xl Bully that needs taming or destroying. The sonic energy coming from the stage is immense, but the crowd is absorbing it. Not reflecting it back and feeding off it. I look ahead, stretching on my toes to see those at the front. There is a dis-balance. The raw power of angle grinder guitars and apocalyptic drums are not making the cut through with those watching. There are some movements, and pockets of activity. Some arms are in the air, scattered throughout. There's singing back of lyrics, sure. I see faces in awe too, but behind the shield of a phone screen. They're witnessing it as though not truly present at all. This isn't live music, for them at least. I feel an obligation to get into it more, to counter this disharmony. Punch the air more when I sense a bass drum coming, try and catch a snatch of a lyric and shout it back to them. But, much like when watching a film that Mia isn't into, it affects my own experience. I find myself getting frustrated at the scene. I can't unsee it. The lack of immediacy between artist and observer. I turn and look at Jasmine and Shaun, they themselves flat footed and unaware of any lyrics. Shaun's arms are folded, taking it in alongside sporadic sips of beer. I find it frustrating. I need to relax and just watch. But the phones have really got to me.

After a few songs, I begin to settle. Feel slightly less restless and emotional. The punky songs all sound very similar but engaging enough to keep my attention. I find my gaze falling onto the guitarist. Her mannerisms and talent are at odds with the personality portrayed in the papers. Well, newspaper websites, read usually on the toilet in the morning. Certain songs strike a chord with the audience, but rather than getting everyone more riled up, there's a split. A gulf between people getting more raucous and people pulling phones out of back pockets and filming the song they know. To consume at a later date. To show friends they were there. These are our lives and we're too busy committing megabytes of data to a repository that we'll eventually cease to look at again. Time is disappearing before us. I find myself checking my phone, during a re-tuning break between songs. Not even bothering with chatter. When in Rome. No new messages. No new WhatsApps. No new emails. Signal's poor here mind. Probably the trees. The music starts again and so does the mixed feelings. During the next few songs, the pace is slowed a bit. The angsty punkiness of the first album makes way for the more melancholic and brooding second album tracks. They're calmer. Contemplative. There's a couple of lasses behind us that we've been sort of chatting to in between songs and whatnot. They have accents that, for the last hour, have bugged me because I can't quite work it out. Finally, I ask.

'Sweden,' they explain. I did think it was around that part of the word. 'Are you from around here?'

'Newcastle, east of here. You ever been?'

'No, but our friend Maja studied there. It has a good university, no?'

'Ah great. Yeah, it does. Two actually,' I say. And from there, the flick-book of my conversation skills stalls. I only have ABBA, IKEA, Isak and Zlatan Ibrahimovic as go to reference points from here. None of them conversational silver bullets.

'I bet Sweden is beautiful,' I offer after a pause.

'Some of it, some not so much. Like everywhere, I guess,' then that's it. My chat skills as blunt as those plastic scissors the kids use at home for crafts, bought off eBay because I don't trust them not to lop a finger off. Dear me. Is that what I've become? A social freak. Unable to hold an adult conversation with strangers for longer than two minutes. I firmly believe Covid lockdowns have killed off that particular skill. At least I formulated some words in this exchange. Usually resorting to a nasal forced laugh and 'hurr' noise in acknowledgement. The Swedish lasses smile then check their phones to break the silence and awkwardness. Bloody hell, everyone's at it. The quiet ballad finishes, singer straps on a V-shaped guitar and threatens with three strikes of a fuzzy chord. Crowd let out a shriek and we all turn back around. An audio onslaught resumes.

*

Cassady Way leave the stage chucking drumsticks and plectrums into the sweaty hands of the front rows.

'Thank you, you've been amazing!' The singer shows her gratitude, but in truth, I feel it's ill deserved. They disappear behind the stage. Lights raise and background music plays. – *I stand accused just like you, for being born without a silver spoon* – With it, there's a great shuffle. A shift in positions. The audience begins to split and surge towards the various exits. The dads stay put, humming along to The Verve, showing off their second-hand purchases of retro Adidas tracksuit jackets and paisley bucket hats. The leavers are heading to get food, drinks, or maybe an early night in the campsite back at their tents. There's not much else happening away from here tonight. The Dance Tent finishes early tonight with the weekday curfew. The main stuff begins tomorrow. I could do with an early night myself to be fair. Day drinking and sun are a lethal combination. But I can't quite justify an earlier bedtime than when I'm at home. Jasmine comes back from the bar and thrusts a luminous looking drink in my hand.

'What's that like?' asks Shaun looking confused at the drink, 'Is it Irn-Bru?' Can't help but think an Irn-Bru would perk me up a bit.

'Ha, no it's not, it's an Aperol spritz,' nods Jasmine, 'thought you's looked like you could do with a refreshment.'

'Smells funky, what is it?' Shaun has his nose to the rim of the squidgy cups taking in big honks. Never seen him look so suspicious of a drink before, 'The colour looks unnatural.'

'It's fruity stuff. With sparkling wine. It's Italian, everyone drinks it there.' She then takes a mouthful of her own, maybe to convince me and Shaun that it's drinkable. I duly follow. It's not particularly nice. Bitter and cackly. But then again, my tongue feels furry with all the lager today, the bitterness provides something of a change of scene for my tongue. Shaun is pulling a face I can't quite work out.

'Aye, it's not bad that actually.' I can't tell whether he's lying or not, but Jasmine looks relieved.

'My treat,' she says. Continuing a day of generosity.

'Look at that family,' Shaun says, looking over to the now clear grassy embankment that some ten minutes ago was trodden flat with teens witnessing Cassady Way. I turn as does Jasmine and see a family walking towards us. Beautiful father and mother flanked by two kids. Boy and a girl. Must be about 8 and 6 or so. All clad in matching knitwear. All earthy colours and wooden toggles. Like a walking Dulux colour chart. They look class. Bet they have their life in order. I'm amazed that Shaun noticed such a thing.

'That's family goals that like,' I'm further surprised to hear him say. That Aperol must have something remarkable in it.

'Look at that knitwear,' I marvel at their look. Thoughts go to my own back home. They'll be in bed now. I begin wondering whether I'm depriving my kids of my company and life experience by not bringing them here. The knitwear kids look happy to be there striding alongside their mam and dad. I can imagine mine just moaning and demanding we buy stuff for them. Mia and I frustrated at the distortion between imagined experience and reality. Parenting is sometimes a constant cycle of guilt. I know we do our best and leave nothing on the pitch, but still, the guilt creeps up. Sometimes I just need to be told I'm doing a good job. Then again, I suppose pride does that job. I feel that in buckets.

'What's it like to have kids?' Jasmine asks, her eyes also fixed on the knitwear flock. We must have all been made soft and squidgy by today's rosé.

'It's good, it's really good,' I stutter. But in reality, it is much more than that. There are not enough hours left in the day to try and explain the complexities of it. The sheer pride I feel when I look at the two little munchkins I've had a part in bringing up. The moment you look at them finally sleeping, facial features all miniature and perfect. You consign yourself to the fact that there is nothing in the world quite so peaceful and beautiful as that. The unreasonable arguments forgotten when they wrap their little arms around you and say, 'I love you.' The damp eyes of happiness you feel when they come out with quips that are funnier than anything you have ever seen on telly. The crushing sadness you feel when they hurt themselves and the fact you would do anything to take that pain away from them. The loneliness you feel when they're not home and the house feels like a tidy mausoleum just waiting for unrelenting energy to be unleashed onto the freshly hoovered carpets. A frenzy of imagination. The impossibility of remembering what the former version of yourself resembled, wondering what on earth you did and cared about before they even existed. The bollock ache you feel when you get your vasectomy done and are holed up in bed for three days knowing you will never gift this planet with any more. Glad that's the case when they come to greet you and bounce on your midriff. Saddened when you realise, they'll never stay like this forever, 'Yeah, it's good.'

'I look forward to being able to bring them to places like this, you know,' I add. Imagine standing with older versions of them, sharing memories. Their minds being captivated by songs and sounds not yet created. Maybe future headliners are among us, kids picking up plastic cups or being held aloft by proud looking parents, young eyes dazzled by the lights.

'I think I'll get another of them, anyone want one?' Shaun asks, holding up his empty Aperol. That's gone down quick.

'I'd have one please, Seb?'

'No, you're fine thanks, I'm going to head to the lavvy. I'll get something else on the way back,' I say.

'Not a fan?'

'Was alright, bit too fruity for me,' I head down the embankment and off to the right where there's a small queue for the men's toilet area. It's obscured by a chain link fence and some of that netting you get on scaffolding. It's got a strong smell of piss. Before long it's my turn. The urinal has three banks of troughs, each with one facing another so six pissers in total. No wonder it smells like that. I settle in to concentrate on the task in hand. I think of that bloke on YouTube who washed his hands in the pissy water, thinking the yellow bleach toilet biscuit was in fact soap. You'd be distraught.

'Having a good night, mate?' the towering fella opposite me says. Eyes look manic with cider and coke.

'Aye canny, you?'

'Grand, shame about all these young'uns here though, eh?' Nailed on nutter alert.

'Hmmm,' I'm non-committal concentrating instead on the stream of piss. It's taking forever to stop this.

'First time at FestiFell?' he probes.

'Aye, it is like. Seems canny'

'Not what it used to be mind.'

'Oh really?'

'Yup, used to be a proper festival full of like-minded folk, not this corporate nonsense full of kids. It's a shame,' he leans back as if his piss is reaching a crescendo. Limbering up to swat away the dribbles.

'Hmmph,' another nasal snort of acknowledgment. Why do I always attract these people? Always have. The amount of bus journeys I've had perched next to some nutter reeling off opinionated nonsense, whilst I gaze out the window wanting it to all end. I finish off my piss and shake. Nightmare, the bloke does so too. Big hulking shakes. As if he's putting his whole body into it. We're in a strange shuffle out together where he's continuing the chat.

'Off to see Lorenzo L?' he asks.

'Yeah, we thought we'd check him out.'

'Aw mate, it'll be good. His earlier stuff was better mind.' Glass half full this bloke.

'Yeah. Hopefully, it'll be a good one,' I say as we reach the opening from urinal to arena.

'I'll see you round man, you're one of life's good ones. Don't forget that.' He puts his big shovel hand out for a handshake. I hesitate for a second, knowing fine well he hasn't washed, he's practically wanked away his piss dribbles. Then again, I haven't washed either. We shake. His grip is fierce, bone breakingly strong. Like the roofer we had last year, the bastard who never even fixed the bloody job we paid him for. His eyes look wild and terrifying. I wonder what he's been on today.

'See you later mate,' I say. Then we part grips and ways. I walk quickly to the bar area sliding into a gap. The bar is wet with spilled drinks. I find myself pawing at the alcoholic spillage, giving my hand something to clear the thought of piss from the toilet bloke off. I then dry it off on the arse of my shorts.

'What you having?' pierced eyebrow and nose asks, catlike eyes and porcelain face.

'Beer please.' I'm served, then I head back to the patch where Jasmine and Shaun are, all whilst keeping a periphery eye out for the toilet bloke.

'Ah here, how old you reckon he is?' Shaun is stood with a group of three or four people who he's chatting too. The group looks at me with the gawp of visitors to a zoo. Albeit a shit one with sad uninspiring animals inside. I take a great mouthful of beer whilst they think it over.

'I would say early thirties,' one says.

'Yeah, probably around that. Younger than you,' nods the thick bespectacled lass of the group towards Shaun.

'Maybe even younger than that? Late twenties?' the top knot wearing fella says.

'Ha, I like you!' I smile at him.

'Fuck off man! You reckon I'm older?' Shaun protests, the group are laughing, obviously pissed. They must be to think I resemble anything other than a crumbling old wreck in the latter stages of my thirties. Feels nice to get some validation though.

'Hard paper round pal?' top knot confirms. Jasmine slaps Shaun on the back and laughs.

'Don't worry, I've got some cream back at the tent. Anti-ageing,' she laughs.

'You'll need a fair bit of that.'

'There's seven years between us! He's seven whole years older!' Shaun protests, aghast that they've put him down as older.

'Seven years? Bet you weren't planned!' one of them chirps. Shaun grins and turns stage bound.

'Aye and not wanted either,' he scoffs. I know he's only half joking with that retort. I know how he feels.

The lights on the stage signal something is about to happen. Crushing sounds, bassy booms play through the speakers. Lorenzo L's logo appears in a huge motif on the stage. Dazzling how bright it is. There is a huge applause. Whistles like farmers do to sheepdogs. Stage goes dark. Music begins. Clanging cold chain sounds and stabbing tones. Suddenly, Lorenzo bursts onto the stage like a greyhound out of a trap, microphone pressed against his mouth. He's wearing a cap, vest, baggy pants. He bounds and bounces across the stage as he raps about an absent father. Strobe lights show the steam rising from his glistening skin as his lyrics undulate and spin to a dizzying speed. Never missing a word. I'm captivated by his presence and the songs, cherry-picking out the odd word that he fires out with ferocity over a canvas of juxtaposed sounds and intense stage lighting. I think of my own relationship with my father, think back to how he made me feel on Wednesday, how he's made me feel most days I've spent with him in recent memory. He wasn't always like that. Think of all the trauma he's experienced that's made him who he is now. Big bass drums thump through me, feel like my teeth chatter in my head. Vibrations that make you feel like your fillings will fall out, a melody that sounds like it's in the middle of a rainforest. The crunching sounds of autumn leaves crunched underfoot a few months from now, to the bubble of a womb or even the embrace of a lover back in the early days, when you're both blinded by hormones and hope. A complex soundscape. Back into the present and the dust and crackle of the backing tracks. - *Automation rules the nation* - He repeats. Fragments of metallic moans, chops and loops of silky soupy samples. The hint of a female voice amongst the broth of noise. He's not messing about with his lyrics, potent and venomous, injected into the ears of us who stand nervous before him. The words I pick out are raw and unwavering, but with an underbelly of vulnerability. Hyperactive implosions of sound breathe and burst between the trees as he unleashes track after track upon us. Nobody moves.

The set is intense and raw. The crowd visible in staccato as the strobe pulses over and over, punctuating the tracks that play over his enunciated words. I'm fixated on the set, desperately trying to hear as much as possible, ruminating over every word he spits into the microphone. By the time the set is finished to great commendation, I feel emotionally drained. I also know why there were epilepsy warnings on the screens before he took to stage.

'How good was that?' Jasmine says when the feedback from the amps begins to subside.

'Isn't usually my thing, but I thought that was class,' Shaun confirms.

'Yeah, it was, he was amazing actually,' I say almost stunned, before adding, 'Not as good as last night though.' Unsure of my opinions. And then we head off into the night, looking for a place to rest our aged bodies.

'I know just the place,' says Shaun as he holds his lanyard aloft, we're about to be indulged in his map reading skills once more.

Thursday
Shaun

'What did you study?' Jasmine asks, face obscured by the slow smoke trails, eyes dampened from the sting, but appearing fixed, interested in me. Genuine. Pop, crackle, pop of wet wood. The lungy whoosh of flames gathering pace, heat on my knees, my hands, my face. - *Didn't I take you to higher places you can't reach without me?* - Piano and Stratocaster major keys tremolo through a distant speaker, washing up on our circle of chatter. Feels calm as owt being here.

'Business,' I reply with a slight hesitation, halt then continue. Could really do with a bump of coke the way this conversation might go, 'but I really wanted to do fine art,' pause, 'believe it or not.' My head bows, eyes down to the ring-pull of my can, fiddle with it to distract from the vulnerability and awkwardness I feel.

'Oh really?' genuine shock sounding, 'Bit of "Paint me like one of your French girls" is it?' she chuckles putting her hand on my forearm for a moment, before pushing away again. My cheeks flush and plump in a smile. Never have painted a lass with her bits out like. Don't think I'd be any good painting under those circumstances. Can hardly pour a decent pint for a fit lass.

'Yeah, I er, I even had a place at Goldsmith, like er, kind of bottled it though.'

'No way? How come?' she leans forward, face orange with the proximity of the fire, embers reflecting in her eyes. - *You're in ecstasy without me, when you come down, I won't be around* -

'I suppose,' breathe, 'I suppose it was down to the old man, truth be told. Like me dad strong arming me towards business.' Then again that's a weak as fuck excuse, but I can't face blaming myself.

'Yeah, Dad is pretty stubborn,' Seb pipes up as he returns to the log stump seat he's left to go and grab a beer from the nearby bar. He hands them to each of us. I down the rest of my can and cast it aside. 'At least you went to uni though. Forever the disappointment me.'

'Cheers,' I lazily raise my plastic cup and suck down the foam. 'I'm not so sure about that now, Seb,' I say. Head leaning forward, I'm conscious of my body language, all crunched up like a crisp packet. Rubbing my thumb over white knuckles. I lean back slightly, open up my body. Muscles feel knackered as fuck though. Too much drink and not really a great deal of food.

'He is a stubborn bastard,' I continue, 'I remember the day I told him about the art course.'

'I can imagine that,' Seb offers, 'tactful as ever no doubt?'

'What did he say?' Jasmine leans forward. Both hands clasped around her beer, foam bubbles popping on her top lip.

'I was nervous telling him, you know. But, I built up the courage eventually and told him. He started with "What the fuck you want to do something like that for?" Like he was visibly repulsed at the idea like. Said stuff like "Hitler studied art" and "only homosexuals study art," that kind of thing. "You want to do a proper degree lad" was said many times,' I mimic his voice poorly. But Jasmine is none the wiser, never having the pleasure of his company.

'Wow. Okay,' Jasmine gasps.

'Kept banging on about Hitler doing art, as if there was some stupid link. As if that was a compelling argument to not do it. Yeah, ironic really that both his kids have the initials SS. Really funny for someone who loved anything to do with Churchill. Daft twat. He's all "Two world wars one world cup" bollocks!' I spit, pressure builds in my chest, a punch as I realise the emotion is still quite raw, despite the years that have passed, 'Yeah "Hitler wanted to be a painter, look how he ended up" shite,' again, my voice mimicking his voice, head wobbling side to side in mockery.

'Bet you can guess which way he voted in the referendum?' Seb nods towards Jasmine, she eye rolls in acknowledgement, 'You should see some of Shaun's work, he's really good you know.'

'Really?'

'Yeah, he's really good. We've got one he painted in the hallway at home. Beautiful actually.'

'I haven't done it in a while,' I interject.

'That's a shame,' Jasmine says, 'you should pick it up again.'

I nod, but know I won't.

We all have a collective sip of the beers as the crackle of the fire splits the near silence. - *I can love enough for the both of us* - Wafting through the tree line. Just audible enough to keep the tinnitus at bay.

'Did you enjoy it?' Jasmine asks, 'The business, I mean.'

'Not really, I was alright at it like,' another gulp of the beer, gassy in my stomach to sit alongside the receding chest punch, 'I mean, it's a bit of a shitter because my mother, our mother, took ill when I was in third year, that made me struggle. Dissertation wasn't up to scratch and whatnot.'

'I'm sorry to hear.'

'Yeah, she got ill. Then iller,' the smoke hides the pinching of my eyes, the prickle of tears fighting through, a long-suppressed emotion, 'I took refuge in going out and getting battered basically. Stopped going to classes in the end. Reverse sleep patterns and shite output. Somehow scraped a 2:2. Only just mind.' I mock celebrate with an unconvincing airborne punching fist. Eyes look down at the squidgy plastic. Rock the beer in a centrifuge, gripping foam dragged into the whirlpool. 'I mean my second-year grades carried me through, but yeah, that was my uni experience.' I stop the whirlpool of my beer and meet Jasmine's eyes for a hairline second. I've divulged more than usual there. That was hard. She smiles at me without a hint of humouring or pity. A look of genuine humanity. The punch in my chest replaced with a different feeling altogether. Longing. There's a long pause as we watch the hypnotic dance of the flames, there's a scattering of others around the fire, some standing, some sitting on the chainsawed log seats. I read about this place when indulging in my dump this morning. Draft up my jacksie was a pleasant way to start the day. The mood here is one of reflection and restfulness. Like I imagine decent therapy would be like. Subdued by the warm glow of fire. Welcoming respite. Seb is chatting to someone on his right about something I can't quite pick out, there's excited hand gestures and a few rallies of 'You're joking? No way!' I turn again to Jasmine. Feeling like I want to keep talking.

She looks reflective as she offers, 'My issue with university was that it never really met with the prospectus image they try and pedal. I mean, I never sat cross legged under a willow tree discussing Descartes with like-minded people in flannel shirts. I never played lacrosse or netball. Never joined a society or protested for something I believed in. None of that, no. I basically sat miserable in a box room freezing my tits off. I sat in the corner of seminars crippled with anxiety without even knowing what that was back then. Wondering why my brain was failing me. It was a really tough time actually, now I mention it,' Jasmine concludes.

'I never knew you went to university?' Seb replies almost looking offended.

'I never make a big deal about it. Maybe I'm embarrassed a bit, I'm not sure. The problem is, everyone went to university, didn't they? We were the generation that did. I'm still paying off the loan, but I've seen no benefit from it. I'm not really using my qualification at work, am I?'

'What did you study?' I ask.

'Philosophy?' she replies, face twisted and skewed almost ashamed, expecting a mock in response. She grimaces, 'I know, I know.'

'No that's cool that,' I offer.

'Yeah, I mean, I was really good at school, could have done anything really, but the careers advisor at school was shite. Totally shite.'

'We didn't even have one.'

'They basically want to get as many people into university as possible, all so the school can boast about the numbers in next year's prospectus. They do that without any care for what actually leads to a career or what actually interests the clueless sixteen-year-old kids they sit in front of. Once you're out the door they couldn't give a crap really. Rinse and repeat.'

'Ay. though to think of it, our careers advisor sided with my dad and pushed for business. I don't think interest ever features in the decision making.'

'Exactly!' Jasmine enthusiastically gestures, a slop of beer falls on her thigh, just below the denim. She brushes it off with her left hand. My eyes are drawn to her legs, they're a pale pink in the fire glow. Sun from today looks like it's had an effect on the skin. She continues, 'I suppose business leads places, unlike silly philosophy.'

'You'd think, but not with a Desmond. Not with graduates ten a penny.' Not with a thousand other reasons.

'A Desmond?'

'Yeah... Desmond Tutu,' I pause. A look of confusion and puzzlement, '2:2,' I spell out.

'Ah,' she laughs, I'm unsure whether she really got the reference like.

'A Desmond and a distinct lack of any real career goal. I mean I've been pulling pints on and off for seven years, not exactly a glittering career.'

'Likewise,' she pauses and looks at Seb appearing back to being engrossed in conversation with a black Regatta rain jacketed bloke with khaki pants and bristly black stubble, Red Stripe can in hand, 'If I'm honest, I really can't stand my job. Look at us two rotting away in insurance.' She jabs him in the arm, he looks as the bloke continues the last of his point in a deep sonorous voice.

'I reckon it's a symptom of our generation,' Seb offers. He has been listening, showing great lucidity he turns to us with a swivel on the log and continues, seizing his opportunity to get on his soap box, his pal now looking engaged in our chat too, 'We are worse off than our parents, not that they'd ever admit it. We've been fucked by financial crashes, wars on terror, and austerity. Fucking Covid. Now the planet is going to cook us alive, or the sea is going to swallow us up first. Fucking one thing after another, grinding us down. We're all just treading water trying to make a living, scurrying around looking for meaning, all while the pennies in our pocket get us less and less and our working days get longer and fucking harder,' he finishes with quite some energy. He's quite impassioned by that. Something must have been building up in him inall. This is turning out to be quite the confessional. - *Since I met you, I found the world so new* –

'It's our kids I feel sorry for the most, inheriting the shite our parents have left them to deal with. It's not fair,' his pal adds. Seb nods slowly and forlornly looking.

'True words,' I utter, 'living from month to month, isn't it? I live in an extortionate flat. It's basic. Needs stuff done to it, I report it to my bellend landlord, but nothing really gets done. Cheap patch up jobs at best after months of waiting and texting and harrying. But my rent is paying for that bastard's pension pot. I'll be lucky to afford a cup of tea and a loaf of bread when I'm old and fucked. It's not right man. The rent's gone up a load this last year inall. Once I've fed and watered myself, then fucking heated the thing, I've got next to nowt left.' Seb is nodding along with every word I utter. Venom and angst building in this otherwise serene corner of the festival site. The flames growing and dancing as a larger log catches and a worker in a green tabard chucks on a flexi-tub of bark and sticks. A ricochet of crackles.

'Same,' nods Jasmine, an air of defeatism in her utterance.

'I mean this weekend has basically been funded through saving up tips over the year, like a charity case,' I find myself saying, not entirely correct, but some truth in it, 'That and my overdraft,' I finish with, guiltily conceding more honesty.

'Hooray for the 21st century,' cup raised by Jasmine; a big mouthful follows. Cheeks full of peeve deflate as she swallows it down, 'We have fuck all but the now.'

'Hear, hear!' I clink cups with her. Not so much of a clink with plastic cups like. Seb remains in thought, him now scrunched towards the fire, his turn to foam up his beer with a flick of the wrist. His face now pointing at the fire. We drink in quiet solitude for a moment, for that's all we can do. - *In my arms baby yeah* - Repeated synth tones pulse from afar. Despite knowing I'll struggle the next month financially, I'll look back fondly at this moment, a one of clarity and candid conversation. Bullshit cut and honest confessions. Proper chat. Can't remember the last time I had that. We're all fucked in our own little lives, at least tonight we can share some of it together.

Thursday
Jasmine

'I'm going to call it a night. Think I've hit it too hard today, or the sun's got to me. Want to save myself for tomorrow.' We've gotten back to the tent and Seb's already shuffled into his cell. I get the feeling he might be a little homesick today. Think he's missing the kids. He's mentioned them a few times. Seems to be there sometimes and then off in his own thoughts at others. But to be honest I'm quite happy to have a chilled one tonight. It's been quite tiring today. Some drum and bass DJ thing is going on over in the silent disco. Too much like a migraine for me. None of us are too bothered by that. Shaun even said silent discos are for 'tossers' before, so he's nailed his colours to the mast early doors with that one. It's only day two. Want to pace myself. Shaun's handed me a warm can I don't really fancy, but I'm settled in the camping chair and looking forward to some more conversation. He's taking a nip out of his hipflask. A teardrop shaped silver thing. An engraving I can't see. The sort of thing someone who really cares about you buys you. Gestures it over to me.

'No thanks. What is it?'

'Just whatever whisky I had lying around in the kitchen cupboards. Probably some cheap blend. I'm not usually a whisky man like.'

'I like my whisky like I like my men. Aged at 18 years and single.'

'I like my women like I like my whisky. Cold over rocks,' a pause, 'and full of coke.' We laugh. He's got ABBA on at a reasonable volume. Wouldn't have expected that from him, but it's certainly doing its job. Nearby there's some dance music coming from a competing phone or little speaker. - *Around the world, around the world* - Probably more my scene actually, but I'm not going to complain. There's shuffling all around. Seems quite a lot of folks are happy to have a chilled one back at their tents tonight. It's dark but warm enough. I've got a hoody I've borrowed from Seb, it looks huge. The material is awful, catching the little hairs on my arms, like that cheap epilator I bought from Home Bargains.

'You having a good time?' asks Shaun, inhaling as the whisky he knocks back hits his palate.

'I am, today's been really chilled actually.'

'Nice to just sit and talk sometimes, isn't it? To just be.'

'Definitely. If I were back home, I'd be busying myself doing something, I can't just sit and chill usually.'

'There's nothing to really busy myself with back home.'

'You must work quite a bit?'

'I do yeah, the hours are a bit random like. Needs must, but I don't really have any hobbies or anything to occupy my spare time. Think that's half my problem.'

'You should get back into the painting you were talking about.'

He doesn't respond, just looks down at his hands.

'I'd love to be one of those people who has all sorts of activities in their week. Those super fit people who have things like squash on a Tuesday, running club on a Wednesday and whatnot. Do ultra marathons on a weekend and shit.'

'Sounds exhausting.'

'That's the problem, I just simply can't be arsed with that sort of stuff. Life is too tiring.'

'I used to be really good at football. Did 5-aside a couple of times a week, but the lads are all getting married or having kids now, we can't get five people who are available anymore.'

'That's what happens, some of my girlfriends from my younger days have been married, had kids, and been divorced now. I'm still floating about wondering what I'm going to do with my life.'

'Yup,' he pauses, 'I hope one day it becomes clear.'

'I hope so too.' I crack the can and take a gulp of the cider. It doesn't get any easier to drink. I think back to the morning and the massage I had. I think of the sights of the day and take stock of what's occurred. It seems to have zipped by without a great deal of anything happening.

'Excuse me?' I turn and see the real ale fella from the tent next to us.

'Hi,' I offer, expecting a request to turn the 'Super Trooper' down.

'Would it be so rude as to pull up a chair and sit with you fine people for a bit? It's a bit lonely since the wife went to bed.' He's still sat in his vest, sunburn spread across the tops of his arms now. They are hairy in the way only a man of a certain age can be. That kind of hairiness is earned over many years.

'Of course,' says Shaun, 'take a seat here.' He points to the chair Seb's been using this weekend still moulded into his shape.

'That's very kind,' the fella stands up, shuffles over and then plonks himself down with a groan as he slumps back.

'Cheers!' We all clink drinks and sit for a quiet moment, enjoying the simplicity of being outside on an evening, sharing a moment with strangers. Suitably drunk that silence isn't an uncomfortable thing.

'Are you guys having a good time?' he asks, twirling his beard between thumb and forefinger. It seems to be the default conversation starter these days.

'Yes, thank you, are you?' I reply to the bloke.

'Very restful, great being outside. It beats being at work,' he says.

'What do you do for work?' I seize.

'Ah, that's totally irrelevant now, isn't it?' he says, 'Our jobs are nothing but circumstantial. I hope you don't think I'm rude, but I find people much more interesting beyond their occupation. I would like to think you do me too.'

'That's very true,' I am taken aback, surprised, and in agreement with his sentiment. Ecstatic I don't have to divulge any details of my own job.

'I will tell you though that I'm tremendously excited to see Origins of Sound. That latest track is...' he gestures a kiss on the scrunched tips of his fingers, then like a firework they explode out dramatically, '...chef's kiss!'

'No way?' I'm taken aback, 'Same. It's an epic tune, isn't it?'

'Oh yes. Do you think I look like a dance music fan?' he leans towards me, eyes deep blue harbouring a gentleness that is the antithesis of his rugged face.

'If I'm honest, I am surprised.'

'There's more to people than what's on the surface,' he continues. He's reminding me of an old RE teacher I had. Philosophic and engaging. He did however go berserk one day and locked some year 11s in the stationary cupboard for a whole class once. There were also strong rumours he got a year 10 girl pregnant. Stacey Cliff. Never substantiated though. He was always peddling all sorts of conspiracy theories when going off on a tangent, ranting on about the difficulties of monotheism. Maybe he turns out to be a nutcase, but I'm enjoying his company so far. This is the place for nutcases after all. His quirkiness silently seen by Shaun who nods and smiles as he talks. 'Who else are you looking forward to seeing?'

'The Red Eyes.' I say, hesitant with the rest. I'm kind of just here to escape.

'Ah, Sunday night, yes?'

'Yes.'

'Do you mind?' he asks as he produces a rolling tin, one of those old things my grandpa used to roll his own cigarettes. This man, on the other hand, has a few pre prepared spliffs inside his, along with a baggy and tobacco pouch.

'Knock yourself out, mate,' Shaun says, looking buoyed by its contents. Eyes widen slightly with glee. Ever so subtly sitting up in his chair, like his brother looks when a cake is brought out at the office.

'Fine by me,' I nod.

'Much obliged.' He then continues to light the spliff with one of those proper Zippo lighters. Abrasive scratch and inch long orange flame. Three massive inhales to get the thing properly alight. Great clouds of smoke lit by the moonlight and nearby lighting rigs. He takes them deep into his lungs, closes his eyes. - *There's nothing special, in fact, I'm a bit of a bore* - Enormous exhale through nose and mouth. Slumps back further into his seat. It's almost as if the creases in his forehead iron themselves out. He then offers me a toke.

'Thank you, cheers,' I say after a moment of hesitation. I take a small inhale, gauging the strength of the things. Not having properly had a spliff since my uni days. I suck it back into my lungs. Hot smoke burns the back of my throat. I remember that feeling suddenly, not one I've missed. Picture reddening tubes. Fight the urge to cough and then exhale. A wave of relaxation comes at me, first in the shoulders, down the spine, then into my limbs. A stab of nausea in the pit of my stomach as it mixes with the cider. Goes again. We keep passing the spliff around for several rounds and talk dance music. Real ale man compellingly retells tales of his youth. Turns out he was actually a massive raver in his youth. Got arrested a number of times for organising illegal raves in old industrial buildings in Carlisle back in the late 80s to early 90s. I sit drinking in his tales of a lifestyle I cannot imagine being part of.

'I suppose it all changed when I met her in there,' he uses the glowing end of his spliff to lazily gesture towards the tent of his sleeping wife, 'She was a keen raver back in the day. Met her one night at a warehouse party shortly before the pigs raided us. We all ran out into this abandoned industrial area. Nobody around for miles. Ravers were hiding out everywhere in the scrub. Under old machinery. Everywhere. Everyone trying to remain incognito whilst tripping their nuts. Dressed in all crazy outfits. We were sitting ducks really. Anyway, back to the rave, was such a good night. Was one of those ones you never want to end, you know. The tunes were dirty. The place was alive. Then the torches and the shouting started. All "Police! Everyone remain where you are" bullshit as they do. Dogs barking like bastards. I managed to escape with the kitty for the evening, being the organiser I had overheads, you know. I scarpered out the side door and made a run for it. Coppers were flooding the place from all angles. I managed to get past one and vaulted a brick wall. The E must have given me super strength. Never jumped like that before or since. I kept running and running and running. I ended up near some substation thing. Was whirring away. I tried the door, and it had been kicked in, so I slipped inside. And there she was again. The girl I'd been dancing with just a half hour ago. We hid out there till morning. I mean it was morning already, but proper morning when we knew it was safe. She wouldn't mind me saying but we made love in that substation, which was bizarre and beautiful. After that, well...' He takes another toke on his spliff and looks up at the sky, the stars are bright, and the moon is full. His story never resumes as he disappears into his own memories. Massive exhale, 'Are you two together?' He finally asks as he hands me the spliff again.

'No thanks,' I say feeling pretty battered from it. Limbs are heavy like when you've woken in the night, and you've been sleeping in a way that the blood pools in your arms. He then passes over to Shaun.

'No, we're not,' Shaun says, as he takes a toke. I on the other hand laugh nervously at the question. Unsure why I find it funny. Must be the drugs.

'Shame,' the guy says after a moment, his face still pointed skywards, 'Look at those stars.' I look up, my head feeling heavy flops back into the canvas backrest of the chair, I'm slumped back at quite some angle now. I find it a struggle to focus on one star, they all seem to be moving so fast. There's another quiet moment of reflection as all three of us observe the great expanse of space above us. - *Young and sweet only 17* -

'I think I just saw a shooting star,' chirps Shaun, a sleepy childish enthusiasm in his voice.

'Wish upon a falling star,' our campmate annunciates with each syllable lazily.

'Could be a ballistic missile,' I find myself saying. Raising smoky laughter from real ale fella.

'Oh, imagine that,' he says, once his laughter subsides.

'All of this would be irrelevant,' I say.

'Very true. Such is the case,' he says, 'Only then would you truly know if you regretted how your life had been.' Another silence falls upon our conversation. Eyes fixed up. The spliff sitting nestled in the fella's fingers, burnt down to the roach.

'What would you wish for?' asks Shaun, 'If it was a falling star?'

'I have no idea,' I say, after thinking about the question for a bit. Nothing and everything comes to mind as to what I would want that I don't have in my life. Like the problem I have when given a menu in a restaurant with too many choices. I get stunned into indecision. The question remains unanswered, radiating into the sky that we all observe.

'I think it's time I head to bed. But thank you for your company.' Our campmate starts shuffling and finding energy to propel him out of the seat. He struggles at first but after several attempts encouraged by mine and Shaun's laughter, he manages to get himself prone. 'Good evening, friends,' he says.

'Good night. Thank you for sitting with us,' I say.

'Goodnight pal, sleep well mate,' Shaun says. An open palmed regal wave and then he shuffles through the chevron of tents before he reaches his own abode. Zipper sounds and fabric squeaks. Then he's gone. Me and Shaun look at one another and smile. Presumably, he's as amazed as I am at the difference between what I thought this bloke would be like and the reality. I've enjoyed conversing with him.

'Can you hear Seb snoring?' Shaun asks. Big proud grin on his face.

'Think we've knackered him out.'

'He's not used to it these days.'

'Has he always been that tidy? I've been dying to ask.'

'Oh aye. Not noticed it before?'

'His desk at work is always organised and his car is usually immaculate, but I never realised how much of a neat freak he is.'

'Yeah, he's always been like that. I'm the opposite. It's probably driving him insane having me in his tent.'

'And me,' we chuckle together like naughty schoolkids.

'You don't seem scruffy to me like.'

'Ha thanks, you should see my flat, you'll soon say otherwise,' we both laugh. Eyes locked, reddened with fatigue and weed.

'Tell you what, here's something about him. When he needs to buy diesel, he'll log in to his online banking app on the forecourt, right? He'll see what he needs to get so that there's no decimals on his balance.'

'You what? What do you mean?'

'Like say his bank balance is 427.63p. He'd make sure his diesel bill gets to 63p. Says it gives him satisfaction when it's nicely rounded up.'

'Wow. That's bad that.'

'Lunatic behaviour, isn't it?' We're laughing again, confident he won't hear us over his snoring.

'Different strokes for different folks, I guess. We all have our own little daft quirks.' His snoring getting louder through the polyester. I pull a face at it, snort out a snigger. Noticing a nearby voice say, 'fucking hell, listen to that.' Shaun takes another nip from his hip flask.

'Don't think I'll be finishing this can,' I say to Shaun.

'Yeah, that spliff has finished me off. I'm done.'

'Think it's time to head for bed,' I say, chucking the can half arsed towards the limp black bin bag near the entrance to the tent. Red liquid splashed onto the polyester and dribbles down slowly. Can missed by about a metre short. 'Him in there wouldn't be happy about that.'

'Ha, no. Yeah, bed sounds good,' Shaun says, stretching out wide and beginning to stand up, 'Good shout.'

'Would you mind giving me a hand?' I ask, noticing my brain isn't talking to my legs properly. Like the earth is trying to pull me down more than normal.

'Of course,' he puts his hand towards me, I grip it and he pulls me upright. I steady myself and wobble into him. My head at his shoulder, left hand holding his arm as I gain my faculties before heading to bed. I notice a smell of stale sweat and aged deodorant on him. Not unpleasant though, weirdly.

'You alright?' he asks as I wobble. I look at his face, there's a kindness in his eyes.

'I'll be fine. Just need to get to bed.' I lunge forward towards the tent flap.

'Let me get that for you.' He helps navigate the entrance zips.

'Thank you,' I say as I wriggle into the darkness of the tent, feeling my way through the boxes and bags toward my own sleeping pod, 'Goodnight.' I say as I kick off my shoes and pull my sleeping bag over me.

'Goodnight Jasmine, sleep well,' he says as the colours under my doughy eyelids dance and bleed, merging with the darkness, enveloping my mind.

Friday

Friday
Seb

Tower-block missile strike, royal family illness, humanitarian crisis, misper's partner arrested, abducted child reunited with parents, police accused of racism, footballer affair, death of an 80s popstar, misogynist Youtuber bailed, rioting, striking, hating, hurting, lying, dying. The usual morning routine, same news apps in sequence, order of articles shuffled. Next, the sports apps, transfer rumours, and accompanying betting odds hyperlinked. Emails. WhatsApp. Fitbit app. Loading taking longer than usual, struggling for signal. Reveals '7hrs and 23mins' of sleep. Decent for me these days. Didn't feel that long mind. A broken sleep punctuated with vivid and weird dreams, a sharp inhale, and violent flip in my bag every so often. Soundtrack of the hubbub from the life around me. All Yorkshire accents, zips, and polyester shuffles. Cans clinking, lighters, and farts.

My eyelids blink with gravel strokes. Sleeping bag feels damp inside, sweaty bacteria laced. Lucozade bottle, which I have hazy memories of using as a makeshift bedpan last night, sits taunting me. The wider opening conveniently minimising the risk of pissing all over my quarters as I crouch in shame, euphoric with relief in the dark hours. I must remember to dispose of that, first I must hide it though, in case of any mistaken consumption by those two. Lucozade at this time of the morning would no doubt be a temptation to someone. The green fabric of the tent and the angle of attack from the morning sun create an eerie backlight as I survey my little pod. There's a couple of them horrible fruit flies on the inside, my airbed is already deflated, its limpness reflecting how I feel. I don't even think I drank that much last night, but the hangovers after 30 are brutal nowadays, I really struggle. Heart always racing and pulse feeling tickly, as if thick treacle or that slime the bairns play with has replaced my blood. I've found myself often googling 'alcohol allergy' after a night of increased consumption and scanned the article with one aching eye through the duvet, looking for some confirmation and validation that there is another explanation. Anything to explain the dis-balance as to how I feel after a few peeves. Anything to explain the desperate need for grease, sleep, and rest, other than the incontestable fact that I am getting older, my body has been made inefficient through time, kids, and attrition. When I was a young man, I could be out until 3am in the morning, get back plastered with tongue stained red with sickly alcopop film, T-shirt reeking of tobacco, ears would be ringing from being stood at the mouth of a Funktion One sound system belting out the lyrics with my face to the dancers, as if it was me channelling the indie bangers. A frontman wannabee. I'd get my head down for a couple of hours of sleep, then spin off a shift in a clothes shop, starting at 8am without any great fear other than the sheer monotony of the shift. Nowadays the prospect of being out beyond 10pm on a work night is unthinkable. Any more than two beers profoundly affecting my sleep quality and my mood the following day. The Fitbit app confirms this, I'm a sucker for data. I do a mental mind map of the drinks I had yesterday, totting up a tally. When I get to drink eleven at around 9pm, I concede that perhaps I do indeed deserve this stabbing pain behind the eyes. A textbook mid-30s morning after. I visualise the yeasty sludge fatbergs in my body, the carbonated bubbles in my blood. I understand why my ticker is working overtime in my chest, petulantly bashing about its work in a huff at how I've betrayed its trust. Like a huffy kid loudly cleaning its bedroom, showing it's working under duress. My mouth clacks as my jaw untethers itself from clinging to the top teeth. I make that well-worn vow to myself, to cut down on the sauce once this weekend is over. Just the one glass of wine with Mia when I'm back.

I'm dressed in shorts and T-shirt from yesterday's festivities. I reach for the nearby water bottle, the one with FestiFell branding and logo of the local water company. Confident it's not been used as another urine receptacle. Unscrew the tin lid and welcome the cool liquid as it drains down my grateful gullet. Pop the foil on two paracetamol and down the remains of the metal water vessel. Sit up, airbed dispels more air. Like a bus does when it draws level with you when you're walking on the pavement. My bag is still neatly packed, only having changed my pants and a T-shirt so far. None of the rainy-day prepping required yet. The bag acted as a pillow last night and goes some way to explaining why my neck adds to this morning's long list of ailments. The paracetamol has a few fronts to fight on today. An ibuprofen reinforcement may be called upon in due course.

I unzip the inner door of my pod, shuffle out through the cardboard mess of a sitting area, adding a mental note to deal with this mess later. Then wriggle out through the tent door. As I stand, my knees creak like a rusty garden gate. The full extent of consequences of a particularly deflated airbed sleep manifesting in my joints, as I unfold and stretch into the morning. I lament the resilience of a younger version of myself as joints crack. A great exhale, then gulp down the freshness of the morning air, awakening. A contrast to the stale hotbox of my pod, which received the Eastern sun from around 5am. Good morning, Vietnam.

I glance at the surroundings, observing the scene. I'm greeted by the poignant smell of a sports-day school field cut grass. Memories of coming last. Tents, rows and rows of tents like a lovechild of a Dulux colour chart mated with the Normandy war graves. Flags scattered across the horizon catching the rising sun's uplifting effect. There's a nearby circle of lads under a gazebo. A clear disregard for the rules, as described quite clearly on the FAQ section of the FestiFell website, but who am I to judge. The lads are playing top trumps with cigarette packets. L&B, B&H, Sterling, and Marlboro lights. Milligrams of tar, offensiveness of safety picture, power of the warning slogan. One lad with a Polish looking packet google translates the meaning of his slogan, growing frustrated with the speed of his internet connection. They're slumped in camp chairs, perhaps been there all night. Piss-hole eyes and sallow faces. The great Bowman Crag looms behind them, the sun not yet high and confident enough to light up its slopes, to light up and reveal all of the crevices, show all the dimples and scars upon its face. A ripple of laughter erupts as one lad leads forward and intonates something I don't quite catch. Another pal protests loudly, slurring and squawking. It makes me think of Shaun. Remember when we had such stamina, slowly chipped away through years of work, bills, and responsibility. They laugh again like machine gun fire. North Face joggers and jackets their uniform this morning. Looks like a lot of young'uns these days, I'd be terrible picking out at an identity parade. I look at the two pods in our tent usually occupied by Reuben and Emily, occupied instead this weekend by Shaun and Jas. Thoughts drift to home, teeth brushed, and porridge fed they'll be bouncing on beds and resisting getting dressed. The line between laughter and frustration. Eventually, Mia losing her cool, wrestling the bairns to herd them into the car for the school run. The last of the week. Car door slams. Another explosion of laughter comes from the circle of lads and snaps me back into the present. The first proper day of FestiFell.

Friday
Shaun

The long drops are a bizarre place of solitude. There's fresh air whipping across my balls as I sit there feeling like a sack of shite. I always feel like a sack of shite in the morning though. It's par for the course. There's a chorus of grunts coming from around me. A communal chorus. Splattering sounds. Scat Songs of Praise. Strangely calming actually. Fellas and lasses alike, all dropping their morning bait. There's something levelling about that. Doesn't matter who the fuck you are around here, you're shitting into a massive communal pot. The bang bang bang of doors closing and opening, the rustle of the toilet paper, and the retching noises. Hockling and throat clearing noises, the wet slap of phlegm hitting the shitberg. It's like an avant-garde track they'll be playing on the periphery of the dance stages at some point today. Proper stupid that they say the festival doesn't officially start till today like, some of the people I've spotted on my way here look ready to head back home. Casualties to temptation and strong cider. I'm quite comfortable here, in this little shitbox haven, even getting used to the noxious nose pinching aromas. Smells like a farmyard, always an exciting trip to go to see the animals when you're a bairn. Listen to the left, I think I can hear a goat wailing a few traps down. I think that this shitter here in some ways represents the place I've left behind back home. A squalid smelling hole, surrounded by noises coming from all sides. Muffled by crumbling concrete and plaster. A draft that blows through when there's a wind, because the windows barely fit. In strong winds they rattle, so I can't sleep. It's warmer than my flat inall here. My morning crimp is usually rushed because the bathroom is colder than a fridge. Funny, the fridge is fucked, so it either freezes everything or does not work. Packets of sliced cheese and wafer-thin ham bulging and blowing. I know from my mandatory bi-annual e-learning at work, that that's a bad sign. It's 95% condiments in my fridge anyway. Dijon mustard with one scoop out of it for a recipe a few years ago. Tamarind from fuck knows when, not even sure what I'm meant to do with it. Can't bring myself to chuck it though, it'll come in handy one day. When I host that fantasy dinner party with Alan Shearer, Liam Gallagher, and Scarlet Johannsen.

After a while, I get up and wipe. The paper is cheap and painful, maybe even worse than a Spoonie's toilet. I leave my little smelly cell. I take a slow pace back to the tent. I'm in no rush. Try to drink in the sights, squinting because I've left my sunglasses somewhere in the tent. People are walking at a half pace. A saunter walk. A pace you might see on a Sunday somewhere. A waddle out a pub, or an amble along a front street. 60 bpm. Like a slow jazz beat. Nowhere in particular to be. All sorts are kicking about. Young and old. Dancers and rockers. A right mix. Unsure where I sit in the demographic. I can smell bacon from all angles. People having epic morning barbecues or using them little blue gas stoves that they had in Tesco. We opted against bringing owt like that. Remembering back to Wednesday and still feeling the ache in my arms now, I'm glad we brought nothing else. Even if it does mean forgoing food, I do that plenty enough usually anyway. - *I should have kissed you, by the water* - Someone is playing Bloc Party on a little speaker. Sounds like a cheap one, no bass. I remember that song as a teen. Retro as fuck. Had it on a CD that I'd burnt after downloading the album. Can still picture the permanent marker squiggle of the band and album title on the shiny rewritable CD I'd liberated from the ICT studio at school. Wasn't as good as the first album mind. It takes me back to Nikki, the barmaid from the local. I don't remember whether I actually listened to it with her, or if it was just released around that time. Still takes me back to that time regardless. She was two years older than me, maybe more actually. I was drinking underage, so must have been seventeen, because I had a provisional license. Fuck knows why, as there was no chance I'd be able to afford lessons, never-mind a car and insurance. Can't even do that now. It was a provisional we doctored with Photoshop and laminated in the back of the graphics design class during detention. My mate Cloggy made a bit of a business out of it back then, I remember. Big market for IDs that show you as old enough around that time. Was easier back then. He always was entrepreneurial. Had an eye for creaming a few quid off the desperate. Dinner money swapped for a 3-ply pritt-sticked ID. Still seems to be a man who makes money now, based on his Facebook profile. Looks loaded. Nikki took me in her burnt orange Clio up to a beauty spot car park. Pitch black except for the stars, the moon, and a phosphorous light that illuminated the little map that shows dog walkers and runners the designated routes. We drank a half litre of voddy sitting on the bonnet. - *Oh, oh, 'fessions do I, do, I, I, I do* - Drowning out the sound of a nearby river, or stream, or whatever it was. I never saw the water like, because it was too dark, and I wasn't really interested in anything other than getting a kiss or a shag. Knob already sticky with pre-cum at the prospect of some action. Maybe I just craved the company. It was confusing. Drinking and stumbling nervously over my words, directionless and clueless instead of studying for my A-levels. - *I'm heartbroken, without your love* - Then again, I could coast my way to grades back then. 'Naturally clever,' even with a hangover. Teacher's words them, not mine. Gave me licence to do what I wanted. We did this a couple of times, me and Nikki. She'd take me after last orders on Quiz nights. Different car parks in the half hour vicinity. Some brown signposted, others through her own memory. Was this her thing? - *And I don't know what to say. I never felt this way* - Always near water, if my memory serves correct. Maybe it's this song that's rewritten memories. - *I still remember* - The delay on that guitar is proper noughties indie championship. Must remember to mention it to Seb, to reminisce. I think back with a feeling of embarrassment, how I was so convinced that I had a chance with her. Maybe I did? I told all the lads as much inall. Divulging all the details about our late-night drink driving and voddy escapades. Lads scrambling over one another in morning registration, 'Did you shag her?' To which I shook my head defiantly. A mere formality, I thought. Though, I had no fucking clue how to initiate and engage. Then it happened. Not that. The inevitable. Dropped from a great height. Messages stopped. The trips to car parks ceased and the pints got pulled with a rancour. It's only now in my adult life, I've come to realised that it was probably due to my infancy and lack of confidence with women. Nikki had grown frustrated with me. Me and my persistent need for attention and unspoken, unearned entitlement to her affections. For whatever reason that may be. Maybe she was just lonely too, just thought of me as company. Who knows eh? A flick-book of embarrassment inducing faces of girls from the past I pursued. Women rather. Nikki was one of the many ones I thought were the future other half of a young me. Romanticising every detail of them. Believing in some divine fate. 'What, you like Radiohead Idioteque too?' That's a sign. Women who I thought were the one, those thinking otherwise. Turns out, they're not mind readers, nor are they attracted to shy but cocky kids who expect them to do all the courtship effort. They don't know what a hormonal pubescent mind is thinking, despite how predictable I thought it all was. Boy meets girl meets sex. Turns out, there's a bit more to it than that. Fuck me, how naïve I was. Always misreading cues and ending the same familiar way of spectacular disappointment. - *I should have kissed you by the water* - Never was a lyric so accurate. Funny how a young version of myself seemed to have a knack of finding really nice lasses who wanted to spend time with me, for whatever reason. Now that particular personality trait has dried up. Shame.

I keep walking the slightly longer loop route back to the tent, more towards the border where there are a couple of food vendors. Carbonated kids kick a little penny floater about wearing Mbappe and Ronaldo tops. Chucking in some meaty slide tackles on spindly legs. Proper ankle breaking stuff, lovely to see. Smells of coffee and fried meat cleanse my nose from the shitters experience. The sound of Bowie's Greatest Hits comes into reach with every slow step I make, as I scan the people wandering about. - *It's the terror of knowing what this world is about* - There are some fucked up looking people, looking like they smashed the peeve too hard last night. - *Watching some good friends screaming 'Let me out'* - Once they've had a couple of liveners they'll be alright again. Some smart looking lasses and handsome bastards walking about inall, gripping coffee cups to their faces. Hand in hand as they laugh at a shared memory. - *Pressure on people, people on streets* - Bloke eyeballs me for looking towards his Mrs. Envy. Don't worry mate, I'm no threat.

I get level with the crumpet stand and stare at the blackboard, need to squint a bit to read. Partially because the writing is all scrawly and twee, partially because it's fucking bright. Some lasses in flamenco outfits are dancing behind the counter to next door's Bowie tunes. I see now why it's playing nowt but his tunes, they sell eggs in all sorts of ways, and the stand is called 'Eggy Stardust'. I don't know how I feel about that. Turn back to the flamenco lasses. Three of them looking like they're having a great time. Flogging expensive crumpets to a load of hungover zombies. Fair fucks to them. I think of Jasmine's generosity providing us some sustenance yesterday. Think for a moment about returning the favour, but quickly decide against it. They're extortionate and the three flamencos look intimidating. I feel small right now. I keep on walking, now thinking about my chat with Jasmine last night. That stomach flip flop feeling of whether I said anything stupid or weird to her. Never helps when you've had vivid and disturbing dreams that night. She featured in my dream, actually. Don't need Freud to tell me what it means either like. We were around the fire. She was laughing at everything I said. Even when I started shouting on, crying uncontrollably, pleading for her to stop when I was trying to say something serious. She just sat laughing. Seb then turned up as a pirate, cutlass and hat. That's when I knew it was a dream. He doesn't do dressing up. Well except that stupid fucking wig he bought the other day. Bet he regrets that now. - *Why can't we give love, give love, give love...*-

I trawl over last night's conversation, the one around the campfire, then the one with that beardy bloke. I don't think I said anything dodgy. Don't think there's anything I need to be fearful of facing when I see her. Is that why I'm doing this elongated route back to the tent? Could have been there now sitting back and resting. Something has compelled me to wander. Fucking hell man, what a mess. - *Under Pressure* - Aye, about right there Freddie. Have a word with yourself man, Shaun. Man the fuck up. Get back there. Instead, I'm flat footed in an area where folk are milling over what to order for their brekkie. - *Under Pressure* -Youthful and fit folk, confident and calm. Not like me. No, I remember telling her about Mam. Felt comfortable enough with her to mention that. Didn't quite divulge the full details, as far as I can remember. Fucking hell man, what is it with peeve and mind blanks? - *Under pressure* - Never used to have this when I was younger. Can't even trust my own memory, how on earth is a man expected to trust anyone else? Mentioned Mam in relation to uni, that was it. I think. - *Pressure* - Didn't tell her about the daily fucking breakdowns, when I'd rake around the fridge for something to shove in two slices of bread and be faced with products that had a longer shelf life than the doctors gave her. Didn't mention the lectures missed, because I was holed up in the Student Union toilets unable to stop wiping away tears with whole rolls of lavvy paper. - *I'm happy, hope you're happy too* - Throat aching with the great gulps I was making, hoping no one would hear me. Flushing the toilet over and over to drown out the world. The cistern taking an age to fill, a time where my mind sloshed and filled with sadness too. Fruitlessly searching Google for any medical articles, forum posts, or alternative treatments. Using my university library card to access the plentiful resources. Anything that might go against the absolute irrefutable fact that she was going to die, and painfully. - *Ain't got no money and I ain't got no hair* - Neither did she. Fuck it, I will treat them two to something. I'll get the morning coffees in at the very least. - *Ashes to Ashes, funk to funky* -

*

'Ah, I like my men like I like my coffee,' Jasmine's smiling reaching towards the steaming cup, 'Thank you,' she smiles, looking buzzing when I arrive back at our camp.

'Mind, it's hot.'

'Like I like my men,' jibes Seb, 'Thanks, bro,' he adds. Seb's got his phone on an upturned shopping crate in the middle of our camp, it's playing some proper trance tunes from yesteryear. I plonk myself into my camp chair and notice the beardy guy from yesterday is sitting in his spot, whilst his wife is standing in the doorway of the tent applying sun cream to her face.

'Morning!' I holler over to him. Keen to make the effort to be a fully functioning human being. I give a two finger to the eyebrow salute, thinking I'm cool. Regret it instantly.

'Ah, good morning,' he raises a can of ale, 'Cheers to the first of the day,' he says, then lowers the drink back down to his knee. His gaze then settles in front of him. His wife says something as the last of the sun cream is applied to her forehead. He replies with a grunt. Jasmine whispers, likens her to a cat in the way it cleans itself.

'She's like my Cindy cat, thorough as anything, not like Barbie though, she's a lazy cat.' All I can imagine is the horrible wet noises and fur all over the place. Rancid things.

'Probably quite handy being a cat, having that range of flexibility.'

'You mean licking your own bum?' she asks grinning.

'I like my women like I like my...' I stop for comic effect; she knows where I'm going with this, 'Saying that, it's probably nicer than that toilet paper they have in the long drops.' I then realise I've just dobbed myself in it that I've been for a shite.

'Today's the day for dance peeps,' announces Jasmine, changing the subject with a look of faux disgust, 'Got to bring your dancing shoes today... and your dancing sunglasses.' She points at some new neon wayfarers she's produced. Looking buzzing about them. Like a kid when they've got themselves some of them light up shoes.

'Got this on to get us in the mood,' Seb nods to the phone which is spitting out snare drums and piano hooks, with epic delay and reverb. Proper retro trance. I love it. Tonight, Origins of Sound are playing. Going to be huge this like. Huge.

'Takes me back this, you know. To them great big nightclubs you used to get. Massive things. Sticky carpets. I still remember the sour smell. There were a few of them in Newcastle, you remember?' Seb's on another nostalgia trip. Jasmine is nodding along. He continues, 'Had to queue for hours to get in them. Had like loads of rooms. Used to have to wear a nice shirt and smart shoes to get in. Well, at least that's what I thought. Were stricter them days. Would come home stinking of tabs. They were always packed. Don't get places like that now, do you?' I find myself nodding. I do remember going to these sorts of places. There was one, in particular, I remember going to when I started hitting the town with the lads. Back when they were on their way out in popularity. Great vast spaces with few and far between punters. Reeking of yesteryear's good times. Almost eerie. Craggy faces from years of late nights and students adorned with fancy dress. Not much in between. Luminous paint and luminous drinks. Thinking I'd meet some gorgeous lass and we'd fall madly in love, go clubbing all the time and fuck off the world. The only thing I'd ever wake up with the next morning was a pizza box and a stinking gob. A few slices remaining for breakfast if I was lucky. Coagulated garlic sauce. Would microwave up alright though.

'No, it all seems to be late bars that sell expensive cocktails. I don't think people go out as much these days,' Jasmine agrees. To be fair, she might have a point. I'm not sure. Can't remember the last time I was on a late one in town, just stick local or back in my shitty flat nowadays. Lost that yard of pace it takes to dance and spend a ton on going out out. Taxis to my flat are too dear to justify. Wouldn't know who to go out with these days anyway.

'It's expensive nowadays.' There he goes, on about the cost of things again.

'Listen how old you both sound,' I scoff, 'Back in the good old days,' I mimic an old codger's voice. A stupid attempt to hide the fact I agree with them.

'Alright young'un,' jabs Jasmine, another textbook poke in the ribs from my left. The next song starts on Seb's phone, hooked up to some speaker he's brought, a familiar composition. Snare drums, electronic melody, and in your face bass. A silence descends and there's a mutual slurp of coffee and appreciation of the uplifting feeling of the high energy music. There's still a little snippet of Bowie present, somewhere over there, little snatches of - *As long as we're together, the rest can go to hell* - During a refrain in the tinny trance tunes.

'I've always been partial to trance music with a Spanish lass shouting on over it,' Jasmine offers, as - *Liberta* - echoes and decays into a string synth and a snare drum uplift. High end keys spraying out spikes of energy. Picture the green lasers and smoke machine of the clubs we have just been talking about. - *Liberta. Liberta. Liberta.* - I nod in agreement. Adds an authenticity to a track. Picture the sweaty superclubs in Ibiza and maddened faces in strobe light. Semi naked bodies flexing and bouncing into one another. Elite levels of beauty necking on and grappling with muscles and tight arses. Olympian level people. Fuelled with high purity drugs and ungodly levels of testosterone. Knowing I'd never fit in. The tune finishes with one final - *Liberta.* -

We sit for a few more tunes, basking like cats in the sun, sharing a mutual love of the music. Thoughts drifting between past and present. Strong feelings of anemoia on my part from the thoughts the tunes stoke. Coffee cups are strewn into the bulging black bin bag. Like a fat black frog.

'I'll take that when we head off,' Seb notices the bag's size; veins start pulsing in his head.

'Howay then, let's go now. Let's go and get entertained,' I take the lead, grabbing a few cans for the road and a couple to smuggle in my trouser legs. See if I can beat Checkpoint Charlie today.

'Let's go and see some music,' repeats Jasmine in an excited voice, as she stands upright and stretches like a cat. A nice one.

Friday
Jasmine

Warm hessian and incense scent wafting in the warm morning air, deep purple, and rich red linen drapes ripple. We're enveloped by a low-level swooping ceiling, Asian style embroidery, stray threads dance in the waft, backlit by decorative chandeliers sprayed neon colours, themselves glowing under a stage spotlight's insistence. A mass of crossed legs and knee kneelers invade one another's personal space on the potato sack floor, but it's different rules here, no one is offended by the stray elbows of shoe rubber touching their person, it's merely an invitation for a smile and a phatic conversation. Like a school assembly, before the teacher takes the mic, there's jabber in pockets around the crowd. An animated fella dressed in park ranger gear bounces, as he tells a story to a circle of sniggering friends. He himself struggling for air as the story reaches a crescendo, I pick out a few key words of 'photocopier' and 'boss was booting royally off with the wrong lad!' The recipients seem genuinely amused at such a tale. Park ranger seems to raise from his knee sit as the laughter volume increases, arms reach a Christ the Redeemer statue pose as the tale finishes.

There's a perfume smell of various fruity cocktails on offer, the recipes which are scrawled haphazardly in pastel coloured chalk on a blackboard hanging over the bar, attached to the frame of the tent by brass hooks and bungee cord. The bar is opposite the stage, me and Seb with our backs to it, Shaun facing it head on. Occasionally the sound of a milk frother screams over the hubbub, the waft of bitter coffee mixing with the opium incense and fruity syrup. An attack on the senses.

We chose here as a shelter from the morning's intense heat, the sun a 'big ball of bastard' as we trooped from our tent to the heart of the festival, feeling the sweat beads accumulate in our crevices. 'Howay, let's shelter in here and grab a drink'. We're now jabbering about nonsense. Seb and Shaun rallying with tales of when they were younger and when they went to gigs together. Stories about drunkenness and piss incidents, some of which befell themselves. I listen as they collapse about the place, as a long-buried memory is dug up by the other brother. The conversation drifts to future events, musical ambitions, and who we'd like to see before they die. 'How much you reckon a ticket for that would be?' and 'Nah, their new stuff isn't so good.' Sharing guilty pleasures, Shaun declaring a love for Taylor Swift, a dying ambition to see her live. Wouldn't have guessed that of him. 'Her early stuff is actually really good!' he pleads.

'Would be you and ten thousand kids screaming on. Nah, not for me.'

'Still wouldn't mind, I'd want to be at the front inall.'

'Would the court order allow that? Being so close to her, and all those kids. Could be problematic.'

'Stupid twat,' Shaun looking at his brother with scrunched eyes and sneer whilst annunciating in a petulant tone, 'For the record Jasmine, I am NOT a convicted paedophile, nor a 'nonce' in any way, shape, or form, regardless of what this bellend says.' I laugh.

'Tell that to the judge,' quips Seb after a short pause.

'Cock,' replies Shaun looking away now. Marking the end of this brotherly battle. More will follow, I am sure.

Seb seems at ease right now, which is good to see. He's surprised me a little with how on edge he seems at times, something I didn't expect of him coming here this weekend, but then again everyone has their own ways. He's laid back with his elbows to the ground propping him up diagonally, legs are stretched out to Shaun's left, Adidas Sambas pointing towards the stage which, as far as the lanyard describes, will not see anyone grace it for a fair few hours yet. Not that it would appear anyone in this tent cares. He hasn't checked his phone in quite some time, which is a huge deal for him. One of my great annoyances with him is that when I'm talking to him and he appears to lose concentration, he begins to rifle through his phone checking no one has messaged or rang him, no push notifications have passed him by, and something remarkable hasn't happened in the last minute, something more important than the conversation happening right in front of him hasn't occurred. I don't think he means anything by it, just a habit he has, but then again so do a lot of people. This behaviour led to a failed attempt at making the nickname of 'Texty' stick. I tried it for about a week with the team at work, as an attempt to politely address my upset at it, but save for a few initial nasal half laughs from the older members of our team the name died, as did my confidence that he'd change anyway.

His hand is now on his brother's arm as he has sat upright with an audible groan to hear better, as Shaun begins reciting a story about when they were kids. It followed the usual introduction of 'Remember when?'

'You pinned me down and farted right in my face, I was fucking screaming for Mam, she was busy hoovering downstairs and never heard!' Choking on laughter as tears emerge in both parties' eyes, Shaun looks at his big brother admiringly, despite the subject of the anecdote. For a fleeting moment, he looks vulnerable, almost young. He quickly resumes his usual presence, composing himself with a swig of his fruity cider, condensation clinging to the matt black and purple can. Hand over mouth, he cushions a belch.

'Excuse me, sorry, that was disgusting,' he says to me with genuine self-disgust. Manners. I smile as his eyes stay on mine, they convey a kindness and vulnerability, that the bravado he's veneered himself with, betray. I see his eyes flick to my lips as I whisper, 'It's fine.'

Friday

Seb

First band of the day are due up, skinny jeaned and bearded roadies have finished '1,2,1,2'ing and turning knobs and striking chords in short bursts. I check the time on my phone. They're due any second. Photo of Mia and the bairns embossed with app tiles. Love. No new messages indicated. 67% battery. Full bars of signal. I place the phone back in my short's side pocket. The one with a button on, to add an extra layer of security. Could be a good place for an opportunist pickpocket, this place. But then again, I'm not sure whether people still steal mobile phones, best not to find out though. The new employer has this number, don't want the kerfuffle of chasing that up. God, I still need to tell Jasmine. Need to find the right time. Not here. I don't know why I feel like I have to protect her, she's probably fine about it all.

The big logo of NE:Pomuk! is emblazoned on the backdrop screen of the dome shaped stage that stands before us. Bright Barbie pink handwriting font on black. The exclamation mark punctuated with an 'X'. The stage is stood over by ancient oaks, leaves lime green glowing in the midday sun's rays. Flags of a multitude of colours and geometric shapes ripple in the gentle prevailing breeze. There's an air of excitement, clouds of vape smoke around us smells like a fruit platter at a continental breakfast bar in Greece. Peach, blueberry and strawberry clouds waft from different directions, muffled coughs the only clue as to the perpetrator. To think this is the new norm for cigarettes. Wouldn't mind a cig now actually. I'll be smoking by the end of the day, I know it.

There's a chorus of enthusiastic chatter. Shoulders seem loose around us. Straw hats and white T-shirts, fluorescent tank-tops, jorts, plaited hair, retro trainers, jelly shoes, and fake tan. The best versions of people. Carefully curated and planned in the past few months, heaped on spare beds, packed, and repacked. I glance back, the crowd goes as far back as I can see. Looks like all the way back to the food vendors. Decent turnout. Cheering, I turn back and see black clad lads in pink feather boas appear from stage right. Four pairs of black jeans, four pairs of black wayfarers. Only the design on the black T-shirts and the hairstyle of the lads to differentiate, as they throw timid waves to the audibly excited crowd. One launches his feather boa into the front row. Cheers from that section of the crowd, as a young lass in a retro Sheffield Wednesday football shirt and bucket hat holds the boa aloft, before wrapping it around herself and cuddling into it. Stage side screens display the whole thing. The introductory Oasis tune - *She's electric, she's got a family full of eccentrics* - volume decreases. Shaun singing along to that one loudly. The sound of the lads behind their respective guitars, undoing and redoing the tuning the roadies had just finished. A buzz of a guitar in hand, hi-hats followed by a bass slide.

'Alright?' the dark curtain haired singer mumbles. Crowd whoop and whistle, then the lights illuminate the stage alternating red and blue, red and blue. The sun numbs the effects slightly. Uplifting keyboard melody starts, and then the drums roll in, I can feel them in my chest. A smile paints itself onto my face, a feeling I'm becoming quite accustomed to this weekend, excitement. Synth gets louder, steps up a note building tension and anticipation. Guitar announces itself into the mix, like a dangerous dog barking from the stage. Jas turns to look at me and Shaun, brown eyes and nude lips mouthing the intro lyrics, her arms rhythmically raise into the air as she turns back to the great dome. Sun shafts bouncing off her pale fedora and freckled shoulders. Shaun looks to me with mouth gaping wide, like the face he used to pull on a Sunday when the ice cream van's chimes could be heard a few streets away. Poor bastard always got his hopes up, only to be told 'It'll spoil your appetite' and the brutal, 'Anyhow, if they play the music, it means they've run out of ice cream.' Queue door slam and the Nirvana CD getting turned up to the loudest his little Alba portable stereo would allow. He's swaying intently to the synth and guitar duel. The crowd ripples, like the Mediterranean on a lazy afternoon, sunbathing on a family holiday. Now that was a time he could have ice cream. Big fuck off knickerbocker-glories, smiling from ear to ear on each of the photos of him developed in Boots the Chemist photo lab express service. 30 exposure film for a week in Majorca. Had to be economical with cherished moments to be remembered forever back in those days. The splashing pockets of excitement in the crowd glisten, as the sun meets sunglasses and phone screens. We're all waiting for the big drop chorus. A young couple squeeze through the gap between me and Jas; him dragging her by the hand over a sea of Converse Allstars and empty plastic cups and cans, his T-shirt emblazoned with the NE:Pomuk! logo, the very same font and colouring projected 6 metres high behind the four young lads from Middlesbrough.

'Excuse me,' and 'Sorry, can I just...' precede, 'Thank you,' and 'Cheers,' becoming less audible, as they dig through the crowd like moles. Edging forward to get a better spot to share their love. No tuts or disapproval follows them, the crowd are in good spirits. Egos and aggression left behind, in dull lives beyond the chain link fence and way across the fields and hedgerows. I think of Mia back home and when we were that young, pushing to the front for a better view. Getting the music before everyone else. As time went on, eyesight diminished, as did the desire to get beaten up by a front barrier at a gig and we drifted further and further back in the crowd with each passing gig. Truth be told, seating is now our preferred experience. I look left to where she would normally be nestled, replaced by some grey haired, goateed fella wearing a brown cord maths teacher jacket, khaki shorts, and wellies up to knees that resemble Homer Simpson. Mustn't be very good at meteorology judging by the outfit, it's cracking the floor this heat and he's got a jacket and wellies on. He's mouthing every lyric the skinny lads of NE:Pomuk! bellow at him. He catches my eye.

'How then! Good inte't,' he shouts over the vicious guitar soundwaves in thickest of Yorkshire accents. The outfit makes sense now.

'Aye, cracking,' I reply with smile. My own Tyneside accent more pronounced. Snap my head back to the stage. High fretboard play and Marshall amp feedback. Red, blue, red, blue. Cobralike movements from Jas, Shaun nodding to the bass beat. Cigarette smoke curl smell merges with crushed grass pungency. I could murder a cig. Wonder where it's coming from. Red, blue, red, blue. Beer shampoo hits stage right monitor and skids out of view behind the sweating black vested drummer, long hair whipping like a Newton's cradle to the sound of hi-hat crash. Frontman gestures to the crowd with an overhead clap motion. Crowd obliges. Serpentine claps from Jas. Multicolour painted fingernails make a rainbow against the blue sky. Shaun flat palming his chest, instead of clapping, he's still grinning, his eyes obscured by sunglasses. His mouth open like a fish chewing gum. The tribal synchronised clapping gets louder, as the synth stops and frontman unhooks mic, heading towards the crowd. He's pulling out all the moves early doors I notice, and the crowd seems to be lapping it up. He strides towards them with confident steps. Pausing to eyeball them, as the bass and drums chug along, battling for supremacy under the red and blue strobe. 'Yeah!' he shrieks, doubling over in the moment, as if possessed or nursing a bad cramp. Guitars and drums up their pace, fretboard and feedback reach a piercing crescendo as they merge and collapse back into themselves, ready for the next song. An audible increase in collective approval as the great sea all around me begin to sing along to the words of NE:Pomuk's recent banger, a banger that I didn't actually realise was theirs. A song that has reached a decent level of success, due to exposure on a recent TV advert for none other than MGM Insurance. Jas whips a bemused glance at me, before snapping back to the stage. No words needed. Balls, forgot for a second about the whole new job thing. Must tell her at some point. She probably won't be bothered.

Leave No Trace

Friday
Shaun

'Nah, I don't drink mate,' the Brummie lad declares loudly in my ear over the sound of someone called GoH! rapping on the stage. Bit of a change from that NE:Pomuk just gone. We're chatting about his epic Adidas tracksuit top. Black with stitched strawberries all over it. Looks fucking class like. Told him so too. Said he picked it up in an old vintage market in Camden. I initially thought he said he'd pinched it because this rapper is loud as fuck. I high fived him inall, saying he had some balls to nick something so big and bright. He corrected me. I am well jealous like. It looks insane. He's not even sweating in it, despite the fact it's red fucking hot today. He's a good-looking bastard inall, got that Johnny Marr sort of hair, the hair I associate with Mancs rather than Brummies. I could never pull that off. He's a Villa fan. Say I forgive him that, on account of his jacket. Wouldn't say that sober, I think. We have a good laugh about stuff, I offer him a drink. That's when he tells me he doesn't drink.

'How the fuck can't you drink?' I feel taken aback, 'You must do gear then?'

'Nah mate, nothing. Nada,' he smiles.

'But like you're at a festival, how do you do it?'

'Easy mate, never drank.'

'Fucking hell.' I can't quite believe it. To look at him you'd think he was a proper sessioner, occasional coke dabbler. Turns out, his poison of choice is smoothies and herbal tea. I'm fucking aghast. How on earth do folk deal with life without peeve?

'Fucking hell,' I repeat. The thought is so bastard alien to me. I feel betrayed almost, 'So, what do you drink on a night in front of the telly? Or when you're out with your pals?'

'Tea, soft drinks, water.'

'Couldn't do it me like,' I feel saddened by that fact as soon as I say it. Look to see Jasmine proper going for it, chucking her arms in these weird imitation rap moves. Seems to be well enjoying the girl on stage. Now joined by someone called K2 apparently. Seb's looking awkward, as usual, thrusting along to the music. He's moving like I'm feeling, fucked. I've never properly woken up today.

'Nah, my family were all bad drinkers mate, my mother had a terrible time with it. Liver transplant, she's in care now. Drank away her mind. Dad followed with a stroke a few years later. I was only young.'

'Fuck me, mate, that's tragic.'

'Yeah, I was just young, never touched a drop to this day.'

'Fuck,' I pause, 'I don't blame you.' I then instinctively take a swig out of my can, as I do in these situations, totally oblivious until I'm doing it how insensitive I look.

'Sorry mate,' I say, pulling the can away from my mouth, as if that's any fucking better.

'Don't be mate, you enjoy yourself,' there's no hint of any animosity from him, his big strawberries as bright as his smile. I begin wondering, seeing the benefits of tee-totalling in his face. Skin looks fresh, eyes look white. Looks young but could quite easily be in his 30s. He seems confident. And as it turns out, you can pull off wearing outlandish clothing stone cold sober. I guess this is a lesson. I then take that sip out of the can, seeing as he said it's okay. He turns to, who I presume is his lass. Picking fluff out her hair and saying, 'Hold still.' I leave him be.

There's a rustle of movement up ahead, as a policeman sort of ambles and scans the crowd, who parts like the sea did when that Moses fella lifted up his stick. Or was that Gandalf? He's got the yellow Day-Glo stab vest on and a capped black copper T-shirt underneath. Looks young as fuck. Still got acne. Bet he's boiling fucking hot in all that get up. Looks like he should be in the crowd going radge, as opposed to looking for any troublemakers. He reminds me of that liquid terminator in Terminator 2, a spottier version. Got a smug bottom jaw and snake eyes. Dodgy vibes. Proper ruining the mood. What the fuck's he doing here? Meant to be a place to escape this sort of shit. I become totally conscious of the fact I've got a bag of pills and a wrap of coke in my pocket. Didn't trust some little scratter to rob from our tent. They're not exactly the most secure things around. Couldn't be hitting up The Dance Tent later without the pills like, that would be a huge anti-climax. I imagine he's got like X-ray vision, like one of them airport scanners. Picture him spotting my stash, quickly tot up what year I'd get out the clink, and wonder how many football world cups I'd be missing. Don't want to find out like. I'd be shite in prison me. My arse doesn't accept a spicy curry, I highly doubt it would tolerate an endless succession of criminal cocks very well. The copper disappears from view and goes deeper into the crowd. You can see where he's been as the crowd stops dancing for a second and takes one step back. Paranoid about all the crimes they have ever committed. To think, I thought about becoming one of them. Even got quite far in the police recruitment drive. Applied in some self-reflection crisis where I had my bi-annual 'What the fuck am I doing with my life?' moment. 20,000 new coppers, and they didn't want me. Quite right inall. I couldn't do what spotty copper is doing. Couldn't trust me not to confiscate, then consume contraband. Then again, I can't rightly say I trust any of them. I suppose I always pictured having a police dog, he'd do most of the work. It would be company for me too. I'd call him Neville.

After a few more raunchy tracks the rapper finishes. Her hair dyed deep red, straightened to fuck. Glittery vest top and military shorts. Got great legs. Shame about the Nikes like, loses point on brand choice. I've not been paying massive amounts of attention to what's going on, instead just scanning the crowd. I'm feeling a bit restless. Tired and wired at the same time. Can't be going on like this all day. Something is wrong with my chemistry. I need to sleep, I think.

'I'm going to head back to the tent for a disco nap,' I say to them two when GoH! has finished her set, thanking the crowd, leaving arm in arm with K2. We do that thing where we're stood around waiting for someone to make a decision as to what to do next. Shoegazing.

'Ah, baby need a nap?' Seb says in some whiny ridiculous voice. I'm still reeling from him embarrassing me in front of Jasmine again before. I regret not bringing up the time I walked in on him with his cock in a yogurt pot, wanking using chocolate mousse and banana skin wrapped in electric tape around his chap. Chasing me out the room smearing chocolate all over the bedspread and across the walls. Dirty bastard's probably forgotten that little gem in my arsenal. But no, I didn't mention it, I'll keep that in my locker for another time. It's a proper nuclear ace card that, to be fair. Been brewing it for twenty years that one. Again, I choose to say nothing in reply to this attempt to belittle me.

'You know, that sounds like a good idea. I'm feeling a bit knackered myself,' Jasmine says. For a moment, I feel a little put out that she's going back too. I was kind of hoping for solitude, even if I didn't sleep, at least I'd be alone for a bit.

'Well, I'm going to explore the sights. Goodnight children,' Seb says. I feel like pulling his nose and twisting hard. And with that, he's off heading through the crowd in the direction of the big tower. There are plenty of nooks and crannies we're yet to explore, so he'll be occupied for plenty of time.

'Let's go,' I say to Jasmine. We're heading back across the fields towards Checkpoint Charlie. Legs feel lazy, it's as if my body knows it's getting sleep soon, so has started the shut down early. We're weaving past bodies and bins, trees and tents after Checkpoint Charlie where the confiscated drinks pile resembles a boozy cash and carry. It'll be some post festival party these lot will be having at our expense.

'I hope I can sleep,' Jasmine says with a feeble mock yawn as we start approaching the tent, dodging guy ropes and bin bags.

'I just need an hour or so to sort myself out.' The zip on the tent a welcoming sound. Shoes kicked off into the entrance and I collapse into the airbed, sinking towards the ground. It's unbearably hot in here. Horrible.

'Sleep well,' my mouth squashed into the bed muffled. - *Let's Dance, put on your red shoes and dance the blues* - Let's not dance, David. Let's Sleep.

'Sweet dreams,' comes back from Jasmine. Her airbed hisses as she makes herself comfortable. I imagine what it would be like to be next to her.

Friday
Jasmine

I know I won't be able to sleep. My mind is too active for such a thing. But just laying here will do the trick, away from all the stimulation. Started feeling a bit panicky before, unsure why. The noise got overwhelming all of a sudden. I wish I could sleep during the day, but never can. Ridiculous scenarios play out in my head, arguments from years ago, catastrophic consequences of my actions. It's all symptomatic of an anxious mind. Did some mental health app thing that was going around for free at work during Covid. Knew fine well I had anxiety anyway. That silly little app confirmed it. Not that I ever did its recommended exercises when Ellis was around. Did it when I was sitting on the toilet, or when he was out at football. Didn't want him to think I was troubled. Couldn't deal with that.

I walked back with Shaun before; he too seems a bit troubled. I can't quite work it out. He's a canny lad, great actually. Funny as anything. He's a bit of alright. You can tell him and Seb are brothers. Obviously, they look just alike, but also you can tell they love one another, and love to wind one another up. I wonder what life would be like if I was closer to my brother. Wonder where it went wrong. Here comes the chugging train of today's mind talk scenario. Choo choo.

There's a long snorting sound from Shaun's pod and a thrash. I wonder whether he's sleeping or choking to death. It would be rude of me to barge in and check either way, so I'll hope for the former. Immediately panicking it's the latter.

How on earth would I explain that? He's looked knackered for the last few hours. Good to see he has no trouble slipping off to sleep.

I scanned the lanyard before and didn't really feel much of the mid-afternoon line-up. I don't feel like I'm missing anything by lying here having some respite. Seb called us lightweights before when we said we were going for a lie down, but he neglected to mention the fact he had about three hours more sleep last night. I wonder what he's stumbled upon out there. If that were me, I'd be exploring the woodland area, seeing some of the art installations and shielding from the sun. Bathing in the trees. I love being outdoors. I don't think I've been out in the sun as much in England for a few years, don't really get the chance.

I lie there for a bit, getting increasingly frustrated that I can't sleep. Scrunching my eyes tighter, like some petulant child, whipping from front and back on the bed to try and find some miracle position which makes me drift off into slumber. It's not coming. Typical. Fuck it, I'll make use of my time alone, with Shaun snoring away. I slowly reach towards my bag and fish out some baby wipes and some deodorant, the crumple plastic noise sounds so loud. Then I stealthily zip the door flap of my pod all the way round. A breath held, as the zip ticks down slowly towards the end. I don't want anyone spotting my cleaning ritual. I shuffle off my clothes. If Seb comes back now, he'd have full view of my arse. Poor bloke wouldn't look twice. It's not my best feature. Bit of a saggy mam bum, minus the mam bit. I pull a chunk of baby wipes out and start with the armpits. The cool wipes are fragranced, it feels nice as I dig them and spin them against the stubble that's growing through. I repeat the process with the back of my neck, my stomach, and then my legs and feet. Grab new wipes for my fanny. Another clump for my arse. It feels great wiping away an invisible layer of dried sweat and imagined bacteria. I lash on a liberal spray of deodorant and stifle a cough as my pod becomes a solvent user's paradise. Consider how many years I've knocked off my life expectancy. Sit for a moment to listen if I've woken up Shaun with the ruckus, whilst the hazy aerosol floats down onto the groundsheet. I treat myself to new knickers and trainer socks, but wear the same vest top and the jean shorts I travelled in, they pass the sniff test. Then for the dry shampoo. Lashings of spray on my hair, then finger brush the strands as snow falls like bad dandruff in this green tinted snow globe. The smell of coconut and lemon. Refreshing.

I feel regenerated. More human. I lie there looking at the ceiling of the tent, wondering what sequence of events led to me being in a random field in someone else's family tent with a virtual stranger in the pod next door, snoring and thrashing away like a crocodile. I listen to all of the laughter and life that is occurring on the other side of the fabric. Families, couples, friends old and new. The nearby hum of diesel generators and bashes of long drop doors. - *We can be heroes, just for one day* - A familiar song from the nearby food van. I've heard it probably ten times on loop since we've pitched up here. They must only have one CD, or playlist, or whatever it is they are playing. I don't know why, but for the second time this weekend, I begin to feel the stinging sensation of the start of tears. Again, I am flooded with emotion, this time I can indulge in the feeling, and I let myself cry. I have no idea what's brought this on. Great slavering wobble of the jaw. Scrunched cheeks. Tears form lakes that I wipe away with the baby wipes I've discarded by my bed. Hoping it's not an arse or fanny wipe, as cry turns into a momentary pathetic laugh.

'Pull it together, Jas,' I whisper to myself, then exhale one great breath, then try again to see if I can fall asleep. Putting on my eye-mask and hugging my rucksack, opting not for the earplugs, instead focussing on all the different sounds. Focussing on my breath. Try to block out the heat and the thoughts.

Friday
Seb

Elevated a whole story above the crowds of bucket hats, hysteric faces, and energetic stumblers. 90s hip-hop eases out of the speakers in lo-fi laziness and saunters around the veranda arrogantly. In my hand is a glass, an actual glass! In it is a fruity cocktail, a panic purchase from a complicated menu. I spouted out its name in haste, anxious at keeping the bartender waiting. I hate making people wait. The order meets his approval, a ducking and diving lad, Italian looking, with dark features and handsome jaw, he proceeded to effortlessly show off his degree in mixology. An arc of chrome flashes, all tinks and taps of metal on the laminate bar, spinning glass, and twists of fruit rind. All for the benefit of the young lass next to him working the quiet bar. The jury is out on whether she is impressed, only momentarily breaking her gaze from phone screen scroll, before returning to whatever it is she's fighting off boredom with. I reckon she'll truly be sick of him by Sunday, mind.

I sit in and get wrapped in a wing back chair, like one of the ones I've always wanted, but couldn't bring myself to spend quite so much dollar on new living room furniture. Like a Barker and Stonehouse one, but original. A cut crystal glass sat in my hand like a 20s New Yorker. I could get used to this. Glass covered in condensation, dampness from the heat of today, and ungodly amounts of ice the bartender whacked in. Must have cost its weight in just ice this thing. Some fruity syrups and a small splash of whiskey. £12. I must be mad. Well here goes, to my health.

Packs a punch that.

Quite a lot going on there. Refreshing. Like a fruit platter in one of those semi decent hotels me and Mia used to go. Aftertaste, a kick of smoky spirit, ever so slight hint of a pub ashtray, me old enough to remember the big glass bastards sat in the middle of a sticky table in the Bay Horse, Sunday dinners, soft drinks, and tar-stained curtains. The hum of a football match or horse racing in the distance, coughs and splutters of ill lungs. Crumpling of betting slips. Orange and red flashes of a fruit machine ready to take someone else's weekly wages. 'Mug's game, waste of bloody money', Dad saying as he chows down crackling. Collar button bursting around meaty neck. 'Mind your elbows lads.' Drink down the Coca Cola. Drink again. A sip this time.

Yeah, that's the ticket, just what the doctor ordered. I feel myself easing further into the cracked leather of the chair, parched desert cracks of well-worn arms. The whisky, whose name evades me, starts working on my legs. Warm rush of poison hitting the backs of my knees. I embrace the space, the calm, and the quiet. There are only a couple of tables occupied, and each occupant looks to be in a state of easiness. The sun is chucking down some serious heat. I detect a burning sensation on the top of my head. A trickle of panic. Nondrinking hand inspects hairline, and, satisfied that balding is not commencing any quicker than I've managed to accept, returns to resting on the deep red leather armrest. I'm regretting wearing black today. My Origins of Sound T-shirt. Torso feels as if it's wrapped in a heat blanket. Some twelve years ago I bought this T-shirt, print still holding strong and showing no signs of peeling off. Twelve years since the show at The Roxy. An impulse purchase that still sits uneasy with me. I recall it was a time of personal austerity, but that T-shirt pinned to a blue felt board spoke to me. I wanted it. A younger version of me, back then. World seemed like one big opportunity for stimulation and experience. I'd gone with an ex-girlfriend, lost her in the crowd the moment the lights went down, and the lasers started. The crowd surged and the arpeggios poked and pricked eardrums. The hypnotic swirling bass took us on a journey. That, and the pre-gig nourishment. This same black T-shirt appeared from the crowd sweat soaked and euphoric, some ninety odd minutes later. Tussled from the physical battering I'd had, the crowd was like a choppy sea, wave after wave of unimaginable energy and power. My massive wide eyes and bewildered grin met her disapproving hostility. We went out into the autumn chill, the curfew hour of the night. Ears screaming like valves. Eventually, we went our own ways.

My neck is getting burnt up quick today, but I suppose that is inevitable in a place like this. There's sun cream back in the tent where the sleepers reside. I'll get some later, if I remember. I look over the rails, which are basically scaffolding covered in colourful fabric, the sort of stuff truck curtains are made of. Looking over I see scores of people milling around, drinking in the stalls and food vendors, the smattering of artwork, and looking to see what next can entertain their hungry minds. 'Dilated Peoples' squeeze and pulse through the speakers - *get shit off my chest, extra stress, three-four over the score* - battling and winning for supremacy over the multitude of other PA systems in the 25-metre radius. Funny how it feels so calm here. The crackling sample sparks nostalgia. Tape echo floods my brain, the school summer holidays as a kid, endless time. Endless time has a negative connotation now. As a parent, it can feel like a jail term when the schools break up. Back then, we'd have bike rides, flat footballs, nettle stings, and my father's greenhouse. His pride and joy, his own personal sanctuary. A place he most seemed at ease. A heat inside not dissimilar to today's temperature. The smell of tomatoes and cucumber, concentrated flavours and fragrance dangling on vines, tethered with twine by my dad. He'd usher us into his place of refuge, to see the fruits of his graft. Prickly heat rashes and water fights on a squelching lawn. Laughter. Then I think of my kids, their laughter. Their jabbering and their demands also. None of that here, in my Shangri-La. I look at my glass, swirl the rapidly melting ice, watch the droplets of condensation streak and crash down, teardrops, then take another sipful of fruity kick. Smokey kick in the bollocks to follow. For a moment, I think about ringing Mia, then think better of it.

Those two are napping now, or at least they said they planned to. Peaked too soon. Overdid it with the breakfast cocktails and hair of the dog. The exuberance of youth. It's a hare and a tortoise sort of deal at these festivals, got to approach it with a level of sense. Not like them too, all gung ho. Then again, they're not my problem. For now, I feel quite settled on this veranda with this music and this drink. The weekend before me. Aye, amidst the chaos around me, I feel close to relaxed. This'll do me.

Friday
Jasmine

The sky is as blue as my nonna's bathroom suite was, a bizarre choice by modern standards. But back then totally normal. 'You do you pet,' she'd say, 'I'm doing me.' Her looking proudly over her freshly installed bathroom. Silicone beads still tacky, grout still bone white. Now, the sun is towering above us. Tremendous levels of heat. My hair feels hot on my head. White wine in a bloated bladder not cooling me down. Instead doing a great job of making me not care. I'll grab that hat when I can be bothered. I've recently woken from a disco nap still feeling a bit drunk. I'm slumped in my camp chair waiting for my senses to return to full capacity, or as best as the wine will allow. Be it through vitamin D or alcohol I'll alter my state. The huge angry rock backdrop looks stunning in this afternoon glow. No clouds shroud it, the crevices and rocks well defined. Its full imposing majesty is for all to see today beyond the CND flags and chain link fence. I think of those who dare to climb it today. Sweat beads and throbbing heads, aching legs, and regular breaks to cool down. Soreen and water, or an isotonic drink to replace lost electrolytes. Checking GPS and hoping for PBs. All so foreign to me, but terribly alluring. Easy to navigate from afar, in the comfort of a supermarket camp chair. No way could I even manage to ascend the first few metres in this current state. I'm envious of other's physical prowess. Envious of the outdoor types, the walkers, the healthy ones, the happy ones. I long to have the drive, the determination, and the attention to dedicate myself to something like that. I bet it feels amazing, to stand on top of that and see us little bugs with our little tents and our little lives. I wonder whether they look down and long to be amongst this.

I look closer to home and look at the neighbouring tent, sensing movement and life close by. A blue inflatable pole-less tent across the way suggests life for the first time I've noticed since we got here. A pair of white feet, blue veined, poke through the little door flap. Toenails painted neon green, one heel is dug in the grass, the other stacked on top of the right. Soles illuminated with the sun, a crescent of dirt on the bottom. Not heavily soiled, but enough to notice. A wooden ankle bracelet on the left, the loose patterned fabric of pants, and higher up a glow of a cigarette peeps through the flap, between two fingers. The rest of the owner is obscured by shadow and tent flap door. I find myself fixated. Obviously, a female form, I build an image in my head as to fill in the blanks. I picture great waves of surfer girl hair, a leather wrist strap, and plump Angelina Jolie lips. Maybe this Californian wine is taking a heady effect. The orange firefly glow of the cigarette dances in an arc, rests, then returns in a reverse arc. A sensual machine motion, like a steam train's wheels. The smoker lying prone on their back perhaps. Totally at one with the world, I imagine, listening to music on them big over ear headphones. Her surfer girl hair hiding half of the muffs.

I look back at the mountain range, a solitary cirrus cloud above the peak, an etch-a-sketch jetstream, or to some others a chemtrail. It inks the blue with white chalk. Normal life goes on above us. Burning up carbon in search of heat and escape. I trace the silhouette of Bowman Crag, studying its curves and edges. Appreciating the jagged formations, the bulges, and the drops. I trace it all the way to the fence, then look around my immediate vicinity again. Cowboy hatted lads, biker jackets and skinny jeans, Fred Perry, and stonewashes. Retro football tops, day-glow boob tubes, university sweaters, Adidas Originals, all the colour spectrum of H&M's 100% sustainable cotton T-shirt rail. Pride colours, Rasta hats, football colours, and plenty of neutrals. Vests, sweatpants, leopard prints, hoods up, hoods down, baseball caps, and fedoras. Jack Wolfskin elders and Spiderman costumed kids. This could be the evening rush at a train station, if it were not in a field under nothing but sky and the ambient buzz of portable speakers, diesel generators, and laughter. If it were not for the smiles and the ease and the lazy pace that doesn't exist in normal everyday life.

After a moment I turn back to the blue tent, then a head pops out, reflective sunglasses, nose ring and cigarette smile greet.

'Hi, neighbour.'

'Hi, there,' I chirp nervously, not at my surfer girl, but someone equally as endearing and unique looking, her hair bushy and volumous.

'Fancy a toke?' she , as she takes what I now realise is a spliff from her lips, into her slender hands and reaches in my direction.

'Aye, go on,' I find myself saying, leaning out of my chair. A great physical endeavour. I meet her friendly face halfway.

'Northern girl, yeah? Sound. Enjoy babe,' she says, reflective glasses hiding her eyes intent, but smile on nude lips warm and genuine. Easy. I inhale from the spliff and feel the immediate waves of THC ride through my arms. Feels, on first impression, stronger than the one from the bloke last night. I slump further back into the chair as the girl climbs out of the tent, stretches towards the sky in a sun salutation yoga pose, and asks, 'Can I sit here babe?' gesturing towards a vacant seat.

'Yeah, of course.'

'One of them lads your boyfriend?' At who she is talking about in her posh sounding accent, I'm unsure, I'm not in any way inclined to turn around and find out, but I can see the periphery figure of Seb, he's returned looking a bit lobster coloured. There is some form of rustling and rummaging going on from the tent. I guess Shaun has awoken from his own disco nap. He's who I pictured first when she posed the question.

'God, no,' I spit a bit too quickly.

'Ha,' she pauses, 'good,' she says, without further explanation or elaboration. Face towards the sun like a solar panel. I see her eyes close through the gaps in her sunglasses.

'Lovely day, isn't it?' The great conversation filler of weather chat.

'Boys are bad news,' she chooses to ignore my phatic talk, 'Bad news,' she repeats slower, which makes me definitely think she's had a raw experience with one recently.

'Hear, hear,' I say, holding my plastic wine glass aloft into the air, then settling further into the chair after another inhalation from the spliff, facing the sun myself, allowing my eyes to close too. I pass it back to the girl on my right, she takes it gently.

'Just came out of a bad news relationship, hence riding solo this weekend,' she explains. I inwardly celebrate my observation skills. 'So far, it's liberating. Meeting people and doing my own thing. It's good.'

'Me too. Well, not riding solo, but I've broken up with my boyfriend recently too,' I splutter.

'Too bad,' another thoughtful pause, 'Solidarity girl, single sisters,' she utters with the spliff nestled between her lips, taking the sibilance away from the 'S's'. She raises a fist, still facing the sun, and we fist bump, neither with a great deal of power. Probably because of the strength of the weed we've inhaled. She's calming, I feel chilled with this girl. We produce wide smiles and proceed to laugh, at what I don't know, turning toward one another as far as the arm rests of the camp chairs will allow, and revealing a new side of our faces for the sun to burn. This girl is someone I'd want in my tribe; I can know that. She reminds me of a version of myself I imagined, once upon a time before, well before...

Friday
Shaun

God, I can't stand this lass. Fucking woke up to this. Jesus man. Nailed on only child, this one. She reminds me so much of those 'rah rah rah' girls from uni. Swooning about as if with a lead weight in one ear, constant tilt of the head in their Oxfam 'vintage' clothes, spitting out Keynes quotes, and applying Marxist theory to fucking everything. They always drank Black Tower wine, even though everyone knew there was no cash flow problem. Fucking armed with the Amex from the bank of mummy and daddy. Holidaying in the South of France in their 'humble' holiday home, they'd come back to the campus with a new set of batteries and a new French boyfriend. All 'Aw my gawds,' and 'No way that's so randoms,' emphasis, always applied to the last syllable. Champagne socialists, getting dropped off at the beginning of term in Daddy's Lexus, a car that Daddy probably got his bollocks polished off in by his fucking secretary, whilst Mummy was at Pilates. Nowadays seen retweeting, or X'ing, or whatever the fuck it is the local Conservative MPs latest propaganda bile. A full toothed grinning idiot stood beside some teachers in a local school. Framing the image in a way that didn't reveal the peeling paintwork, dodgy fucking ceiling about to fucking cave in, or the malnourished poor kids. Posting inspirational bollocks about making one's own future and hard work the key to success. Bollocks. 'We all have the same 24 hours.' Fuck right off.

I remember them and their leafy suburb campus dwellings. Great imposing beautiful Georgian townhouses with endless streams of these characters spilling out of them. Hugging their knees in bay windows of high-ceilinged rooms whilst drinking twee fucking nettle tea, basking like cats with phone and book in hand. All whilst I trudged further on where the buses daren't go, into my rotten terraced accommodation. Not lucky enough to be flattened in the ever-sweeping wave of gentrification, these houses provided ruthless bastards with a second income. Like printing money, a regular supply of willing idiots looking for cheap accommodation, too young to complain about squalid conditions. Slugs and mice crawling through shoddy pipework that leaked and let in draughts. Thinking it was fucking normal. Cracked mortar around the backdoor haphazardly plugged with screwed up scratchcard and fag packets. Shame none of my housemates were studying engineering. A bachelors in History or English Literature is not handy when you have the cold Manchester winters making their way into your sitting room. That and the threat of a serial rapist working in your vicinity. Needless to say, they never found the bloke. Police were under resourced at the time. Try retweeting that.

As far as I'm aware, this land is still not deemed valuable enough for a developer to raze in favour of better housing. I went down last year for an old school friend's stag do and drove through the area. Still looking glum and miserable. Year after year of student shat into its cold box rooms, breathing in century old mould spores and dust. Ever developing cracks in mortar to plug with whatever material they have at hand.

This lass is wearing some obscure vintage band T-shirt. The Stocksfield Tantra Club. Sound like utter shite. Her yoga pants and wooden beaded chain add a more wholesome nuance to her attire. She's barefoot and has greasy looking hair. There's a roll up cigarette in her hand, an accessory to punctuate and emphasise whatever she's saying, experience with these lot has taught me. Who the fuck even smokes roll ups nowadays? Social club blokes, street beggars, and this strange middle class who have fetishised impoverishment. Let me tell you, folks, it's nowt worth aspiring to. A generation geared up to think it's cool or edgy or provocative to deny their own privilege. A fucking cancer of our society, as far as I'm concerned. Wanna feel akin to the poor? Pay more tax and stop ripping the heart out of the most in need. Maybe don't tick that box so those dickheads don't get in government ever again aye? Good to see the nap has sorted out my head. Needs something more than sleep, evidently. That Class-A bulge in my pocket, it's feeling very tempting right now.

She laughs with Jasmine like old chums. Look at her man. She's the kind of lass who scoffed when I dared to speak, or even look at her in a bar. Offering to buy a drink met with an eye roll and a laugh. They'd speak over me in seminars with counter arguments that were total tripe, but met guaranteed support because they spoke in a posh Southern accent, and spoke loudly. Never taught the rules of conversation by doting parents who never dared challenge demanding behaviours. Looking down on me with pity, when my considered point eked out before the staring eyes of the students. Looking on in pity at the poor Geordie lad, as words tumbled out of his brutish head and past pub piano teeth. They'd give a 'there there' nod of acknowledgment, then move on past my roadblock comment. Dismissal of my views. Might as well have patted me on the head, probably didn't want to touch me in case class is infectious. They made me feel like going from being a big fish in a little pond at school, to being a little twat in a massive ocean at university. Never before was I aware of my own class, or Northerness, until I was surrounded by these characters. They made me nervous; they made me struggle with a thing that wasn't really a thing back then, but only now I'm aware of such a thing as mental health. I'd drink for certain seminars, just a couple of pints, to build the courage to speak with more conviction in these classes. My inhibitions lessened meant my facial restraint was lessened. Expressions probably not giving off the friendliest vibes when they talked. None of this helped. It just made me bitter, evidently.

I receive the same 'there there' look from this lass, when I not so subtly stifle a particularly bassy lager belch halfway through her telling us, or rather lecturing us on some secret set she'd read about on some blog I've never heard of. 'Lovely,' she addresses the belch in the same way a schoolteacher addresses the class knacker who does minging stuff, like turning their eyelids inside out for attention in an infant class. Exclaimed with a cold annoyance, she isn't used to being interrupted, or not having full attention from all her subjects. She launches back into her declarations of, 'You've totally got to see these guys, but fingers to lips, yeah? Keep it on the d-low.' I sit here, cheeks aching from feigning a smile, stifling the want to be sick all over, and scream at the top of my lungs. I'm just waiting for this fucking monologue to finish, so I can politely excuse myself and vacate the area to relieve myself. Or rather this painful situation. A few peaceful moments in the long drops, in the baking heat with two days worth of barbecue, tinned food, and alcohol shites as my company, a more favourable proposition. A metal tank filling up with human excrement, a place I'll not be questioned on a burp, a jollier way of spending the afternoon. Might even take a can to drink there. Read the ingredients and warning labels as entertainment. Could even message Sara. Then again, maybe not.

Jasmine seems to be buzzing to be chatting to this lass. Her conversation gestures take on a more feminine character immediately. Laughs are an octave higher and more prolonged. Plenty of knee touching and whispers between the two of them, too quiet for the boys to hear, before launching into the next lecture. Quiet chatter and giggles obviously aimed at me and Seb. Me sitting on my arse like a pleb, him in the last chair nearer them. He's hard to read, must remember to catch him separately later and probe his opinion of her. He used to be like me, but now I'm not so sure. Would be a great bonding experience to rip her apart and slag her off. I'll do it later when we're in the arena, when Jasmine's queueing for half an hour for a Portaloo.

'Anyway, I'm Jasmine, but I prefer Jas.'

'Such a pretty name babe!'

'Thanks, was my mamma's favourite flower. Mine too actually. My nonna, grandmother, was from Verona originally, they're everywhere there. We went back a few years ago, I loved it. Have you been?'

'Oh wow! No, but I'd so love to go, it's on the list. It is a big list, believe me.'

'You totally should, it's so beautiful.'

'Yeah, wow. And my name's Aurora everyone, nice to meet you guys.' Of fucking course that's her name.

'I'm Shaun, and I'm just off to the lavvy.' I'm up off the floor, dusting grass off my arse, and off away rapid speed, mumbling and huffing as I make my escape.

Friday

Seb

It's getting towards the time. I've got some noodles from a van, and we're huddled under a tree chowing them down. The roots covered in other pods of people also chowing down their meal of choice. Jasmine opted for some fried rice, and even Shaun has got himself some food. Chips and gravy from the van next door. He's always been partial to that. Simple tastes. Twelve quid for some noodles is steep as anything mind, but they are nice. Could buy a cocktail for the same price. No nicer than the ones Mia does from a jar either. I couldn't work out whether it was hunger or a nervous belly knowing that soon enough we'll be dropping pills and heading out into the unknown of the night. Shaun floated the suggestion after Everest 1922 had finished their set. A vacuum of silence filled with Jasmine saying 'Yes,' after a moment's contemplation, she was up for it.

'Reckon they need testing?' I asked him. Knowing from the FestiFell website FAQs that there's a free testing service on site.

'Nah, they're sound. I've had them before. The fella I buy them off is sweet.' Does little to make me feel any less nervous, knowing fine well I'll be swallowing one down regardless. He's been using the dealer for years and we've never been let down by Shaun's guy in the past. That counts for something, I suppose, even if it was about five years ago the last time I dropped a pill. Remarkable the bloke hasn't been arrested in that time. Remarkable I'm trusting a purveyor of poison.

Everest 1922 were exactly what a mid-afternoon slot should be. Two DJs playing some great uplifting tunes on The Rabbit Hole stage. Grinning Aussie blokes behind the mixing desk, looking cool as anything, chucking out some class tracks with little clips of old films interspliced over the top of them. The crowd a similar age to us, on account of the fact they have been going for years. Quintessential summer tunes. Great. Got chatting to some aged raver who told me about the nights they had in somewhere called The Phoenix, retelling tales with a smile and expression that suggested there was still a little bit of permanent E that runs in their blood, keeping on taking them back to that time.

They followed on from Chilli-X. A young rapper who commanded a great grip on the crowd. Her hands held a thousand invisible strings attached to the audience. Mere puppets to her mastery. She was tremendous, made a note in my phone to give her a listen when I'm back home. Once the kids are in bed mind. Was a sweary set. The lyrics visceral and punchy. The music tricky and infectious. Her performance assured and bullish. She'll be a future headliner, without a doubt.

After Everest 1922 we started getting itchy and headed to The Main Stage, but the band The Fallon Deer didn't satisfy, their sound too small and plinky for the big stage. Anyone following on from that set would struggle, but those lads with violins, banjos, and ballads didn't cut the mustard. We wandered off after a few songs failed to inspire.

I scrape all the last remnants of teriyaki sauce off the paper plate with the wooden fork and scrunch up the litter. Grabbing Jasmine's and Seb's plates as I head to the nearby bin, which by now is overflowing with paper plates, cans, and plastic cups. I head back to the tree; it's stood noble and vast before me. Another nervous pang as I think, as I always do, that death could be a few hours away once we've dropped the pills.

'You guys ready?'

'Aye, howay then.' We head off towards the dance area, shuffling with a nervous pace.

Friday
Jasmine

We're standing close to one another, by the chain link fence and wooden perimeter boards, we're shifty close. Can feel my heart beating hard in my chest. Spray painted image of a pirate ship in deep red adorns the wood. See the sails, full and magnificent, fixate on the crow's nest. It feels like bunking off school, the giddiness that comes with breaking the rules. More than that actually, more like a sort of sexual tension, exciting and nerve-racking, racked with anticipation as to what might happen, like the first time. Shaun has a little polythene bag down low; he's fingering inside it, pulling little individual pills out. They're purple, like the shade of Parma Violets you have as a kid. Little perfume sweets. But these look smaller. Tiny little things, actually. He looks around and scans for anyone watching. Nobody will be. He hands Seb his pill, then struggles as he fishes another out. Fingers wiggle and dance into the corners of the bag. He's got it, deep breath audible. He passes it to me; my thumb and forefinger take it from his. Hand is slightly trembling. Hope he didn't see.

  Right, here goes. Fuck it. I picture Ellis's face. His self-assured cocky face, as I pop the pill onto my tongue. It curls instinctively. Seb passes me the scrunched-up bottle of water he's just necked a mouthful from. He whips his head back. The water is cool as it meets my lips and fills my mouth up. I swallow hard, hoping the pill went with it. Tongue explores the depths of my mouth, tracing teeth and prodding the gums. No pill left anywhere. It's done. The die is cast. What's the worst that could happen? Death. Such a prospect isn't frightening for someone who would have welcomed it with outstretched, bleeding arms not so long ago. If I die,

I die. I wonder what death would look like in these circumstances. Picture a sudden heart attack in the middle of The Dance Tent, the last thing I see, a swirling spectrum of colours and skewed faces that fade to black. Carted off on one of them little golf caddy cart things I've seen bombing about the site. Pissed up revellers wondering what all the commotion was about, then losing interest.

The sun is losing its intensity. It's that time of night that you get on your summer holidays. The time when Pa emerges from the bathroom after a shower and shave, wrapped in towel and gets Mamma to slap on the aftersun. He smells of Aramis. Leather and spice. You're all on the balcony, watching the glittering chromatic dance of the sea as the day comes to a close. A figure stacks up the plastic sun loungers swinging the metal chain around, ready to lock them down for the night. Music from the pool bar - *and all the love I have is especially for you* - rattles over the kitchen fans and the sound of taxis pulling up at reception. Cream paintwork, black bonnets. Greasy aloe hands smear on the dappled wine glass that Mamma's poured whilst applying her makeup for the evening meal down by the harbour. Seafood freshly caught on a little boat that bobs and makes slurping and slapping noises, as little tiddler fish swim up to the surface. Bougainvillea blossoms floating in the ripples. A serene scene. Tranquillity and harmony. The recent adultery pushed deep into the recesses of the shared conscience. The silent resentment. There's plenty of time for that to resurface and explode. Maybe death is just reliving all of this, forever.

I wonder how they'd react to the death of their darling daughter. Would the same silence befall them when the coffin was lowered down in front of them? A handful of friends snot and sob into paper tissues. Hand in hand, another setback to deal with together. A feeling of 'Now what?' as they turn and walk to the waiting cars. All black. There are three different types of sarnies at the wake. The fading sound of earth hitting wood, as the spades get to work. No, it's the sound of the plastic water bottle scrunching as Shaun washes down his pill. The die is cast. We head to where the bassline oscillates deep, and anything can happen with Origins of Sound.

Friday
Shaun

Fuck me, that come up was strong. I'm fully torqued. Could jump 10ft high. The last rays of the sun light up the entrance with a golden glow. This tent is packed, absolutely buzzing. My brain stem squealing like a dodgy garden tap. Brain bubbles dancing. Freaky dancing. Folk everywhere loving it the most man, all my music brothers and sisters. I feel close to everyone. This ain't me right now. Seb and Jasmine are looking great. Absolutely going for it. It's like another planet in here, Origins of Sound are dishing out all squeaks and beeps, crowd lapping it up like hungry cats and a big fuck off bowl of cream. Every note I feel in my neck. - *Ride the sound, ride the sound* - Electric. Like one of them spectrograms from gadget shops in the noughties. All wumph wumph to the beat. Colour floods in like one of them two grand tellies you see in Curry's PC World. Vivid and stunning. Slo-mo images of the Hong Kong skyline and a close up of an Iguana. Only difference is everything is soft around the edges. It's all pink and yellow lighting in here, right now, proper bright. And that bass. I can feel it in my heart. Head's rocking side to side like one of them car dogs. I see Jasmine looking at me. Fuck me, I feel it right there, right in the fucking heart alongside that meandering slutty bassline. She's a fucking goddess. Stunning. Her head leaning forward, stupid neon sunglasses barely on her nose, I see those eyes. Them lips. As pink as the lights in this gaff. She glitters, liquid dancing skin, sun-kissed from today's activities. I can't take my eyes off her; I don't even feel the need to. I've lost all sense of fear. The crippling anxiety and awkwardness that blights me most days is absent. In its place, a warmth and assuredness. Confidence, albeit chemically enhanced. She's looking at me smiling, sunglasses pushed back onto the bridge of her nose. Body gyrating and glowing. West Side Story. That scene, Mr. Brown, the science teacher, banged on about, just before his mental breakdown. Wheeled out that big telly on its frame for our Christmas wind down week. That scene, I remember it in the recesses of my drug addled mind. The Cuban lassie Maria and the Tony bloke. First time they clap eyes on each other, the whole world stops. Everything didn't matter anymore. Just them two, love. Loved that scene. Watched it a few times on YouTube when I've been feeling on a downer. That's me and Jasmine right now. I'm seriously rushing and can see only beauty. She's amazing. Three notes play in succession, all majors, uplifters. It's hypnotic. Her dancing is sensual, each limb moves leaving a trail in my vision, brain too flooded to process images properly. Flooded by her sight. Her eyes are still on me, mine on hers. This molly man, I feel fucking alive. She nods to Seb in a gesture to take a look at him. He's got his arms outstretched and eyes closed, he's loving his life. Loving it the best. And I love him. I love her inall. But I'm going to tell him.

Friday
Seb

A snippet of - *I am, we are, I am, we are* - repeats over and over, battering about the neon lit tent, bouncing off the weatherproof fabric and bounding into the sweaty ears of the happy souls. Repeating over and over. Like it did the first time I saw them live. It's growing in intensity. Treble turned down, so just the bass reverberates. A loop of the chorus, teasing the crowd. Some majestic sounding bassy harmony hides behind the drum loop. Like the sound of a drainpipe that someone is warbling down. Gushing liquid sound. Distant. The energy in the room is electric, whoops and screams, fingers pointed in the air, strobe lights and green lasers ascend, illuminating beautiful faces. Everyone is smiling, shimmering. A steel drum raps introducing another bass drum to the equation. It's hot in here, sweat beads visible as light pulses in the saucepan eyes of the possessed souls in this cathedral of music. My palms are folded into a fist and I'm punching the air in time with the undulating repetitive beat. An electric beep, a tone, and some form of gospel vocals announce themselves out the speakers. - *It's a groove thing* - The words I pick up. Punching the air. Yes, it is a groove thing, that's all we need in here. Punching in the direction of some floodlit silhouettes elevated from the crowd. They're furiously nodding and bobbing behind mixing desk. Technics and an Apple logo glowing alongside red LEDs. Images of something liquid, maybe colourful liquid oil mixing and merging projected onto the massive screen. Lazily flowing, whilst the music springs along with infectious vigour.

    I feel like I'm in the centre of the universe. Smiling faces appear and disappear with each strobe flash amidst our circle of sweaty dancing. Each face welcoming. Each face I trust. I could kiss. I smile easy, honestly, contaminated with a tremendous feeling of happiness. Joy. I feel loose, the base of my spine like it's hooked up to a slow trickle battery. Back of my head feels like when Mia plays with my hair, my neck like when she kisses it from behind. Shoulders like the first time we embraced. Sexual energy. I lift my head to the blue and yellow swirl pattern ceiling. The curves smile down upon us. I close my eyes; strobes still illuminate through my eyelids. Swirls of green and red retinal action. 'Ahhhhhhhhh,' I breathe, as I feel every cell in my body is carbonated, fizzing through knotless muscles and supercharged nerves, they're hooked into the moment. Blood circulates through my veins to the bpm of the piano scale, dished out by the two geniuses behind the mixing desk, elevated ahead of me. Eyes closed, I feel the music more clearly, fist is stretched out towards the air like a chemical revolutionary. Did Che Guevara dabble in ecstasy? Imagine all the powerful people feeling like this, the world would be a better place. I picture Mia and the kids as I breathe in and out, nose and mouth. Love. Absolute love. Thank god I'm not dead.

'Woo,' I snap my head forward, intense headrush, jaw clenched tight. Eyes flick open, greedily taking in the beauty of everyone and everything before me. Look at all the people of all colours, all fashions, and ages. They're all so beautiful. This is the world on a good day. Stroke of strobe illuminating an array of rhythmic movement. Shaun has his sweaty arm around some lad in green, he's laughing. Shouting in the guy's ear, something I can't hear. Not that it matters. Look at him, my kid brother. Known him since he was in Mam's womb. A crazy thought, that. He's a beautiful soul. This is his natural habitat. I love him. Love him like the day he was born, smell the bleach of the hospital ward. Remember the vending machine tea. Three sugars. The soft glow of my parent's features. The hushed words, to not wake the new life. Sucking cheese and onion crisps, so as to not make a noise. 'Ahhhh,' punch the sky to these drums, those teasing strings. One note. I think I know it. Illuminated green under floodlight, the crowd knows it too. Jas has her hands behind her head, twisting side to side. Elbows at 180-degrees. Eyes closed behind those neon sunglasses sliding low down on her nose. She's taking it all in. Black light makes her white top glow like magnesium burning bright. Got to hand it to the lad, he's delivered with these pills, absolutely top class. I feel light, agile, and empowered. Glance around, Shaun is back pointing to the heavens, he sees me. His eyes like dinner plates. Bounds over to me, like a big Tigger, and wraps his arms around me. We almost fall backwards. Sweaty hug feels good. Body still bouncing to the music. He can't stop. I'm his anchor. He switches direction, left arm remains over my shoulder as he turns to face the DJs. As one, we punch the air emphatically as hues of reds and blues dart over the thousands of moving bodies. His face turns to my ear. Shouting he declares:

'I fucking love you man. Love you!' he grins, eardrum tickling with the volume.

'I love you too man!' I reply, with not an ounce of cringe, because it's true. Jasmine beside us. Looking the best I've ever seen her, full of life. Glowing. She's in her own little world at the moment. Chewing gum rapidly and blinking slowly. Me and my brother embracing. We keep on punching the sky, fighting the invisible enemy of inevitability and time. Fighting the certainty, that this beautiful moment will pass and echo into the eternal darkness of time, only remaining as a fleeting untrustworthy smudge of a memory that we will regurgitate and misrepresent each time we feel nostalgic.

Friday
Jasmine

I'm not dead, far from it. Probably the most opposite to dead I've felt in quite some time. Wow, I feel good. All the colours have been turned up in brightness. Contrast knob has been turned to twelve. The music is like a silk sheet wrapping itself around my skin, can feel it stroke all of the tiny little hairs on my arms, down my back, and across my stomach. Like good sex. White sheets in a Parisian apartment, wind drifting through opaque drapes and stroking exposed skin, smell of the florist stand in the street below seeps in. The lights are so bright, I'm still wearing sunglasses to shield my eyes. The music I recognise. But it sounds different. I can pick out all the little micro sounds hidden below the surface, warming tones I've never heard before. Little Easter eggs, hidden back at the studio. All oranges and reds, yellows and greens. Sounds and lights stronger, pulsing. High notes penetrate deep. Speaker spitting out the mid, bass engulfing me like a sonic hug. Treble zipping off the walls. Synth fed directly into my brain. Trills and whoops explode like artillery fire from the crowd that packs into this great hall of sound and light. They're drawn to the allure of positive sound waves and human energy. There's a great positivity in here. So much love, it's dripping off the walls. I've hugged more people, all randomers in the last twenty minutes, than I have in the whole last ten years. It all feels natural. Like this is how we're all supposed to be. We're a communal species. Why do we choose to rot in boxes when we could have it this way? Suddenly, a polyphonic discord screech knocks away that thought, and I'm possessed by movement and the present moment, as the notes decay into an electronic rattlesnake sound accompanied by some cosmic fairy wings. - *Till we meet again. My love* - A hyena cackles in the background. The night zoo in Singapore, Jungle Book baddies. Calm it, Jasmine. A great wave of the pill washes through me. Brain firing off in a thousand directions. Take a massive breath in through the nose. Out through the mouth. Again. Heart prominent in my chest. Colours bleed together. Marching ant's drums dominate the soundscape. - *Where do you think you are?* - Indeed. I look to see Shaun. He's beaming. I can't help, but bound over to him and wrap my arms around him. His body is warm. His arms safe. I remain in his embrace for a moment, and then, as I release, I feel compelled to kiss him. Because I can, so I do. Our tongues meet in sync with the freight train tearing down the philharmonic track.

Friday
Seb

Hard to focus on my phone screen, turned the brightness down to preserve battery. Fumble to unlock, all the icons floating in front of me like sea creatures. Focus is fuzzy. Brushed around the edges. Mia and the bairn's photo from a camping trip earlier this summer. Massive grins. Mia fuelled by wine, kids by chocolate, and Pringles. Pride pang in my stomach. Total pride. I've found myself heading back to the tent, or at least in the general direction of it, so I can call Mia. I miss her, and like a homing pigeon, I'm drawn to her, albeit through the medium of a phone call. I want to share this moment with her. Origins of Sound have left the stage and been replaced by some young pup I haven't heard of before. The bass is still reverberating through the grass as I head away from The Dance Tent in the opposite direction. I'm still intoxicated by the music, swaying sporadically as the sounds waft to me on the nighttime breeze. I'm nodding my head as the music slowly turns down in volume, with every rhythmic step I take away. There's a load of people darting in all different directions, going about their respective evenings. It's like a scene at central station train platforms at 8am, but they're all smiling, showing teeth. Beautiful. I spot a retro 98-99 Newcastle football jersey on someone in the crowd heading towards me, bucket hatted and sunglasses.

'Toon, toon!' I point and shout.

'Black and white army!' he reciprocates, curves his walk towards me. I'm glad he's heading towards me; I'm feeling in the mood to chat. 'Alreet lad?' he asks, as his arms wrap around me. The shiny polyester cool on my arm. Never met this kid before, and yet I feel as close to him as I do with most family members.

'You having a good night, mate?' he asks as his hands grapple my upper arms. Broad Geordie accent making me yearn for home.

'Fucking mint mate, proper class,' my own accent slightly exaggerated. Something Mia says I do when speaking to tradespeople and mechanics.

'Good man, love you, fella!' His forehead meets mine then he whacks a massive kiss on my lips. Then he's away, knees dragged by the gravity of The Dance Tent, arms swinging like a Geordie chimp. He's ready for the love in there. Fuelled by Class-A serotonin rush. God, I'm rushing. This drug. Prescribed as a marriage counselling drug in the olden days. I can see why. The peak is over, but now I'm chugging along feeling fantastic. But, I'm yearning for my wife. Imagine sharing this feeling with her.

I look down and fumble through my phone again. That task shelved previously by the excitement of human interaction. Attention span like a pinball table. Unlocking the screen is hard, but I get there after a few attempts. Swaying on the spot for full focus. Eyes are blurred, icons hard to centre. More smiling faces appear and disappear from the campsite entrance just ahead of me. Start walking again. Voices and voluminous laughter in stereo. Call log. Scroll. Stop for a second again to try and focus fully. Takes a fair few finger drags to get the Mia 'Woman of My Dreams' contact. The name she changed many years ago, never changed it back, despite my insistence on everyone getting surname and first name treatment in my phone book, even my dad. She's special.

Press.

Pause. Screen brightness increases as 'Dialling' appears. *Ring ring.* Start walking again, smiling and gurning. Jaw aching, I'm stumbling through the campsite gate, Checkpoint Charlie. *Ring ring.* Scaffolding and header board emblazoned with sponsorship. Burly fellas frisking down people heading in. The grass here well worn, flattened underfoot. *Ring ring.* Through the other side a shanty town of tents everywhere. *Ring ring.*

'Hiya darling,' voice groggy, an undercurrent of white noise from poor phone signal. Hear her voice and I'm home.

'Alreet pet, how are you?' my voice more Tyneside than usual, hasn't reset after my previous encounter.

'I'm good,' clears voice, 'missing you,' voice sounds more normal but muffled, presumably by a pillow. She breathes in deeply, a muted yawn, 'Having a good time?'

'Absolutely...' drawn out emphasis, '...class' stress put onto the 'C' and the 'L'. It occurs in my mind, that I might sound a little inebriated, how annoying for her at this time, I imagine.

'Glad to hear. You looking after yourself?'

'Of course,' I retort, my childlike intonation betraying me.

'I'll not ask,' her nasal laugh into the pillow. Bless her for answering the call at this time. I love her.

'Sorry it's late pet... Just wanted to hear your voice. Wanted to check you and the kids are alright?'

'We're all good,' pause, 'They're missing their daddy. I am too.'

'I miss you.'

'It's only 11:34 by the way. Just been reading in bed... Think I just drifted off.'

'Aww sorry.' Time works differently here; I thought it was the small hours of the morning. 'It's been a long day,' I add. I don't know what to say in response. People shuffle past everywhere. Smiles and sounds skewed. Finger in my other ear to mute some of the ambient clamour. Pause in the conversation. White noise amplifies the silence.

'How is everyone? Is Jasmine okay?'

'She's fine, they're both fine.'

'They getting on okay?'

'I think so yeah, seem to be.'

'That's good. That's good.' She sounds so sleepy. White noise returns as I feel the pinch of emotion just hearing her.

'I love you,' I say.

'Love you too.'

'I'll let you go, just checking in.'

'Look after yourself. Make sure you eat.'

'Love to the kids. Kiss them in the morning for me.'

'Will do darling,' she yawns, 'goodnight.'

'Goodnight, love you.'

'Love you,' and we part. The portal to my normal life is closed with three beeps as the screen dulls, image returns to twelve app icons and the time, which indeed confirms it's only 11:39. Mia and the kids grinning away, as the brightness fades to black as I shut off the phone. I keep walking, betrayed by my own sense of time, I'm now buoyed to stay out. I feel the need to explore, to share love. Wanting to stumble upon some mischief. As I walk, I begin hearing dance music coming from a pizza van near our campsite. Makes a pleasant change from the same Bowie tracks that have punctuated my sleep and idle time around these parts. I notice flashes. Bright lights. Blue. Electric blue. Someone must have brought their own light rig. They're pretty intense. Must have cost a fortune. Fancy bringing something like that camping. Might be my imagination. Never mind. It's like being in The Dance Tent again, but with fresh air. Al Fresco. Old school raving. The smell of post-party food and diesel generators. I get nearer, the music sounds good. Feels good too. My brain hooks back into the beat. Ecstasy fuelling my muscles and nerves into movement again, I'm compelled to move. That punching arm destined to salute the sky again. Freaky dancing Che Guevara is back, powered by the phone call home, I have my second wind. Dancing freely in a field in the middle of fucking nowhere, loving life. I'm in sync with the blue lights, strobing and illuminating the shanty town rave I've created for myself in my own mind. I can sing along; I know the lyrics. Force fed into my cerebral cortex through a plasterboard wall, as I dredged for sleep many years ago in my dancing days, living with a night owl pal that I no longer keep in touch with. - *I've got so much love to give. I've got so much love to give* - Mixes into another high energy, love-soaked tune. Must drop him a text sometime, maybe meet up and rekindle our friendship.

'Oi Oii!' Two lasses, blonde and pretty shout, the memory of Michael Gibbs flits and disappears from my mind which flips back to the present, and the punching the air in total euphoria. They join in, all woos and giggles. Yellow and orange neon face paint dots adorn their porcelain faces. Flashes of blue in the blacks of their eyes with every other beat. Wine bottles in hand, switched between one another as they mirror my moves. I don't feel mocked. I feel complimented. The old dog still has moves. Wine bottle becomes a makeshift microphone as we dance and rap along, doing jaunty hand gestures to the barres. Our blue strobe pizza van rave the centre of the universe.

'Stop it you fucking bastards!' I think I hear from the epicentre of the blue light rigging, followed by an awful sounding scream, 'Show some decency.' I pick up. But I can't be sure. It fades into all of the other voices and sounds that adorn this beautiful and ephemeral night. We keep dancing on for some time after.

Friday
Jasmine

Hues of orange, decaying synth. Gaining fuzziness. Boundaries soften. Tracks blend. Berroca fizz. A robotic echo. A tubular bell. Something new. But familiar. Commuter train bass, chest explosions. Heart eager. Deep breathing. Almost orgasmic waves of pleasure engulf me. Five simple notes, beautiful.

Repeating.

Tubular bell clangs, like a Sunday morning. St Cuthbert's across the way. Welcoming. Not aggressive. Familiar. A summer fête. White linen and cream tea. Smell of grass. The rustle of oak trees. Children's laughter. Handstands and tags. The wings of bees and wasps.

Repeated lyric over and over. The commuter train rattling on, lazily. There's no rush. Words unclear. Oranges, reds, and yellows. Warmth. Comfort. Cosiness. Wrapped in the blanket softness of the edges of my own vision. Passion, love and togetherness. Purples and blues. Happiness. Is this how it feels? The warmth of the lights on my face. Eyes happy to be closed. Taking in the music. The feeling. The now. A string synth starts quietly. Barely audible, but it's there. I feel it. I'm back on a jet plane, heading back from a family holiday, the cool air vents above my head. They blow relief down onto my skin. My hot skin. Burnt skin. Peeling at the shoulders. They flick the pages of my book, rippling the paper, like the waves lapping upon the golden sands we leave behind. The pages mottled with moisture from the pool. The smell of chlorine. Cleanliness.

The synth weaves around. I go with it. Hinted at over the blend of bells and distorted lyrics. The beautiful commuter train tapping along a coastline. Low summer sun casting dapples of gilded sunlight. Never stopping. Never ceasing. Chugging away. The bell now a whitewashed basilica, a wedding overlooking azure seas. Atop a crumbling ancient cliff. Rows and rows of sailing boats tied up tightly on the shore. Bobbing lazily like apples in water. Prosecco hisses in crystal glass. That family wedding when I was just small.

A sudden squawk. A seabird. The lyric repeats, more distorted this time. Choppier bells, the sea plumes foamy froth on a rugged coastline. A buoy tilts, but does not fall. The five simple notes explode louder and louder. The homely feeling approaching. A change.

Synth gets louder. Steps down. More confident. No, more at ease with the world. These surroundings. This life. Louder, a hint of green. A skittering sound of a deer retreating into the bracken. The foliage of a forest, the trees, and the fields of home. Beyond the jagged cliffs from before. Neatly drawn squares and oblongs, mostly green. Some yellow. Others orange. Through the round window of the jet plane. A little hole in the outside pane. Condensation. A hum of an engine, and a whistle of the vents. The sight of home soil. Youthful eyes flicker looking for Nonna's house from up high. A wave hello. She said she'd be keeping an eye out. Through her window. An open window. She'll be cooking up a lasagne for my return. Wrapped in foil. Stored in a washed-out ice cream tub. A great grandfather clock, never ceasing to stop, like the bassline. - *Tock, tock, tock* - Furniture polish smells and an ironed pinafore. Lettuce waft and balsamic vinegar. Cup of tea, two sugars. Make it a pot. Show me the photos. 'Ooo lovely pet, bella.' The horns bring me back to the present, but not before the hint of Corrie on an old portable telly, the cat slinks out of sight.

The pitch changes. My eyes open into the now. The crowd a rhythmic puppet. Willing subjects to warm major notes and warm radiating tones. Same rhythm. The diehards amongst the sunglasses and swaying eyes point to the stage. Pupils like dinner plates. Like them big black CDs Papa got out on Sundays. The massive sound system wedged into a sideboard. They recognise the next track. Ready to be taken to somewhere else, with this deconstructed chord progression. The nuanced sample recognised. Snaps of a chorus teased. Then it disappears, leaving just a metronome tick, to build up the anticipation. - *Tick tick tick* -Feels in tune with my heartbeat. This DJ knows me.

Finally, the hollers and screams reach the rest of the crowd when the melody slithers out and announces itself in its familiar glory over the speaker's stacks. Heralded with a blinding white flash of light from the rig. Rapturous reception. Colours pink and neon green, as the journey begins again. There he is. Shaun. His skin shines with perspiration and joy. He looks glowing. Buoyed by the music. His arm reaches around my shoulders. The pricking pain of sunburn replaced by the feeling of lightness and pleasure in my neck. We've been kissing. Holding each other. The sledgehammer feeling compelling me to him, and him to me. A primal surge of desire I haven't felt since puberty hitting me. The drugs. The music. The colours. This night. This moment. The most alive I've felt in a fucking age.

I turn my head back, nose pointing to the swirling pattern of the roof, I speak without any sense of dread, with nothing but pure reason and instinct. 'Should we have sex?' I say. Me doing me.

And as he turns on heel to face me, kissing me hard. I smell that stale sweat smell from last night. It feels familiar and reassuring. Feels amazing being away from my own mind. Mouth dry with excitement. Stomach quivers. Hands rake through my hair, he pulls back and meets my eyes with a, 'Okay, let's go. If you're sure.' And we're off towards the tent. I am sure. Holding hands as we pass through face after disappearing face of smiling revellers and lovers who vanish into the night. This night.

Friday
Shaun

Fuck me, I can barely see. Seriously rushing. Ecstasy rush feels like feathers are stroking down my spine. My fingertips feel like they're made of light. Seriously good drugs these. Jack did good. Wonder whether I'll regret that second one I bombed in the tent. She is in front of me sitting on her knees, legs kicked to one side, shoes kicked off in the entrance. She pauses for a moment and takes a breath in. She'll be rushing too. Her eyes are closed as she deals with a wave of molly. Deep breath in and out. Those lips man, she looks like she's fucking glowing. Shimmering. She is the only real light in this stinking tent. Illuminated like an evening moon with the battery-operated lantern that dangles pendulum like from the ceiling hook. Batteries exposed. Gaffa tape holding it all together. Shapes and shadows are projected onto the fly sheet from outside. She leans back on her airbed and gestures with her arms towards me. I go towards. Our bed for the evening moulds around us as we clasp. My knuckles contact the flocking top of the airbed. The ecstasy makes even that contact feel like pure pleasure. The touch of her skin, warm and soft, like a fucking thousand volts through my veins. My left arm is now a pillow for her head, hair sprawled all over, like an Orthodox Russian icon. My fingers on her arm, tracing the tiny contours of her limbs, feeling every freckle and hair follicle. Feel the ribbed scars on forearm, pull it towards me, and kiss it softly. To make her know it's okay. I see her. My heart is going ten to the dozen, racing like a bastard. In a good way now. Her chest is rising and dropping. Ribs visible above the deep plunge of her white T-shirt. Our breathing synchronises, the Class-A rush forcing me to commit deep breaths, for fear of floating off into space, hers obviously too. Someone, somewhere in a tent nearby is playing some Trance classics, late 90s tracks. High bpm, the synapses in my brain tune into this and it becomes the internal rhythm of my mind. We lay there as shapes sashay across the green polyester film screen. Lights dance around from passers-by, a million voices whorl about. We're silent in all but the breathing and blood rushing in my ears. Entwined together, we are one mass waiting for the music to dictate the next move.

She unhooks her head from my arm, sits slightly, and turns her face to mine. Airbed hisses. Decaying drums in the distant sound of 'Meet Her at the Love Parade', seriously deep bass. Our noses meet, cold to the touch. Feels like mine is damp, like a dog. I've been sniffing quite a bit on account of hay fever, or maybe a cocaine allergy, slug trail streaks on my bare arm drying over the day. But the drugs take any form of self-consciousness away, along with the electronic pulse of the soundtrack of our embrace. Her eyes are open, meeting mine. Fucking hell man, they are immense, fucking galaxies or something. Supernovas. The big fucking bang. My arm runs a hand along her back, the white ribbed top soft under my fingertips. Her eyes close, head tilts back. I look at the lips, glossed with lip balm or something now, her face immaculate, reddened under the eyes from today's sun, tiny little freckles barely visible under the LED light. Her neck, slender, scented florally as my lips go down to kiss the left side. Brush the hair to one side. I savour the smell, like an airport duty free tester. My fingers rest at the base of her spine, circling slowly around the finest of hairs, then shamelessly write my name over and over as I gather up the momentum for the next move. Listen to her body.

She takes a deep breath and then rolls me onto my back, her right arm propping her up over me, as her left hand moves down my body. She's rummaging, I can't work out with what, but I know she ain't dealing a pack of cards. Lights flash around again. I hear the sound of a belt buckle as she rocks left then right, bottom lip bitten between front teeth and the faintest of giggles, almost playfully mocking in its sound. One more rock to the left and the belt is free, she holds it aloft with her left hand, proud like she's slayed a great beast. Belt buckle clinks as it hits an empty lager can en-route to the ground. My hand moves down her back again, but where previously was the rib of jean shorts is now bare skin. My hand grasps arse cheek as she leans in to kiss me, bringing back the floral scent, glossed lips meet mine. Watermelon flavour. Tongue massages mine, slowly. Her nasal exhales breeze through my facial stubble. Lowering down onto her side of the airbed she's met with another hiss. Left arm behind my head, her right arm tugs my hand gently down, gesturing. She wants me at the lower end of the bed. As I oblige, she shuffles across and lays prone. Knees 180-degrees, soles of feet pressed together in prayer pose. White ribbed top still clinging to midriff and breasts. Stomach muscles faint under the soft light. As I shuffle down the airbed, accompanied by staccato hisses, she smiles with her eyes closed, at peace with the world. My hands grip her pronounced hip bones. Heartbeat battering as the serotonin in my blood floods my brain, my tongue meets moisture, her body jolts slightly as I explore, urged on by the sounds of 'Beachball'. Taste reminds me of a rare steak in a fancy restaurant. Canny. Snare drum, as I breathe and snatch a look at her prone body, goddess like. I take my weight with my left arm, hiss follows. My eyes close as I let instinct and music guide my exploration. Images and colour still streak my vision despite being closed. I move confidently, pulling her closer, switching hip with buttock, then begin unbuttoning my own belt and shorts. Pause for a second as I wrestle off my pants. Semi. I feel the evening air around my balls. I return my mouth to her clit as her left leg raises up and twists. Suddenly I feel the cold sensation of something stroking my shaft and balls. Her knee tenses and contracts in time with my tongue. Like one synchronised machine. Tiny movements. I become more aware of my breathing. Lights all around. Shapes and colours. Bass vibrating through the floor. High energy hooks and feminine voice, - *'cause it's easier to fly, than face another night in the southern sun, and you're love is all around* - I feel her stroke me tenderly, cold and stunning. Hooking me with a tense ankle. Pulling me upwards. Towards her goddess body, but I remain here for a moment. Ravaged blood pumps from wired brain to cock. Gentle strokes, gentle tongue. Battering heart. Finesse. Cold softness. Warming with every wave. I take a deep breath, resting for a moment as my old chap throbs. A fucking miracle on ecstasy like, my subconscious reminds me in a faraway thought. Her arm reaches suddenly down my side, then a gentle pull towards her face.

'Come here,' she whispers. Airbed hisses again. Cock now resting somewhere between her thighs. Slight worry of pre-cum dribble dissipates when she hands me a gold square packet, she's produced from fuck knows where. What a lass. The lights, the bass, and the bpm swirling around the atmosphere as she utters, 'Put this on,' just as - *piece by piece, I release* -

Friday
Seb

- Isn't it a pity, you already have a wife- Bouncing vocals ring around the wooden forester's lodge, converted this weekend only into a late-night hub of gyrating bodies and party casualties. Faces hidden behind cigarettes and sunglasses. The stimulated, the unwell and the horny seek refuge in here tonight. Many gurns and dilated pupils, sweat streaked hairs, two-day old T-shirts, and sunburnt forearms in the air. I've left the other two, who knows where. Admittedly, I did have quite the wander looking for mischief, enjoying the freedom, stopping at regular intervals, just to take in the beauty of everything and ride the rush of the drugs still going strong in my blood. I left them two somewhere between the dance stage and the cheesy chip van, if I remember correctly. I did return to The Dance Tent eventually, to where I thought we had been dancing, but to no luck. Faced instead with hordes of jean short lads chirpsing girls in fancy dress. My memory not to be trusted tonight, my judgement skewed. The music had changed, drum and bass by my reckoning. After a few tracks and attempts to tune myself into it, I left. Almost a hint of fear came with it, in my mind. Too aggressive.

    I bumped into this Aurora lass who is camping near us and told her I'd lost my pals. She said I should come with her. She'd been doing it alone all night, she was tripping heavily and wanted to skank out to some reggae DJ in The Hut on the Hill. Hill is pushing the definition slightly, but it did take a little effort getting up it, hey ho anything goes here. She's now stood in front of me, body hooked up sonically to the downstroke of a spiky reggae guitar. The room feels smoky and close. *- It's a pity -* the singer declares, as Aurora closes her eyes as though lost in the moment. Elbows pointing to the wooden rafter roof, fingers slowly dragging through her mousey hair, lifting the whole lot up as her forearms reach vertical. Hair is left to fall, slow cascade, two chords, horn, and a slow seductive bouncing. - *It's a pity* - I get a small waft of dry shampoo, coconut and some other fruit I can't quite work out. Intoxicating. She smells fresh compared to the sweaty fug emitted by the two chord twitching bodies around us. I am finding myself possessed by some dad dancing, left right knee bounce. I'm semi-conscious I look like a man with no rhythm, dancing to music with its own specific way of dancing, the drugs in my system tuned into a higher beat, a little out of its comfort zone. Feel-good doing just enough flowing to keep me going though. Calves feeling the burn. This setting suits Aurora.

The song changes. Again, two chords similar to the last, slow steady rhythm, male voice singing about being a - *Ganja farmer* - the rest of the lyrics I struggle to understand. I swig from my Red Stripe can. One that cost more than a 4 pack from the Co-op back home, something that'll gripe me come Monday, not today. I glug from it to hide my static lips unaware of the words, the feet of mine don't know where to put themselves, clumsily shuffling back and forth feeling weighty and judged. The fuel light is on for the ecstasy, I reckon. Early warning signs of running low, reality will start penetrating my mind again. Real feelings will return to haunt me. Been an age since we dropped. Wonder where the other two are at? I don't know where to put myself to this song, no idea of the words to sing along to, no idea what to do with my arms that hang sideways like heavy pendulums. Knees are doing all the legwork, so to speak. Aurora holds her eyes on me, mouthing the lyrics to the chorus as her tongue curls, her body shifts, and twists at one with the music. This is her natural habitat. Her eyes deep pools of hazel, the sclera of her eyes still lily-white. No sign of fatigue or stress in her on this Friday evening. She's still sporting a daisy hairband and band T-shirt from before. Her naked feet twist heels on the black and white chessboard linoleum, hippy pants swishing and sweeping across the floor. She's her own person alright. I'm drawn back to her eyes, she's confident, I like that. My own eyes keep darting away, struggling to keep contact. I break off again and look at the bouncing figures around me wielding Red Can stripes and spliffs. Smoke cloud in the rafters. They're convulsing to the bichord beat that fills The Hut on the Hill, dished out by wide smiled DJ complete with Rasta hat and sunglasses. His face revealed by the glow of his MacBook screen, as he shuffles, and rearranges his setlist. Reading the audience and choosing where to take them next. He turns the treble down, so the bass resonates deep, bodies around squat lower on this queue. Lowering themselves to the earth. Treble returns like a sharp spike of sound, like when you wake up from a deep sleep. Aural clarity returns.

I turn again to Aurora, who smiles at me behind a freshly lit roll-up. The smile lingers as she cockily exhales through the corner of her mouth. Is she just friendly? Or more? Stop thinking that. You're an old man. The ecstasy definitely stuttering to a slow burning stop now. Mixed thoughts and the familiar feeling of overthinking and worrying returning. Suddenly, the familiar drum intro of Dawn Penn - *No no noooooo* - batters through the speakers. This, I am familiar with, a surge of confidence returns to my moves, I mouth the words back in Aurora's direction with sureness. Her to me too. She places her right hand complete with burning roll-up onto my shoulder - *I'll do anything you say boy* – I'm worried I'll be burned. Feels too nice to move it away. - *I'll get on my knees and pray boy* - The lyrics go, the words from Dawn's mouth to my ears, via Aurora's tingling hushed tones. Cigarette smell almost choking along with the tension I'm feeling. I stifle a cough to remain static except for the sensual bounce as horns play and Aurora places her left hand on my shoulder. Absorb the smoke. Bodies closer. The DJ turns the treble down again, bass reverberates through each other, pulsing as I place my hands on her lower back. Nervous. Pulse of bass and drum. Legs lower us together, Aurora's thighs parallel to the floor, mine ache, but through sheer will almost make it there. We return to standing. Two chords, devoid of treble. Slow beat, fast heartbeat. Hand off shoulder. Blue cigarette smoke curls to my side and brown eyes are within a foot of me. - *No no no* - a long drawn-out suck on her cigarette, head flicks back to exhale, then returns to my face with that same ambiguous smile. Tobacco, dry shampoo, and some floral fragrance mingle together. I'm conscious of my own smell. Is my breath okay? What does it matter anyway? The room is stifling hot with moving bodies. I feel a sweat bead trickle down the back of my neck. Hands and eyes return to me. A thrilling feeling in my body. Confusion. We're just dancing. Only dancing. With an aching in my balls. Only dancing. I take the cigarette from her hand, she obliges, and I take a long, drawn-out inhale, letting the nicotine calm the tremble I feel inside.

DJ throws back the treble, life returns to the room, the wooden beams of the roof stop vibrating the nuts from the bolts. Song fades and changes, same stabby staccato guitar, horns, and - *Bam Bam* - Aurora breaks off her hand again and pulls a phone from her back pocket, the screen brightness breaking through the dark smoky air. For a fleeting second, I see the unmistakable image of a young child in their mother's arms, smiling at an unknown cameraman. My heart sinks. I think of my children. It was only dancing.

Friday
Jasmine

Spinning sights. Torchlights from stumblers by shadow play on the green canvas. Concentrate. Think. Bring yourself back down onto earth. Yes. I always used to like playing along with Deal or No Deal. That programme where they open red boxes and win what's inside. Always guessing what the contestant had in their box. A pointless exercise, but fun to do. Used to watch it at my grandpa's after school. Crossed legged in tights and skirt, secondary school blazer chucked over the armrest, sitting in my nonna's old seat. It felt intrusive. As if the cushions and the walls still held traces of her voice, the faint whispers of 'You do you pet. Always stick up for yourself.' When I got to sexual maturity, I naturally applied the game to a sexual context. Looking at prospective partners and wondering what was inside their box. Is it a £250k shag or a 1p cock? Just a bit of fun to occupy my stupid adolescent mind. My judgement was never great. Had a couple of £100 cocks at uni. All piston action and no rhythm, tongue rammed into my mouth and wrestling with my own tongue. A frantic and stressful encounter over all too quick. I'd found myself earlier today wondering what Shaun had in his box this weekend. Opting for a guess of £25k. Now I lie here, holding on to the edge of the airbed, hanging on for dear life, feeling I'm going to float off into space. All things considered, I think I got a £7.5k cock. Maybe a £10k one. Less than expected, but not a resounding disappointment by any stretch. Different. Very fucking different. Maybe I'm being unfair.

He's laid behind me, we're spooning and I'm watching shapes dance across the fabric of the tent. Trance music in the background. Voices everywhere. He's stroking my back, and it feels nice, almost better than the actual sex. The little pill I took still doing its thing with me, for now. I can feel goosebumps on my skin, his breath rolling over my neck. One of the few thoughts that I have is, that I'm pleased I had a freshen up today. We'd been having sex for I don't know how long, it felt otherworldly. Like I was a passenger in my own skin. Almost unnerving at times, as though I was watching myself in a parallel universe. Could have been going on for hours or minutes, who knows? Problem with trance music is there are no markers of time. Just a constant beat. Wonder whether the lads with the speaker know they provided the soundtrack to a psychedelic shag. The drugs making everything feel amplified, good and bad. It was slow and sensual. Breathy. I've read about tantric sex before, think it was as close to that as I've had. Totally unlike anything I've had in as long as I can remember. Tuned in to the nearby music, eyes closed, our bodies twisted and wrapped around each other with each 8th beat of the track. Spanish girls shouting on. My eyes closed; I picture them in similar situations. In tents yearning for a climax. Something that neither me nor Shaun reached. We kept going until it naturally slowed to a stop. A steam train rolling into a station, just short of the platform. I felt the chemicals in my bloodstream run clearer at that same moment. The peak was out of sight. Whether or not I would have come, given a bit more time, I'll never know now. Was it New Year's Eve sex? A load of build-up, fireworks and light shows, but fundamentally a letdown? No, not at all, but now it's done, I'm left wondering whether the anticipation was greater than the experience. When fantasy becomes reality, I am more often than not, left hollow. Always have been actually. Probably explains why I am always quite so disappointed in life, always wanting to reach the unobtainable. Never mind, I'm just confused, that's all. Trying to sift through and forge meaning out of things, with a mind ill prepared to do so. The spectre of Ellis is vanquished though. Once and for all. Him and his sometimes violent and always passionate £25k sex, which I hate myself for having enjoyed. A total contrast to the experience I've just had. Yeah, it was sensual, but I don't like the fact I wasn't me in that moment. The feelings were not real, were they? A chemically altered state. As the pill stutters and spits out its last influence, so returns the self-consciousness, the anxiety, and the feeling of vulnerability. The look for the exit. The breath on my neck becoming more of an irritant with each exhale. Fingers grip the airbed and dig nails in for different reasons now. I need to fall asleep now. I need to be unconscious.

As if by telepathy I feel the movement in Shaun's limbs as he shuffles and unhooks his arms from around my body. Now he's clattering around in the dark, sounds of fingers dragging across groundsheet. I sense he's looking for his clothes in the dark, only the opaque backlight of the fabric to provide any visibility. I hear the sound of a belt buckle clinking as he rocks and thrusts his shorts on. Airbed projecting me up and down violently with each few inches he pulls up. I can't help but think that the particular motion was lacking from before. Then the sound of cotton meeting hair, then stubble. The stretch and contraction as he pulls his neck through the T-shirt. Another bounce on the airbed. Fingers gripping the airbed more. I find myself irritated, feigning sleep. Trying to be as still as possible, so as to not encourage interaction. He pauses for a second as if he's looking at me. I feel that weird prickle you feel when you're being watched. Then the zip of the pod opens and he's out into the entrance area. The pod then gets zipped back closed. Outside I hear shoes getting put on, cans rattle, and boxes crush as he flacks about. Another zip, and then he's off out into the night. I then find it's my turn to look for clothes in the dark. Hand doing its own scanning, looking for knickers and vest. Feeling awfully naked right now. Finding both quickly enough. Pull them both on in case he comes back. The vulnerable feeling now real and strong. Will he come back? I spread out over the mattress and find a comfortable pose. Willing sleep to come.

The front door zip starts again. Fuck, he's back so soon. I roll back into the position I was in before, but no door zips go. The breathing is different. A crash of cans again, a stumble, and a rub of fabrics.

'What a pigsty,' I hear. It's Seb muttering and slurring under his breath as he begins the zip orchestra of his own. He then starts laughing to himself whispering 'Fucking hell,' as he shuffles into his own pod. The hissing sound of his airbed, then the long period of nothing. Nothing but breathing getting slower and heavier. I match my breath with his and will sleep to come soon. Spanish lasses and pulsing tones still audible over yonder, as the smears of reds and yellows still dance in my closed eyes.

Friday
Shaun

Fuck man, that was surreal. Did that really happen? Needed to get out of there pronto. Need to walk it off. Get my head in the game. At one point I thought I was with Sara, as I stroked her back and everything. The tent was her flat. It's like it was when we first met. She even smelt like Sara. That's fucked up man. I shouldn't have done that. That second pill came up during it all. Too much man. I'm shaking my head as I trudge up towards the long drops. Proper big head shakes. Like a footballer who's missed a sitter. Jaw clenching like a cunt. Guided to the lavvies by instinct and the smell in the warm night air. I've been needing this piss for a while. Not ideal shagging when you need a piss like. Especially when you're fucking wrecked. Why should I feel guilty about it all? We're both single. Aye. Wey, technically. Feels dishonest for some reason though. As if it was behind Seb's back. It's only his work mate. It's not as if I've been shagging Mia. Now that would be wrong. I think of Sara, even though that's dead in the water. Feel bad for her, even though she's probably shagging someone new now. For some reason, I think of the time I shagged that Mel lass. Felt like dirt after that. Pure fucking bastard's trick. It's not the same here like. But I still can't help but think about it. Thinking about shagging my mate's ex with barely a semi on her sofa, all the while knowing fine well it shouldn't be happening. Probably only really doing it because it was forbidden fruit. Don't even think I found her attractive. Absolute scumbag. No, this was not the same. We're both adults, single, and attracted to one another. Fuelled by chemicals. - *If you've lost your faith in love in music, oh, the end won't be long* - Well whoever is listening to that in their tent is just winding me right up.

I'm near the long drops. The little yellow light rig above the area shows there's no one queuing, but plenty of people floating around, stumbling, looking unsteady, waiting for mates. Proper severe faces all over. Trench beards. I head straight into one and sit down, even though I only need a piss. Pleased to have somewhere to sit and think. Not that I've got much capacity to think like. Try and replay what's happened. I mean, it was fun. She's fucking gorgeous like. Absolutely cracking body.

Hang on what the fuck is that?

What an idiot man, I've still got the fucking condom on. I'm filling up a big pissy water balloon, cascading up over the latex ring like a pan of boiling pasta. Stop the flow, testing my prostate, and snap the latex back, then drop it into the pool of mankiness. Bombs away motherfuckers. What a fucking tit I am. Pathetic. Piss resumes.

'See that bird in The Dance Tent? The one with the tits?' I hear someone outside saying.

'Ahh mate... Fucking gagging for it her,' another says.

'You get her number?'

'Yeah, I got her digits man. Sweet as you like.'

'Definitely worth a go,' they say. We're simple disgusting creatures, aren't we? Driven largely by our knobs. I think back to the events that led up to me and Jasmine shagging. The Dance Tent. The kissing. The music. The sex was trippy. We were good together tonight, riding that high together. I sit there and picture whether we'd work beyond tonight. I picture her flat. I imagine it laden with soft furnishings, cushions, and soft lighting. Easy on a tired mind. Scented candles, fairy lights, trinkets collected from vintage shops. Nice dresses and knitwear. Order and calm. Pink and green fabric. A white cocoon of a bed where we would discuss our careers, our future plans and share body heat. I'd be sober and rested. Happy. Fresh faced, like that bloke in the strawberry Adidas jacket. I know this could never be. I know me. I'd only ever fuck it up.

Piss finished, I finally get up, the relief helps the feeling of shame to take centre stage. Self loathing can now sit dominant in my mind as I head back to the tent. Dragging my feet over the dusty grass. Was only a shag, I never normally feel this conflicted. Should I go back into her pod? Is that what she'd expect? Bit creepy that like. No decision is the right one here. I've shuddered in the past, crippled with cringe from overstaying my welcome with previous conquests. Don't want Seb to feel betrayed, waking up to see me and her emerge from her pod grinning and nude. No, I'll leave her be. She'll want her own space. It would be creepy if I went back in there. Just don't want her to feel abandoned. As if I've humped, then ran. I would love to have someone to hold tonight, but no, I'll go back to my own bed. Aye. There's a very real chance I'll not sleep tonight with that second pill coursing through my head. Fucking idiot, I've got no self control. She'll probably be asleep anyway. I see the tent as I do the well-trodden course back to the doorway. Fiddle with the zip and open slowly, so as to not wake anyone up. Wonder whether Seb is back. Help myself in and look at the doorway of Jasmine's pod. Vision cloudy and wobbling. Wonder whether I should go back in there, knowing fine well I won't. Head instead into my own squalid pod. Collapse into the airbed and zip up my door. Wrapped in fabric and my own thoughts. Pull off my socks and shorts, kick them to the bottom of the sleeping bag. I'll just sleep in this T-shirt. Mind replays the scene of her curves, her lips, her taste, and her hands as they grabbed me. The nails in my back. The sound of her breathing in my ear. Feel a stirring. Consider getting that orgasm after all. Think of how she felt when I was in her. Her eyes when she looked down at me. Grab the sock I've just pulled off. Would make a suitable mop for any jizz. No. Pack it in man. Absolute fucking scratter behaviour. Grotty little man. Think of Maggie Thatcher. Think of something else. Anything. I lie there staring at the ceiling. Sock still in my hand as I try and settle my battering heart. Closing my eyes and trying to chase away the thoughts of what had happened. But it keeps floating back up into the front of my mind. Push it away. Think of something else. Relive Newcastle United's best goals last season. Walk around my childhood home. Count up sheep, or regrets, until it all fades to black.

Saturday

Saturday
Jasmine

The first thing I register is the light, then the heat, followed swiftly by an awful thirst. Dull aches. Then comes the question. Did last night really happen? A question pondered, as I scrabble around looking for a bottle of something soft to quench this horrific thirst. An awful forehead pain throb gets worse, as I swoop and swing bat-like scanning the floor for a drink. Heart rate at anxiety attack levels already. Liver sifting over the rubble, assessing the damage from last night's carnage. Thoughts shooting, misfiring, and radiating into the stifling air. I am in the realm of the unwell. A half empty bottle of water presents itself at the foot of the airbed and I greedily drink it down. The crumpling sound of the plastic collapsing on itself deafening. That same sound heard twelve hours earlier when I swallowed down a little pill and entered a different land. Bottle scrunches more, piercing the ringing in my ears. Bottle emptied, I survey the scene, try and gain some composure. I haven't felt this fucked for years. Let's assess the facts. It's Saturday morning. I drank far too much yesterday and the previous two days before that. It's been incredibly hot and sunny. My skin is obviously burnt. Cheeks hot. I'm at a calorie deficit. I took drugs and danced for hours without any water or food. Screamed at the top of my lungs along to songs. I have slept on this shitty airbed for three shit nights sleep, and last night I had sex with Seb's brother. I think that pretty much explains the state I find myself in now. I feel the walls, if you can call them that, envelope me. They feel closer this morning. I feel cooped up, aware of the lads in the other two rooms and how they might wake up at any moment. I need to get away for a bit, to compartmentalise my thoughts. I need coffee. Knowing fine well that it could very well accelerate and derail my fragile mental composition entirely this morning. But that's a problem for later. I must leave. One swift move or I'm done for.

Creeping out of the tent, then standing straight is a struggle. I go light-headed immediately and have to lean back down, nausea follows. Floaters and black shadows enter my vision. A metallic taste in the back of my nose. Take in deep breaths. The morning air feels moister this morning. The grass feels damp on my feet as I stamp and kick my shoes on, crushing down the backs as I do so. I begin to walk. Don't even bother zipping the door up, there's nothing worth stealing in there.

The usual route looks different this morning. Whether it's the different light with the ominous clouds, or whether it's my dull tired eyes. The figures that are milling around look more awkward and laboured today. Slower and more cynical in their movements. Limbs and minds are fatiguing. The ambient sounds seem turned down and the white noise turned up. Chatter more of a whisper than spoken with gusto. It gives me quiet comfort that my neighbours all look as fucked as I feel. Even the speakers of the food vans in the distance seem more muted this morning. I head towards my usual coffee vendor, the amusing 'Au Lait and Au Night'. The main pathway is well trodden and there are streaks of damp mud in patches, confirming the moisture in the air. It looks like it rained a bit. The climate has changed overnight. A lot can change overnight. I now have a new sexual partner to add to my list. One I cannot ghost or avoid contact for a few days, to assess where we go from here. No, it's someone who I'll be sharing a tent with for the next couple of nights. I curse my boozed up, drugged up self. I shudder at the cold light of day invoice that happy and carefree Jasmine has lumbered me with. Jealous of her break from anxiety and self-consciousness. As is always the case with me, sex fails to solve any problems, but creates a whole host of new ones. It all needs a radical rethink. I must be doing this all wrong.

I'm walking slowly, partially because I'm in no rush to return to the tent, and partially because I seem to be a bit more unsteady on my feet this morning. A couple walks past, heavy arm over shoulders, eyes underlined with dark rings. As they pass, I smell a strong reek of BO. Feel immediately paranoid that the smell is me. As I always do. Couldn't have sweated that much last night in my sleep. I don't recall building up much of a sweat during the sex either. Shudder at the thought. Was a new experience doing it that high though.

The peak of Bowman Crag is enveloped in cloud. It's hiding its eyes from the scene below it. I wonder whether there is anyone up there right now, wild camping in the crisp moist morning air waiting for the visibility to improve and to keep on ascending or descending. Peak of physical fitness that I can only dream of. Steady hand and feet over rock, while I can't even walk straight to get a convenient coffee. I suddenly remember a dream I had last night, that of a runaway car. I was a passenger in it, screaming, the tyres screeched as we skidded into the side of a deer. It lay for a moment in the road in a crumpled heap, then slowly struggled to all fours. I was powerless to help. It cautiously approached my passenger window. Black eyes looking straight at me. Brush-like eyelashes. Bloodied nose and cold air steam. We looked at one another. A moment. Then it hobbled off into the trees, as I struggled with the door handle of the car, impotent to help. Locked inside, the driver stunned into paralysis. A dream so vivid and a night so surreal, I struggle to differentiate the two.

As I approach the coffee van I'm frustrated to see a queue. The biggest queue for this place I've seen so far. As I stand, the nausea and the light-headedness become stronger. I shift weight from foot to foot. Deep breaths and fidgets with belt loops and hair to occupy me. Avoid eye contact with the strangers in front of me. I needn't worry. There is little to no chat between even the people who stand next to one another. The queue goes down quick enough. I find myself stood small in front of the ordering hatch. The person I've ordered from daily looks less friendly. Perhaps flustered at the queue that's formed. I place my order, the words seem to come out, but I feel disassociated with them, as though spoken by someone else. Like I'm in autopilot and a passenger in my own body. The beep of a contactless card and the relief that the transaction is approved, and that I don't have to remember four simple numbers.

Shifting cup from left hand to right hand, due to the fingertips burning. The vendor not putting the little insulating cardboard sleeve on this time. I'm in no mood to go back and get one. I'll make do. Pain reminds me I exist. The walk back slower than the walk there, I take in the scenes and try to place myself in the present. Two kids passing a ball to one another in the pathway, a girl in yellow and a boy in red. Contrasting colours to the monochrome scene. A stubbly dad fries sausages, a column of steam rises to merge with the high cloud above us. The weather could go either way today. Further along, there is the sound of a radio coming from inside a tent. It's the traffic announcements. Too much reality for my liking this morning, I tune my ears into some reggae from two lasses sitting, scrolling on their phones in university hoodies, knees tucked inside. Sporadically turning the screen to one another. 'Oh no, delete that please.' Then nods of approval that a photo is good, or a meme is funny. Take a sip of my coffee through the little drinking hole. Far too hot. A while till it's drinkable. I'll be back at the tent then. Anxiety twinge in my chest. I wonder whether Shaun will be up, or Seb.

A lad with a green mohawk is crouched with a hand pump cranking air into his airbed. The inside of his tent looking ordered and tidy, with a little drawer storage unit. I think how much Seb would like that sort of thing. As would I. Finding a water bottle would be a bit easier in the morning with something like that. He has some guitary stuff playing on his phone, too quiet to pick out what it is. Thrashy and violent even turned down low. Beyond him, further on down the path, I spot a spliff being passed around by some lads who look like the kind of people Ellis would surround himself with. I wonder whether a spliff would settle me today. Temporarily, maybe. Their voices battle over one another for their chance to talk, too busy waiting for their turn to speak, to listen to what their friend is saying. Recalling hilarious events from the night before. Competing for airtime on who was drunkest. As I look over at them at a slow amble pace, a couple of them look back at me. Dark eyes and dark clothing. I turn quickly away, aware of a mood of suspicion and dissonance in the camp. From here I know I am near; I turn to my right and spot the top of real ale bloke's head. I cut off the main pathway and start the slalom back to the tent, bypassing him entirely, so I don't have to acknowledge his existence in this state. As I pass a few tents, coffee sloshing through the drink hole and burning my hand, I see Shaun and Seb in the camp chairs. Another anxiety sting. I pause. They haven't spotted me yet. I could keep walking in the opposite direction. Put off the inevitable. Could head to the gates, leave this place, and hitch a ride back home. I'd be home for lunchtime. Back with the cats. Keep my phone switched off in its drawer and put off real life in the comfort of my own cell for another few days. Could draw up my battle plan as to how to approach Seb at work, without a feeling of betrayal. No, I'm being ludicrous. I've dealt with far more hostile situations. It was only a drunken, drugged up shag. He might not even remember it. It's no big deal. I walk with purpose and slip on my mask of faux confidence. Stepping over guy ropes and litter.

'Morning campers!' I find myself saying in some stupid high-pitched voice. Pleased with my own acting skills.

'Morning,' unenthusiastic rumble from Seb. Is he angry with me?

'Morning,' Shaun sheepishly smiles as I walk towards them. I allow a glance at him and a smile, as I place my coffee down on the upturned table of a home-shopping crate.

'I would have got you both a coffee if I knew you's were up,' I break away and throw myself into the tent. Then back to the scene of the crime. Heart going at an alarming rate. I make more noise than necessary, to make it sound as if I'm getting something from my bag. In reality, I'm gathering myself ready for the next interaction. Deep breaths. Slow the battering beat of my own nervousness. Thumb and forefinger pinching skin to distract. All the techniques I was taught on the phone by that therapist that time. I head back out after a few seconds and get into my chair. Hiding my face with a coffee cup, my hot awkwardness shield.

'Canny night last night, wasn't it?' Shaun offers.

'It was,' I say, 'I had a fun time.' Fighting the sensation that I'm going to flush red all over my face. Luckily, the sunburn will hide that somewhat.

'I lost you's after Origins of Sound finished,' says Seb, who looks tired and gaunt, 'Had a proper panic before, I've only gone and rang Mia late on last night when I was totally fucked.'

'You tit,' Shaun scoffs, 'What did you say?'

'Nothing too cringe, I don't think, just wanted to speak to her. Not sure what I said, but I'm sure it was nothing stupid. I hope,' he pauses, looking evidently panicked by the phone call. He shakes his head and his internal dialogue, 'What did you guys get up to?' A silence descends.

'Stayed in there a bit, had a bit of a wander, then had a couple of drinks back at the tent. I crashed after that,' Shaun explains. I'm working overtime on not flushing, also concerned at how easily it seems that lies fall out of Shaun's mouth. Don't know where to put my face, I'm terrible at hiding expressions. Finding myself nodding along to the tale. I suppose it's not untrue. Just misses out on the bit where he went down on me, then fucked me.

'Where did you get to?' I find myself chirping up with a squeak, desperate to shift the conversation along.

'Ended up at that place on the hill. That old hunter hut place. Hut on the Hill or something? There was some reggae night on. Was canny. Bumped into Aurora,' he quietens down when saying her name, opting to mouth it instead along with pointing at her tent which sits lifeless and showing no signs of anyone awake in there. I can't help but think mine and his night got somehow mixed up and skewed in a really surreal way. Reggae with Aurora seeming like the more probable outcome of my day yesterday. I suppose oral and shagging from Shaun wouldn't be ideal for him though.

'Canny?' asks Shaun.

'Aye,' replies Seb non-committal. Another silence descends. The lads swallow down mouthfuls of warm breakfast beer and I chug down slightly hotter than ideal coffee. Impatient that I've waited long enough, the slight burn is a price I'm willing to pay. Why do they make them so bleeding hot? I drink it down quick. Willing on the caffeine to jump start me. 'Some kid called William died here last night.'

'Fuck, really?' I'm shocked.

'Yeah, saw it on the BBC app this morning. Poor bastard. It doesn't give any details. Looks young though, judging by the photo they used.'

'Fuck,' I say before chinning the rest of my coffee. Brain is too overloaded to take in the magnitude of what's happened. We sit in collective silence once more, staring at the floor as one does in these situations.

'Poor bastard,' Shaun hushes during the lull. We sit for a while as life occurs around us. The only sound from us is slurping lagers and stifled burps. Deep breaths and sighs.

'Fancy getting into the arena early this morning?' Seb asks.

'Aye.'

'Yeah, can do,' I say. Everyone seems anxious to get moving this morning. No one wants to linger on last night too long. The lads drain their cans and replace them with full ones once more.

'Want one?' Shaun asks, that vulnerability in his eyes again. Avoiding too much eye contact. Seems shy talking to me, as I am with him.

'Cheers, thanks,' I say, cracking it open and drinking a big mouthful, 'chin chin.' Awful tasting after coffee, and warm, but I'll welcome the effects. With each mouthful today, I'll edge closer to the carefree Jasmine of last night again. Things will get a little less tense; I'll be able to deal with my shit better. The action plan today is to keep demolishing myself and keep on powering through.

'Let's go,' Seb says and we're all to our feet heading towards the arena. Shaun stuffing cans down into his usual hiding spaces ready for Checkpoint Charlie. We head towards there, me lingering a few paces behind, intending to vanquish the feelings, the residual regrets, and emotions of last night. Pause them for Monday afternoon.

'We go again.'

Saturday
Seb

The screens on the side of the stage are adorned with 'Drug warning – Red Ferrari Pills – These pills have been tested on site and contain potentially lethal levels of adulterant'. Screens are bright against early morning retinas, the morning attendees squint through tired eyes to the grainy close up of a pile of pills, various poses, pressed indeed with the famous prancing horse of the Ferrari badge. A tape measure beside. The photo is clinical, crime-scene-esque. The brightness hurts my eyes, I look up to the prevailing high clouds, elevated in the atmosphere. Intimidating, swirling, and marching over the ceiling of the world.

There is no mention of William, but the subtext is clear, as is the mood. Sombre and mournful. Remembrance Sunday vibes as the collective penny drops, this is what killed that poor lad. 180mg of concentrated and debased death. There's a collective shoe gaze, a shuffle. Muted chatter, the occasional ripple of laughter emerges cautiously as the screen blares away. Meanwhile five metres inside the screens, there is a rummaging with microphone stands and speaker monitors. Fluorescent inspections of the stage scaffolding and black T-shirted men rearrange the instruments ready for this morning's opener. Much like a motorway car crash, there is a blood intrigue buried deep inside the human brain, a morbid fascination, the collective pockets of chatter speculating about the details of the death. Phones are refreshed, and various news outlets are cross checked for any more details. 'Have they caught the dealer? Was he spiked? Was he the only one? Apparently, another three were hospitalised.'

The mood remains subdued, a total contrast to the scenes in this field some twelve hours ago. A whole world can change in a few movements of a big and little hand. The evidence of last night's euphoria, just an echo in the cosmos now. The remnants all cleared away under torch light by a team of hi-vis clad volunteers, bug eyed from the string of nightshifts clearing away other people's enjoyment. In one of those bin bags, grabbed by a long arm litter picker, maybe the little cellophane bag that held the lethal pill. A pill taken perhaps as a totally new experience, a rebellion from parents, or a peer pressure impulse action. Something he'd seen on TikTok, or saw on a film, read in a book perhaps. Maybe it was to impress a girl he's fancied since maths class. A young soul who wanted to enhance the enjoyment of his weekend, turn that wattage up just a bit more, make those lights a little brighter, that music that bit more touching. Squeeze that orange for every single drop it was worth. Little was he aware, as his stomach lining digested both his grandmother's home-made pasty and a bright red pill, poison fragments were being distributed by a dilated heart. Toxic molecules sent to extremities, whilst fuck knows how many miles away some dickhead sits quite unaware after cooking up a batch and combining with caking agent. A batch laced with whatever shite they had lying around the kitchen, or lab, or whatever the fuck they used to make these trojan horses with, just to fatten that profit margin a tad. That's all life is really, when it all comes down to it. Profit. A succession of scams and flogging snake oil. An endless list of taking that little bit extra, stepping on those fingers a little harder. Grabbing that pound sterling. Scraping from thy neighbour. A few extra quid on the bottom line. Everyone's guilty of it. This one just so happened to be an illegal venture, but there's examples of it fucking everywhere. Christ, we do it at our work. MGM Insurance, one big fucking scam artist trooping about with Trustpilot approval and a positive brand name. Looking for any old loophole to get out of paying out. Supermarkets, banks, paperboys, fruit stalls. We're all subject to exploitation, ripping off and shafting in favour of a few quid. Widening that profit, for what? A blowjob and a better life? Status and power? Is this what we've evolved to? Fuck everyone else. As long as there is greed, there is no trust. As long as there is no trust, we're all ultimately alone. Insular, silo wanderers, looking into the distance and not budging, as we walk past beggars, junkies, and yesterday's newspapers. On it, the photo of a smiling young man in a Carlisle United football top. A lad taken too young. William. Everyone turns away, we have somewhere to get to.

I look back up to the grey cirrus cloud up above, hiding how emotional I suddenly feel, dewy eyed as I think of home and the bairns. I dread to think of the horrors and heartaches that are waiting in the wings that I have to face with them. Picture them now. Curled up watching cartoons or painting at the kitchen table, still in their pyjamas. Munching on cut grapes so as to not choke. Crusts cut off cheese toasties. Mia pottering on, maybe they're in the garden burning off their endless energy, in the warmth of the morning under the very same clouds. Maybe it's turned to the promised blue sky now back home. Mia applying thick layers of sun cream to wriggling arms and scrunched up noses. A nostalgic smell, one of freedom and fun. I survey the crowd and simultaneously wipe my eyes with my sleeve, in a well executed movement to hide my emotion. Well practised over my years on earth.

Suddenly, the screens switch from the warning to a band logo. The Thunderhawks. Overlaying the image is the footage of three boot-cut wearing hairy types. A bottle of some brown spirit swinging in each hand, big gulps as they swagger to their instruments. The drug warning mood now replaced with a gentle joyfulness as the feedback screech of a Marshall amp and Fender combo pulses out of the speakers. The crowd more than ever wanting to be taken away from reality. Quite unaware down country lanes, a few junctions of a motorway, and just over the bridge, inside a hospital crouched over a mortuary bed, is a mother crying over the cold motionless remains of her only child. William.

Saturday
Jasmine

Something has changed. The mood is different. Anxiety rises even more. It's like it's reached fever pitch. There's a nervousness, a paranoia. No amounts of coffee and alcohol have helped so far. Made it worse even. Those friendly pissed up faces smiling freely from last night are replaced with cynicism. A hostility. 'Who the fuck you looking at' eyes, shrouded in bags and cloaked in darkness. Chemical imbalances all over the field. Very unsettling, a feeling I'm all too used to.

The hair of the dog isn't working, and the wine bladder draining quicker than my budget will allow, but it's barely touching the sides. It's meant to last all day, but at this rate, it'll be done by the time this singer has finished her set. I've seen Shaun eyeing up the drink, at least that's what I think he's looking at with a hangdog puppy eyed countenance. Look away, this is mine, I don't want to talk. I want to lose myself in music and wine. Just leave me be. He's looking fucked in his own way right now too.

The female artist leans back onto a pub style stool, sporting a black guitar, chords chiming over the muted crowd. Really soul cleansing chords progress, and her voice punky and satin at the same time. Like a cat's fur stroked one way, then the other. This is hitting the spot. Soothing. Energising. I really dig her dress sense too, unique; dress pants and blouse, padding about barefoot on Persian rug, white rimmed sunglasses. The sort seen driving about in classic car passenger seats alongside floral head scarf in old black and white films. Driving off into the sunset with the love of their life. Her sunglasses reflect back hunched shoulders and blank faces, glowing cigarette ends, and the dull metal bottoms of cider cans. I know it's not music to dance to, but the crowd's lack of enthusiasm annoys me. They've obviously overdone it on their respective Friday nights. Live and let live, I suppose. She growls a lyric - *trick.... meeeeeeeeeee* - going from tenor to soprano and holding the last syllable. I love it. I feel it in my chest.

'Here, she looks like my Aunty Doreen!' squawks some gobshite from nearby. Half arsed reply of forced subdued laughter from the vicinity of the comment. Laughter sounds more appeasing and polite than anything else. Like you do with an inappropriate customer. Laugh it off and hope they move on. The sort I've employed myself to placate Ellis, in relatively recent history. The sort you make to your boss, when you want him to go away so you can get back to funny cat videos on YouTube, or suicide tips from online forums.

'Shite this!' he goes. Even less enthusiasm bounces back. I see both Shaun and Seb pull faces at one another, they silently convey their own disapproval of him. He continues, 'At least me Aunty Doreen can sing, and she's been dead five fucking years!' He's wheezing and laughing at his own rudeness. I look at the beautiful lass baring her spirit in front of several thousand zombies. She's doing it with elegance and power, but now I see her through a vulnerable lens. The one where she's not protected by a stage, a crash barrier, and five cross-armed stewards. She's the woman standing outside a nightclub toilet, anxiously waiting for a friend, the woman in the back of a taxi planning her escape route when the red light indicates doors are secure, the woman in a work meeting spoken over by grey-haired, red-faced men in bad shiny suits. She's me on the bus late at night, she's walking down a street in the dark, taking a run in a park. The woman who workmen don't even bother telling the details of what they've done with your boiler, the woman whose arse is pinched on the way to the toilet in a busy pub, the one who gets messages asking for nudes from random men, the one who is paid less than her male colleague on the same work level, the one who is asked if she's planning on having a family in her annual review at work. She's every fucking woman that has ever existed, and she's every fucking woman that will ever exist. Her guitar is now a shield, sunglasses her mask for hunched gorillas beating chests and dragging tiny cocks in the undergrowth. Testosterone levels reaching meltdown with this bloke, that, and lack of education. The feeling in my chest, the soothed soul is replaced by a fist knotting up my insides. Wine circulates my bloodstream, faster now as my heart begins to flood with adrenaline. Not today.

'No wonder the lass can't afford shoes if this is how she sings!' he huffs, 'Give it a rest love, find another job, eh?' Shaven head owl-like turning around, looking for approval, or more likely disapproval. Spoiling for attention. There is menace in his vicious eyes, gingery beard failing to hide a grimace. Not receiving any nibbles proceeds to belch out, 'Cunt! Fuck off ya shite!' spat with absolute venom, saliva dripping lips lingering on the Ts of both curses as if taunting the stage. The vitriol cuts through all the major, minor, and 7th chords the small girl on the stage can wrangle out of the fretboard. A collective inhale. Teeth clasp. A ripple of uneasy silence in the ten-metre radius of this gaping arsehole. The fist of rage in my stomach punching its way up through my diaphragm and out of my mouth. I've got to stick up for this little lass on this great big stage. For women.

'Haw, do you fancy giving it a fucking rest mate?' I find myself saying, adrenaline shaking my extremities, I'm shocked at the voice that comes out of my mouth, 'Don't like it, just fucking piss off somewhere else yeah? There's plenty going on around here.' Both 'mate' and 'yeah' are not normally in my repertoire, but this is no time for soft speak, do it like they do on the telly Jas. His rotten gammon face snaps towards my direction, eyes lock on to mine. Oh shit, what have I done?

'You fucking what there little girl?' he spits.

'You fucking heard, man. Don't like it mate, leave. Simple.'

'Is that right? Is that fucking right? You're one of them, aren't you?' he probes, getting louder, the beer slopping out in a spray as he barks. Clearly, this man has not slept in a number of days, his face twisted and distorted, fist like. I reckon he hasn't felt the love of another human being in some time, or perhaps not with their consent anyway. No partner is visible by his side. Then again, all faces in the vicinity are fixed on the stage, obscured by awkward angles, they're not getting involved. Ironic really, that now they pay attention to the singer. Drinking in her words to drown out the melee. Cowards. His gaze is still fixed on me as she finishes her song, she's taking a while to start the next one. Hear the blood in my ears like an underground train approaching at speed. A quick glance sees her handing her acoustic guitar to a roadie and swapping it for a blood red electric. I look back to the wanker and he's still eyeballing me, mouth moving like he's chewing the cud. Bovine idiot. He slowly mouths 'Mate' in my direction, or at least that's what I guess he's saying, the electric chords bulldozing through everything as she attacks the fretboard. My heart is drumming, I feel vulnerable as fuck in this crowd of gutless mutes.

'You're bang out of order, absolutely bang out of order mate,' I double down across the wasteland, hoping he hears, or perhaps not, but rather sees I'm not backing down. He punctuates this exchange with a drink of whatever awful shite he's jacked himself up with. Tar like liquid, the colour of his eyes.

'Cunt!' he mouths again.

'There's absolutely no need to go on like that.' I bellow, adrenaline now wobbling my voice, guitar salvo hopefully masking the waver. His eyes are still fixed on me, my throat. Veins visibly pulsing, I bet. He's wobbly on his feet, disappearing between bucket hats, caps, and heads, then re-emerging. He ponders a bit, as the singer begins shredding the hell out of some major chords, chorus, and delay pedal applied, echoing around the pit. The next bit, I do not expect, he proceeds to stick his tongue out towards me, blowing a raspberry. Like a petulant toddler told they can't have another biscuit by a parent. Nearby smirks hint on the faces of those around him. He's disarmed, exposed for his pathetic behaviour. He then proceeds to stick his arm into the air flicking two fingers at me, head bowed. Shuffling to the right he continues to weave away from my direction, away through the crowd, and disappears from view, presumably off to climb a tree and wank himself silly. My heart's still going, a feeling I'm used to with Ellis and his rages. A new feeling appears, one of standing up for oneself. A kind of pride and fear cocktail. The wine bladder is tight with the vice like grip I have on it. Down the rest of the crushed cup in my right hand. A celebratory toast. Turn to the stage and watch the artist bounding about the stage, belting out arpeggios and pitch changes. Feel the fear ease slightly, tell myself I won't see him again. Must be cautious though. Thirty thousand people here, odds always were there would be one wanker. By the time she's taken her bow to the crowd I'm clapping arms aloft, the wine bladder wedged between my knees, its contents fuelling a throat pinching cheer. The screens fade back to the drug warning message. That poor kid.

'Well done for that,' a random crowd member says to me during the break, 'That was really brave.' I feel a hand on my back from one of the lads.

'Top lass.'

'Aye, that was something else that, Jas. '

Saturday
Shaun

These farmboy fuckers are not really my vibe like. Yellow Stone Country Club, they're called. Shite like their name. I'm feeling Premier League paranoid. Champions League finalist fear. Those screens keep coming up with pictures. Can't escape them. Them and Jas having that barney. It's shaken me up big time. Those Ferrari pills, I saw them. I nearly fucking picked them man. In that crowd in The Dance Tent, there were those lads peddling. Not particularly incognito either, sales strategy more market greengrocer than dark web. All green Adidas trackies and bucket hats, assured and aggressive in your face transactions. 'Don't fuck with us,' kind of stances. All limbs and angles. I was six sheets to the wind and wanted to restock my disco biscuits, having sneakily dropped the last of them. I was breaking my own cardinal rule of not buying shite from strangers. Don't know what you're going to get, and more importantly, I'm not made of money.

Preston, that's where he was from, the bloke said he was from Preston. 'Some cunt from Preston.' The punchline to my dad's favourite joke, shock factor when he told it to me straight faced when I'd barely entered my teens, rebelling when my mam was out at the shops, a punch in the arm in stitches. Bruised my spindly arms. Anyway, the dealer, blatant as owt, he wasn't there for pleasure, purely business. No sweaty dancing or stupid colourful attire on him.

'Red or blue?' he said, like a casual Morpheus. Brazenly holding a zip lock sandwich bag stuffed with ecstasy tablets, there was probably fifty odd pills in there, like the fucker had cleared up at a bootleg Halloween. Probably about fifteen years in the nick that, if they get caught. More now, I suppose. His eyes were fixed on my face, as the battered brain of mine chose which design to have, he was serious man. I made some quip about Sunderland being red so, 'It's a big no no for them from me like.' The joke didn't register, muscular frown didn't budge. This fella isn't the comedy type, I thought. His resemblance to a malformed Colin Farrell not something I should bring up. 'Then again, I do love a Ferrari, Michael Schumacher, eh?' His eyes boring into me, and even through the serotonin overload, I sensed the lack of love in this man.

'Blue please mate,' I shouted over the sound of a pounding high energy 150 bpm track. An industrial sound like spinning band saws or something, like the woodwork block back at school. High alert and plenty danger. He handed me two of the three ordered blue DHL embossed pills. Sixty quid, extortionate. Remember the days it was two quid a pill and good stuff inall. His bony fingers fished out another blue into my upturned palm, but not before one of those red ones rolled out inall. Ferrari, my favourite car when I was a bairn. Had an Enzo poster on my bedroom wall, Dad went mental that I used duct tape to stick it onto the wall, tore the lining paper when it came down, and was swapped with a bikinied Kelly Brook once puberty struck like a fucking steam train. Colin Farrell's ugly brother looked on as the red pill, which lays in the crease between my thumb and index finger.

'This one on the house?' I quipped.

'No,' he replied matter of fact. The 'don't fuck with me' tone was clear, even over the pounding woodwork soundtrack in the background, all fucking techno saws and power tools. I was tempted to purchase, but not at those prices. My left hand clumsily fiddled my damp palm, dexterity purely buggered from substance abuse. Between scruffy thumb and forefinger, I handed it back to Colin.

'Nearly scored!' I said to him, again totally fucking clunky in judgement with communication, but I couldn't help myself. His face like a fist all stoic as he placed it back in his big zip lock bag. Then bag into green Adidas hoody left pocket. Cash shoved in the right. He disappeared as quickly as he came into the crowd of ravers. No goodbye. I shouldn't have felt surprised.

Now some twelve or so hours on, I have those blue pills wedged in my wallet back in my rucksack at the tent, shoved in the little window bit where normal people have loved ones. Mine's usually blank. Today it's reserved for potentially fatal Class-As. Sixty quid's worth of potential death. What a fucker, eh. Best call at those testing facilities Seb was chuntering on about, before all inhibitions disappear with this premium lager.

Saturday
Jasmine

'I've been looking forward to these lads.' The next band are up, Vita Nova. The lads look enthused, buoyed by the prospect. It begins with a primal howl, a blood-curdling scream. Hi-hats gnash sticks, gnawing like bones and echo into the ether, hissing amongst the oak branches, whistling through their leaves. Bouncing and bounding, larynx battling with the hubbub and wind. Bass punches through my soles, my crotch. Diaphragm contracting in the hollow of my chest. Hormones course through my throbbing veins, the angst I've felt so often, but this time I'm not alone. Thousands of brothers and sisters beside me in joy, not anger. The only fist striking me is that of a guitar hook, a bass slide, and a kick drum. The guitar is given free rein to bob and weave through the crowd, jabbing and stabbing eardrums, high notes on the fretboard indiscriminately grabbing and shoving random members of the crowd, screaming in their faces, and possessing them, shadowboxing and arms windmilling back in dance. Some crossed arms watch attentively with intrigue, smartphone light peppering their nodding faces, screen scroll reflected in dust film sunglasses. A gunshot scream sing-along - *way low below the ground, deep below the roots* - where the bass penetrates and probes. Confusing worms and moles who pray for rain in the crumbling earth shook into action. The vibrations beneath a thousand stomping pairs of rubber soles meet rock. Stranger Things haircuts thrashing, boot-cut jeans, stonewashed and torn. A single bead of sweat down the forehead meets the mesh of the microphone, as a final scream is ejected upon the awakened crowd. Hi-hats give a final bash, sticks breathe a sigh of relief, fibres crack. Song over. Applause. Acceptance.

Saturday
Seb

I'm devouring little bits of pineapple and peaches from a little plastic tub. Really obscene teeth rotting sweet stuff. They're dripping in syrup which makes my fingertips sticky. A wet wipe perched on my knee for quick removal. I hate being sticky. Sugar and acid revealing what feels like a thousand mini lacerations in my mouth, as I welcome some vitamins into my body. Like my face felt when I've rubbed in sun cream before, the cracking skin drinking down the moisture like a dog eating chips. They're both much needed. I feel the cells in my blood slurp up the goodness. It's the same little fruit pots I urge the kids to eat, never having tried them myself. I'm wondering how healthy this supposed fruit actually is. Another thing to feel guilty about as a parent.

We eschewed breakfast this morning and now I'm feeling the hunger descend. Jasmine has gone off to get a communal margarita pizza for us all and Shaun is making a racket in his pod. I have no idea what he's doing, but it seems flurried. Quite at odds with the weary rest I find myself indulging in, sitting in this camp chair with this sickly pot of vitamins, feeling almost close to normal.

He's muttering, 'For fuck's sake,' and 'Bastard,' repeatedly in increasing volume and huff each time. I try and block it out initially, I don't want to know, but it's absolutely insisting on my intervention. I'm too tired to make whatever problem he has my own. I'm in no mood for responsibility. That's what I'm relishing the most here. Then comes a frustrated moan, 'Argghhhhh,' and the sound of something thrown into the communal area of the tent. It sounded heavy.

'What's the matter, man?' I snap, aware at once how violently frosty I sound.

'The pills,' he says, loudly enough to make me scan around in case any nearby stewards or coppers were in earshot.

'What pills?' I ask in a quieter tone, leaning towards the door flap of the tent. Hushed, but assertive in my query.

'Them pills I bought last night. I had them here,' I can't see where he's pointing, nor was I aware he'd bought more pills. So much for being skint. He moans, 'I cannot find them at all.'

'I never knew you bought any more.'

'Aye, in that tent last night,' he huffs again, 'For fuck's sake they were here man.' He starts scrabbling around again tossing things about. He'll never find anything going on like that.

'You mean you've lost them in the tent?'

'Maybe, probably,' he pauses, 'I thought they were in my wallet in my bag, but they're not here.'

'Well, they've got to be somewhere,' I say, hearing the voice of my own father as soon as I say the words. Shuddering at the audio likeness. Then, a realisation that the pills bought last night, as well as the tragedy that has befallen the festival, I put two and two together. I feel a great sense of fear. I add, 'They weren't them ones on the screens at the stage, were they?'

'No, no,' he says. I feel a relief somewhat, until he continues, 'But I saw them ones in the same bag. The fella in The Dance Tent who was flogging them had those ones. Them red Ferraris.' His head pops out of the tent flap, his face reddened with exertion and stress. He squints as the light hits him.

'Hang on a minute. You know the bloke who was flogging the ones that killed that lad?'

'Wey, maybe. I mean he had ones that looked similar in there. I can't be sure like, y'know?'

'Not reckon you should speak to the police about it?'

'Are you fucking mad? As if I'd dob myself in it when they start asking questions.'

'But someone died Shaun.'

'I'm aware of that.'

'Surely that's something you can help with?'

'Bollocks to that, I'm not going to rat on anyone, it'll only end up on me that.'

'Also, you've lost pills that might be deadly? In my family tent? Have I got that right?'

'Wey no, they'll be somewhere, like you say,' he stumbles, 'or maybe I dropped them somewhere last night. Fuck's sake man.'

'Well, that's no better man, what if a kid picks them up and thinks they're sweets?'

'Well, then The Kidzfields area will have someone having a belting time,' a wry smile testing the waters.

'Or dead! Honestly, man, this isn't time for jokes. Seriously, have a word with yourself will you.'

'What's up, man? I'll find them if they're in here. Just give me a minute. It's not the end of the world. I'm wounded at the cost of the things. They weren't cheap like.'

'What's up? What's up? The fact that some kid died last night and you're going about losing the shit that might have killed him in my family fucking tent,' I see his face flushing redder, he knows what's coming, 'Honestly man, you are so irresponsible. It is embarrassing.'

'Here man, these things happen,' he barks back.

'Yes, they happen, but not to people who are responsible. But these things always seem to happen to you. Honestly man, do you not think sometimes?'

'They'll turn up man.'

'They fucking better, or you're buying me a new tent, honestly. I can't risk Emily or Reuben finding one of those things in a little side pocket that you're too fucking irresponsible to find.'

'I've checked the side pockets actually,' he's getting agitated, scrunching his face childlike and petulant as he says those words, 'Your kids aren't stupid man. Is it because you're precious about the tent, is that what it is? As if you're not going to be sweeping and hoovering out this place before you're next trip. I know what you're like.'

'No, it fucking isn't,' I say, that narks me more, 'You don't get it do you?'

'Aye I do,' he's getting to his feet now, kicking on his trainers, the backs getting crushed under heel. Aggressively tying his laces, he's all combative movements. Then stands erect above me. Red bloated face, chest all puffed out. He exhales with a 'Loud and fucking clear.'

'You stomping off now? Leaving me to sort out your problem?' All peaceful solitude has evaporated. The field is back to being our three-bedroom semi during the Easter holidays. Bickering and flouncing, whilst Mam and Dad graft on all week. I'm left as the responsible adolescent looking after my kid brother. Frustrated.

'I'm going to get some air,' he says, then heads off through the tent slalom over ropes and pegs.

'Pathetic, aye run away from your problems,' I say, loudly enough for him to hear as he disappears from view, knowing it's unhelpful, but compelled to have the last word on the issue. I am fucked off. But almost immediately I feel bad. These confrontations between us are rarer nowadays, but always result in a feeling of guilt and remorse. Like when I berate the kids for things that kids do. Yes, these things happen, but then they suddenly become my problem to sort out. I dart into the tent and start searching through his gear. Checking pockets of discarded shorts and jeans. Lifting things up high and shaking them upturned. Making a checked pile and shoving it about as I scan the floor, avoiding a crispy looking sock by the airbed. Lucozade bottles scattered everywhere. I couldn't live like him. I spend a good few minutes crawling through foul-smelling socks and flicking underwear by the waistband, to no avail. I feel dirty sifting through the clothes. I feel intrusive rifling through his bag, but most of all I feel heightened and on edge because of the argument. Plus, it smells like an old pub carpet in here.

We used to have hundreds of arguments when we were younger. Over anything and everything. Like siblings tend to do. I don't look forward to mediating Reuben and Emily after their future barneys. Being much older, and with a more developed vocabulary, I usually won these arguments. It was easy prey. Slicing him down to size with a parting shot that led him to exit the room, slammed door into the garden where he'd loudly kick a ball against a wall. Or to play Nirvana, Blur, or Oasis loudly on his headphones if it was raining. It was always something aggressive, for my benefit. There would be a period of silence, passing one another going through rooms without eye contact, and ignoring one another over a tense family meal. Mam and Dad knew fine well what was going on. We'd put on bravado and speak to our parents individually as the Frey Bentos and home cooked chips cooled. Smug smiles over mushy pea mountains, puffed up chests and shoulders back to hide the remorse and a means of doubling down and winding up the opponent. The period of silence could last anything between a few hours and weeks, if memory serves correct. Then they would be resolved, or rather we'd be reconciled with an unspoken peace offering. An offer of a sweet from a packet, or a games console controller slid in the direction of the other. The rebuilding would begin, and the reason for arguing forgotten. For the sake of the festival experience, a peace offering will be needed rather quickly. I'm too old and tired to be putting effort into conflict. Nowadays, the silence lasting months when we're on good terms, it could go on indefinitely if not sorted here.

'Pizza's up!' Jas is back at the camp, hollering through the door flap.

'Ah, champion,' I say. Except now my stomach feels raw with anxious nausea.

'Shaun in there with you?' she asks. Tilting her head to one side.

'No, he's gone off for a walk.'

'Oh,' she looks taken aback and concerned, as if she herself was at fault for him leaving.

'Think he's just struggling a bit today. Needs a little break, he gets like that,' I offer, hoping it will put any mind talk of hers at ease. I know she thinks she's intruding this weekend, but if anything, she's going to be the glue today. My words don't appear to have the desired effect and her stance drops a bit, as though she is burdened with something.

'We'll save him a few slices,' she says, as she lowers into the camp chair.

'Yeah, I'm sure he'll be back soon enough,' I hope.

Saturday
Shaun

A flat cap wearing bloke mockney drawled, 'Champion champignons,' his mouth all disgusting like an insole that's fallen out a shoe. He handed me a polythene bag stuffed with rank smelling wrinkly mushrooms inside. I chewed down the foul-tasting bastard like a hungry dog, washed down the bits that refused to budge from my tongue with a swig of the slavering bloke's energy drink and vodka cocktail. Him watching on all hur hur hur. His drink a 50/50 mix ratio. Rocket fucking fuel. That was an hour ago, just after my barney with Seb, or more accurately, the attack from Seb. Cunt. Honked down a key of the Columbian stuff in a Portaloo whilst I gathered myself. Then got chatting with these fellas who looked decent enough craic and hung around their tent a bit. Obviously, a group of hard sessioners. Knew they'd have drugs on them. I have an instinct for it. Now I'm laid on my back, peering up at the clouds in some random arse end corner of the site. I could be on Mars for all I know. The clouds forming shapes in rapid speed man. Trilby clad men embracing cocktail dressed women, they melt into each other in love. Kissing passionately. Every single cloud pairing off with a perfect other. No cloud left alone. Then they zip off the conveyor belt to be replaced by another trilby and cocktail dressed cloud. It's like a 20s speed dating scene. Above me, nothing but blue sky and lovers. Me gawping in amazement, mouth open and not blinking. I'm aware of a sick feeling brewing, but I don't think I'll be hoying up imminently like. Feels like how I felt as a wee'un in the back of Dad's Escort after a long car journey. Me too restless to just look out a window, insisting on reading a magazine, playing on my Gameboy, or drawing jet fighter planes, fucking about, like I do. Air stuffy and my arms too puny to wind the little handle to crack open some ventilation. I'd instead moan to no avail, until Dad would whip the Ford into a petrol station, cranking up the handbrake rat-tat-tat in frustration. Disappearing into the kiosk and appearing a few moments later, stomping gorilla-like with a new packet of Regal king size for himself and some Fishermen's Friends to share. Back in the car, he'd silently gesture the open packet to me. I'd take one, them bastards were nuclear. He'd then contort himself into the back and manage to wind a few centimetres of airgap for me. Then we'd be off again, my head like a polar bear's arse-crack. To be fair like, the searing pain of my mouth under attack from menthol overload did take away the sickness feeling. Even as I watched, through watering eyes, the cars in the slow lane disappear in the wing mirror. My Dad on a mission to make up for lost time. Just like Seb the other day. He doesn't realise how much he's like him nowadays. Then again, I see myself in him too.

The earth is rotating too quick, eyes can't catch up. Clouds whipping by at the speed of those slow lane cars all of them years ago. All the lovers are floating by. I grip the spiky grass, in fear of floating off terra firma. Disappearing off into the deep blank loneliness of the universe. Eaten up by a black hole, ripped apart, and shot through the cosmos in a great supernova.

'You alright there mate?' It takes me a second to register. I hear it from the nearby bins, sounds stereo though. I hear it again, 'You need some water or something?' Tie dye vest and frizzy hair sucking the end of their fingers as they dispose of a paper tray. Their movements exaggerated. The finger sucking sexual. In the deep recesses of my mind, there's a porn soundtrack, all fake orgasms, slurps and wet sucking. Slap bass. Slapping flesh. Gets louder. Groans of pleasure and exploitation unbearable. Hair turns to snakes, like that ancient Greek lass. Medusa, that's her. The food tray floats on like a paper aeroplane, beyond the bins and up into the direction of my cloud gods. It leaves a trail, a soft white contrail that loops the loop, curls, and zigzags on the blue chalkboard. 'You look a bit peaky.' All echoing and distorted, like it's going at half speed. My head rolls back. Tie dye pulses to the sudden loudness of the plucky guitar solo playing from a nearby food van. I need to get out of this trench. Across no man's land. One quick move or we're done for. - *Forward March!* -

'Aye, sound,' I muster, barely a slur, tongue feels fucking massive, like a big raw chicken breast, tastes like it too. I roll over on the prickly grass and get myself upright. Must walk. Get that blood moving. - *Stop children, what's that sound?* - There's drumming coming from somewhere. Follow it. I picture a human sacrifice, naked sinewy people gathering around a pile of twitching corpses. Keep walking. Head to the sacrifice. Faces, faces, faces everywhere bustling by. Bug eyes and blood-streaked mouths. Millions of people. Like Terry and Julie, Waterloo Station. - *Sha-la-la* - Tinny speakers on an ice cream van. Am I really hearing that, or just imagining? The blue and white of the van like a hospital corridor. - *You've got wires, going in* - I'm back in the sterile surrounds of the day my youth was lost for good. My mother fading to grey. All bleach and chrome instruments. Shiny linoleum flooring. That sickly green paint of the corridors. The Twix bar I split with Seb in the waiting room. - *But I don't, feel no shame* - All mid, bass disappears down a foxhole. Treble bouncing off a nearby tree. Sparrows and blue tits scarper from the sonic onslaught. Up into the sky, which the cloud lovers have abandoned, the plane long since landed. '*Sha-la-la*', did I say that? Or Ray Davies on tape. Take a breath, and focus.

Drumming, follow the drumming, towards the trees. The ancient trees. Scenes of swordfights and ancient settlements. Bows and arrows. Deer hide clothing and mead. The smell of smoke from the settlement burnt down, the women and children raped and murdered. No, no, it's from that German sausage grill over there. Perspective. Nausea pangs, as the torture rack of sausages rocks over the hell coals, a deafening fizz. Fat globules drop like my leaking bathroom tap. Drip drip fizz. Rat-at-tat-tat, bud-um budmph. There they are, the drums. Clad in military tunics of black and gold. 80s neon headbands and legwarmers. Wellington boots. Their faces are pale. Walk closer. Use an imaginary walking stick to stay upright. Fight the urge to fall. Slowly does it.

There's a crowd. Wriggle through that gap. Barge a toddler out of the way. Waaahhh. Maybe a dwarf. Who cares? To the front. Squinting. Eyes burning. Takes a few seconds to register. Sunglasses on my head pointing skyward. Flick them down. Rat-at-tat-tat-tat. Dum Dum. Bass drum. Cha-cha- rat-tat-tat. The drummers. There are about thirty of them, swaying side to side, rhythmic, like the pendulum on a grandfather clock. Tic tic. Hypnotic. Look up, I swear the trees are mocking me. Got Seb's angry faces in their trunks. The Smith scowl. Pines rocking and swaying in unison. Slow exaggerated movements. They're in sync with the drummers. Tic tic. We're all connected by the invisible force of sound. Left right left right. Unrelenting. Faces are pale man, that's the most disturbing bit. Their lips are so pink. Like the waxed fannies, a young me tugged himself silly over, at the family computer, when the rest of the household was asleep. Stuffing soiled tissues into a toilet roll tube under the desk. Tic tic. The sound of dial up internet and puberty. Tic tic. Those pink lips, is it makeup? They been eating them lollies that stain your mouth? Is that their gimmick? Fucking radge. The conductor stomping about, bald headed and bearded. Looks like that old France goalkeeper. A lethal combination of masculinity. Like a bouncer. The facial expressions of scrunched muscle and testosterone. He commands the band of pendulums, tic tic orchestrating the big bass I feel in the hollow of my chest. His arms whip and jaunt to rat-at-tats, the dum-dums, and everything in between. They're beating the fuck out of these instruments; their life must depend on it. A stunning rhythm. It may go on forever. Let it. The constant Newton cradle of infinity. Time and space irrelevant in the right here and now. My eyes are fixed on all the pink lips. Left. Right. Left. Trees and drummers like school rubbers. Bending and bowing. The intensity increases. They appear to be chewing now, munching on something. Big cowlike chews, round and round. Mouths reveal black tongues like giraffes. Hanging out all leathery. Calloused and drooping. Wobbling in the ever-swinging motion. All thirty, bashing shit out of the drums, crowd clapping along all gormless. Faces lit up with a phone screen version of the events before them. Gawping at this random moment in history, in the corner of a fucking field between trees, food vendors, and the shadow of The Dance Tent. Purple puppet phoenix on sticks swoops over the horizon followed by a procession of colourful characters. Disappearing into the sanctuary of the wooded area. The final galactic bang of the drums decays into the cosmos, as the cloud lovers retreat under crisp white sheets. Fuck me. Champion champignons indeed. The nausea makes a reappearance, as my body prepares for the next stage of this strange and wonderful trip. Joe Strummer sums it up: - *What have I done? What have I done?* -

Saturday
Seb

'It is something I've eaten,' gasps Shaun, in between the awful retching noises he's been making. Scrunched pose over a black bin bag. The bin bag I had been using to separate out my dirty and clean clothes, to make Monday's big sort easier. They're strewn aside in haste. He's got strings of saliva and bile dribbling down his chin, resting bubbles of spit in his half week old stubble. He got back twenty minutes ago.

'Seb man, I am so sorry. I do understand you and I apologise,' he spoke slow and controlled, as if reading off a script generated by AI. His eyes damp with emotion and red with heaving. I hugged him, and said, 'You daft fucker man.' Not convinced, but not wanting bad blood for the last couple of days here. He then withdrew and proceeded to start hurling his guts up, firstly into the Sports Direct bag that had all the food in until recently, then upon realising it had anti-suffocation holes in the bottom, he switched to the bin bag. Not before he'd unintentionally decorated the felt fur of his inflatable bed with little teardrops of puke. Jasmine had helped hand him the bin bag, arm outstretched after upturning and pulling out my dirty laundry, not so fresh boxer shorts, and bad smelling trainer socks landing on the floor in a shameful heap. She scrunched her nose and mouth in an attempt to avoid the stomach-churning stench. 'I can't deal with sick,' she gagged, as she turned herself away from the carnage.

'It's something I've eaten,' he repeats. Funny that, I don't recall seeing him eat anything all day. His pizza slices long gone cold in the box, as me and Jasmine sat slagging off colleagues and working practices, laughing at our own viciousness as the wine bladder became baggier and Bowie's Greatest Hits did its cycle again and again. - *All the young dudes, carry the news* – Kept on bottling mentioning the job news though.

'Get it all up, it'll make you feel better,' I state, sounding like my bloody parents again, cannot help myself. A phrase passed down generation after generation of pitying bystanders looking over a twitching gurgling person. A phrase, which to my knowledge, has little medical research either way. This here is not a rare sight, he's always been a sickly drinker, or more accurately an excessive drinker. But, even in his youth, he was one of those kids forever wiping snot bubbles onto sleeves and coughing great barks into the faces of those he shared a soft play with. The routine always follows like this: drink to excess, have a power half hour of violent sickness, a half hour respite, maybe even complete with an 'I'm not going to drink any more today,' speech, before finally relenting to his own dependence and indulging the rest of the day in just as intense fashion as he had done in the morning. His stomach emptied and ready for the next salvo. There have been few times to my knowledge where this playbook has not been followed to the letter.

Jasmine and I have stoked up a barbecue. Some tactical food during a lull in the line-up and a lull in energy. The lull lasting longer than we initially thought, we haven't seen any music since before the argument. Our camp chairs becoming more and more comfortable as time proceeds. Getting our money's worth out of them. Our food bag empty of everything except condiments. 'Much like my fridge,' Jasmine scoffed. And ten inches of pizza failing to keep us full for long, 'Much like my sex life,' she joked. We picked up some chilled, and very nearly out of date vegan burgers going cheap at the mini mart tent nearby, on the way back from the toilets. Them and some buns bought, along with a pack of Lucozade bottles, we're longing for some calories to replace the ones we've left amongst the blades of grass these last few days. Some energy reinforcements not to go amiss. Truth be told, it's been quite restful sitting slumped in the camp chair, sharing a moment of silent contemplation as the charcoals turned from jet black to silvery grey. Jasmine's eyes affixed on the mountain in the distance, the imposing beauty not lost on me either. Quite stunning actually. Makes me feel quite small when surrounded by terrifying nature like that. Went to Iceland with Mia for the weekend once and got scared by it all. The total vulnerability of being a bag of blood and bones, and nothing really much else. Totally at the mercy of nature to not crush, burn, or suffocate you. A couple of tents away, some lads are playing music on a tinny little portable speaker. I've barely got around to using ours much, relying on the community around us. Their tunes are hitting the spot, really matching up with what I need at this moment in time. The uplifting steel guitar pluck of a 90s garage anthem - *How you like my, how you like my style?* - I'm transported back to the six weeks holidays, hearing Radio 1 through the open window, as I kick a ball about on the lawn with Shaun, him in goal. Someone's cutting grass a few doors down, the drone growl of the mower, the trebly scream of the strimmer. Cream soda refreshments, with a Rocky biscuit bar chaser. Even young Shaun drank too much cream soda, knocking back a good chunk of a two litre bottle, then embarking on a sugar and E number fuelled rampage. Firing plastic M16 machine gun at crows, hurling stone grenades too close to next door's conservatory. The scary old woman neighbour eyeballing us through bifocals, cardigan and jumper combo, even though it's scorching. Hiding out in the branches of an apple tree. The smell of a lilac tree and the freshly cut lawn bewitching to a young brain. Hardwiring memories that have come to the surface today. I look at him now, same kid, just bigger and with a bit stubble, trying to present a harder demeanour. Hard to keep up when you're wiping your mouth of sick with the closest absorbent thing to hand. Unfortunately for him, it's one of my rotten trainer socks. At least it's not that crispy one of his I spotted before. I've seen plenty of single socks scattered around his rooms over the years. He sits up and stares into the middle distance, his eyes look lost as he tries to bring some function to his brain. He looks pale as fuck, enveloped by the greenness of the tent fabric. His skin impregnated with a sage hue.

'I think that's it,' he finally states, pausing for a pathetic belch. I look at my phone, pretty much thirty minutes since he came crashing back from his adventure, reaching for a receptacle. He looks as pale as he did on Wednesday.

Jasmine is arranging her burger in a bun she's halved by hand; it doesn't look too blackened. She grabs the sauce bottle and shakes. Mayo flicks big fat blobs onto the white baps. She leans forwards, 'Reminds me of an ex,' she says, stifling her laugh, before exploding into fits of giggles. She lifts the burger and takes a great bite out of it; her eyes again drawn and then settle on the vista beyond the site.

Shaun shuffles forward, replacing the lid of a Lucozade bottle that he's taken a sizeable gulp from. 'Any spare of these going like?' he says, gesturing towards the other burger. I pause. Then that parental caring instinct kicks in.

'Aye, go one,' I say, reluctantly, 'but eat it slowly.' I say again, shuddering at how much I remind myself of my parents, I might just stop talking. It's annoying me profusely.

'Champion, cheers man,' he says, before getting to work constructing his own burger, all while Jasmine chews slowly staring, trance like, ahead. He smirks, as he tries subtly to add his own mayo, failing with the little shakes, he gives the bottle three great slams. Big wrist actions, that which saw his sock get spoiled, I bet. Without breaking her stare, Jasmine swallows her mouthful, then utters, 'That remind you of any exes?'

He smirks, 'There's a few come to mind like,' grinning whilst looking at her, hoping for a reaction, eyes fixed on the back of her head, hoping for clues to a response. There is none. I must be missing something.

'There's a few slices of pizza left over for you inall, just over there,' I nod towards the box. A reply of a timid smile, as he remembers back to the argument. That's all behind us, for now. The music from the young lads to the left again churning out some greatness. Curtis Mayfield is yelping - *move on up* - an absolute unmistakable sound of summer sun to me. Late night beers and hope. Sitting up until the early hours of the next morning with Mia drinking by the little chiminea. Watching the orange and yellow flames lick up the wood, we had that previous day pulled from the building site, of whichever room we were renovating in our first home. Old gloss drips and screws blackening and burning. Fingers bound with plasters from all the knocks my knuckles had sustained. Still wearing the scruffy paint clad tracksuits from the graft, we'd fester by the fire. Revelling in the moment and the break from the work and dust. Building a home together, a life together, discussing plans, hypothesising about the future with enthusiasm, until the flames died down, only embers glowed, then we'd shuffle off to bed smelling of smoke and beer. The house got finished. We then filled it up with stuff. Trips to shops filled our Friday evenings, along with a TGI Friday's pizza, a trinket here, and a picture there. We eventually filled it up with kids. The trinkets were replaced with toys, and the pictures replaced by world maps and ABC posters. Now the plans we discuss consist of tip trips to remove all the cheap shite we filled it with, that and

the rusty chiminea, rotting away in the garden. It saw too many winters uncovered.
- *Rust never sleeps* -

'You know,' Shaun begins, as though about to say something profound, 'one thing I've witnessed in my many...' emphasis on the 'many', suggesting that this point, may not be as serious and deep as first thought, '...many years on earth, is the progressive thickening of eyebrows.' He pauses, allowing his audience to take in and absorb what's been said. No wonder that burke got a 2:2 if these are the pearls he's producing. 'I wonder whether it's a trend that will continue. Like, is it an evolutionary thing? Or more of a fashion thing, like flares?' I look down at him, mayo and bile on his chin, but colour has returned to his cheeks. He nods forward, gesturing for me to look. I turn and see three young lasses, maybe 18 or 19, all bikini top and jean shorts, hair in plaits, and fluorescent paint dots on face. A load of tit and teeth on show. As promised, they do indeed have quite pronounced eyebrows. A bit more Guess Who, as opposed to Vogue. Reminds me of the faces Emily draws. 'Mammy, Daddy, Me and Reubs,' she'd point out, all with massive black monobrows and sausage fingers. 'Awww lovely darling, which one am I?'

'It all started with that Cara-whatsername.' states Shaun, buoyed with calories, 'Same as Lady Gaga making it normal for lassies to wear leggings with nowt over them. Not complaining on either like. I'm a fan of a decent eyebrow, me. Think it makes a face interesting.' He takes another chunk out of his bun. Still, the same kid I played soldiers with in the garden, just as divvy. He continues, 'As long as they're not like that, marker pen brows owa there.'

Jasmine stays silent, wiping the remnants of the burger on a wet wipe, eyes still mesmerised by the mountain being enveloped by clouds on and off. The staggered blueness of the sky fading to white and greys. I wonder what he makes of her brows. Neither bushy nor thin.

'I'm sorry Seb,' Shaun whispers towards me, as the silent gap gets too much for him, his own eyebrows arched like a Labrador that got caught eating the post.

'I know man,' I reply, 'Let's just have a good time, yeah? After all, it's my birthday gift.'

'Ah, I heard about that,' Jasmine pipes up, with a chuckle slightly moving her head backwards. Shaun looks embarrassed, says nothing in return. Begins looking at the floor and looking away from us.

'We'll finish these ones and head in, yeah?' I say, guilty feelings of all the music we've missed this afternoon, think of the pound-per-artist ratio getting more expensive with each passing minute.

'Yeah, yeah,' he hesitates, 'I'll just get changed out of this gear and freshen up. Give me a minute.' He disappears into his pod once more.

Saturday
Shaun

Did I know he wasn't fucking 40 on his last birthday? Of fucking course I did. My constant throbbing anxiety, my impending doom feeling of being left behind by every-fucking-one, the driving reason for my Bafta award winning, 'Ah no, really? I thought you were older, sorry man.' Whilst incubating this stereotype tag that I'm bad with numbers. Alienation man. Always been there, even as a bairn. Probably second born problems, Mam and Dad not fawning over me as much as over a first born, been there and done that, isn't it? Not quite as exciting, another lump of crying flesh screaming at you whilst you try to sleep, you're not going to be as forgiving the second time round. Want attention lad? Go elsewhere, we're busy. Dad even prides himself in telling everyone how he got the snip straight after I came along. Those sorts of vibes jabbing into my subconscious all the time. Nah, alienation got a whole lot fucking worse when shit went down in that seafood market in Wuhan, or that lab around the corner. Whichever you believe. Different strokes, different folks. Come to think of it, it started even before that, maybe even when Mia said, 'I do,' to Seb under a floral arch in some fucking country manor, which cost about seven quid a pint. Followed a few months later by 'have you seen this house that's for sale?' A couple of bus rides for this little brother to contend with, aye not a bother. Typical sod's law though, that we live in 21st century Britain and profit rules, the first bus fails to turn up and the latter eventually ceased to exist due to: 'Realigning of our routes to suit changing customer demands'. Aye sound, no bother. Bastards were on separate operators inall, couldn't get a day pass because of that, the round trip used to cost an hour and a bit's wages.

Champion. Can't bike that far either, I'm not Lance Armstrong, organically or doped. So now, I'm reliant upon a lift there, if someone's passing or the charity of them calling in to see me on the way back from some National Trust picnic and fucking cake day out.

No. The alienation really hit home when Sara was legally and morally forbidden from seeing me. 23rd of March 2020. Bound by duty and humanity to her patients. Visibly shedding weight, sweat, and mental resilience as bruising arranged itself around her eye sockets, facemasks leaving their mark. All displayed in WhatsApp's shoddy definition on video calls when she could snatch a break and a cuppa. Those who she ran herself into the ground for dying, gasping their terminal breath through charcoal lungs whilst those cunts in power dillied, dallied, danced, and drank. Pub quizzes with laughter like carrion birds squawking into the night, as colleagues pushed one another up against oak panelled walls and French kissed under our noses. Cold sores and sweaty genital rashes shared, whilst we clapped on doorsteps and paced rooms looking for something, anything to do. Tigers in cages watching Tiger fucking King.

Six months or so, I saw the bags under her eyes grow dark, the veins in her eyes swollen red through the grainy resolution of Teams on an old iPad. Freezing from time to time, as we staccato spoke about our days. There was a great disbalance. Mine dominated by boredom and tedium. Hers of sheer exhaustion and tragedy, a hopelessness. Her days off were spent sleeping, we'd watch Netflix together in sync whilst our phones were on loudspeaker. Me in my shitty flat, her in her childhood bedroom. Pink paper with butterflies. We'd chat as Money Heist, or whatever shite we binged, played in the background. It was not uncommon for her to go silent, as the day's toil took its toll and her battle with her eyelids failed. Heavy breathing played down the speaker, loudening into a snore as the REM came quick. I'd hang up with a gentle 'Goodnight darling,' then a hesitant, 'I love you,' growing more painful to say with each solitary day that passed.

Sometimes, we'd share a few bottles of wine if she was off the next day. Quite beneficial at distance, as we could cater for our different tastes without need for compromise. Mine an Argentinian red, hers an Italian white. We'd chug down great beakers full whilst we laughed along to comedy shows, growing courage as we built up to the great finale. Masturbating on camera to one another once the wine had removed enough self-consciousness to allow. Practising the best angle before the call, so that my knob and bollocks didn't look like a butcher's bin to my darling girlfriend. Sometimes, when boredom forced, I'd shave myself on the day of a camwank, getting overzealous and making my chap look like a sad, plucked chicken complete with small lacerations from a blunted Gillette. She'd never say anything. We'd both do our thing over the internet to one another, her quiet in her speech so as to not notify her parents of her escapades. Gave me comfort knowing she turned her volume right down. Made me feel less self-conscious. We were desperately trying to stoke the fires of passion and were both desperately lonely. It wasn't even so much horniness, more a remedy to the total lack of human love that I craved. Once we'd both come, the post orgasm void normally filled with pillow talk and embracing, was replaced with a deafening awkwardness, maybe it was the within reach baby wipe pause, as I cleaned away the slime trails of shame and she'd wipe down the blue silicone phallus. Bought off her Amazon Wishlist as a distant birthday gift, along with some self-help books to get it up to £25. Free delivery and discreet packaging.

When restrictions eased and we could see each other again, things felt slightly fractious. We'd both changed. We'd lost the art of fluent conversation and social energy. Both respectively mentally fucked. Affection felt like a massive vulnerability, one more fearful than the virus itself. A hand on the hip at risk of rejection or repulsion. Netflix, wine, and eventual spoon sex became the routine of the relationship when we did see each other. Self-isolation cases and the onslaught of the daily grind getting in the way of each other. We messaged one another less and less, perhaps we had less to say, or rather not enough energy to keep it going for any length of time. Attention span centre of my brain turned to porridge with midday alcohol and American reality TV. Never a massive cannabis fan, I turned to it out of desperation, anything to numb the daily routine. Luckily, dealers around my end didn't adhere quite so strictly to the social distancing and essential travel rules. In my own world, it was pretty essential. Over time, the Netflix and wine inherited a larger share of the pie chart of our relationship. Razor burn on my balls was replaced with stubble, replaced with wire brush hair, and then cloth.

Sara's conflict, between looking after herself and looking after others, a total lost battle in regard to her health and appearance. Never a big girl she grew thinner and thinner with more pronounced collarbones and ribs each time I opened the flat door to her. The frequency of which was decreasing and decreasing. Nothing spoken, just a gradual slowing of whatever ride we'd been on. Maybe, on my part, it was my evident drink issues? The residual scent of weed in the corridor, as she clopped up the steps to my flat. Me doing my best to remove any evidence from the flat, scrubbing it, bleaching, and sanitising on a visit day so it was a sterile environment, to make her feel comfortable coming. Maybe it was my inability to fully sympathise with the horrors of her daily life. Mine a trivial nothingness, strung together with fridge trips, box sets, and wanks. Maybe, and likely, she found me boring, as I was only ever particularly passionate about music, and not even convincingly with that anymore. Eventually, the pubs were reopened. I had to start earning my own kebab, drug, and peeve money. I was deployed on an evening shift, to serve tables of six or fewer. Small plates of food accompanied pints, as I saw that the inability to socialise was not just individual to me. Huge swathes of the Friday night crowd now fiddled nervously with beer mats and chugged pints to hide their own social impotence. Forced laughter and repelling eye contact. It wasn't just unimaginable amounts of normal people who died in this time, the art of conversation went too. But me working all the time, chucked a big fat fucking bucket of shite on whatever embers were still glowing in mine and Sara's relationship. Honestly, since then we have been more like an occasional mate, a convenient other. Using one another for sex, usually on a pay weekend where one of us suggests a curry at my flat. We are a partner for those rare social occasions that exist nowadays, usually a baby gender reveal or someone from school getting married and having a social club reception. Both getting smashed out of our skulls, collectively mourning what could have been, what once was, and what never will be. Facebook still says we're in a relationship, and Dad still asks about her. The poor bastard pinning all his hopes of my redemption, all his hopes of having something to be proud of, on a woman who will inevitably disappear from my narrative once she builds up the energy and self-confidence. In all honesty, I think we're both too tired to have the conversation and call it a day. But it is. I don't even think last night was the final nail in the coffin, more like the first step in moving on from a tragedy of what could have been. God, I loved her.

    Fuck, that was a bit deep, the mushrooms from before still doing something to me. My burdened mind snaps back into the tent, the green glow of my little pit. Around my sleeping bag are more piss bottles than in an Amazon car park. Minging really. Anyway, numbers. Seb and his 40th birthday caper. Really narks me this stigma against my name. I'm not shit with numbers. Got a GCSE A in Maths, fucking statistics A-Level B grade. Great with stock take at work. Can manage to cadge a certain percentage of wastage for my own consumption, without a fraction of my colleagues noticing, whilst sub one level crouching in the cellar. Can minus the lost property bags of coke stuffed under chair cushions and add a few quid to my own back pocket by short-changing the very drunkest arseholes that come late on a Saturday night. Now watch me divide this remaining portion of coke and multiply my heart rate two-fold.

Saturday
Jasmine

'Anyone for a line?' Shaun appears from his tent pod in a fresh T-shirt and demonic eyes. Expression twisted and distorted. The face a battleground for many issues. A man unwell, and unlike anything that I saw last night.

'Go on, why the fuck not,' Seb slurs in agreement, without much thought, 'When in Rome.' Leaning towards his brother. Then turns to me, as if looking for permission. He's lost some of that assuredness. This isn't the first time he's looked at total odds with the Seb I know at work.

'Not for me, thank you,' I resist the new experience in favour of intoxicants I know. As experience has taught me, cocaine is only good for turning people into insufferable arrogant arseholes, who talk incessantly. Ellis used to dabble on a weekend. It doesn't appeal. I'm bad enough after a few Red Bulls. Once they've sniffed up lines from the back of Shaun's bank card and I've drained the last of my white wine, we're heading out again. The lads are walking with great strides, Columbian marches. I'm breathless trying to keep up as they trudge and bound into passers-by, looking rattled and refusing to say sorry. I feel like a Henry Hoover they're dragging behind them. My little black castor legs struggle to keep up, frustrated faces turn when I lag too far behind. Then, respite when we reach the arena entrance. Bouncers look fatigued from the repetitive nature of their role. Only so many frisks you can do with enthusiasm. Only so many times you can sniff water bottles to ensure it's not strong spirits. The lads are fidgeting in the line at Checkpoint Charlie. An even more apt name at this juncture. Wiping noses and shifting weight. Muttering under their breath. I feel isolated from their experience.

Shaun looks far from the person I kissed last night. He's lost that playful tenderness. I'm almost fearful of him now. He looks volatile. Like Ellis when his team lost.

In order to avoid the belligerent feeling of the day, I decide to immerse myself in the music. It's what we're here for after all. It's already gone 4pm and we've only seen a couple of bands in the morning before an extended break. A much needed one, though it was. We saddle up to The Main Stage after buying some drinks and stand on the downward slope, a good distance back from the stage. People are sitting on blankets beside us. I'd happily sit on the grass, but the lads look to be keen to keep standing. They seem happy embracing the new sense of energy and urgency their powder has given them. On stage, there is a band called Wildflower Soundwave. I recognise the name from my youth, though they were never a band I opted to listen to. A bit too uncool for a younger version of myself. There are a couple of acoustic guitars, a bass, keyboard, and drums. The people behind the instruments are unremarkable looking. Beige. I'd struggle to pick them out in a police line-up, but their songs are quite soothing. What you might call easy listening. Wholesome. Smooth FM friendly. The acoustic guitars convey a warming sound, like we're huddled in a cosy pub around an open fire, that pops and spits, sending fireflies up a boot black chimney. Orange fire and brown wood. Brass bar rail and bone white beer pumps. Ceramic tankards and sailing boat pictures. A pub of yesteryear. The drummer uses brushes on the skins of his drums, as though aware of a collective headache in the crowd. The singer's voice cotton soft tone, conveying songs about relationships that probably ceased to exist some quarter of a century ago. I wonder whether he still feels the pain, or whether time and his art has healed the wounds. Even the lighting on the stage is muted, a simple warm glow spotlight on each band member, a Next:Home lighting section feel. The organisers knew what they were doing booking this. It's like a collective hug. A parental knee to sit on for the unwell souls around. It's doing the trick for Seb and Shaun too, their fidgeting decreases. Maybe it's the drugs wearing off, but before long Shaun sits back on the grass leaning down onto his elbows, legs outstretched watching the chiming sunburst guitars strum out four chords of pleasant sounds, coupled up with simple choruses that the front rows sing along to like children do with nursery rhymes. It all feels very cleansing.

'Ahh, this is canny,' Seb plonks down beside his brother cross-legged. I think I hear Shaun whisper, 'I'm sorry man, I'll sort it.' To which Seb smiles, nods, and looks back to the stage. I get the feeling these two might need some time alone later, or perhaps I'm craving some respite myself. It's been quite the slog. Some time to sift through my own meandering thoughts and take in a change of scene from these two. I sit myself down cross-legged next to Seb and watch the rest of the set, letting the calming sounds wash over me and take me somewhere else.

'Thank you everyone, god bless,' the singer says, blowing kisses to the crowd as the band depart the stage. I watch the pull and compression as the crowd shifts and scatters from the slope, as they head off into the rest of their afternoon. The folk that remain take a collective shuffle forward into the vacant spaces. Like a human game of Tetris.

'Who's up next?' I ask towards Shaun. One of the few direct questions I've asked him today, despite sensing no real awkwardness on his part towards me. He readjusts his stance and pulls out the lanyard from his pocket. It's looking worn and tatty now, the punched hole now looking frayed.

'Let's see,' he flicks through the pages towards the purple page of Saturday, 'These were Wildflower Soundwave, aye?'

'Yeah.'

'Well, after them it says it's Lyrikal Lotus.'

'Never heard of them, it, her, he... they?' Seb says.

'Nah, me neither,' I agree, 'but, to be fair, I'm quite comfortable here.'

'Doesn't look like there's anyone special elsewhere. Should we just stick around for this?' Shaun asks mainly pointing towards me.

'I'm happy here.'

'Yeah, fine,' Seb agrees. So, we sit there watching the clouds float above us, and the people mingle before us.

*

Lyrikal Lotus came bounding on to a dread inducing white noise rasp over the PA and a police siren wailing. The sound of a window smashing and screen visuals of Molotov cocktails smashing onto pavements. As we deduced from our time sitting watching the stage being set between acts, she's a rapper. The crowd bulging and bursting, as if connected to a compressor, as the time got closer to her stage arrival. We're stood again, as the crowd goes far behind us, up the hill towards the food vendors, and is packed far closer together than before. A great roar as she enters the stage, sporting a horse whip, wearing knee length leather boots and leather corset, walking some collar and leashed bloke to centre stage, like a human dog. I feel for him, but find her stagecraft amazing, good on the lass. Her hair scraped back tight into a ponytail that flows down to the bottom of her back in a plait. Looks expertly done. Bet it takes a team of five a good chunk of time to get it like that.

'Motherfuckers make some fucking noise!' she bellows at the crowd, as the police sirens reach fever pitch and the cymbals of the drum set behind her crash like the Molotov cocktails. Clouds of smoke emerge from the crowd. It smells pungent. The crowd bellow back an octave lower than her. The contrast in performers is extraordinary. She launches into her opening track. Pacing the stage as she goes, microphone to her face and riding crop by her side. The man dog scurries off after a kick up the arse from her. I feel quite quickly this is the wrong kind of music for my mindset right now. The calmness split in a second with the arrival of this woman. As handsome and goddesslike as she is, I'm not ready for something quite so aggressive. I look towards Shaun and Seb, to gauge their reaction, only to be faced with Shaun passing a house key laid flat to Seb. They're back on the coke, almost oblivious to the world around them. It's time for me to go elsewhere.

'I'm going to go for a wander, this isn't really doing it for me,' I say.

'Want me to come with you?' Seb asks, with feigned concern, whilst wiping his nostril of the remains of coke.

'No no, you're fine. I just need a bit space.'

'Sure, you don't want some?' Shaun asks gesturing with his key.

'No, I'll catch you's soon. Enjoy,' and, with that, I'm uttering, 'Excuse me,' and 'Sorry,' in an alternate roll, as I bob and duck through the sweating bodies of the crowd. I'm faced with a spectrum of smells swinging between fresh from the shower block soap smell, all the way down to stale armpit. Reek of belch, cigarettes, and sickly-sweet drinks, as I aim towards the great tower that marks the way away from this claustrophobic nightmare. I keep my head low and keep marching on, waiting for the clear space of a green expanse, where I can breathe away from others. Finally, it arrives. I dance over several picnic blankets full of kids watching

YouTube and dummy past camping chairs on the periphery, then I'm out of the thick of it. The sound of Lyrikal Lotus clearer from afar. I can actually make out the lyrics from here. But I'm in no mood to listen to them. There are far too many 'Motherfuckers' to count. I seek solitude.

It's found in a wander around the woodlands. It shames me that it's taken me until Saturday to fully explore the furthest edges of the site. It's not even that big. I walk through the bark serpentines that ebb and flow around banks of bracken bursting with wild fruit bushes and thorns that sit at the foot of fat tree trunks. Take in great lungfuls of woody air and pollen. Waft away flying insects. The rough bark, the cracks, and the knots of snapped branches conceal tales the tree will never reveal. The ambient din of the site can still be heard from here, but the walk feels more like being on a country walk that backs on to a festival, rather than being inside one. The area is quiet, I can even hear birdsong high up in the jagged branches. A few people stroll leisurely through, similar souls seeking refuge for a moment. I look at one tree, it must be a few hundred years old. I look at its stance, its majesty. Tracing my eyes up its trunk until I spot wooden carvings of different birds of prey hanging from its branches. The carvings are beautiful. Crafted by someone who takes pride in their work. I envy those who can do that, rather than willing the clock to spin faster towards 5pm. Sitting in the toilet cubicle, seat down, extra-long to wind down time. Checking Facebook for the nineteenth time and see nothing has happened since the last compulsion to check. As I stroll further into the woodland area, I see all manners of sculptures and installations. There's a succession of mirrors on either side of the walkway, creating a sense of an infinite woodland with an infinite repetition of myself. A portal into parallel universes just like ours, getting smaller and smaller as they go. There's metal craft with rusted sculptures welded together placed in the middle of pathways, the bark path then splitting off either side around it to allow for closer inspection. Makes me think of the Notre Dame in Paris, the way the walkway goes. A modern incarnation of such a building. Seine splitting around it. In front of me, there's welded washing machine drums, corrugated sheets, shopping trolleys, tools, and car parts creating a great imposing beast that stands taller than any person or beast that would grace these woods normally. Industrial lights strung up inside it casting eerie shadows. A small speaker in its mouth plays ominous sounds, droning notes on a keyboard. A smoke machine giving off just a wisp of smoke. Enough to make it look alive, and angry. I stand and drink in its beastly appearance, letting the smoke drift into my nose and fill it with the bleach scent. Willing it to cleanse my insides, cleanse my mind. I wonder what they do with it once the festival is over.

'Quite a sight, isn't it?' A woman states who stands next to me, hands on hips looking at the metallic beast.

'It really is, quite beautiful actually,' I reply.

'The artist is from around here; all the installations are done by local artists.'

'Oh really? That's cool.'

'Yeah, I mean some of it stretches the meaning of the word "art" as far as I'm concerned, but it's good they support local. There is not much for young ones around here.' She's an older woman, looks well maintained in terms of health. She's wearing Patagonia fleece adorned with geometric shapes in natural colours. She looks as though she lives in these woods and lives off the land when the festival leaves town. Foraging for mushrooms and setting snares for squirrels. She could be anywhere between 50 and 70. The creases in her face like the lines in the tree bark that surround us. More weather beaten, than wrinkled from age. A face that has a story. 'It's going to turn soon love, hope you've got your waterproofs ready,' she adds, looking skyward to the ever-greying clouds that poke through the leafy canopy.

'I don't actually,' I grin, biting my bottom lip, thinking back to my rucksack in the tent which is ill equipped for anything other than ideal weather. There's no way I'm conceding to that awful poncho unless I absolutely have to. She just smiles back at me.

'Take care of yourself, love,' she beams. Then she sets about walking with her arms crossed behind her back around the sculpture and deeper into the woods. For a second, I think I feel a droplet of rain on my nose, but realise it's only a flying insect. A gust of wind breaks around the trees, and I hear the heavy bassline and hollering of Lyrikal Lotus come back into focus.

Saturday
Shaun

God, this lass likes swearing. Feels canny good shouting 'Motherfucker' at the top of my lungs. Feels like a release, like when you scream into a pillow. Something I'll probably end up doing on Monday night. When I can't get to sleep and can't shift the voices in my head and the ringing of regret. The coke has taken the edge off the comedown from before and settled the mental visions of the mushrooms. I feel like I'm close to what level feels like, if I remember right, despite having various substances at different stages of potency floating around my system. Some fucked up chemical ballroom dance is going on. The odd key here and there to fend off any lapse in focus and down-gear in energy. This lass providing the perfect musical accompaniment to let off some anger. Throwing violent punches into the sky shouting obscenities into the heads of the people in front. It's good to see the crowd looking like they're of a similar mindset. Thousands of poor fuckers nearing the finishing line of a big bastard marathon of drink, drugs, and social anxiety. It's fucking exhausting and relentless. All you can do is keep powering on through, or you'll get gobbled up and hockled right fucking out. Jasmine's gone for a wander, and I'm pleased to be honest. Feels canny intense spending the whole day with a lass you've shagged the night before. Not talking about the thing that is dominating the unspoken air between us. The big pink elephant in the room. And Seb seems totally unaware, which only adds to the weirdness between us. It'll take some serious amounts of drugs to approach the subject with her later, if she comes back at all. Wonder whether some more pills will help. Remember I've lost mine. Bastard. Back to the music. Not shy of a sample or two, it's full on. A brutal assault of noise and savage lyrics. She's fucking epic. I feel impotent just watching her. Can imagine she takes no shit from some gimpy pleb like me. Seb's looking like he's enjoying it inall, he's cadged a cigarette off someone nearby hungrily sucking it down. Dealing with his own chemical imbalance. Good to see there seems to be no bad blood after this morning's attack. He's chucked his arm over my shoulder a few times, a silent gesture of peace. It's not been mentioned since I've apologised. I wonder whether he'll apologise for how he spoke to me. I doubt it. But one can hope. Back to the music. There's a whip crack sound that shatters over the speakers, just as this Lotus lass strikes out her horse whip towards the crowd. It sounds just like the whip crack of my father's belt that time I came home from school just after 9am playing truant, forgetting that he was on nights. He emerged from his room primate like, all leathery and fuzzy hair. I didn't forget after that. Not one fucking bit. I feel the need of another key coming.

Saturday
Jasmine

The smell never changes in these places. Foist, moths, and death. I wonder what it is. Every charity shop I've ever visited has it. Like a plug-in air freshener for that line of business. It's a nightmare to wash the smell out of any garments you buy too. I've got a bomber jacket back home that's infected the rest of my wardrobe with its smell. Marinated in it. I'll never rid the wardrobe of it, no matter how many stitched lavender bags I hang on the rail. Death beats life, I guess.

The dull metallic squeak of clothes hangers getting shifted along as I indulge in some retail therapy in the Oxfam vintage stall. Forgetting I'm in the middle of a festival and casually browsing like I'm on Northumberland Street in town. I've gravitated to what I know best. When faced with time for myself I always end up in a shop. Thinking buying something new will somehow make me feel better, will solve all my issues. Like the good little consumer that I am. I crave something new. If the weather is going to change, I best layer up. There are all sorts of jackets, mainly military style cotton numbers with German flags on the sleeves. Khaki green is never a good colour on me. I always find it draining, makes my eyes look tired. There are big grandad coats with Greenwood's labels. A shop I haven't seen on the high-street for at least twenty years. My grandpa getting his best shirts from there, ironed to perfection by my nonna, ready for him to head to the social club for a few jars. Her just finished the washing up and plating up another meal for his return. He was buried in one of those shirts. Alongside his wife.

I scan through the jackets, flicking quickly, eyes darting down willing something to jump out to me. Then I see it. Check the label. Yes, as I suspected. Faux fur. Just as well, and it's in my size. I'm in luck. It's leopard print. Leopards are waterproof, right? Massive fluffy thing like those huge dogs people have. Big beasty collar. I pull it from the hanger and try it on. Feel the immediate warmth, the immediate feeling of being wrapped in a clothing hug. Better than any man can make me feel. Swing my head like a cat, looking for a mirror. The person on the till notices and gestures to my right with a nod. I smile and go to where she gestures to find a full-length mirror hanging on one of the stanchions. I stand in front of it. Pouting with confidence knowing no one else is around. As I suspected, I look fabulous. Leopard print totally unlike anything I've ever owned. I look more Parisian model than cheap hooker in my opinion. It could have gone either way. Now, for something to top it off. The headwear is over near the till. A plastic mesh box full of all sorts of hats. I rummage past the beanies and Russian flappy eared hats. Past the Peruvian woollen hats and trilbies, further down and lay my hand on a black fascinator. I pull it out. Looks like something one would wear at a wedding. Probably was. Wonder whether that marriage is still going. Classy hat to be worn at an angle, wide rimmed, a sort of dome with a black mesh detail that hangs over one eye and a crimson red bow on top. Head back over to the mirror and try it on. Readjusting until I'm satisfied it's at the correct angle. Yes, that's the ticket. I look epic. Me doing me. That's who I want to be. I'm as far from real life Jasmine as I can imagine, as I look at the person who stands in front of me. Not exactly the waterproof clothing I came in for, but there's no way I'm not leaving wearing this gear now, this will overwhelm the weather this. I head over to the till reluctantly taking it off so that lady on the till can scan the tag.

'You're going to look amazing in that,' she smiles, as the red light flashes on the scanner.

'I know,' I say, confidently.

'Would you like a bag?' she asks.

'No, thank you. I'm going to put it straight on.' I pay by card, again pleased to see the transaction is approved after that little cheeky delay that those machines like to tease with. Then walk out into the early evening with a new sense of confidence about me. Girl got swag.

Saturday
Shaun

Intense as fuck looking singer, face pulling these grotesque expressions like a bad drug trip. Like them lads and lasses on spice, who used to knock about near the Monument. Mental a human can look like that like, all Ivan Drago heavy limbs and twelfth round Rocky Balboa face. Skin mottled like rank corned beef. She jostles with the microphone, flicking her hair with the other hand. Sand in your teeth sort of voice, abrasive and punky as fuck. Mustard gas stage smoke rolls across the band and out into the front rows of the crowd at The Plantation Stage. It's a horizontal kind of performance. She's fully into it, bounding round the stage looping her helicopter arms around the bassist. He's a total contrast to her. Looks like he's on his holidays in some bright green Hawaiian shirt. Plucking out some naughty thumping bassline for her to hide her face with her hair to. Scraping out the words - *We're finished, fuck you and your show and tell* - His stance is that of a man devoid of any worry in the world. Proper grinning and white Turkey-teeth, boshing along to the words. I'm surprised to see that he's not wearing flip flops like. Instead of a bass guitar, he should be holding one of them big inflatable whales. Or scranning a snack, just finished queuing up for a hot dog at the all-inclusive pool bar. Wouldn't even be the most radge thing I've seen this weekend either. Nah this band, Roughshod, they're called. Proper magnetic. Can't not pay attention to what's happening on the stage. Can't even work out whether the singer is fit or not, but I find her well attractive. She's confident and unique. Emphasising the lyrics of self-loathing by hitting herself on the back of the head geet hard with the microphone. Sonic whumps mingle with the cymbals. - *I'm nothing, I'm nothing* - Raking her bleached hair and yanking it, pulling it hard at the grown-through dark roots. Eyeballing the crowd, face contoured like an armpit. Getting Harley Quinn vibes from her in her dressed in the dark mismatch outfit. Looks class like.

She glides over to the other side of the stage, to captivate the other side of the crowd, expressing all the polar emotions with a face that tells a tonne of stories. - *Who are we?* - She asks psychotically through gnashing jaw. Fuck knows pet. Honestly, fuck knows. She's backing up to the guitarist who has a proper shagger tash and little pot belly. Looks sweaty like a Spanish taxi driver. He's proper wanking his fretboard phallus. A gorgeous Rickenbacker 330 in walnut. Stunning thing. Cost a bomb them things like. He's proper making love to it, squeezing and thumbing out some seriously rolling thunder hooks and lightening solos. I'm no good at finger work like, more of a rhythm man. Wonder if Jasmine noticed. He's twitching and convulsing with his eyes closed as his Orange Crush amp bellows and cries. Manky come face, as he spunks all over the crowd with sound. Proper epic like. Another contrast with the lassie who stands beside him on backing vocals and maracas, wearing one of them twee vintage dresses that look so unfashionable and dated that they're cool again. Got dark noughties helmet hair like Noel Fielding and reminds me of Samantha Reed from back at school. Necked on with her in the empty kitchens at my school disco. Didn't get nowt. She's doing all that shoop woop sort of dance, with twister arms and hips sway. None of these band members match, yet it fucking works. It's class. Didn't expect this at all at the start like. Couldn't see past the key and the powder so far today.

I start feeling the dull ache in my lower back. Take a moment between songs to stretch and shift my weight about. Glance at the overprotective boyfriends shielding short arse girlfriends. Tot up badly faded tattoos on the people in front of me. Glance at the student flat dweller lot peppered in the crowd, stroking beards, and drinking down craft ales in little stubby cans. Take a look at my brother standing beside me, he's just messaged Mia a selfie of me and him captioned 'brotherly love.' Big stupid grins and reflective sunglasses to hide pisshole eyes. Big heavy arm around my back and the other outstretched, 'Say cheese.' Must admit, it makes me feel good that like. Message sent, he turns and looks at me, giving a proper warm Christmas morning smile.

'Good this, isn't it?'

'Aye really good,' I say. Feels like old times.

Bass drum thumps, demanding everyone's attention. 'We're Roughshod, and we're from New York. This is our last song, thank you FestiFell!' Makes sense they're New Yorkers like. They've got that swagger and look, that only bands from there can get away with without looking like wankers. Long stomping build-up of bass drum as Samantha Reed twirls and twists. Broaches catching in the spotlight and twinkling. Bassist still grinning like a simpleton, effortlessly plucks out some slap bass solo thing and the guitarist prepares for multiple orgasms again. Stroking his shagger tash then thrashing out some delay and reverb chords proper aggressively. E string snapping speed, it's frantic and furious. Singer squats low on her hunkers and points to the horizon. - *You, and me, we're no good you see?* - She rolls and whorls with an abrasive throat. Repeats. I can't help but think Jasmine needs to see this. The drums are twatted and kicked as I stand pure mesmerised by it all. Blue light from the stage hits the back of my eyes, proper bright. Going straight into my brain.

By the time the last note fades on the Orange Crush, and the band have left the stage, there's already a bottleneck shamble towards the other stages. A slow foot shuffle. There's a big rush for The Main Stage starting in half an hour, some shite poncey pop band that think they're edgy. Appeals to angsty adolescents. Fuck that. Nah, not for us. We're off elsewhere, buoyed and energised by what we've just seen. That gig right there though was exactly what I needed. Huge surprise like. Proper good. Was the sort of gig that makes you go straight home and pick up your guitar, thinking you could do it. Makes you reckon you could start a band and one day play Glastonbury, if only you knew others who played instruments and had any semblance of musical talent. Look back at my brother who has one clasped hand on my back, so as to not lose me in the crowd.

'Was amazing that.'

'Aye, it really was like.'

Saturday
Jasmine

I head back to the tent fully expecting the lads to be in their usual pose, discussing football and chinning cans and chatting shit. But I'm almost disappointed to see the camp just as we left it this afternoon. Bin bag in the same place and no sign of life. Grey looking and lifeless. A melancholic scene when there's no one there. Maybe I should have called them on this ancient relic phone. I stand in my new fur coat looking at three empty seats, unsure what tonight looks like and what to do next.

'Hi Jassy, oh my god, look at you!' I hear a familiar voice. I turn and see Aurora in the doorway of her tent rolling a cigarette. 'Jassy' is something Ellie Graham used to call me back at school, some condescending know-it-all who feigned friendship merely to make herself feel even more superior. In this case, I'll let Aurora bear the burden of desensitising the nickname and giving it new meaning. A hard job.

'Oh, hi there,' I say, 'How are you?'

'I'm great babe. Just heading out. Came back to reload,' she says tapping her tobacco tin.

'Cool, cool,' I say, not entirely sure what she means by reloading, presuming she's had a spliff.

'What you up to?'

'You know what? I'm not actually sure. I haven't thought that far ahead,' I dodge her eye contact, look up at my mountain, picture the scene up there, and imagine the silence and solitude. Bet this coat would keep me warm even up at the summit.

'You been up there before?' Aurora asks.

'No, no,' I say, laughing as if the notion is a ridiculous one, 'I'd like to though,' I add. I can feel her eyes resting on me, trying to work me out, 'It's really quite beautiful, all of it,' I say, gesturing towards the horizon and the ever-greying silhouettes of the hills and valleys that dominate the skyline.

'You should come with me. I'm off to The Rabbit Hole for a bit boogie. Fancy it?' she asks after a moment, whilst clicking her lighter several times until it catches and her roll up glows bright. She gestures the spliff towards me.

'You know what, yes. I'll come with you if you don't mind?' I take the spliff confidently and inhale a bit too much, stifle the cough, and feel the familiar rush of weed hit my bloodstream.

'Absolutely girl. Let's go.'

'Is anyone actually in that tent?' I ask, pointing towards her neighbour, noticing it hasn't shown any sign of life since I've been here.

'Oh, it's a sad story. I'll tell you about it when we're walking.'

We walk off towards the arena again. It feels good to be in female company. She's chatty as anything, telling me about the lads who were staying in that tent getting bullied off site by some bigger lads. Then she's telling me about the bands she's seen today and the people she's met. She's flirty with the blokes at Checkpoint Charlie who seem to recognise her. As we get through, she almost immediately produces a clear bottle that holds a black liquid inside. 'JD and Coke babe?'

'Great.'

'So, what is it you do for a job?' she asks as we walk side by side. I think for a moment, hesitate in my response. Think of the real ale bloke and his wisdom a few nights ago.

'You know what, it really doesn't matter, does it? I am who you see here,' I gleam in my new robes.

*

We're at The Rabbit Hole, it looks more colourful than previous times there. The crowd looks kookier.

'It's queer night tonight,' Aurora tells me, as we make our way through figures draped in colourful fabrics or shiny skinned and topless. Thems and theys, hes and shes, and all in between, basking in red searchlight and sound bath. We stop near someone who has red latex pants on and has nothing but duct tape covering their nipples. God, imagine the pain when they take that off. They dance with their arms in the air, breasts looking perky with their dance pose. They spot my gaze and smile, pursing lips into a kiss. I almost hear it. A silver suited man with bleached blonde hair wraps his arms around them and they bounce together to the sound of - *dripping and dropping and dropping and dripping* - For once, I feel dressed appropriately for my scenario. The tunes are blasting, and the lights are bathing the area in a kaleidoscope of colours. The rainbow hues emphasising the brightness of those under it. On the stage is a DJ clasping headphones to their ear, grinning at the scene before them. A one of togetherness and joy. Aurora is spirited, thrashing to the music, urging me to join in. I close my eyes and try to chase away the morsel of self-consciousness that is buried deep in my psyche, trying to channel the newfound confidence the fur jacket has given me. I open my eyes again and mirror Aurora's moves. Her confidence and enthusiasm is infectious. I find myself giggling and wrapped in glee, the weed and JD doing their thing. Drinking in the sights and the stimulation around me. There's a feeling of total expression around me. People free to be the people they really want to be, here in this moment. I look to the sky and see the matted cloud and blue and yellow shades of another day ending. I look to the ground and see the feet of those around me pounding the earth. Aurora's feet bare, twisting soles into the bark and grass underneath. Unaffected by the uneven ground. I then look at her. Assured and unique. Enthralling. We dance together, basking in the mutual love of the moment and the music, totally at the mercy of the DJ who lines up tune after tune that keeps us and those around us smiling and dancing as the blue and yellow above us turns black. We share the strong JD and Coke until the bottle is empty, then her hand is spared to put her arm around my waist. We dance close. It feels tense and exciting when she first does it. The drunkenness keeping me from recoiling. I'm unsure, but her feminine expression and gentle smile puts me at ease, and we share body heat to the sound of Bernard Sumner singing over Kylie Minogue's - *La la la, la la la la la - How does it feel, when your heart grows cold?* - Singing the lyrics back to one another, as does the rest of the crowd. Howling at the trees. We're putting off hangovers and comedowns for Monday. A Blue Monday, as the song forebodes.

'Fancy another drink babe?' Aurora asks, when a less exhilarating tune is played and figures head to the bar or the toilets. I feel conflicted. I could happily spend all night and the rest of the weekend with Aurora. She's like an enigmatic ghost who will drift in and out of my life for this one weekend only. Intrigue would like to see how far down the rabbit hole her company will lead me, but I also feel compelled to go and see what Seb and Shaun are doing.

'Go on, I'll have one more,' I find myself saying, as I sense her disappointment in me for not immediately replying with a yes. A pet lip expression, to show her faux sulk. 'I'll get them. What would you like?'

'Something strong babe. I'll meet you back here.'

I head to the bar, she heads to the toilet, and I find myself grinning at the strange situations I've found myself in. Whilst queuing up for drinks, I look at my own attire and then at those around me. Feeling proud that people can be individuals here. Free of judgement and ego. This is the world on a good day. Before long, the queue goes down and I'm served.

'Next please?'

'Two JD and Cokes please.'

'Single or double?'

'Make them double please,' I find myself saying. Let's see how far the rabbit hole goes.

I head back to where we've been dancing, Aurora is back already and she's chatting to someone in yellow vest and red shorts. Looking very Baywatch, he's even grappling a rubber ring.

'Jasmine babe, meet Sam!' she grapples me towards him.

'Oh my god, look how amazing you are!' he says whilst grabbing my fur jacket with his spare hand stroking down with the pile, 'So soft!' he says, 'Is it real leopard?'

'Hunted it myself, yes,' I joke, 'Was the last man to wrong me,' I continue, 'Luckily not, no.'

'Isn't she amazing?' Aurora's asking him.

'Mhmmm,' he nods, 'so pretty.' I find myself feeling good taking the compliments. Drink them in and store them up. From those two, a gay man and a woman complimenting me meaning more than any straight lad, I know they're genuine when they're saying it. Not trying to woo me into dropping my knickers.

'Thanks guys, you look good too Sam, nice rubber ring.' I find myself reciprocating.

'It's for my piles, they're giving me gyp today. Hazard of the profession, I suppose!' he states with grave face.

'Oh,' I'm taken aback, 'sorry to hear that.'

'I'm obviously joking! Jesus. Well, it's fancy-dress night tonight isn't it babe? Can't really tell in a place like this though, who is dressed up and who is just normally fabulous.' I nod and hand Aurora the JD.

'It's a strong one,' I say.

'Thanks, darling.'

'How do you know each other?' I ask.

'Just from here, we met on Wednesday night, didn't we girl? Aurora is an angel, she played with me when I lost my friends. We got up to all sorts of mischief, didn't we girl?' Aurora is nodding and grinning through her plastic cup, sipping down JD and coke. Moving her hips to the - *and it hurts with every heartbeat* -

'Are you guys together?' he asks.

'No, no. I don't think I'm Jasmine's type,' jibes Aurora to Sam who is looking well engrossed in the conversation.

'Such a shame, she's a catch,' he says towards me.

'I wouldn't say she's not my type,' I find myself protesting, immediately retreating behind a glug of JD. Jesus Christ, it's strong. There's a moment of silence and Sam pulls an excited face. His skin now green with the above lightshow. Eyebrows raised and mouth scrunched into a tight 'O'. Aurora takes another swig down, then breaks the silence with a, 'Let's dance guys.' We oblige and leave the conversation there, lingering in the ether as we move our bodies to the last barres of Robyn and the opening barres of Sunshine Anderson. - *Coming home late, it feels you've barely beat the sun, tapping my shoulder thinking you goin' to get you some. Smelling like some fragrance that I don't even wear* - I think of Ellis. I also think of Shaun, not sure why. Remembering back to what Aurora said the other day, 'Boys are bad news.' - *Heard it all before. All of your lies, all of your sweet talk* -

*

Sam has danced off into the night with another bloke, leaving me and Aurora empty cupped and in search of a change of scene, the feel-good energy has dissipated and been replaced with downright cheese with the changing of the DJs. - *Babe, I'm here again. I tell you I'm here again. Where have you been?* -

'I'll ring the lads and see where they are,' I say, digging deep into my fur jacket pocket in search of the unfamiliar device. Aurora nods, looking about. The phone requires a * and green button press combo to unlock it. Simpler times. Hard, when you're thick with JD and THC though. I dial the only number saved to the phone and duck by the side of a tree, at the entrance to The Rabbit Hole, to block the noise bleed from the arena. It rings several times. I'm worried he won't answer. As if he's going to hear that anywhere around here. But, on the fifth ring, I hear the sound of someone answering.

'Hello?' the voice sounds confused.

'Hi, Seb is Jas.'

'Ah Jas, I didn't recognise the number. You alright like?'

'Fine, yeah, where are you?'

'Just heading towards The Dance Tent with Shaun,' a pause, 'You coming?'

'Yeah, I'm with Aurora,' I turn to her and ask, 'You fancy The Dance Tent?'

'Sounds good.'

'Yeah, we'll meet you somewhere.'

'Erm, there's a big tree near the entrance. It's lit up green. Want to meet us under there?'

'Excellent yeah, we'll be five or ten minutes.'

'Sweet, see you then,' the phone line goes dead, and we set off to our next port of call. Aurora links arms with me, as we set off onto our next part of the evening.

Saturday

Seb

Jas has been on the phone, I forgot she had her little burner phone. Didn't know who on earth was calling me. For a second, I thought it might have been the recruiter with news. Fair play if he's working Saturday night, but alas it was not him. Makes me feel a bit knocked, thinking about it. The change and the fact I haven't told Jas yet, definitely gone on too long now, not telling her. Looks deceitful now. Another theory was it was a paramedic ringing me to tell me Mia and the bairns had been in an accident. The world being amazing, and then crashing down all in the space of a few rings of a telephone. Funny how the mind works. I'm pleased to hear from Jas, but it's been nice bonding one on one with Shaun. He's remorseful for the whole pill saga, so remorseful in fact he's gone and bought three more pills from some fella in the long drops. 'Cheaper than last night,' he said. What is it with him making friends whilst having a piss? I get his logic that he's replacing the ones he's lost, but it doesn't necessarily sort the issue of the missing death pills, but we've covered that, and there's no purpose in crying over spilt MDMA. We've since been to The Loop testing area. Never done that before, but seems like the reasonable thing to do considering what happened yesterday. Had a bigger queue today than I've seen all weekend. They were dead professional. Crumbled off a little of the off-white pill presented by Shaun and taken away for testing. They come back a couple of minutes later with the results. A little print out for us to take away.

'The test shows that the pill contains a high strength MDMA, but there are some traces of amphetamine in there too. About 10% of it in fact.'

'Oh, okay. That's speed, right?'

'Correct,' the tester replied, whilst handing over a little receipt print out which details the findings.

'Thank you very much for that,' said Shaun as he stood upright and left the tent, 'Keep up the good work. Honestly, thank you,' he parted with, as I followed him out.

Now we're stood under a green uplit tree, it's a glowing beacon in the darkness of the field. A great place to meet. Many a person is waiting here for someone. The air feels moist and colder than it's been all weekend. A wind is beginning to blow, and the leaves are rattling above us. A cheerleader's pom pom sound, announcing something about to happen.

'Sad about that lad, isn't it?' a bloke with shaven head starts.

'Aye, it is,' I agree, 'Really sad.' He looks shifty this bloke. I don't like the feeling he's giving off.

'No age that. No age.'

'No, it's not. So sad,' I continue. Hoping he meets the person he's waiting for, or picks up on my lack of desire to talk about it to him.

'In the end, I suppose none of it matters though,' he says, before launching into asking, 'You looking to buy anything then?' his eyes lingering on mine. I can't believe this bloke has used that as his opening pitch. His expression is blank. Waiting for my response.

'No, you're alright,' I almost laugh in disbelief at this bloke's front, shaking my head as I shuffle a few paces away from him.

'Have a good night, man,' he says, before working the other side of the tree, approaching a group of young lasses, 'Hey, girls.' I'm stood in astonishment whilst Shaun finishes his chat with some bloke nearby, the sky is getting much darker as night is in full swing and the clouds look full of anger, ready to erupt at any moment.

'He used to be in The Palmers him you know?' he says, as he swaggers back to me.

'Really?' I casually say, still reeling from the dealer.

'Who's your mate?' Shaun asks.

'Some bloke selling drugs.'

'Get any?'

'No.'

'Shame,' he says, then looks around and does a deep exhale as though nervous about something, hands in pockets like he's about to get bollocked.

'You alright?'

'Aye fine,' he says, evidently not.

'She's bringing Aurora,' I state. He pulls a face, then rolls his eyes, I blurt, 'What?' I am surprised at his reaction.

'Nowt, nowt,' he says, before turning away and looking at the flashing lights on top of the great tower over in the distance. I sense he doesn't like Aurora. Then again, I'm feeling a bit apprehensive about seeing her tonight. Not that anything happened last night. Still, a bit awkward though. Then, I feel the unmistakable feeling of a raindrop on my face. I put my palm flat and feel the specks begin to fall.

'It's raining,' I state.

'I know,' says Shaun, looking back at me. Scanning the faces of those who pass for Jasmine's and Aurora's.

'We still going to drop them pills?' I ask.

'I am, just a little bit speed, nowt to worry about,' he reads off the little Loop receipt again. Before I have time to think about it, I spot the figures of Jasmine and Aurora walking towards us arm in arm. Jas is wearing some big pimp jacket and some wedding hat. Looks like she's had quite the afternoon since leaving us. It's only been a few hours.

'Hi, lads,' she shouts as she approaches the tree. Sounding all buoyed and confident. Unlike her.

'Hello, guys!' follows Aurora full of gusto.

'Alreet?' says Shaun, hands still in pockets looking anxious to get moving.

'How you's doing?' I ask as they stop in front of us. They look close and giggly together.

'We're great,' Aurora answers for both of them. Like married couples do. Like me and Mia do. I don't want to know.

'Where are we headed?' asks Jas, looking at me and then Shaun, 'Dance Tent?'

'Aye,' nods Shaun.

'You got anything for a pick me up?' Aurora asks confidently, obviously briefed by Jas.

'Only got enough for us three I'm afraid. Some bloke is selling around there though,' Shaun seems more than a bit standoffish with Aurora.

'Don't be silly, we can split a pill, can't we?' Jasmine says turning to Aurora face on, 'You okay with that?'

'Yeah, babe that sounds good. If that's okay with you guys?'

'Aye,' Shaun replies, 'nee bother.' I can tell it is a bother. He emphasised the 'nee.' But it won't be once he's dropped. He sees this as his queue to dig out the pills and hand them around.

'They okay?' Aurora asks.

'Pure as the driven snow,' he gestures. I notice he neglects to mention the speed. I'm not in a position to speak out and show him up. As long as she doesn't die, I'll be okay. He gestures, 'here,' as he hands over a half empty can of warm lager for the girls to wash their half down, Jasmine biting the little pill into two with her incisor.

'Ugh doesn't taste nice,' she says, before swallowing down a mouthful and sticking her white tongue out in celebration. Then handing the other half and the beer to Aurora. 'I've missed you guys.' We simply smile back and concentrate on swallowing down our own pills. Myself first, then Shaun.

'Let's go and have a good time,' I say.

'I'm so excited guys,' Aurora is squeezing further into Jasmine as we head away from the tree and towards The Dance Tent. A thud thud thud getting louder as we approach. Shaun leading the way and the two girls behind. Me in the rear. Nervous belly, anticipation? Or wind? Lack of food? Who knows anymore?

*

It takes about half an hour to kick in. Just enough to start thinking we've been sold a dud. Despite knowing through testing, it's near enough pure. Long enough for me and Shaun to bounce into one another and me to shout over the music an, 'Are you feeling anything yet?'

'Not yet, you?' he shouts back. We look at the girls, thinking we're letting them down somehow by the drugs not working yet. A tetchy moment.

Then it comes. The upgrade to HD. The bleeding of colour and music. The heightening of senses. The rush of pleasure down my neck. The closing of the eyes and the deep breath in. The relaxing of my shoulders, the straightening of my spine, and the raise of the arms to the sky. The feeling of the music. Bass in my chest. The relief. The deep breath out.

'It hit you yet?' Shaun's in my ear. I sense him bouncing like Tigger now. He's feeling it too.

'Yes, fucking yes!' I'm laughing manically as he wraps his arms around me, and we rock side to side in time of the beat. His embrace doting. I forgive that knacker everything.

'I'm sorry I was a cunt before,' I shout to him.

He pulls back and puts his finger to his lips, 'shhhhh,' he's gesturing. Shaking his head side to side looking coy. He doesn't want to hear about that now. He's enjoying himself once more. He wants to be one with the music. He bounces over to Aurora and Jasmine, who look to be having similar sensations. Their eyes wider and their smiles easier. Everything is in soft focus now, the edges of everything blurred. Limbs entwine, I go to join and the four of us dance. Embracing the textures and sounds, bathe in the colour and lights and move instinctively. It feels good. We're all together and laughing freely. Aurora's looking incredible again, but then again, everyone looks incredible in here. Every face I see smiles back. To me, everyone feels as I feel right now. We throw all egos aside and revel in the tunes, hoping the feeling doesn't end. Tone plumbs the depths of my soul.

Aurora and Shaun head off to the toilet together, a positive step in building relations. I've pretended not to see Jasmine and Shaun kiss one another on the lips earlier, it's easier that way. Might have been mistaken anyway. A great advert for the benefits of ecstasy though. Bringing incompatible souls together under one roof. A roof that now sounds like the white noise of an old analogue TV that's not tuned in to anything. I guess it's raining pretty heavily outside. The clouds did as they threatened to do. I suppose it's long overdue. English summer never lasts too long. It'll benefit the lawn back home, if it reaches that far. I look at Jasmine and feel compelled to tell her the thing that's been bugging me all weekend.

'Jas,' I place one hand on her shoulder.

'Yeah?' she's shouting over the shimmering sounds, eyes rolling about the place.

'I'm going to be leaving MGM, you know.'
'What?'

'Looks likely I've got a new job. I'm going to be leaving,' I repeat in case she can't hear.

'That's great,' her face does not betray her words and she genuinely looks pleased for me. A pause. She turns and smiles once more, 'Congratulations.' Then, she pivots back to the DJ booth raising her fur clad arms in its direction. No more is said on the matter. I know it's a coward's way to tell her when chock full of feel good, but at least it's out there now. I feel a release. She turns back, 'Sorry, where are you going?'

'I'll tell you about it later. I just wanted you to know. Let's dance.' I throw my arms around her and squeeze her tight, knowing that after today we'll slowly drift apart, no matter how hard we try and how intent we are not to. - *I am alone* - Distant echo in the layers of sound.

Saturday
Jasmine

Pulse after pulse of cold steel sounds. Coagulated blood swirling down a plughole in the shower, hot steam fizz. Cleansing water twisting into a slurping tornado. A spin. Tones boomerang back from somewhere out in the stratosphere. High gain. A window rattles in a storm. Coiled snake wrapped and poised to strike. Technicolour smears like a squeegee on glass. Discordant klaxons. Robotic hum. Intense and otherworldly. Trampled grass, pestle and mortared into perfume. A jittering voice comes through the ether, a siren on a rock. A ship lost in fog. Wailing over an ocean that's settled after a storm. Waves lap onto concrete breaks far away. Geometric shapes at uncomfortable angles. Pink and yellow. Blue then red. A sweeping razorblade of light orbits horizontally up and down, veins visible in my unsighted eyes. Smoke and steam rise up from the gathering that manoeuvres and oscillates, inhaling and exhaling. Turning I's into us. A collective trance through our own doing, soaking in the music and the being. A celebration of just being here. Sounds we emit disappear above us into the ever expanding and ever cooling universe, to reside in the darkness where we will one day be encloaked. I feel no fear. A jittery, ghostlike voice plays, subduing all other sounds. Drawn-out arms raise into the air, as if possessed in some religious experience, giving ourselves to a higher being. I submit to the sounds, a far cry from the person I was some weeks ago. A person who would have happily watched every tree burn and every river boil. Embers of the earth dancing. - *You can't burn ash. You can't burn ash* - Here I am now showing the greater good to people I've never even met before, than those I squander precious hours and days with. Sweaty hugs and 'oi oi's' of sheer elation.

The only conclusion is that we are innately optimistic and progressively disappointed.

'This is amazing,' Aurora says to me, sounding suppressed and slow. Her mouth to my ear, I can feel it all over my skin, prickling and tingling down my spine, it mingles with the percussion.

'It's not real though,' I mutter back, 'None of this is real, is it?'

Saturday
Shaun

The tunes were immense, and then something shifted. Don't know if it was the undercurrent of speed that brought with it a sense of restlessness, or whether it was the upping of tempo with the changing of the DJ. But all four of us have decided to move on swiftly.

'There's a Bowieoke on at that Hut on the Hill,' Aurora suggests.

'Should know all the words with that van playing it all hours of the day,' I say.

'Fuck, I know right?' she says slapping my arm, 'Get a new CD guys!' She's a very touchy-feely girl. We are sheltering under the same green uplit tree we all met at before, whilst deciding what to do next. All closer now, after a few hours of dancing and dosage of serotonin. The rain is fat. There's a load of people sheltering under here now, waiting for it to stop or relent. I doubt very much it will like. Seb's talking to Jasmine about a job offer he's got. She looks overly interested in what he's saying, as if trying to mask another emotion. I recognise this because it's something I do myself all the time. Never mentioned a new job to me like.

'You going to be alright walking over there?' I ask Aurora, pointing at her bare feet, 'What's with that anyway?' I feel confident enough to ask.

'It's grounding. Don't know if you've guessed, but I'm a bit of a hippie. This makes me feel at one with nature and the earth.' she pauses, as if waiting for me to take the piss. I resist the urge, captivated by her allure, 'Some people think it's weird, but I've been doing it for a few years and have never looked back. It's got loads of health benefits too. It helps me with depression. I feel it switches off my mind, stops it swirling around quite so much.'

'Fuck, I should do that,' I reply.

'I always say people should try it before they knock it. I always get the looks and that, but I really find it helps me.'

'Even when it's pissing down like this?'

'Even then, more so even,' she chuckles, slapping my arm again, 'You should see the state of the towels in my tent.' I feel bad for writing this lass off. She's canny enough, actually.

'Bet you save a load of money on shoes like,' I jibe, 'Right, let's head there,' I say loud enough for the insurance folk to hear me, and then we dart off over the damp field, rain saturating clothes straight away with its ferocity. Proper twatting down. The girls scream as it drenches them. The hut feels further away than it looks. The speed I'm pelting feeling close to a world record pace. By the time we reach the doors, we're soaked, hair is dripping down faces. Jasmine's jacket looks heavy as fuck now. Like a dog that's jumped into a river. As I pull the doors of the old hunter's lodge, I'm blasted with a sweaty heat. We should dry off in no time in here. - *As the world falls down* - as we make our way through the crowd to the bar. No queue here, champion. Looks like they only sell Red Stripe, so I order four cans with ease. Too full of drugs to even look, never mind grumble at the price. I dish them out to my comrades and look around at the scattered people in the room. There's a fair decent amount of people in fancy dress. Apparently, it's tradition on a Saturday here for fancy dress, but either I've been too fucked to notice today, or people are generally dressed like lunatics anyway. The rain has a different tone on the roof here. More metallic and more immediate. Machine gun fire. This feels like our safe haven though. Our shelter from the mountain rains.

There's a never-ending playlist of Bowie songs playing, not a karaoke like described, but a mass sing-along, nevertheless. Could have just sat by our tent to hear all this like. No microphones anywhere, but I'm singing along confident of the words. Already a Bowie fan, I can hardly not know the words after being steeped in it for the last four days. - *I absolutely love you* - Jasmine and Seb are perched up against the wall, seeming deep in conversation again. I hear snippets about interviews and whatnot between songs. Fuck me, even on pills he finds time to jabber on about graft. Give it a rest man. Then again, he's a sound fella and he's on the whole been alright about pill-gate. I've found myself walking slower today, scanning the ground for any clear plastic packets. Fruitless I know, but it bugs the fuck out of me as to where on earth I've lost them.

A bloke stands next to me singing - *Rebel Rebel* - loud as fuck, he's got one of them scratchy voices like nails down a blackboard. Half his face is painted white, and the other half is black.

'What the fuck you come dressed as like?' I find myself asking, 'Apartheid?' falls out. A moment for it to land in this guy's brain. No idea where the fuck I got that from.

'You think that's funny? You think you're clever? Is racism a joke?'

'No no, just being silly,' I should leave it there, 'and it's not really racism, is it?'

'Yeah, too right you're being silly. Not a laughing matter that, is it?' But I can't take this fella seriously, this makeup is ridiculous. He's proper in my face. He looks too old for this caper. I'm concerned some of his makeup rubs onto me and my canny white T-shirt. - *You remind me of the babe* - plays and I find myself grinning uncontrollably at the sheer ridiculousness of the scene. This undercurrent of speed is definitely making me giddy.

'You still fucking laughing?' he is getting right in my grill now; I can smell the garlic on his breath. Pure rank. Others have noticed that this might kick off. I can't stop grinning. - *What kind of magic spell to use?* - The more I try, the more I find the whole thing funny. This just riles him up further. Poor bloke can't just leave me be.

'Here mate, back off and leave him alone, will you?' Seb's on his feet now and pushing this guy away from me. He's my own Alan Shearer shoving away Roy Keane. He barks, 'Just leave it, yeah?' he keeps repeating, as Bowie and his Goblins sing - *Dance magic dance* - The bloke takes one look back at me, shakes his head, then opts to leave the place altogether. Looks like he struggles with the wooden door. Fuck knows how like, because he looks in decent shape. Pulling when it's a push and making a right arse of it all. Flustered to fuck. Well, he's gone anyway. What a man my brother is. Saving his fuck up of a brother from a tanning off a skinhead ghoul, or whatever he was meant to be.

'What happened there?' asks Seb, as he comes back to me with a look of concern.

'Just drunk, isn't he?' I say, forgetting to mention the comedy genius on my part.

'You alright?' asks Aurora, Jasmine just looks on from afar.

'Aye I'm sound, just want to dance to some Bowie. Some people get so irate to Magic Dance like.' I brush off the situation. We share a couple of rounds of Red Stripe. The place feels like a sauna with all its wood panels and warmth. There's a warmth in how everyone is here, loving the alien, celebrating the music of one extraordinary man. The songs keep on coming and the quality never dips. The pills are wearing off big time, but the drink is keeping me just afloat, plus that 10% speed is keeping me jittery enough to maintain energy. But it's on a knife's edge.

'It might be time to call it a night for me,' I find myself saying after a few more hits. It must be getting late. Just as those words are spoken, I hear - *I, I would be king* - A song energising me like a key of coke does. I'm compelled to the dance floor centre, onto the black and muddied white linoleum chequerboard. To sing and move to the funeral song, that one day will see me bid farewell in physical form. Hoyed into a pizza oven to be cast away forever, as distant relatives and work colleagues head off to a wake where they'll raise toasts about the sort of person I was. Hopefully not soon like, but I wouldn't be surprised. Tonight, I'm joined by my brother and two companions as we scream, - *We can be heroes, just for one day* - Until our throats hurt and the lights are switched on. 'One more tune, one more tune.' Fails to come to anything and we're chucked out into the night. Darting through the wet dark alongside the other Bowie pilgrims, back through Checkpoint Charlie, and back to our tents. No sitting on the camp chairs tonight. Aurora darting into her tent with a frantic bid of goodnight. We make ourselves comfortable in our own little pods, pulling off wet clothes and shoving them to the bottom of our pods, getting changed into whatever is close to hand. The darkness disorientating as fuck. Lying on my back, I listen to the rain and wonder how on earth I'll ever sleep with this sound. To think some people listen to this on their phones to try and fall asleep. I hear a constant rummage from the other pods.

'You lot asleep yet?' I ask.

'Not a chance of that yet, I'm wired,' Seb groans.

'Same,' Jasmine chirps up. We sit for a moment; I ponder a subject to address.

'What you reckon the best way of smuggling drugs into a country is?' I ask, already ready and waiting with my own idea of bird migrations and little saddle bags. We chat shite for half an hour or so more until, one by one, the replies stop coming. As the rain sounds soothe each one of us to eventual fucked up sleep.

Jordan McMahon

Sunday

Leave No Trace

Sunday
Jasmine

There will be no coffee run today. There won't be any movement today. This isn't fun anymore. Head pounds, feels like a hundredweight on this bloody airbed, deflated beyond all shape. Heart's been going insane all night, liver scarring as each moment passes. Crystals form in kidneys. Slept awful. Poisonous dreams and intrusive thoughts. The rain providing a constant cacophony. Impending doom. The temperature has dropped. I shiver. I need a wee, but there's no chance of that happening anytime soon. If only I could sleep away the pain, the thoughts, the day. But I know that won't happen. Is this what it's amounting to now? A cycle of unwellness kept at bay with poisons. At what point does this turn into a dependency? I don't want to find out. As of tomorrow, this will all be just a distant memory. A line in the sand for how I treat my body. I really need to do something different with my life. This is not a sustainable course. This isn't me. Then, I remember, the memory emerging like an old photograph developed in solution in a dark room, Seb is off to pastures new. Leaving me behind. Haven't dealt with that news yet, it would be wrong to digest it now too. My mind too biased towards darkness. That's another task for tomorrow or beyond. That in-tray is getting bigger.

It's quite literally a day for The Red Eyes, mine feel bulging and raw. I crave caffeine. Now that's a dependency. A socially acceptable one. My body rewired to not fully operate until it's had its dosage. Roll onto my side. The rocks and coldness of the earth can be felt through the airbed. Reach my hand into the communal area. Stretching. Cramp inducing into the drinks bag consolidated by Seb yesterday. Feel about for a smaller can. There. A Red Bull. Awful stuff, but desperate times. Drink it down. Jump start the engine.

I need to rethink my life. Not today, but I need options. I can't be stuck in this life forever. Maybe a drastic change is needed. Use that Italian heritage and relocate. No, these are fantastical thoughts. It's the drinker's regret. What would I do in Italy anyway? Duolingo did little to remind me of the phrases Mamma desperately tried to instil in me as a kid. 'I don't want to speak that silly language,' a higher pitched voice of mine said, bashing my head into her buttocks in frustration. She smelt of soap and orange blossom. No, can't imagine they need many English speakers over there. But if they did? I can see myself in colourful frocks walking on the polished cobbles of a little sun-bleached hamlet collecting bread and fruits. Stopping off at the central piazza and drinking down a strong bitter coffee from a small thick ceramic cup. Watching my future husband from afar. He just doesn't know it yet. He's planing down a door propped upon two blocks. Brushes his broad hand over it and satisfied, switches to paper. Sanding it down. The treble static whisper the only sound besides the tink of coffee cups, stirring in lumps of sugar, and the colourful birds looking for mates in the trees that burst through the uneven pavement. He's restoring something aged and battered, back to its former glory, he wipes away a misting of sweat on his forearm and looks up, catching my eye and smiling before getting back to work. Making his living working with wood, I'll picture myself as one of his restoration projects. A jewel he's yet to unearth. Over months and years, the close-knit community will accept me, and I'll marry that man after a chance encounter at a wine festival. Flags and the aged folk littering the streets. Songs and merriment. A joyous dance where we bump into one another, his English better than my Italian. It all started with a coffee. Bugger it, I will go for a coffee. Change comes from action. If I'm ever going to do things like mountains, I've got to do steps. Cast the can of sickly bull spunk to one side. Pull on clothes from the bag, they're either cold or damp. Fingers are too cold to know the difference. Make one fast movement to vacate the tent. A scale of greyness faces me. Can barely see ahead. Sunday.

Sunday
Shaun

Sunshine underground. That's it. Spin cycle. Brain won't make simple connections. Synapses fucked. Wires fried. Breathe. Am I too hot or too cold? Could be both. Fuck knows. Is that sweat on me or rain? Hunched. Sitting arsehole to the ground in the middle of a fucked airbed. Was fucked days ago. Too pissed to care. Too fucked to do anything about it anyway. Especially now. Would I feel better prone? Probably die face down. Wouldn't be the worst outcome. Sweet release. Play this song at the funeral. Just after 'Heroes'. I guess it's not a song if it doesn't have lyrics. What do you call it? Track? Tune? Who cares, I'd be dead. Wonder if Jasmine would come, and cry? Don't flatter yourself. Heart. Too fast? Nah, too slow if anything. Bass drumbeat. Yeah, Sunshine Underground. Chemical Brothers, apt name. How long has he been gone? Where is she? Still asleep? Sure, I saw her before, or at least the shape of her. Can't trust this memory of mine though, what's left of brain function rendered unreliable. Shit man.

Sunshine Underground. Did I put this album on? Why? Some fucked up sadist shit if so like. Maybe it's been playing all night on repeat. Wouldn't be impressed if I were our neighbour if that's the case. Handed the baton from Bowie maybe. Nah, I'm too fucked to change it, I'm too hunched on this fuckwit airbed anyway. Sunday knees stand no chance standing up at that angle. Look at my palms, pale. Don't look like my hands. Fingernails dirty. 'You could grow potatoes in those', I imagine my father telling me. Proper dad craic that. Breathe. Traffic jam in my nervous system, struggling to send one thought to another part of my body. Every cell aching.

Sundays, never liked Sundays. Why? Reason evades me now. Did someone die on a Sunday? Might be that.

Sunshine underground. What's that instrument? Must remember to google it when I get back. God my eyes are fuzzy, like a badly tuned analogue TV. Focus! - *Run away* - Is that a lyric? Ah, so it is a song. Sorts that problem out. - *Run away* - Wish I could mate, no chance of that from this fucked lump of matter. - *Run away* - Is it a sign? Did them two run away? Couldn't blame them like, state of this place, looks like an atrocity has occurred. Are they coming back? Is he? Is she?

Tent zip. Is it ours? Aching eyes scan towards the door. Great effort. No. Hunched still, breathe. Where's the water? Too much fucking effort. Tempo begins increasing. Breathe. Drums, or rain. Maybe my heartbeat in my ears. Maybe all three. Bells? I lean forward, bile sloshed forward with me. Reach slowly, fingers spider walk across the floor instinctively towards a can. Any can. An unlucky lotto. Got one. Finger the ring-pull, fingernails soft with moisture and malnourishment. - *Tssst* - That oh so familiar sound to me. As comforting as a lullaby. As terrifying as a church bell. Drum. Can didn't fizz. Cider most likely. Bells. Machine gun? Breathe, breathe, sip. War? Sweet, flavour duller than previous. Tongue feels thick with gunk. Hairy. Stomach burns as I stifle a wretch. Breathe and wait. The bridge. Song calms. Sip, shudder. Is that my pulse? Drums? All? Need to change this music, it's fucking with me. Can't. Sip. Burn. Think. Can't. Move. Sip. Ache. Blur.

Breathe.

Breathe.

Stifle a burp.

Burn. Drums start to build in intensity. It gets louder. Impending doom. Deafening in the great bony cave of my skull. Rain. Breathe. Breathe. Song calms. Breathe. Deeper. Song calms further. Calmer. Breathe. Sip, a larger mouthful. Calmer. Then, silence. Silence falls on the speaker. Metro train pulse in my ears and rain the soundtrack for the three seconds relief. Over. Next song begins. A female voice. Jasmine? No, maybe Mam? No. Breathe. Drink. Tension in my shoulders, my neck. Be aware Shaun, relax it, man. Breathe and drink. You're going to get through this. Your faculties will return, sometime.

Tap, tap, tap.

Is he coming back? I look again at my palms; they look different from what I remember. An older version of me. Use the thumbnail on my free hand to scratch off mud from my pants. Anything to kick myself into gear again. Sip, gulp, two glugs. Burn. This voice man, like pure fucking silk. An old Gaviscon advert. Could murder some Gaviscon now. Moss in a forest, flowing water. Drink. The pain man, just fuck off, I need this. Was I stabbed? Bayonet skewered in the trench is my bet. Voice, I hear voices. Please be them. I think it's someone else, lingering about. Probably talking about me. Might be the police, or the security. Someone complained no doubt, about the noise. About the drugs. Imagine the German Shepherd pulling no punches. Me a mere snack, probably start at the bollocks and work its way north. Take away the pain.

Drums. Lasers. Fuck. Drink, glug. Stifle. Got Glint? Eyes fuzzy, like looking through the steamed-up winter windows of a drive time bus from town. Crowded and flustered. Phone screen condensed. Time? Must be early. Screen dull. Too dull to read. Focus man. You fucking idiot. Focus. What was that voice? Psychedelic robot. Part of the song. Skin on my hands looks yellow, jaundiced. Wouldn't blame my liver packing in, I would give up on me too. Everyone else has.

Breathe.

Metallic taste followed by sweet taste. Burn. Can feeling lighter. Maybe it's my strength returning. Popeye spinach. Was never a fan of him mind. Stupid balloon armed cunt. More Seb's scene.

Knocking knees together, movement is good. Thoughts begin to cross my mind. Stand up, get the blood moving Shaun. No fucking chance mate. You know me. Aye, you're right there. - *Hey boy, hey girl, hey girl, hey boy* - Always mixed that one up. Winded Seb up no end. That and a thousand other things. Wonder where he is. Ran away maybe, back to the home comforts of Mia. And Jasmine? Maybe she's still asleep, best let her stay asleep. Or perhaps she's lying there, quietly watching this pathetic excuse of a man trying to rouse himself, too polite to intervene, or even scared. Regretting ever letting me get near her. Pitying me. Using me as a life lesson, a junction in her life.

The speaker is too far away, across the ravine in the bear's lair. A rickety set of ladders across a raging torrent of white water and jagged rocks. Still hunched, I breathe deeply. Why the fuck did I put this on? Maybe I'm in purgatory, forever in this state, juxtaposed to the surroundings I find myself in. Anxiety inducing. Riddled with fear. Drink Shaun, drink your medicine. A little more and you'll be able to reach that speaker. The source of this mindset. Drink your apple a day. What day is it? Sunday? Ah fuck. Just a little more until you can reach that speaker.

Breathe.

Leave No Trace

Sunday
Seb

This site is now starting to feel like what I imagine a prison yard to feel like. The watchtower, the fence, the grey, and the expanse of nothingness beyond it keeping me from my family, my home, and my kids. People walk around in quick circles avoiding the gaze of one another. Hands in pockets. It is Sunday. Normally a National Trust wander and a Sunday roast sort of day. Thick gravy and giant Yorkshires. A family day of tuna sandwich picnics under the shadows of a lighthouse, watching container ships and ferries melt into the horizon, the kids dragging their feet on scree path, placated with expensive slabs of dry cake. 'The sea air will do you good,' and it usually does. Kids asleep by 9pm, Mia and me might retire to the remains of last night's cab sav and slow sensual sex. Coming, cuddling then brushing teeth, and doing a chapter of our books before bed. 'Love you, darling.' All done by 10.30pm if executed correctly. How I'd long to be home doing that tonight. Bed the most attractive proposition.

Woke up with a jolt this morning, an awful panic about changing jobs and whether it's the right thing. Whether it's the best for all of us. Whether I'm good enough and whether it's me. Then had my usual panic, wondering what even is me?

I've been to the long drops for my morning ritual, spending longer than needed just on gathering my own senses. I feel mentally and physically empty today. With a little luck that'll be the last time my arse sees that pit of hell. The smell never yielding. My nose never getting accustomed to it. I'm walking back to the tent now, rain running down the back of my neck. Legs working half speed, but far harder as each step creates a squelch vacuum that feels like the earth is trying to keep hold of me, drag me down. 'Don't leave me', it says. Threatening to steal my shoe as a memento. It can have them both on Monday, there's no way they're salvageable after all of this. But I know I'll try with a hose and a hard brush back home. Several spins in the washer-dryer. Might settle as garden shoes. My forehead is scrunching out the cold wetness. Makes the morning headache an all-rounder. Bodies clad in rippling ponchos and Mountain Warehouse jackets dip in and out of tents with haste. Weak voices ask each other where things are. Kids expressing hunger. Parents begging for a few more minutes of sleep. Floppy boxes of beer and full bin bags flung to the saturated ground to create more space in people's tents. I hear the nervous sound of people using camping stoves in doors. Shiver at the danger. Festival goers hunker down and wait for better weather. My weather app is saying it won't change until the early hours of tomorrow. Today will be a challenge.

Sunday
Shaun

Foist and fart smells in our polyester coffin and serious stomach burn. Proper peeve acid man. I can smell the vinegar in the back of my throat and nose. My faculties have somehow returned after their earlier departure, remedied with cider and chaser of a sickly energy drink and hellish measure of some white spirit. Furry tongue too abused to appreciate whether rum or vodka. I bet my breath honks like. Them two are back now, but I'm giving them plenty of space, so they don't smell my gob. Must remember to give them a courtesy brush before I get too close to anyone.

I'm sat like a Kappa logo (sans acquaintance) on the seriously deflated airbed. Damp socks and hoody creating a dam from the rain leak, or perhaps it's condensation. My body literally steaming and sweating out all of the poison, alcohol fume breath, and Class-A sweat trapped in this tomb of squalor and smell. Sausage roll crumbs from Wednesday pepper the groundsheet, stuck with moisture. Finger drum tap of the rain above hints at childhood memories of caravan holidays. Wet dog smell. Cold, wet, sad UK beach resorts that reeked of Sundays and yesteryear. Me and Seb swinging Day-Glo buckets and spades made in China, digging to China. Calor gas bottles hiss, sickly fish and chips that sat on your stomach. Much like the 100 plus alcohol units I reckon I've consumed so far. As if I'm wondering why my brain won't get out of 1st gear. The only reason I haven't stalled altogether is because of peeve though. Funny old world.

Them two look as fucked as I feel. All silently accepting the collective unspoken suffering with occasional 'humphs' and 'hurs', before leaning back, swallowing down warm lager, wincing, and returning to a blank stare. Shuffling and twitching. Breathing deeply and glancing anywhere, but into one another's bug eyes. Waiting, like Everest climbers in the death zone, tent billowing and bowing. Coughing and spluttering as clocks tick and cells die, waiting for that window to leave towards either death or glory. Tell you what, I'm on the fence as to which we'll achieve today like.

Feeling conscious of the silence in the tent, I fumble into my bag which is a total shitshow of detritus accumulated over the weekend; underwear I have no idea whether clean or dirty, a sunflower pin badge which I have no idea where it came from and the dead speaker, thank fuck it stopped eventually. Almost makes me think there could actually be some divine being watching over me when that thing stuttered then stopped. I bring out the lanyard, now beginning to decompose with edges returning to pulp due to moisture and wear. I flick through it, and despite studying repeatedly all weekend, I pour over it, intrigued. Avoiding the uncomfortable silence. Are they in a huff with me? Did I do something wrong? Did I say something bad? I've been in this drinking game long enough to know these are irrational thoughts. The questions every dedicated drinker asks more and more regularly the further down they plunge, a bad chemical imbalance. The weather matches my mood. Glum, grey, miserable, uncertain. End of the world sort of shit. I look at the lanyard again. Study the adverts, the sponsors, the organiser's introduction, headliner's testimonies. There's no one I'm arsed about seeing until 3pm today. Especially in this weather man, who wants to see some novelty tribute dickheads in daft clothing when you're piss wet through and in the awful grips of the fear.

'What's the time?' asks Jasmine, breaking the silence. I feel vulnerable, a crushing responsibility, fumbling like a knacker with zips to find some timepiece.

'Erm, almost 12 now,' I splutter. Taken aback at human interaction. Is she humouring me? Did she sense my uneasiness? Is it that obvious I'm crippled with paranoia and anxiety? We've been sat here for hours, no one wanting to venture out into the arena. Flip flop between hunger and nausea. 'Humphs' and 'hurs.'

'My word, I feel like shit! Never felt this bad for a long time,' she says, catching my eyes. Hers still bright and white despite the deep dark circles, there's a warmth in her smile. Her lips scroll into a semi-circle before collapsing into a teethy exhale. She mutters a 'Cheers gents, there's only one thing for it.' Her head flicks back, and with it, the remains of the warm lager can she's been clutching for what seems like an eternity empty. A faint gulp audible over the rain tap sound. As the can drains, so does a morsel of the uneasiness I feel. I force a laugh and proceed to do the same with my cup of sickly sticky medicine. Acid, acid, acid. Fuck me it burns as it goes down. I picture my poor oesophagus crimson red, a blistered and burnt mess. A problem for another day.

'Nah, bugger that for a laugh,' Seb is gurning, as he half arsed chucks his can down into the black bin bag that's laid flaccid in the middle of us all, containing five days of fuck knows what in there, but it reeks. Any self-respecting vermin would stay well clear if they had any hope of surviving this apocalypse like. Must remember to take that out en-route to brushing this horror show mouth of mine. That's if Captain Clean doesn't get there first. He's wearing that fucking mullet wig again. Then I realise it's probably been a godsend for keeping his mush warm last night. Fucking terrifying though. A hint of hallucination going on in my vision. Fuzzy eyes and paranoid shapes. Each in turn, we shuffle in a micro movement to indicate intention to move on soon. A trait I know both me and Seb inherited from our paternal grandfather. Images of him pocket jingling car keys on Christmas day, telling Betty to whip down the remains of her sherry and say her goodbyes. He'd had enough socialising for one year. 'Cheers for the socks and scarf.' Stuck in a drawer alongside last year's.

'Once more unto the breach,' utters Seb, somehow mustering enough energy to even sound passable as a lucid human being, and just that little bit pretentious. The rain in its infinite bastard-ness begins drumming even more intense upon our polyester coffin. I zip my rain jacket all the way up to my Adam's apple. Beard whiskers meet thumbnail. Jasmine's unpacking a poncho thing she's got in her bag, makes a plastic crinkle noise as she unfolds and whips it open. Looks defeated that she's got to resort to it. I'd be devoed too to be wearing that like. Horrible yellow condom looking thing.

'Howay then,' I encourage, more to myself than anyone else. And with that, we venture out to the chorus of zips on jackets and tents, welly boot squelch, and squeak and nylon rub. The wind whips and rattles Jasmine's poncho with each gust that blows. It's cold and really fucking wet.

Sunday
Seb

The air smells of frogspawn and pond lilies. A childhood garden or a city centre fountain, back when they were switched on and working. Geosmin is the word. I know that from a Guardian crossword a few months ago. We're walking three abreast. A sorry bargain basement version Reservoir Dogs. If you ordered a Tarantino film off Wish. If there's a Mr. Brown, that's me. There are people dismantling tents already, their weekend brought to an abrupt end by the weather. Hooded and miserably gathering tent poles and tying neon green guy ropes, as fingers ache in the cold. Snapping at one another for pulling too hard or not keeping hold properly. It's just gone afternoon, but we needed to get out of the tent. I could feel the anxiety and tetchiness. Could practically see it pooling on the groundsheet. We were entering the domain of the unwell. Out here we can breathe. Ankle deep in slop. Wellies and sturdy walking boots replace sandals and trainers today. Hoods replace straw hats and mullet wigs. Passers-by ripple with each movement, as pound shop ponchos catch wind and rain. Eyes fixed on their footing; energy sapped. Conversation depleted. Jasmine conceded to the festival gods and now adorned with the poncho she swore she'd not need.

'Anyone wanting any food?' I ask, as a courtesy more than anything. We've been on a major calorie deficit all weekend, no point changing that now. But a sense of responsibility is juttering back into me. I have zero intention of eating myself, but best to check on them two. My stomach is in no fit state for solids any time soon. I'm met with scrunched faces in hoods. That'll be a no. They remind me of the little monsters back home. It's cold today, the heating undoubtedly will have kicked in, and then there's the Sunday night baths. Goodbye money. British bloody summertime.

We walk past the bank of food vendors, now with aggressive scribbles through certain things on the menu. The spices smell stronger today, sharper with the clean air of the rain. The sizzle of the fryers and grills more aggressive. Angered snake hiss of steam. The music played is quieter, blurring into one merged track, more melancholic. Aware of the inevitable. The well-worn grass has now given way to mud, streaks of slip marks evident like kerplunk on the ground. They act as warnings, making examples of those who fell before us. The tower looks distant in front of the grey backdrop. Colour fades. To the right of us is the red and yellow shiny rain-soaked fabric of The Big Top tent.

'Should we head there?' I ask, directed towards the hunched hoodies.

'Aye,' shouts Shaun. No response from Jasmine, whose chin shivers violently poking out through the flap of her wrinkled poncho hood. Great veins of rain on Nylon streak down. She's still sticking with the shell toe Adidas trainers. Now largely brown puddings she's dragging about the fields. Come to think of it, I never saw her unpack any other footwear. The sickly stench of the nearby bars more visceral today. The rain changes the smells of the landscape. Like a drop of water in a whisky. Poisonous stench of acidic cider and yeasty beer.

As we approach The Big Top tent, we dive through the doorway waterfall that engulfs the threshold of the tent. A yelp from Jasmine as it skids off her saturated hood. We're in. A moist humidity. It looks steamy in here. But my vision isn't to be trusted. The place is pretty full, no doubt the attendance is aided by the weather. A band is already playing. Primary colour clad ripped jeaned musicians, gender unknown. Androgynous, their performance is acrobatic, sweaty, and energetic. Totally at odds with the three of us. Dyed haircuts with asymmetric angles and poker straight styling. Glitter and body paint. Guitars scream and feedback loops and shudders through the amp, squalls and undulating rumbles, dark baritone voice grumbles - *let us stay here forever, until the earth drags us down.* - The weather suits the apocalyptic sound, but the stage craft and sound are conflicting. The reverb and chugging bass mingle. The sound of the rain twatting the roof a constant.

'We're Ludo, are you there FestiFell?' the enthusiastic singer tries to inject some energy into a crowd, which responds back like a key stage one class of children. A discordant salute reply. Solidarity in a communal feeling.

'What do you want from the bar?' asks Shaun. But he's already halfway there with a hunched shuffle, 'The usual yeah?' he shouts back over the speakers, not waiting for a response. He's drawn to the backlit bottles and frost coated chrome pumps.

I turn to the stage and will the tempestuous sounds to blast the clots in my mind and body away, hoping it to sonically recharge me for one more day. By the time Shaun is back from the bar, there is a double vodka coke thrust in each of our hands. My eyes do not move from the stage, in some unblinking daze for the rest of the set. However, I am some passive observer, unable to recall if the band are any good or not. More trapped in my own meandering thoughts of home and my own awareness of my uneasiness. A bloke near me looks as though he wants to talk, looks like he's built up the confidence to reach out and speak, only for it to fall in on itself. Like one of them big waves you see at the beach. Looks like it's going to be enormous and spectacular only to collapse in on its own disappointment.

Leave No Trace

Sunday
Shaun

I'm safe in the Portaloo. Make sure the twist lock is secure. Safe from the rain, safe from everybody and everything. It stinks in here, but that's just normal. I stink too. Sit on the seat, don't give a fuck about the germs. I'm immune. Pull out my phone, barely looked at the thing all weekend. No point. No one has contacted me except EE with offers. I don't care. Fuck them all. Scroll with no purpose, fingers hovering in stasis. Look at the little recommended things that the phone learns about you. Fall into a clickbait hole, 25 things that the Simpsons predicted. I don't even watch The Simpsons. Haven't done in years. Doesn't stop me from reading intently. Could spend hours in here. Drowning out the noise of everything. Someone tries the door. They move on. My cold thumbs fidget in pockets to pull out the bag of coke. Much smaller now. Just a key will do. Just a key to level me right out. Can't be much left in there now. Enough to last. Hopefully. Then the sadness that I actually do have a reasonable chunk left. This is only going to end one way. I need a radical reshake on life. This is no good man. Need to get out of this hole. Ten years later and I'm still hiding in toilets. The blue walls glow. The smell of shit and bleach. Honk down a key to keep me from falling off this tightrope. Try not to die in here, it would be a fitting end though. From somewhere outside some fucker keeps singing - *this is the life, the life we love.* - Then whistling in that way that old cunts do.

Sunday
Jasmine

We've found a dry spot. Up near the woodland area between two of the smaller stages that we've yet to really explore. We've been here for a while, our spot too precious to lose. Sitting talking shit; how you'd kill someone and get away with it. Nice cheery topics for a wet Sunday. I've shocked myself at how much of a clinical killer I could be, if my plans worked. Shaun disappointing with his efforts. I thought he'd be a master killer, but shows I'm not a good judge. He'd definitely get caught with all the weapons he is planning to use. There's a huge sheet of tarp above us held taught by trees. Their broad leaves darkened with the drenching which they have been receiving. Shaking like a dog in the wind, dispersing the droplets onto those not lucky enough to be under the makeshift roof, but just outside. Every so often, a great pool accumulates on the top of the material, the sheet bowing lower and lower as if the fabric is going to rip and cover us all. Bowing and bulging until a great gush is released from one side. Wet slap sounds, a collective gasp, in case anyone is stood under it. A huge pile of woodchip tipped into the lake which it's creating. Smells of mouldy pine. A futile attempt by the organisers to stop the inevitable. Like rearranging deckchairs on the Titanic.

We've got a pile of a few of the remaining alcoholic drinks from the tent by our muddied feet. Shaun has been back to the tent for a 'livener' then come back laden with warm cans stowed upon his person. Apparently, the lads at Checkpoint Charlie have lost all sense of duty. Sick of the repetition and the rain, it seems to be a free for all now. He was grinning like a hyena as he pulled them from various hidey holes. Fair play to him, he used some inventiveness. 'Mission accomplished', he states, with a genuine look of pride on his face. First time I've seen him smile today, looking a little like the guy I met on Wednesday. Admittedly, I'm glad he's gone and got them as it's going to make today that little bit cheaper. The fear of logging on to my NatWest app tomorrow is one of real worry. Our conversations naturally gravitate towards the week ahead, to normality, as it's now firmly on the horizon.

'Shower,' and 'Bath!' barked all at once from all of us.

'Yeah, I'm looking forward to my own toilet.'

'Mhmmm,' I agree, picturing the bright white porcelain, the wooden seat, the orange blossom soap, and the fluffy towels.

'You know, it's daft, but I'm going to miss fresh air on my ring piece,' cackles Shaun.

'Go for a shit in the garden then,' I find myself scoffing back at him.

'Second floor flat I'm afraid. Neighbours would complain if I did it out the window into their yard.'

'Yes, that is a problem admittedly.'

'I won't miss hiking for five minutes just to go for a dump, or even just a wee,' Seb adds, 'especially in the middle of the night.'

'Yeah, it's refreshing mind,' Shaun proposes.

'How do you know? You've resorted to exclusively pissing into empty cans and dumping them outside the front door of the tent,' Seb's laughing. This time Shaun laughs along after a moment of it looking like it could go either way. Apparently in a good enough place to not take offence and fight back at Seb's jibe.

'Work smarter, not harder,' Shaun comes back with, 'Don't hate the player, hate the game,' smiling again with an expression of pride, 'I didn't know if you noticed.'

'You're not the most subtle,' Seb replies.

'I'm going to take some time away from the drink and that,' Shaun offers casually. Almost blasé. Seb raises his eyebrows. Takes a second and turns to him.

'Like actually? Or is this the Sunday regret?'

'Way aye actually,' he puffs out his chest defiantly, 'I can't keep on going like this. I'll wind up fucked. I've never felt as bad as I did this morning. Something needs to change, this isn't sustainable like, is it? I mean, I'm not stupid, I know I need to get my head out of my arse, have been for a while. Might start running or something, you know. Get on them herbal teas and that. Sort my body out before I hit the big 3 – 0.'

'Bloody hell,' Seb's fallen about laughing at the notion, whether it's the Shaun without drink or the Shaun the runner that's tipped him over I'm not sure, but after spending a few days with him I am inclined to think it's the former, 'You sure you are in fact turning 30?'

'Har har. Seriously though. I need to do something. I've gotten into a bit of a bad rut,' Shaun protests.

'Good for you man. Good for you,' Seb composes himself, 'Honestly good for you, I'm proud of you,' he nods and gives a loving smile to his brother, then continues, 'I'm going to spend some quality time with the family me, especially if I'm going to get a few weeks between jobs. Might book a last minute cheap one. See if there's anything going,' he's nodding with eyes closed, 'Might even find a hobby or something, something for me.' For a moment I'd forgotten about Seb leaving his job. But, rather than letting it sit there, I bat it away with my own ambitions for a post-festival future.

'I'm going to climb that,' my finger lifts like ET towards the break in the treeline.

'What? A tree? Like a monkey?'

'No, that,' sensing they're none the wiser, myself struggling to make out the grey face through the leaves, rain, and the chain link fence, I add, as I stand up and stretch on tiptoes. 'Bowman Crag. There. I want to climb that. Imagine it.'

'Really? Cool, cool. Wouldn't want to be up there on a day like today,' Shaun says.

'No, but I want to do something great like that. Be out in nature, use my body the way it's intended to, not just rot behind a desk or on a sofa. Imagine how good you'd feel on top of that,' I find myself speaking passionately about the prospect. I hope I keep that passion when it's held up to the cold light of day and sobriety. 'I want to climb mountains,' I conclude with. Picture myself spending a spectacular summer away from the shitty lonely flat which holds nothing but bad feeling. The room I've left behind is a combination of sadness and squalor. Any prospective burglars that may operate in the area will be put off by the fact it looks like it's already been done over and raided. I've never been one for tidiness. Not like Seb over there who is using a pocket handkerchief to rub the dirt from the lip of his next can. No, I'm not one for keeping things tidy, prefer a more occasional sort before the grave inevitability of everything descending into a shit heap once more. A heap I will be back in tomorrow.

'Not a fan of heights mind, but good for you Jasmine,' Shaun offers after a moment, looking both contemplative and melancholic.

'Time's it?' Seb asks. Funny, times never been mentioned so much as it has today, probably because it's slipping away.

'Nearly half three,' I say.

'Bollocks, we missed Farohk Hussein. He started at three.' A time when years ago I'd have finished doing the dishes with proper Fairy washing up liquid, put them neatly in the drying rack, and thrown the towel over my shoulder, like the body of a slain dragon. I'd retire to the sitting room for head scratches and a film with my nonna. Her stubbing out whatever was left of her cigarette when I pushed through her sliding doors. Stained mahogany and dimpled glass. The morning was spent helping my grandad at the allotment tying up cucumbers and tomatoes with little bits of twine. The smell so pungent on my little lime-stained fingers. By the time Mamma and Papa would come and pick me up, I'd be asleep on my nonna's lap. Gently woken with a paternal hand on my shoulder 'Jassy darling... we're back.' They smelt different, looked tired from the six-day weeks to make ends meet. My brother upstairs leafing through my grandad's old Beatles and Stones records in awe. The sound of a Clint Eastwood film coming from Grandad's room, gunshots, and snoring. Driven back home to a house in darkness, I'd do whatever homework was due. Maybe some reading and comprehension. I'd get my Sunday bath and bed off Mamma whilst the sound of Heartbeat could be heard from downstairs. Greengrass up to his old tricks. The water washing away the green stain and smell of tomatoes from under my fingernails. Nails clipped nice and short. Sponged hair. Mamma singing softly - *stella stellina, la notte s'avvicina.* - The smell of bleach in the toilet bowl, the same clinical smell from the hospital corridors when I said goodbye for the last time to my nonna a few Sundays down the line. 'You do you pet, make sure you look after yourself.' The last thing she always said to me, cracking and barely audible over the bleeps and pips of the machines that plunged into her purple bruised skin.

*

There was only so much doe eyeballing we could take under that tarp until the guilt became too much. Grumpy looking parents with grumpier looking starfish kids in all-in-one rainsuits and wellies, stood looking glum from behind the watery curtain, waiting for some respite from the downpour.

'Here, have our seats,' Shaun had offered, 'Howay you two,' he said, ushering us out into the rain. The parents saying 'Thank you, thank you, isn't the man kind? What a good man,' to their kids who shuffled a few paces into the dry. Perching on tree stump seats warmed by our bums.

'Should we just go back to the tent for a bit?' he's rhetorically asking, knowing fine well that's where we are going. Neither me nor Seb showing any enthusiasm to the prospect of spending any more time outdoors than absolutely necessary.

We get back to the tent and its familiar stench, now with soggy mud undertones to add to its bouquet. I spot Aurora in the doorway of her tent, smoking roll ups. She's looking betrayed by the weather. Rainfall washing the filth from the soles of her feet. I sit in the doorway of ours.

'Alright?'

'Sound babes, you?'

'Yeah, wet.'

'Not ideal, is it? I'm heading out soon. You fancy coming to see some Scandi-Punk?' I think for a second, think another dose of spontaneity might just do the trick for me. I sense a collective refusal from the lads as they retire deeper into the tent.

'Actually, you're alright thanks. I'll sit this one out. Going to chill a bit, then head out later.'

'Cool babes. Catch you around,' she says, as she sucks another mouthful of her cigarette before making evasive action, readying herself for the dart to wherever the band she is going to see is playing. 'Might see you later,' she parts with and heads out into the rain.

Sunday
Seb

The mood has plunged darker, and desperation fills the tent. Outside is a washout, desolation. The weather reflects the despair felt inside. That impending doom feeling of school the next day, shutters coming down at 5pm for shops and dark nights approaching, that football result where the ref has robbed you of a result, a hangover you can't shift. Laundry needs doing, kid's uniforms need ironing, packed lunches preparing. - *Everything is silent and grey* - as Morrissey once said. That Sunday fug. Scraping plates and scraping your own mind, wondering who on earth you are anymore.

I can see my breath as I exhale. Water has saturated my back, creeping down my drenched hood. Shaun is possessed. He's in the last five minutes of a TV cookery challenge mode. He's chopping out lines of coke on my National Trust card. He's borrowed it after glancing at it lying out to dry along with a chunk of the contents of my wallet. Photos of Mia and the kids, a whole host of various loyalty cards I have no use for really, now everything is loaded into my phone. He lumped for the card due to the image of a blue tit on the back. The childish glee on an impish face, repeatedly saying 'Tit' still provides entertainment.

'I'm going to snort coke off your tit,' he threatens, whilst eyes remain firmly on his chopping action. His tongue is pinched between his teeth in concentration, just like Dad does, when he's ironing or doing some DIY, not insufflating hard drugs. Little does he realise it's made of paper. Pulpy bits of recycled, biodegradable eco-friendly paper mixed with the petroleum impregnated powder. He honks up quite the line. Deep breath, head snaps back. Repeated sniffs to drag dregs from his nasal hairs deep into the dark recesses of his chemically saturated psyche.

Jasmine is lying on her back on what's left of the airbed. It resembles a seabed dwelling fish more than a sleeping aid. Her face is illuminated with my phone screen. She's borrowed it to browse the news pages. 'I need some reality,' she claimed, fringe stuck to forehead with rainwater. Her headphones are jacked into my phone, streaming Spotify. Ruining my algorithms, but I let it slide. The tinny tap of percussion audible over the battering polyester rain drumming all around. I hope the battery doesn't drain too quickly.

'Are you alright?' I ask Shaun, using my dad voice. One I've employed when conveying sincerity to the kids, encouraging conversations on emotions. Gentle parenting.

'Me?' He says upright, eyes full.

'Yeah, are you OK?' I repeat.

'I'm fucking bouncing.'

'That's not what I mean.'

'I'm sound man.'

'Sure?'

'Way aye, rights man,' he says, chewing open mouthed on a piece of chewing gum. Another of the procured items laid out to dry from the contents of my pockets. A toothpaste odour drifts across the tent, artificial, but a pleasant contrast to the smell of faecal matter, compost, damp cardboard, and stale alcohol.

'I mean generally?' I say, leaning towards him, keeping eye contact on the black dinner plates that occupy his face.

'How you mean like?' he leans back slightly.

'You know what I mean, like in life?'

'Fucking hell man!' he scoffs. Thinks and draws a deep nasal breath, flecks of cocaine remnants no doubt dragged down with it. 'Mhhmm,' he hums. He breaks my gaze, inspects the seams of the tent, a forced smile. A zealous forced grin follows. Enforced eye contact.

'I'm your brother, I...'

'I know man,' he interrupts, clearly agitated at my probing, but I feel like it is my duty to check up on him.

'...I love you; you know that, yeah?'

'Fucking hell man. I know.'

'So?'

'I'm fine,' he mouths with a pout, like when he'd fall over on the hard ground playing footy and pretended the blood from his shins was inconsequential. I tilt my head to the side mirroring his. His eyes lose their manic intensity, a flicker of moistening. Some human element returns to his expression. One I recognise. That of a younger, more vulnerable Shaun. One that I cradled on my bunk bed top when some kid nicked his bike when he was 9. One that sobbed into a pillow when Dad found out he'd bunked off school. One that I met off the train that Sunday we got the call about Mam. My brother. He sniffs, could be Class-A or emotion flooding his brain.

'Wey, like...' he begins hesitantly, 'Like if I'm honest.' He snaps back to see Jasmine engrossed in an article, headphones playing. She's paralysed with fatigue and a glimpse of home comforts, 'Ah, what does it matter.'

'Everything,' I say.

'Wey,' he continues, 'I'm a, erm. No, not really like. I'm a bit...' he pauses and looks at the drops scatter on the tent roof for a moment in contemplation, '... lost.'

'How do you mean?'

'Everything man,' another pause, an inhale between teeth, 'Relationships. Like, all my relationships feel like they're dying. I mean, ninety percent of the time, I feel a big fuck off void where human... human interaction should be, you know.'

I pause for a moment, grateful he's opening up, but preparing myself for the conversation I've stoked up, but am poorly prepared for.

'What about Sara?'

He laughs loudly and sarcastically. 'Went the way of the dinosaurs that mate,' he sucks through teeth again violently, 'Died long ago... Covid fucked that one up. Well, it's easier to blame something else, so we'll go with that.'

'I'm still here for you man.'

'Hmmm,' he pauses unconvinced, his eyes tracing everywhere but my eyes. Chewing violently. I feel a jolt of defensiveness and shock, but stifle it with all my strength.

'I really am,' I offer, his face contorts and contracts, 'What?' I enquire.

'I know you're like... "there", you're my brother. But, you have your own life, it would be... would be selfish of me to expect us to remain static, the young lads we once were.'

'I'm still the same person you know, just a bit greyer, couple of kids, a bit bigger around the gut...' His nasal exhale seems to laugh; his crescent smile looks uneasy. I continue, 'and a VW,' I finish with, hoping to make that crescent bigger.

'Ha aye, and yeah, I know. The kids are great man, they really are. I do love them. I should probably make more effort to be a good uncle y'know. And Mia, I know you think we don't get on, that I don't like her, but I really do man. She's sound. I don't mean to give her a hard time. I guess... I guess I'm just jealous, I suppose. Jealous of what you have. A proper life, all settled and secure.'

'Of what I have?' I'm genuinely taken aback, 'Mate... shit sleeps, school drop offs, swimming lessons, and constant snotty noses? Fucking fish fingers? No time to myself? No fucking idea of what to do with my time off because I don't even know what I am anymore?' I retort, aware I'm protesting too much, I soften with, '...and a heap load of costs.'

'I love fish fingers. Have them when I can't be arsed cooking. Two slices of white bread. Loads of sauce. Bosh!' Shaun sniffs.

'I envy your freedom, Shaun. You're still young enough to do something. Anything, you know. Can choose to do something mental and change your life like that,' and with the dramatic click of my fingers failing, due to the moisture in my skin, we both grin.

'Yeah,' he ponders, as the grin subsides, he nods. Razor blade still in his hand between thumb and forefinger. 'I guess it's just hard man, I really struggle sometimes. I'm approaching 30, just as fucking clueless as I was when I was 16, you know.'

'I get it. Trust me, I feel the same in a way,' I pause again, 'we all do, I'm here for you though.'

'Ditto man. I figure, I mean, like I guess why I like getting fucked up all the time,' he looks up in contemplation, face screws, 'do I like getting fucked up? I'm not sure. But the reason why I do it, is to sort of delay reality. Kicking the can down the road, avoiding emotional overload, and all of that. Been doing it since Mam passed.'

'Yeah.'

'I know it's bad, I know I do it too much. I like, hit it too hard and do stupid stuff, have big gaps in my memory the next day sometimes. It's just the easier option sometimes, you know.'

'Mhmm,' I nod.

'You're alright though?'

'As always,' I say, unsure whether I am or not.

'Wonder what Mam would think of us now getting coked up in a tent?'

'Speak for yourself, strictly the taxables for me today,' I say, lifting my can as an example, wiggling side to side.

'Not fancy one?' he offers, gesturing with my National Trust card. His face helpless, eyes now resemble that of a child. A sort of 'one more game' kind of expression he'd show when bedtime was approaching.

'Nah mate, driving tomorrow,' I shake my head, shuddering at the prospect.

'Fair enough,' he withdraws his offer, perching the card on his knee, eyeing up the goods again.

'She'd be fuming by the way,' I begin picking mud from my knees, 'Mam I mean, she'd be spitting feathers!'

'Aye,' he semi laughs looking down. Crouching over the card, razor blade dancing about the place. His voice then squeaks out a barely audible, 'I miss you, man.' A voice that sounds pained with fighting back emotion.

'You too man,' I reply, 'You too. We should make an effort to do stuff more.'

'Aye, like I was saying before, I think I need to make some changes like. I feel so lonely sometimes, it's pathetic.'

'It's not pathetic man.'

'Fucking is, supposed adult over here.'

'You could be in a room full of people and feel totally alone. Christ, I feel like that at home half the time.'

'Really?'

'God aye. It's quite easy to forget who the fuck you are when you're responsible for everyone else.'

'We're all fucked, aren't we?' Shaun declared, 'All fucked in our own little worlds.'

'That we are. That we are.'

'I love you though, I do... Thank you.'

'Right back at you,' I hold aloft my half drank warm can for a cheers, 'You're gonna be alright, you know.' We both clink dull aluminium clinks, then swig and look over at Jasmine oblivious, hiking sock twitching to the sounds of Spotify. Algorithms getting mashed on servers as every track passes. She's escaping the scene of this tent in news and heavy drumming. My eyes stay on her, with almost a paternal affection.

'What?' she notices my gaze. She smiles in protest as she unhooks her headphones. Shaun's head is crouched over the National Trust card, the temptation of the line was resisted for long enough as we conversed.

'Did I miss something?' Jasmine asks, as she sits upright, the gentlest of hisses from the forlorn airbed combines with the sniffing sound of my brother.

'Nah.'

Sunday
Jasmine

They look like they're having a moment. They need it. I need my own space and my own moment too. Fat rain has drenched me to my underwear. I can't muster the energy to change yet, probably nothing dry left in my feeble rucksack, a perpetual shiver is the easier option. Hair is cold against the back of my neck. Hate that feeling. I long for the warm air blast of a hairdryer, that smell of the burning element and cooked hair. The wrap of my dressing gown, perched on the end of my bed, mindless telly playing on the iPad. Cats purring on my knees, too precariously balanced and comfortable looking to shift my legs, as they start aching and going dead. A steaming cup of tea. Maybe even a Chinese meal on order. All that, I'll be doing in a day's time. I shuffle a bit on the sorry excuse of an airbed, my arse contacting the earth below it through three layers of plastic, and not a lot of air. Not quite the best grounding I've been doing this weekend, nor the most glamorous.

My phone hiatus has lasted until about fifteen minutes ago. I need to escape escapism. Need something normal. A dose of reality. A phone screen and some recorded music will do. Something that'll recalibrate my mind. I'm aware it's Sunday, but as for the rest, I'm a bit sketchy. What exactly has happened? This weekend has been battering. Emotional overload, need thirty minutes in a cocoon, in a womb. This plastic cave will have to do. My chrysalis rapping with the constant downpour. It's like radio static rain between songs, the stretched polyester caked in dancing droplets is like TV static. Diagonal streaks. My eyes cloudy with fatigue, elongated blinks provide microsleep, split second respites. A brain deprived of rest doing all it can to recover. Prepare for the final act.

My numb thumb swipes clumsily on the phone screen. The Guardian. Yes, I'll accept cookies. No, I don't want to pay for a subscription. Scrolling for something inspiring, past the disgraced TV presenter, his image disappears as quickly as it arrives through the top of the phone screen. A motorway tragedy child's parents speak out. Flick into the invisible ceiling. Past the wildfires, the rate rises and detained MP. An article on the chemistry of happiness, this is the one for me. Headphones are emitting The Red Eyes Spotify playlist, abrasive drums, and relentless guitar hooks. There's something brutally nostalgic about it. Similar to a band from my youth that I can't quite name, not just because my brain's struggling, but more likely because I consumed anything with a guitar back then and the choices are abundant. The sound takes me back to being a skinny jean clad, poker straight hair, and eyeliner curled teen. I used to mop anything like this up, jumping like a white wine fuelled pogo stick thinking I'd be spotted by the singer, or maybe the guitarist from the latest indie band and swept onto the tour bus for a whistle stop tour of Northern gig venues, complete with an acoustic song dedicated to me. I'd be a Geordie Kate Moss. Ah, the folly of youth.

The next track is one I vaguely recognise. I heard of them before, but neglected to properly research their back catalogue, something I intended to do when I booked tickets for FestiFell. One of the many things I've planned to do recently and failed to follow through with. Sending myself to the grave was one of the chunkier things on the list. I frantically added the line-up's top five played songs into a playlist. Origins of Sound and The Red Eyes tracks were the ones I skipped to, impatient to learn the other less familiar songs of the other bands and artists. I named it 'A FestiFell Playlist' so that the alphabetisation didn't mean it was lost amongst my already cluttered portfolio of attempted sound-tracking of my life. There will be some darkness in there, that's for sure. Luckily this is Seb's account, he seems to have his shit in order.

My clothes feel damp and foisty underneath the sleeping bag. I should really change, but the zip is too far from arm's reach to make my pod private. Nothing Shaun hasn't seen before, I suppose. Things are a little less fresh there right now though. I focus on the phone screen, floating specks in my vision, a cloudy aura. Eyes not used to reading up close, a moment of worry about blindness, then they're there, working. Battered. The herculean amounts of poison I've ingested over the last few days ripped through everything good in my body and turned it to shite. Funny enough, this happiness article makes no mention of alcohol, drugs, or loud music. Or sex. My mind has been flicking back to Friday night quite a bit today, fleetingly, snatches of the sounds and the sensations. No shame or anything like that, just surprised in myself, having casual sex in a festival was not the thing I envisaged when I was packing my rucksack on Wednesday night. Well, I guess I did pack a condom. But that's just good practice. No, sex wasn't on my mind when I eschewed the razorblade in the shower on Thursday morning, a timekeeping issue and a misguided confidence that my lady parts would be only for my own viewing. The best way to get over someone is to get on top of them, my pal Gina says often enough, her advice finally penetrated my subconscious mind. The Red Eyes song reaches crescendo, guttural guitars reach boiling point in an old stovetop kettle. Drums crash cymbal heavy and I'm back in the tent in the dead air between songs. The white noise static of the rain above and my own anxious arrival in a brotherly heart to heart. The word 'jealous' delivered, just as a kick drum of another of The Red Eyes song begins. The word gets my anxious mind wandering what they are talking about. Not for me to know. Not my battle. Then again, there's not really much privacy in a polyester tent. Not with the sheer number of ears around at any given time. Am I an intruder on their weekend? It dawns on me that I may have spoilt it for them. Ruined the dynamic. Fucked up the brother's weekend. Is the jealous person Seb for Shaun shagging me? Did he tell him? Does he look at me like that? Snap out of it Jasmine, these are negative thoughts, intrusive. As far as I can tell, the lads have had a good time. You've given them space. Was it too much space? Did it come across as ungrateful of their company? Stop it. It's just a chemical imbalance in your brain. The fear. You're being irrational. In that moment, Seb's phone shivers into life in my hand, the nuclear glow of the screen dimming up and a text box appears at the top of the screen overlaying my article on happiness. It's from Mia, I can't help but scan the text, aware of the gross betrayal of privacy: 'Hey babe. So looking forward to seeing you tomorrow. We all miss...' the preview cuts out the rest of the message, but the content can be predicted. Pangs of emotion hit me, but not before the surprise revelation that Seb is a 'babe', I always imagined Mia would be more of a 'darling' or 'honey' kind of woman, based on the few times I've chatted to her. Her intellect makes me wrongly think she's above a simple 'babe' in a text. The rush of the rest of the emotions follows quickly, killing off this trivial notion. Jealousy? That makes it a majority emotion in this tent, I suppose. Maybe that's just influenced by the word I overheard. I guess it is though, the prospect of being loved. I think of Ellis, how could he have been so broken, so cruel, so inhuman to think that was how to love someone? How could I have been so broken to think that was what it meant to be loved. Love starts with the self. Fuck him. I can see that now. I love myself. Or more, I can see a pathway to love myself. I see things in myself worth loving. I'll grab them with both hands and won't fucking let go. I owe that to myself. I'd sooner be alone than with someone who is wrong for me. Someone who doesn't love me for who I am, doesn't treat me with the respect I deserve. I glance sideways at Shaun, a question mark stance, back crooked down. He's not the one. Yes, he's a good lad, I've enjoyed his company. I really enjoyed his company on Friday, the sex will long lie in the memory of most psychedelic shag for quite some time, I reckon. Looking back, I might upgrade him to a £25k shag after all, but something changed almost immediately after his dick withdrew and the pill I'd taken stopped rushing quite so hard. The realisation that we had reached all we ever would at that moment, a moment in time that was too euphoric to not do it, but too unreal for it to mean anything. Since then, I've observed him, a constant compounding of my opinion; the problem with him is that he doesn't love himself, he's lost. He seems stuck on a self-destructive path that's gone beyond normal function. The reason I know this is because he is me, doing the same things I do, running away from it all. He needs to find his own way first, as I do mine. We'll always have this weekend, but that's the end. We'll drift away again leaving this weekend a mere memory. Come this time tomorrow, I'm focussing on me. I'll climb that fucking mountain and scream from the top. Me doing me.

I flick out of the happiness article, that's not helpful to me, some fashion fad of cold-water therapy and juice diets ain't going to cut it. Absolutely no way am I swimming in the shite that they pump into the waterways around here. I need to carve my own path, I'm the one who needs to figure it out. The synths ripple and pulse, bubbling auras of reds and yellows in the The Red Eyes tune. Click the screen back, one more dip into this alternate reality, put off this beautiful tomorrow one more day. Indulge in the escape. Dig deep and poison this beautiful soul of mine one last time. I feel eyes on me, roll over, hip bone hits the cold harshness of the soil through airbed.

'What?' I ask, as the gospel singers hit their high notes in the headphones.

'Let's fucking do this!'

'One last time unto the breach! Ready to hit up this bastard one last time?' grins Seb. They seem cheery. The air seems clearer.

Sunday
Shaun

'We go again,' coughs Seb, shoulders broad ready to face the final barrage of this Sunday evening. We're stood outside the tent in the grey, glistening with damp as Jasmine zips the door up whilst passing a can of lager to each of us. Top lass.

'One for the road,' a well uttered phrase of the trip. People are appearing from their little plastic rabbit holes all around the site, beady eyes of intoxication and fatigue. Sniffing wet air with scrunched noses, some with cocaine residue no doubt, smelling the rain is softening. We crack cans and retrace the usual route; the path is now obvious to all with its clarts and mud squelch. I'm still scanning the floor in case I spot them fucking pills. Eyes flick over dirty great skid marks. Fuck me, it looks like a scene from Apocalypse Now. That one with the helicopters and the Playboy bunnies. A desolate shithole even the Vietcong don't even bother visiting. There are no Playboy bunnies here though. Just plastic coats and plastic cloaks. Faces obscured with hoods and rain, some with sunglasses, reconfigured to run on low light settings. Low energy mode.

There's a smattering of people packing up their tents, wrestling with tent poles and wind wafting fabric into their frustrated faces. I feel that man, I feel that every fucking day to be fair. But, I feel a big fucking sense of paranoia, no, a sadness at the impending end. I want to scream at them: 'Don't leave! It's not over yet!' like a child at his own birthday party, the guests all leaving before the cake, before the songs, and the party bags. Maybe that was me? That kid. Is that a memory? I don't think so, but can't be for sure. Paranoia man, it's really not over yet, still a good fifteen or so hours left of this ride.

Look ahead at mud-soaked legs trudging towards the main arena, filthy limbs drawn to a religious gathering. Or reluctant souls heading to the gallows. Which one am I? Over the left-hand side of us are the wellness fields, tents browning with rain and weather. No one is heading there; too far gone I reckon. I know I am for sure. We walk in a line, three in attack. As we have for much of the weekend. Me in the middle, leading the attack. Swigging beer, it might finally be starting to have an effect, a small one, a low digit on the Richter scale, but I definitely feel the easing of limbs. Couldn't get drunk before, and believe me I tried. Mixing grape and grain, spirits and mixers. Finally lumping for a little something stronger. Bumped a big fat line to get my engine going, just little dregs left in the bag now for gum rubbing later on. Two young lasses walk past heading back towards the camping area in the opposite direction. They look clean. A smell hits me, fruity and floral. The smell of the pink soap you get in public toilets. The one you have to press hard to get any out, congealed around the nib. Great blobs discharged onto a dirty basin. A smell not normally associated with lust, but today my testosterone seems to be ignited at a mere whiff of such a thing, brain in survival mode, thoughts drift to public toilet sex, doggy styling over a disabled toilet. Blue lights hiding pulsing pumping veins of our genitals. Filling tight fannies up with litres of spunk. Fucking hell, keep it together. The lack of ejaculation for so many days is fucking with my chemistry. One more day. Pornhub will wait. The smell lingers in the moist air long after the lasses have disappeared and I'm aware of my own stench. The filthy look and seedy stench of it all. My arse crack is in dire need of steeping, probably best with Domestos. Could use some of that for my thoughts today too. Pathetic specimen.

'Woah!' squeaks Jasmine, as she grabs my forearm and jerks me into the present moment. My footing lost on the mud with her momentum, she manages to stop her fall, and pulls herself upright, shoulder pulled hard. She utters a, 'thanks,' as her eyes meet mine.

'Your shoes have seen better days', I nod, as her ankles meet brown. A dimpled smile back. God, she's lush man. Despite having the same cleaning routine this weekend, she still looks fresh. Her hair's combed back, wet look. There are a few splats of mud on her shins and she's still sticking with them trainers, despite them being more mud than shoe now. Fair fucks to her. Stubborn lass, great.

*

We hit the food vendor's walk, that all familiar smell of spices not enough to evoke hunger in me. Not enough to tempt me to force some goodness into me. My stomach is only capable of suffering liquids now. My chemistry rewired. The staff are all dancing less enthusiastically than they were the other day. Volume turned right down low on their respective tracks now, or maybe my ears have numbed. Either way, generators pumping shite into the air are the dominant noise now. The great droning chorus of pistons. Half the menus are not available. Not that it matters anyway like. We bear left down to the Colosseum bowl of The Main Stage area, ancient oaks looking like judgemental invigilators in a school exam. Arms folded, watching. Their thirst has been quenched and they look darker and angrier than the previous days. The dance music artist duo Awesome Wells are on the stage pumping out some high energy synths. Beeps and horns. Enthusing the crowd to put hands in the air for 'our last tune, the one that made us big. Let's dance FestiFell.' It looks like a fascist rally, or a peace march depending on your persuasion. Squeezing every last ounce of energy out of the crowd. A baying mob ready to be entertained one last night. We go again.

Sunday

Seb

High grey clouds float over me in the direction of home. I've just received a WhatsApp from Mia, a photo of her, Reuben and Emily in bed. Fresh pyjamas and brushed hair. Pouts and smiles. The caption, 'see you tomorrow, Daddy.' It nearly breaks my heart. I miss them so much, and I miss the me I am when I'm with them. I reply with an outstretched selfie of a soggy me, Uncle Shaun and Jasmine pulling daft faces. 'Love from FestiFell.' Taken earlier by that #Love sign. Just before I bought that packet of cigarettes. I knew I'd succumb to both things eventually. Replace my phone in my front pocket and look around, the roadies set up the stage for one last time.

    Take a deep breath in and turn to look at the faces all around me, thousands of people all with their own story, their own experiences this weekend. Wonder what they all do, where they all come from, and what kind of people they are. Who are they? Linger on that thought as I finger out a cigarette from a packet and let it hang limp in my lips, as I used to do when I was younger to look cool. Often chatting dumbly with it wedged in my mouth unlit for a while to affect my look and personality. Think searching for an identity has always been something I've struggled with. Look at the fella behind and raise my eyebrows in mystery as I pat search myself for a lighter.

    'Here mate,' he holds a flame for me as I suck and get the end glowing strong.

    'Cheers man,' muffled speech, as the tab flicks up and down.

'No worries,' he has the face of a kid who called the English teacher 'Mam' by mistake once and never lived it down since. Just a little bit suspicious. Nicotine and tobacco hit me in the good parts, feel the feelgood.

The stage appears like a spider's form under this light. Framed with speakers, it looks as though it's on its hind legs, angry. Emanating a red and orange light. Ready to spit venom at its prey. An orange glow engulfs the cloud. One mass inhaling in anticipation for the finale. Vibrating with cold and nerves. Steam emitting from the skin of the great arachnid. The soundcheck sounds like a great boulder rolling down a glacial valley, rumbling and moaning. Unstoppable.

Sunday
Shaun

'It's not going to happen... work, I mean,' she hastily corrects in my ear, as the floodlights swoop across the stage and up into the crowd, 'not that you're not great, I just need to clear it up, in case you wondered.' The words, or rather their meaning yet to be absorbed as I focus on the lights and imagine them to be great birds of prey, or even dragons tear arsing about the place chucking great columns of fire about. Totally at their mercy. Powerless to being incinerated, almost willing it to happen. Just to see.

'There's too much...' she continues, with a pause for drama or genuine search for words, I feel her eyes on the side of my head, '...noise,' she concludes. Is that the word she searched for? What the fuck does that mean? I wonder as the dragon does another swoop of the field. I sense the need to respond.

'I get it,' I find myself saying, 'don't worry, it's all good.' Breaking my gaze from the lights, switching to her eyes instead to appear fully engaged in the conversation that is unfolding. I don't get it, but want to move it all along. By engaging, I begin absorbing the words and find myself stifling a hammer blow in my solar plexus. Had plenty of real ones of them off bouncers in the past, a firm hand in the chest. A physical 'fuck off', 'you're not getting in', and 'you've had enough'. I suppose that's no different from what she is saying like. Prettiest bouncer I've ever been battered by. I'm concerned with what my face is doing, don't want it to betray me, giving away a hint of emotion. I used to be a terrible blusher, flushing red with embarrassment. Grassing myself up for my sins with a reflex, and quite often grassing myself up for things I wasn't even guilty of. My eyes watering is another one. Unintentional and unrelated reflexes. My emotions are usually buried too deep to manifest on the surface.

'Sorry, I'm just a bit fucked up at the minute. Too fucked up for... anything,' and she smiles, shamefaced, 'not that I think you want, or don't want that,' she's fumbling. Another hammer blow to the chest, fucking hell she is beautiful. I nod and simply mouth, 'It's okay,' with barely a whisper, reassuringly. More concerned about her own uneasiness than my own emotion, of which I'm yet to digest. I'll package and bury it later. The anxiety from a semi grown up interaction subsides the moment the stage lights beam. A distraction by bright light. It's not the dragon's breath. Maybe it's the resistance, the counterattack lighting up the battlefield. Prepare for crossfire. The light reveals a chrome drum kit emblazoned with the logo for The Red Eyes. They downlight the curves and metallic parts of the Epiphone Wilshire and adjacent Gibson ES335. A glowing thing of beauty, its ebony body highly polished, a curved Goddess. The Fender bass stands erect in a holder poking into sight just beyond the Gibson's slender shoulders. - *So you wanna be a rock superstar...* - begins pounding over the PA system. A bit of red meat for the crowd courtesy of the sound tech getting everyone pumped for the arrival. Bloated and pickled faces in full voice again. The closing act almost due to begin. There's a collective shuffling. People vying for a better view, necks stretched to spot the first glimpse of the band taking to stage. Tracing the faces at stage side for familiar features. Cigarettes and spliffs are being lit. Heads are bobbing and craning with more purpose now, a nervous energy envelopes the crowd, me included. Muscles twitch and stretch. Cramps ignored. Kisses and gropes come to a slurping finale; strings of saliva stretch as flushed faces pull away. Conversations abruptly end. Hopefully, that's the beginning and end of mine and Jasmine's conversation too. Was never one for that feeling stuff anyway.

The intro song thrashes vigorously, riling up the mob - *Don't trust nobody gotta look over your shoulder constantly* - I turn and see Jasmine's eyes on me again, she pulls an 'I'm sorry' face, wracked with guilt. Or pity more like. Mouthing the words eyes widened, brows arch upwards. The way a young child does when they've been caught eating biscuits and they know they're in the shite.

'It's okay,' I repeat, annoying myself, and a bit frustrated at her persistence. Move on. I don't like things lingered upon. Focus, so the eyes don't gloss, the nearby weed smoke could set them off. She leans towards me with arms as wide as the clamouring crowd around us will allow and I accept. Or rather don't fight against it. Never been a massive hugger, always felt awkward receiving and providing them. We embrace, her hair smells of coconut, the dry shampoo she's been liberally applying all weekend, fumigating our tent out. The smell of our psychoactive sex the other day, a long time ago now. A trace of woodsmoke, from our candid conversations. I rub her back, almost a bit too aggressively, the dampness in her garments hasn't gone yet. She fits my arms so well, or maybe not, they're just arms. After the angry grunts of power chords surging along - *so you wanna be a rock superstar* - nearly at the crescendo moment, we unlock. She leans in and kisses me on the cheek, gentle. Tender. Feels more intimate than Friday night almost. I feel my stubble on her lips, but the gentleness leaves a tingling sensation long after her head has turned to the stage. I resist the urge to scratch or to wipe. Let the trace of moisture evaporate into the atmosphere. Crescendo is reached on the PA system and the four members of The Red Eyes take to the stage. Strobe lights and smoke machine. As the kiss tingle vaporises, I feel myself smiling at what's about to come. Excitement. The guitarists both fiddle with the tuning of their instruments despite the roadies' efforts. A familiar sight of the weekend. I acknowledge the humour to myself. An internal smile.

Suddenly, they launch into a stabbing chord cascade down fretboards amidst a cacophony of metallic drums hammering. Gravelly vocals with echo follow, grunted down the microphone, black eyeballs piercing the crowd. - *Raindrop sodden April skies, living fast how young we die, making up for the time we've missed, let's stay young, let's get pissed* - The final line receiving a rapturous sing back of all scales from the crowd. Piercing cold metal guitar chords and headache feedback shaking the audience into a rippling roar of cheers and sky salutations.

- *This is the life, the life we love* - Repeated. Each repetition with more venom and snarl. A sarcastic statement at the futility of everything? - *This is the life, the life we love* - Growled and spewed into the microphone, stage side screens show spittle and dust from the singer's mouth, backlit by the low lighting of the stage. He's hunched over it looking possessed. His guitar hanging like an albatross, pendulum like swinging, strings awaiting their next attack. He looks pained. Crowd sings back in repeat. Jasmine sings back. I look up to the skies and the fuzzy dance of the last of the raindrops as the clouds halt. A ceasefire for now. A patch of yellow punctures the darkening blue sky. Night is descending for the final time as a full moon breaks through the angry looking cloud and works with the stage floodlights to reveal the survivors of the weekend. I look back at the stage glowing with electric energy. Singing back myself with a semi sneer - *This is the life, the life we love* -

Sunday
Seb

The sounds swirl and penetrate deep. A cigarette sucked and blown from my lungs, the nicotine soothing my cells. Right now, there's a slow, steady bass-drum. Nothing more. Bashing like the football against the redbrick wall when we played as kids. Mortar crumbles. Drainpipe is unseated. Goal. Goal. Goal. Thump. Thump. Goal. A single high note from a guitar punctures the scene, sustained and ethereal. The tone hinting at an old indie championship tune, onto the dance floors of my youth, thick with drink and basking in strobe light. The whole world is a playground. Thump. Thump. It steps down, ringing into the night, shattering and lifting high into the air. It heads east with the clouds back to where home is, dying before it hits the forests and farms, which separate me from my family. Drummer hits a jangly bell, just once, waits, then again. Like the buoy in the sea where Mia and me watched the sun rise, on that balcony. A new dawn. Weary clanging from far away. Warning the anglers of rocks. Goal. Goal. Goal. Bass now joins the party. Flowing and bounding, a heartbeat on a screen. Life. Life. Life. Life. It continues in this steady rhythm for some time, building up anticipation. But in no hurry to move on. Keyboard builds up an ascent in sound, growing and stretching. Mind darts between scenes of my life, vignettes of youth. Faces drift and fade. A rim shot, the sound of a walking stick propping up the shadow of what I used to know. The bell is struck louder. The church bell clangs of a funeral. A glassy ting of a champagne toast. Punchy guitar takes over, fuzzy chords rich in treble, bass now with plucked string confidence. I recognise it now, the track I heard over and over on 6 Music, back when I had the house to myself. Pace and pitch changes. A throaty punky voice full of strength. The past turns to present. Digital arpeggios. The set passes by in a frenzied frenetic blur.

Sunday
Jasmine

'This one is our last one. That's your lot. Thank you. And goodnight Lochtdale!' the gorgeous singer declares, before hurling a water bottle into the crowd. A wild clamour, as if it was an aid package for a war-torn village cut off from anywhere. He sweeps his sweaty hair back, then launches into a high fretboard stab of chiselled notes which slice clinically through a collective euphoria. Amplifiers wheeze out their last effort, the rabble notch to a louder volume. Primal screams of approval. A clamour forward. A demand to hear it a microsecond sooner than the person behind you. We're in the centre of the crowd, it's like the epicentre of an earthquake.

'Come on!' yells Seb, beaming as the stage lights lift, like searchlights frantically searching for a convict, or over a train wreck. Cigarette decorating his lips, he launches his wet arms over my shoulder, it feels heavy and uncomfortable, sunburn pricking jolts of pain. He lights the cigarette hanging from his mouth. He bought a pack before, and didn't even complain about the price. He's draped over Shaun on the left of him. Vibrating with excitement, a child meeting Santa. Eyes bedewed with smoke and emotion. A mass sing-along ensues, the singer mouthing silently over the lyrics sung in an array of keys. The reception welcomed by the frontman. A great pride painted on his face, displayed in great brightness on the stage side screens. A laugh, a knowing look to his colleagues. They've made it. Bass guitar simply one note, feel it in my feet all the way up into the hollow bit of my chest. Bass drum duelling with lead and rhythm guitar. Three deadly animals fighting to the death. Stinging and stabbing, biting and thrashing over each other.

Urged on by constant chug of the bass guitar. Swooping and clawing. Distorted lead guitar. All whilst the thousands in the crowd chant them on. Clapping. Focused on the kill.

Something inside me explodes, and I feel a great urge to jump. Propel myself with Seb's shoulder into the air. Previously aching calves find new energy. They feel light and loose as I dig deep and trawl for whatever is left. I leap, aiming to go higher and higher. Pogoing as the bass drums and hi-hats shatter the night. The whip crack tones of the guitars seem to get louder and louder. An urgency. The collective energy of this great ocean I am surrounded by ratchets and builds. I feel free. Enlightened. Stage lights pulse every four plucks of the bass guitar's top string. Chugging along, a level crossing. Lights flashing. Barriers of red and white. Danger. The singer has one foot on the monitor just off centre, suited arm is stretched out towards the crowd. Microphone pointed horizontally. Willing it on. He's grinning. Obviously enjoying himself. Who wouldn't? Feeling godlike, I bet. Lapping up the love. Hearing songs he penned in a bedsit as a student chanted back at him by total strangers. Repeated with total devotion. A thousand voices and a thousand different meanings are derived. All relevant. All real. My arms are in the air, totally undeterred and uncaring about the previously sniffed smell coming from my pits. No one has fared lightly today. Faces around me are all content. Some eyes are closed, absorbing every last bit of this final song. The encore. The last song on this stage for the weekend. For the year really. The peak perhaps. Or the great celebratory return to base camp, depending on how you look at it. The sight of home on the horizon more like.

The singer pulls back the microphone, whipping it close to his sky bound face, and yells the final - *forever* - lingering on the 'errrrrr' like a tenor. Holding that tone, for what seems like an eternity, the screens on either side showing his face screwing more and more pained as he holds onto the note for dear life. Oxygen depleted from burning lungs, a throaty whistle until there is no more to give. But, still, he finds more, moving up an octave as the crowd collapses in applause and wild celebration. Claps merge with the crashes and cracks of guitars seeing in the home straight. Bass still chugging the single note. My heartbeat synced with the bass. Our heartbeat.

Singer whips the microphone away, near suffocation, he turns to his musicians. Over to them now. He grabs a towel from a speaker stack and wipes his face. An overhead slow clap to acknowledge the audience and he's now positioned on stage right, slurping down from a paper cup. The lead and rhythm guitarists now stood in the singer's earlier place facing one another. The song's not over. The guitar brawl is just getting started. The bass note changes. Higher. More positive. Then another note. An ascension. The cacophonous echo of sound retreats. A pause in melody. Just drum and bass. The guitar's filthy distorted noise has been replaced. A cleaner tone. Optimistic. Rhythm playing three simple chords. Progression. Echo and wah decay into the night. The lead guitar plays a single note. Surely the highest the fretboard can go. A Stratocaster. Even I know that. Shaun will know the particulars. Note disappears again. As quickly as it came. Hi-hats. Teasing. The band in no rush here. There's time to build up to the finale. A tantric act. Singer gestures his microphone, like a conductor addressing an orchestra. Rhythm chords.

One.

Two.

Three.

Repeat. For a second it takes me to a place of good sex. Slow, confident, teasing. More about anticipation than anything. Building up good to the crescendo. Taking everyone with you. Bass ups a note again. The bassist's right foot tapping. His body draped over his instrument in comfort. Stage lights get brighter. Pulsing with every 8th hi-hat strike. Lead guitar drops down the fretboard. Up a bit, then back down. Undulating. The terrain they're taking us on is uphill, like that mountain to our backs. Three rhythmic notes repeat again and again. One. Two. Three. Bass up again. Still pounding in my chest. Heart rate increasing. My pulse points in my stretched neck tight like a drum skin. Bass kick increasing. Good sex. I'm present. Someone nearby screams, 'This is it!' and I understand what they mean. They're premature, but I know what they mean. I feel myself going uphill. The band goes for another round. Leaving us on the edge. Fretboard and bass up. One. Two. Three. Crash of the metallic drums then all but the bass decay into silence.

Silence, but for the bass.

A more deafening sound than what it replaced. Thud, thud, thud of the bass. Thud, thud, thud of my chest. Far louder and more arrogant now it's on its own, the bassist's foot still tapping. Hair long and lank on the big screens. Wrists surely aching with each snap, each aggressive pluck of the strings. Only willed on by the collective climactic anticipation. We're on the edge, in the moment, but on a different plane entirely. Just waiting for the crescendo. The great climax. Thud, thud, thud. Then the bassist slips his fingers to the top of the fretboard plucking a startling eardrum busting tone. Shocking us again into the present.

'One, two, three, four!' the singer rejoins his comrades and drums crash back in alongside the uplifting rhythm guitar rappelling down the fretboard. Abseiling tones, cascading chords. Evocative. They sound beautiful. Streaks of electric blue and magpie green. At this moment, this very second, I'm taken to a waterfall I went to as a kid on a family holiday. Sun catching the spray, projecting infinite rainbows in the foreground of moss lined granite. A cove both terrifying and peaceful. The ever-present sound of water hitting water. Happiness.

The lead guitar and bass both synchronise timing and tone. One great awesome descent of sound. Skiing on fresh powder snow down a Swiss mountain. Abseiling at speed down El Capitan into the evergreens. Skydiving. Tombstoning. Deep sea diving. Beauty everywhere. Memories I've never had. The sound gets amplified, louder with each cascade, in itself building to another climax. Hands are aloft and expressions to the sky, a collective inhale and exhale. Piercing warm tones wrapping its sonic embrace around everyone. The survivors of the weekend. This is our reward. Yellow light glows ever brighter, blurring everything in view. My eyes feel damp, like the spongy moss that clung to the granite at that childhood waterfall. Like the mud that is stamped beneath our collective feet. Like the River Oz not far from here swelling and churning peaty foam into swirls.

The sequence of chords ever loudening feels like the most beautiful I've ever heard. Like hearing 'The Lark Ascending' that time in the back of my family car, a child strapped tight into a car seat, as teary eyed back then as I am now. The smell of disinfectant and iodine still raw in my nose. Papa navigating speed bumps, with hearse like care, driving out of the hospital grounds. Classic FM turned down low, his hand resting on my mamma's knee. A silent acknowledgment of love, and loss. Gears screaming as we reached 30, reluctant to change, in order to preserve the physical bond to my mamma. Her head tilted outside, watching the buildings and trees disappear. Curly hair resting on the steamed-up glass. Change of gear, a lower note from the engine, then the hand returning to her knee. Her hand then rests on top of him. Wishing to share the pain through osmosis. The slowing stutter of sniffs.

The violin swooping, lifting with air pockets urged on by the horn section. A shaft of sun in the sky breaks through the grey clouds, light poking through the rear window. My child naivety and primary school frames of reference, thinking this was a window to heaven accepting Nonna's soul, the light her caring touch from the afterlife telling me everything is going to be okay. All whilst the lark soared on.

The screaming sound of something like a gunshot. Several gunshots. Panic. Colour. Blues, yellows, greens, reds. We all look to the sky. Oaks are lit once more with a different light. The crescendo. Fireworks split the darkened sky with hallucinatory beauty, mythical creatures, and great majestic supernovas have us looking away from the stage of falsetto and major chord progressions. Euphoric sounds and sights surround us. Blue, silver, gold. Louder and louder, until there is no distinguishing between the drums and the gunpowder explosions. Gunshot becomes artillery fire. A salvo in the sky, as the guitar reaches as high as it can go, a tone so positive it hints melancholy, for everything else is a step down. The sky is a kaleidoscope of colour, a synthetic aurora borealis. The time between bangs blurs, as flash and spray of colour pepper above our heads. Then, they begin to subside. And the guitar tones begin to work their way back down the fretboard. The lark is beginning its descent. The intensity subsides, the flashes and bangs less spectacular. Then, the last embers fall from a height and disappear out of view behind the great stage. The night has won the battle and returns to the black drape hiding us from tomorrow. The stage pulses a permanent white light onto the crowd and the sound of the band decays into one of white noise, as guitars are slung against amps. Performers stand alongside one another in centre stage, their silhouetted stances backlit by the stage lighting. They steam with sweat as they absorb the adoration and energy from the crowd. Bowing once. Bowing twice. Bowing three times. Ascending cheers from the wide mouths of those before them. Then, they exit stage left, and as they do, the white noise volume slides down the notches, fading in to Vera Lynn - *We'll meet again, don't know where don't know when* - over the PA system. Illuminated, the crowd shuffles at a reluctant pace away from the stage, leaving behind cups and dirt. Grins appear on passers-by. They disperse into the night talking of what they have just seen. Crescendo over. It feels like the orgasm I longed for on Friday night finally came.

Sunday
Shaun

A fuck off great feeling of finality. That feeling you get when it's bedtime at the end of the six weeks holiday at school. Screaming 'I don't wanna go to bed' into a pillow. I feel like screaming that now. I probably will before the night is done. That set was something else like. Felt proper emotional watching it. Those fireworks were immense inall. Not usually something I'm bowled over by, but then again, I'm vulnerable at this stage of the weekend. The crowd stood blind-sided by the end. The big stage lights shine onto the swamp that used to be the grass of The Main Stage area. It's now a brown sludge pit full of plastic cups and cans. Nobody moves initially. Waiting for some guidance. Needing someone to take their hand or to tell them what to do next. We begin the reluctant trudge. Slop, slap, squelch of footsteps in the soup.

'What now?' someone asks.

'I don't know. There's a few things going on after this. The Dance Tent and whatnot.' I say, hopefully.

'Nah, I think I'm done. Don't have the stamina for that place,' Seb concedes, his face looking morbid with the shadows cast by the stage's unforgiving light, another cigarette glowing in his mouth. He's picked up some headphones he's seen in the mud down where some abandoned camp chairs are, they flash blue and red in his hand. They're emitting a tinny faint rattle of - *I am, everyday people* - they'll probably be from the silent disco.

'I might just head back to the tent, see if I can get rid of these. You never know I might get a deposit for them.'

'We could maybe go there?'

'Nah man, I'm done, got driving to do tomorrow, don't want to kill us all,' he grins tiredly. I'm wounded at this, picturing raving until the wee hours, squeezing the night for all it's worth. Putting off tomorrow, forever. Hitting up places we haven't even got around to doing yet. Meeting people we haven't chatted shit with yet. Might meet the future love of my life. You never know. As if. I guess the poor bastard's got to drive us back tomorrow morning, so I'm not going to push him too hard.

'What about you?' I ask Jasmine, who herself is yawning and making faces.

'I don't know.' But, as fate would have it, I hear the familiar drawl of Aurora getting louder through the thinning crowd around us.

'I thought it was you guys. How epic was that?' she enthuses. Jasmine stops screwing her face in a show of fatigue and replaces it with a face of excitement.

'Was amazing, wasn't it?'

'Aye, was class like,' I say, trying to maintain enthusiasm. Hoping for something other than the end.

'Where you guys headed?' she asks, looking at each one of us, as if hoping for a great strategy.

'Seb's going to bed, the poor bubba,' I spit, thinking fuck you Seb, an elephant never forgets. One back at you.

'Aw, shame,' she protrudes her bottom lip, then continues, 'What about you guys?'

'I was thinking The Dance Tent,' I say, hopeful of someone taking the hook.

'I think I've had enough of that,' Aurora states, 'Last night was intense, I need something a bit less full on.'

'Yeah, me too to be honest,' Jasmine echoes. Fucking great. Here's me getting stonewalled.

'Jas, there's a ladies night in one of the tents up near that Hut on the Hill. Proper girly stuff apparently. You want to check it out? That's if it's okay with you Shaun?' Aurora is leaning towards her. Fucking great, totally frozen out here.

'By all means,' I say, reluctantly.

'Fuck it, go on then,' she giggles. Can't blame the lass wanting to leave sleepy Seb and fucked up me in favour of some girl time.

'Great! Sorry boys. It's one of them safe space tents.' Aurora is revelling in this, I reckon. Jasmine on the other hand looks uncomfortable and rueful about leaving us.

'Get yourself there,' I offer, not wanting any bad feeling.

'Enjoy girls,' Seb pips up from his half-closed eyes and a glowing cigarette protruding out his face. Fucker can't help himself on those at the minute.

'Get some sleep, Seb,' Jasmine says concerned, 'Have a good night whatever you's do though.' Then they're away again, linking arms, off to have a night that will undoubtedly be far more exciting than mine.

'You coming back or you staying out?' Seb yawns.

'I'll stay out for a bit, find some mischief.'

'Be careful,' he's got his concerned voice on.

'I will. Goodnight bro.'

'Goodnight.' We bump fists, then I turn and walk off in a randomly picked direction. The opposite of where the girls went.

I'm walking along the perimeter, where people smoke the last of their drugs and the weekend lovers finger each other away from the eyes of parents or partners. There are some lads standing with steaming plates of food under one of the diesel generator perimeter spotlights. As I pass them, I see huge Yorkshire puddings piled high with mash, gravy and sausages. The waft of Bisto is immense. They have the right idea. As I pass them, I see the pointed top of one of the smaller dance tents poking through the trees. I recognise the bassline that's shaking the chain-link fence next to me immediately. I pick up my pace, that's where I want to be.

I get there with no major slippages. It must be the 12" version of Frankie Knuckles' 'Your Love' because it's only halfway through by the time I wrestle into the middle of the tent. Rafters rattle each time the bass plays. Proper bassline that like. The tent's a blue number, small with hundreds of mirror balls on the ceiling and lava lamps behind the bar. Cool as fuck looking. To think we haven't even been here yet. The folk in here look fucked, probably look like I do. It's half full. I'm lead footed in my dancing. It's laboured. All arms and no legs. I spot a lassie in front of me smiling. She looks lush, proper girlfriend material, all nice teeth and cheekbones. Dancing in her own little world, smiling to herself. I try and catch her gaze - *I need your love* - It's meant to be, surely. - *I need your love* - That would show Jasmine. - *I need your love* - She sees my leering and dances further away, closer to the bar. It's not meant to be. Stood in the middle of the dance floor and it hits me, the total awareness of my own loneliness. The song fades into something I don't recognise. I try to muster some more moves to it, but I fail. I head to the bar. Staff look fucked off and ready for the end.

'Pint please.' She's Asian looking, delicate face, and small. Gets to work pouring my drink. Mutters the price, but I can't hear over the sound system. Hold aloft my card and tap it onto the contactless.

Declined.

She nods towards it to try again.

Declined.

I try and put the card in. Put my PIN number in. Pickled brain doubting if it's right.

Declined.

Ah fuck, this was always the fear. I've spunked it all away. Was fucking inevitable this like. She sort of huffs and takes the drink back and puts it on the back bar for the next fucker to buy. Shoulders shrug and I flush in my cheeks. What day's it today? Sunday? Got to survive till Friday with fuck all. Not helping my mood. Bollocks to this. This is no fun. I head back out into the cold rain and stand for a moment. Letting the drops run down my face. The tent is the final destination now. I walk slowly, solemnly. Looking hopeful at each face that passes, probably looking like a dog, hoping someone wants to play or feed me a fucking biscuit. What I really need is a cuddle and stroke. I walk back past The Main Stage, and see the army of litter pickers already getting to work clearing away all the shit that's been dumped. Scan the floor for money or those fucking missing pills. I walk up past the food vendors and see the half price signs. I bank towards Checkpoint Charlie now entirely deserted, no need for any security anymore what with the main bars closing in an hour. I walk beyond it and look over the horizon, wiping rain from my eyes. Trace the endless silhouettes of tents twitching in the rain. Then look to the VIP teepees like war graves on the horizon, fuck them and their proper beds, with proper shitters, fruit platters, and bottled water. Fits eight to a room. Fuck their cleanliness and their money and their ambition. Fuck them. We're all in this together? Don't make me laugh. I stand there feeling totally defeated, for an age just watching the thinning faces flit past me. Finally, I turn back and head towards our tent, piss soaked through. I'm hoping Seb is still awake, just for one more drink together.

Sunday
Seb

I'm peering through the little transparent plastic screen of The Green Goblin, droplets cry down, the walkway diesel generators whirr powering spotlights that reveal the remainers. The base camp survivors all hunkered down; the great hurrah is cut short. No niceties, pleasantries, or Class-As, Bs, or Cs shared tonight. No philosophical knitting circles or enthusiastic world changing conversations. No campfire smoke on mildew chairs. No idle chatter and shared swigs from a bottle of scotch. Survival is the order tonight. Batten down the hatches under lantern light and muster some sleep. There's driving to be done tomorrow, reality to be faced. I must accept the inalienable truth that it is all over. The great arrow of time has won. Monday approaches, save for a small window for sleep, a hundred miles of road, and likely a service station sobering. The weekend is done. My stamina is depleted, even if I wanted to venture back into the rainy evening, my body aches and groans with inflammation. Eyes sting with tiredness. I'm done.

The mud-covered headphones I found, then failed to return, pick up a hint of signal as the battering wind changes direction. They must be from the silent disco. Yet another place we never even went to. Read about it on the lanyard. - *There is a light that never goes out* - appears, then disappears just as quick. The indie channel favoured over the dance anthems. Somewhere, through the hedgerows that develop their infant fruit. Beyond the mighty oaks' rugged shadows, under green and red uplighters are a few final souls, some of the last men and women remaining are expending the last calories of the weekend, spending the last of their energy dancing in the silent disco. Flanked by tree silhouettes backlit by moonlight, they're determined to squeeze every last bit of juice. Maybe one final pair of eyes meet another, to share the final indie tracks and a tongue kiss before accepting the inevitability of it all and retreating to sleep. Maybe one final spliff is lit to 'Fool's Gold' and shared between friends. One last pair of tired arms point to the ceiling of The Dance Tent as - *You got the love I need to see me through* - hits its peak accompanied by a heartfelt chorus from the crowd. Strobe lights cease and the music fades into silence. Floodlights drown the crowds, urging them to the exits. Headsets returned, deposits returned, and the decks are switched off with a static buzz and pop one final time. LED red glow fades to black. Much as our parents discovered in the 80s, we do indeed fade to grey. We slump into sleeping bags, rustling for a comfy pose, fingers drawing the fabric to our chin to keep the ghosts and ghouls from getting in. We hope, eventually succumbing to some semblance of unconsciousness. As my head violently snaps left and right, I try to find softness for my skull, headache approaching. Dreaming of being in the arms of my wife. Cradled. I hear the endless raindrops as well as a thousand voices nearby. Every single one sounds younger and far more at ease than me. They're all having more fun than me; far more sex than me and earning more money than me. None of them have to worry about driving tomorrow, the prospect of a final job meeting this week, and the freight train of responsibility approaching over the horizon. None of them share the fear of when and where to dry this bloody tent, the cleaning of it, the folding it away, and getting it into the loft without setting my neck. Bassy notes of male voices, treble of the females. They all sound like they're on Thursday's vibes, have I been short-changed? Frantically retracing my steps mentally, like a stag do bank statement. Surely that can't be right? Something is amiss. Something's wrong, a scam. Something doesn't add up. Someone has taken more than they should have done.

Anxiety steps in, and voices get louder. I hear the ominous snatch of an argument from nearby, an unfamiliar female voice says: 'I saw you dancing with her!' accusingly, the male defendant replies 'I didn't know she was only 16', a scoff is batted back. I try and tune out. I'm surrounded by vice. I reach into my pocket and grab my phone. Battery save mode, the screen duller than usual, I rest my eyes and my mind on the photograph of my family and focus my thoughts on how lucky I am. How much love I feel and how real it all is. Then, the zip of the tent goes, one of them is back. Headphones play - *That's how it starts, we go back to your house, you check the charts, and try to figure it out -*

Sunday
Jasmine

- Woah, I never meant to brag. But I got him where I want him now - The teenage angst in me screaming out, like one of those camping kettles I've heard all weekend. Aurora and me channelling our inner emos as we thrash our hairs to the songs in this tent. It's full of girls seeing out the festival in style. No lads allowed. It feels good. No risk of being touched up when passing through the crowd. My throat growing hoarse with the back-to-back sing-along tunes. For old times' sake, we're clutching JD and Cokes, hoping it doesn't keep me awake when I'm laid up on that dreadful airbed later. Emo turns indie, turns to rock. Glasses drain from 'Welcome to the Black Parade' to 'The Chain' then get filled up again. Money leaves.

'This is the last song, ladies, thank you and goodnight,' the pink bobbed DJ declares, before setting 'Love on Top' by Beyoncé. This is going to be loud. The place erupts. Fifty pairs of arms lift up and fifty voices work their way through the pitch changes. *- You're the one that I love, you're the one I need -* Screeched into the night. It can surely be heard all around. I surely won't be able to speak tomorrow. Then, silence. Ears ringing. Exits are made.

We head back towards the campsite linking arms again, to stop one another from slipping in the mud bath that has replaced the grassy walkways. The rain is not relenting, my hair is soaked again. I'm less precious about the whole thing now realising that, once you're saturated, you can't get any wetter. We slip, but stay upright as we head past a bank of food stalls, some of them already in darkness, sold out of bao buns or teriyaki tofu. Stop for a micro rest as the walking is taking its toll on Aurora's legs, pulled muscles from the uphill walking. Propped up outside the fish and chips stall, which is still going strong, the yellow light looks warm and dry. I see a man and his daughter thank the vendor and bid them a, 'Goodnight, love,' as they gawp in anticipation of the greasy nighttime treat. A wholesome scene of parent and child. There's a faint recognition of the man who smiles with pride, as he hands his teenage daughter a tray of steaming chips. She utters a, 'Thanks Dad,' then I realise it's that awful bloke from the crowd yesterday. That sexist drunk pig. 'You're welcome, Love,' he says, pure love and adoration in his eyes. I feel sick.

'Let's go now,' I urge. We set off again, my heart feeling the pressure again. I don't want him to see me, and I don't want to see him. We continue on for another ten minutes or so. Next, resting under the big green uplit tree where we all met last night. The surrounds are now eerily quiet. I begin to wonder how much of it is Aurora needing a rest, and how much of it is her wanting to prolong the inevitable end. She's got an early start planned, something I very much doubt will happen based on how late it is now. Under the tree are two young lovers embracing. Teenage dreams who met the one. Perhaps during The Arcadians gig on Friday night and have been inseparable ever since. Black hair with grease and rain, blackened eyes with tears. He strokes her face and squeezes her waist. Both flooded with adolescent hormones and fantasy perceptions of love. They hoped tonight would never end, but their parents are expecting them back, they've texted several times. A tent and a camper van beckon, separated by families and campsites. 'I'll call you,' and 'I'll miss you,' uttered along with, 'no-one-gets-me-like-you-do,' spoken in melancholic hush between bad breath kisses and protracted eye gazing. They'll learn it's not so simple soon enough. We set off again, another ten minute burst and we'll be back in our own tents.

Sunday
Seb

Why is it that you feel tired all day, then the moment you try to get to sleep you can't? You have a stupid burst of energy that gets your brain whirring away. It's as if my body is trolling me, knowing I've got a big journey to do. Shaun and I have been lying in our respective pods laughing into our hands over stupid stories and memories from times we've shared together. Brutal honesty about what we thought of ex-girlfriends or minor grievances from times too long ago to offend anymore. The several sheets of polyester between us like a confession booth. The time of the night and the therapist's chair pose urging on honesty.

'I was always jealous of how you dealt with Mam's passing,' he said, after a gap where I thought he might have fallen asleep, 'you always seemed to keep it together, dealt with it really well.'

'I haven't dealt with it yet, that's why,' I say. The silence continues. I try and conjure a picture of her face, all of us together. The four of us. Panicking that all my mind's eye pictures of her are from photographs. Struggle now to remember what her voice sounded like. 'I miss her every day though.'

Sunday
Shaun

'It's been good craic this weekend though, hasn't it?' I ask.

'Aye,' comes Seb's sleepy voice. I look at my fingers closely under the dull light. All wrinkly with moisture. Like Sunday bath day fingers. Would eat soap once in a while, as a bairn, to make myself sick so I could get a Monday off from school. Spend the day snuggled up with my mam on the sofa watching shit telly.

'Jasmine is canny like, she's good company.'

'She really is.'

A pause.

'Never get easier these festivals, do they?' Seb says with a croaky voice.

'They really don't like.'

'We survived though.'

'Just.'

Sunday
Jasmine

'I might see you tomorrow morning. Depending on when we get up.'

'Maybe babe, got my alarm set early doors ready to go.'

'Well, if I don't catch you, goodbye I guess?'

'It's been epic, Hun,' she says. We're stood facing one another unsure of what to say, 'Nice to meet you.' Aurora then outstretches her arms, I oblige and hug her in a soggy embrace. I'm never good with goodbyes and this is no different. Always expect some Hollywood ending which never comes.

'Goodnight,' she says, as we part and then she crouches towards the zip of her tent.

'Goodnight,' I say, turning to my own.

Once inside, I hear a melodious whisper coming from Shaun's tent, it stops and asks 'Jasmine?'

'Hi, sorry if I woke you.'

'No, no, we're just chatting.'

'You guys okay?' I whisper, as I strive to get into my pod and out of these wet clothes. Struggling with the arms and the neck of my top, stuck to my skin with moisture. I'm glad they're still awake. The noise I'm making sure to wake anyone nearby. After much effort, I finally get them off and slip into whatever dry clothing I find in my bag. It's cold now.

'You good?' I hear Seb asking groggily, after the commotion subsides. Sounding like a man who is already ninety-five percent asleep.

'I'm good.'

'How was ladies' night?' Shaun asks. His own voice weak and muffled by his airbed.

'Decent yeah, plenty of pissed up women singing to Beyoncé.'

'Sounds great,' the voices that return sounding wearier with every passing minute. The rain on the tent drumming them towards slumber.

'Guys?' I ask.

'Yeah?'

'Thank you for having me, it's been great. I think I really needed this.'

'Thanks for coming. It's been a hoot.'

'It really has.'

'Same again next year?' a voice croaks, but only a stifled laugh replies. The rain continues its onslaught. My weary mind moves from retracing the memories of the weekend to strange abstract images as sleep descends.

Jordan McMahon

Monday

Monday
Jasmine

Monday morning desolation. Crows crabbing at the morning dew, pale grass on the horizon blanketed with the cool northerly air of a distant autumn approaching. Brown scorches of ex-tent pitches pepper the barren litter strewn land, like a crime scene. Imposing grey clouds high in the atmosphere, keeping their distance from the incident. Bin bags piled like corpses inside the galvanized gate fencing. A black slag heap, evidence of the weekend's vice. A flurry of bleary-eyed survivors stood over various stages of deconstructed polyester and fibreglass poles. A refrain of zippers and 'Have you seen?'. The spirit of the air flags on the horizon by the chain link fence, colours seem faded, sun bleached, then washed out by the relentless rains. They still whip mist into the air with every south-westerly gust that approaches. The ever-present percussion of the long drop toilet doors, snare drumming awake anyone still unconscious. Like the back of a TV set, some things are too ugly to be on general view.

    A crushed can of a beverage one of us didn't finish, caked in the clay clarts is underfoot, clinging to my boot like a limpet, begging to be taken away. I kick it several times away, until it yields somersaulting towards a yellow patch of grass gasping for sunlight, water, and rest. Parched where our own temporary neighbours lived for a time. Aurora as good as her promise, aiming for an early getaway, has succeeded in her mission. Packing up and leaving no trace before we dragged our sorry corpses out of bed. I feel ashamed of my own lack of motivation to get out of this place. I picture her in the warm orange glow of a service station coffee bar now, coffee steam exfoliating her flawless skin, croissant on a little square of serviette watching the commuters rush back and forth unaware of the life outside of their bubble. She takes a slow sip of her drink, both hands clutched around the paper cup she asked for, absorbing the heat into her palms. Sky News showing atrocities and disasters behind her, as her eyes fix on a child having a tantrum over a magazine they're not allowed outside of WHSmith, parents' minds rifle through mental archives of parenting books they read back in the days when he kicked her spine in utero, on how to deal with this correctly.

The air here feels moist, dew drops are settled on the polyester and on the grass. There's a murmur, an unenthusiastic hushed chatter amongst the leavers. They're resigned to the inevitability of the return of reality, work beckons. Responsibility. Routine. Even real ale man and his wife have vacated the scene, leaving nothing but a yellow bristle footprint where their tent once stood.

Across the way some bucket hatted lads in tracksuits are sitting in circular slouch of a camping chair council meeting, they're holding aloft the last of their Carling cans refusing to accept reality, one last grasp at the dying embers of a feeling. Flogging a dead horse perhaps. Arterial mud trails meet a great racecourse of churned up muck heading towards the exit. It reminds me of Aintree after the Grand National, grandstands empty except for the ghostly shouts fading away, radiating into a distant memory. The mud cultivated by a hundred thousand trips back and forth over the weekend, cigarette ash, spilt alcohol, sweat, and chips, now forever part of the landscape, where in a matter of weeks sheep will roam, chewing up and shitting all over whatever grass shoots manage to establish themselves in this far from bucolic scene.

I look around at the Oxfam appeal around me, a far cry from the optimism of Thursday morning. Humans doing what they do best, consuming, destroying then moving on. We are the survivors. Then, I think of William, poor bastard. His family still soaking Kleenex with tears and snot, screaming and choking as wave after wave of realisation hit them that this isn't some awful dream, but indeed their little boy, their little cheeky chap is lying in a morgue as cold and grey as the peak of Bowman Crag. As I look up to the great imposing summit, I pause. Now for our own climb down, just a few hours of energy needed. Pack, drive, survive. Project and propel myself towards the safety of my flat, cocoon myself behind a locked door cradling my own fur babies the cats. Bed beckons me.

Monday

Shaun

What the fuck have I done to deserve this? Every movement crouched in this stuffy claustrophobic tent makes me feel like I'm going to hurl. Stomach acid sure to burn through, like a chest burster from Alien any time now. Eyes sting with tiredness, sleep was awful. A string of disturbing dreams bookmarked with flipping and thrashing in my sleeping bag, I woke myself up whimpering at one point. Awful. The rain made me paranoid, my dreams soundtracked with an incessant drumming. Doom laden drone. The voices swirling around all sounded the same. Yorkshire drawl. 'Yalriiiit?' Zip, zip, zip. Most of the sounds in my head I'd bet.

My guts are pinching like a vice, but there's no way I'm going up them steel steps of hell today, no way am I going to face the reek. Fuck that for a laugh. That'll finish me off, I'll just drop dead there and then. Breathing my terminal breath face down in a puddle of piss and wet wipes. Another life claimed in these fields. Peace at last maybe. I gather together a few Lucozade bottles that I know for definite contain my midnight piss from the last couple of nights, my shame hurts as I chuck them deep into the bottom of a black bin bag, ensuring the lids are firmly screwed on. Can't have them two seeing that. I already feel disgusting. - *This is the life we love* - Someone is singing nearby, fucking with me. I hear gas bottles hiss and sausages spit fat nearby, all knotting my stomach and I could hurl right here and now in this bin bag, not for the first time this weekend. There's nothing of any substance in my body, I know. Try your best. Sit upright, and take a moment to compose. Bowie has fallen silent for the first time in five days. The crumpet girls and their neighbours must have vacated the site, off to peddle their scran elsewhere.

I pause for a further moment, poke my head outside, and take great gulps of fresh air. I notice real ale fella has packed and fucked off. No doubt devastating the toilet bowl of an otherwise respectable establishment right now, I see him lecturing the fuck out of whoever will listen to him, stroking that beard of his, as he reels off band after band and new beer after new beer he tried. All 'Mark my words, these guys are going to be huge.' I quickly remember that he's nothing like the character I'd built up in my head. He was sound actually. I see Aurora's tent has also gone, free spiriting herself away early to avoid traffic and set off on her next daddy funded jaunt no doubt. Jasmine is making a pile of packed up stuff, her movements slow and deliberate. She looks a far cry from the serpent like dancer of previous nights. Her elbows pronounced as she pauses with hands on hips. Deep exhales as she looks around sadly, staring at the furry heap of her leopard print coat looking more like a dead animal than it probably did when it was a dead animal. Seb is in his tent pod with a dustpan and brush. His rucksack packed and cast outside. Sleeping mat is rolled up and taped with a hefty amount of duct tape. The dustpan is filling up quickly as he rhythmically sweeps away.

'Can I get that after you?' I ask.

'Aye,' he replies, without stopping his sweeping. Pale skin and greying beard are noticeable this morning. I shove a few wet garments into my rucksack, ignoring the blatant brown staining some of my best T-shirts have received, and the further staining that this'll no doubt give my remaining clothes. A few more Lucozade bottles and a decimated lanyard almost entirely returned to its pulpy state are chucked in the bin bag, then I begin shoving my belongings outside. Without speaking Jasmine automatically picks it up and arranges it with the heap. I roll my sleeping mat up and grab the duct tape by the soles of Seb's shoes in the tent's communal area. Soles matted with ingrained mud and grass. I tear a strip and notice how loud it is as I rip it. Tinnitus amplified today. I feel as though I can still hear music, but truthfully, I cannot know for definite. I no longer distinguish sound clearly, there's just a constant 120 bpm. Unaware whether it's music or my syrupy blood pressure. Next is the sleeping bag I roll up, telling myself to, but simultaneously knowing, I'll never air it out. Imagining the awful particles that'll remain in there till the next time I go camping. Could be years now. If at all. Unless gas prices and rent keep going up, in which case I'll need it for when I'm begging for change on Northumberland Street. Might have to do that this week now I've got fuck all money left until Friday. Stuffed into its bag, I rest as my arms recover and the nausea returns, surveying the remnants on the groundsheet in my pod. Amazed I can create so much mess in such a small space of time, jealous of my brother and his tidy ways. Then again, I see the stress mess causes him and find myself lucky I don't have his standards. Bits of cardboard and paper squashed under the sleeping mat, Seb has finished brushing and plonked the pan and brush next to the duct tape. I recover enough to lean again and start brushing, soggy paper mattes in the bristles, dried grass flicks. Crumbs from vegan sausage sandwiches that I've long since shat out. I do long arm reaches and fight the feeling of a cramp that might occur. The sooner this is done the better. I sweep copper coins and a safety pin. I spot the top of a plastic bag poking out of a fold in the groundsheet. Shuffling over on aching kneecaps I finger it out and brush it into the pan. Then it registers.

'Fucking hell, no way?!' I bellow with whatever voice I've got left. A moment of elation. I laugh a hysteric laugh. No one reacts.

'Look at this! I've fucking found it!' I encourage. Seb turns from unhooking his pod from the frame.

'What?'

'The pills man, I've found the little bastards!'

'Really?' he swivels and leans in, two brothers leaning side by side gawping at the little plastic bag. In it, there sits three high strength DHL embossed ecstasy pills. Nestled neatly in a groundsheet fold of Seb's kids' sleeping quarters.

'You spawny bastard,' whispers Seb in total relief. A hidden worry drained from him. I grab the bag and stuff it into the jeans pocket that they have lived in before. A massive wave of relief hits me, and I begin laughing nervously.

'I can't believe that man,' I say, fingers feeling that they're still in their home for the next few hours. My reenergised brain now considering whether I'll be sampling their delights. The Loop testing service is now closed. Would I risk death? Could maybe sell them on, so I can buy bread, eggs, and milk.

Monday
Jasmine

'I can't get over that like...' Shaun repeats, relief on his face as he stuffs a small baggy into his jeans pocket. Seb silent, a subtle shake of the head and a look of mild amusement. The tent lays limp before them, folded in half then half again. Grass cuttings and mud patches cling to the groundsheet. Desperate to leave with us. A 'That'll fucking do,' from the brothers. A fruitless attempt to expel air from the folded tent, bulging frog throat pouch. It's folded and stuffed into the carrier bag it came in, zip never likely to be closed on its bloated shape. With it are folded the flakes of Wednesday's burger buns, the ash from the campfire chat on Thursday, mud, blood, and secretions that I dare not think about now. Folded away are intimate conversations, expressions of emotions, and crippling comedowns. Folded away are creases of laughter, moisture from our sweating bodies, and from the relentless rains. The air particles still harnessing the moisture of yesterday's washout, of the beer and cider and god knows what else we drank this weekend. The grooves of the groundsheet canyons of cocaine, ecstasy, and cannabis molecules, laced with impurities no doubt. Folded away are the dodgy sleeps, earwigging conversations of our temporary neighbours, the wrapping a hoody around your head to drown out the earth-shattering snoring of an unknown sleeper. Scrunched up anticipation and expectation, hopes of entertainment and surprise, of meeting those like us and those who show us what we could be.

The end of my summer? Looks like the end of the world if these scenes are to go by. Certainly, of an earlier life of mine, I hope. These moments always lend to a certain level of hyperbole. But nevertheless, a big fat permanent marker scratch underneath a certain era of my life. We are survivors, in a way. I waft away a drowsy wasp, attracted by the sugary cider soaked into the ground. It's clumsy, blissfully unaware of the inevitability of autumn on the horizon, of its demise. It disappears from me, and goes to bother someone else. Butane blurs from blue hobs, spindly arms whip out from underneath canvas grabbing morning coffee. Strong coffee. Two scoops. Using up the last of the stash. Monday, the day no one wanted to come, or rather have to deal with. Now it's here. Besides the footprint of where Aurora's tent was is a time capsule, a tent vacated on Friday by some young lads, as Aurora mentioned yesterday, who were bullied off the campsite by the presence of some intimidating blokes who came to have a cheap laugh. A relic of a previous stage of the weekend.

A great pile is ever growing beside the long drops, spilling way beyond the designated area. A jagged praying mantis pose of camping chairs, some broken, some not, some repairable without doubt. A great heap of supermarket two person tents £34.99 with a valid loyalty card, available in an array of three colours. Produced on the other side of the planet by some poor bastard, shipped on great container ships across great oceans, and left to rot here in Lochtdale. A half-arsed lie spread about charities picking them up and re-using them. Black bin bags full of cans, bottles, crisp wrappers, and kebab packets. Slug like sleeping bags strewn over rusted fire pits, collapsed gazebos, and bent trolleys. Mountains of pre-loved disposable shite, a great funeral pyre of bric-a-brac people are too tired or hungover to lug back to their cars. Not enough space to store nicely in their homes. The interiors of their SUVs, saloons, and hatchbacks too fucking precious and clean to spoil with this filth. Wellies, disposable barbecues, and cardboard. So much cardboard. This is just the stuff people could be bothered to move to the aptly named 'Recycling' area. No doubt a litany of cast away apparel awaits green tabard volunteers too kind or impoverished, too desperate for a ticket, or too desperate to try and secure a future to turn their heads and look the other way. Unaware of the scruffiness, laziness, and selfishness that engulfs humanity. The 'Not my problem' attitude preventing those from dealing with their own shite. Those strapped with bags and rolled up mats are heading for the exits, leaving behind the destruction they've caused, they seem alien to the ones I danced and sang alongside a few hours ago. Fucking Monday.

Monday
Seb

The baggage seems lighter than when we arrived. Weight distributed more fairly on the way back. I guess food and beer was the main bulk of the weight. Arms still struggle with it, cramps arriving at malnourished and abused muscles. Too determined to get home to stop and rest. The car park is now disjointed with great gaps and skid marks ripping up patches of the field. Reminds me of a drinking man's teeth towards the end of his life. I hope I'm not going to get stuck. I'm yet to use the cheaper breakdown cover I lumped for on my Direct Debit day. Hoping I'd never have to witness first hand why it only got a 2-star rating on the comparison website. The boot is packed with haste, far from the textbook Tetris I crave, but I let it slide, bugger it, I'm too tired. We've been just shoving and chucking bags and boxes in. All wanting to get on the road. Shaun's in the front seat, Jasmine's sprawled in the back dodging muddy limbs of camping gear. The radio is on low, just enough to break the silence. Radio 2. Easy listening. Traffic announcements and friendly patter from callers. The news repeats what I read this morning. Blowers directed to the windscreen, stopping it from steaming up again. Our bodies leaking out fumes of drink and drugs. It'll need a Romanian valeting after all this. The queue out of here is long, weaving down through a farmer's gate and down a farmer's track. A queue I doubt very much anyone is too happy about being in. Message Mia to tell her we're setting off now.

*

'Anyone need to stop?' I ask, as the signs for the services show they're two miles away.

'I'm alright,' Shaun says, looking out of the window, his hand clinging to the little handle on the ceiling above the passenger door. I can smell him, then again it might be me. It's not fresh. I look in the rear-view mirror after Jasmine fails to respond to see her knocking out the z's in the back seat, mouth hanging open, a streak of mud across her forehead. A faint movement in her jaw shows she's still breathing. She looks just like one of the bairns when we've been on a long road trip. 'She's akip.' I tell Shaun. He just nods. Out of the corner of my eye, I spot the brown lump of a dead deer by the side of the road. I'm glad she hasn't seen that.

The service station comes and goes without us stopping there. I could do with a little break, but history teaches me the contrast between the festival and the real world is jutting and disturbing in a service station. You become aware of your own bad hygiene, your muddied clothes, and your total mental separation from reality when you're stood by men in suits taking business calls and ordering lattes, when all you can do is look at the baked goods and feel tears welling up because they look so beautiful. Get PTSD flashbacks when the fruit machines and kids' grabber claw machines flash and light up. Transported back to ecstasy fuelled bliss from a few nights back. Feel now like an alien who has landed on earth, wondering what on earth everyone is doing and how they are operating, forgetting that not everyone is in the midst of a brutal hangover and comedown trip.

The road surface changes to a newly laid stretch. It is smooth. The volume decreases and the key changes to a lower note. I'm only driving 60mph. Radio 2 becomes the dominant sound again. Feel the weight of my own eyelids, the sluggishness of my own reactions. The radio plays a familiar harmonica sound. My brain takes a few seconds to register it as The Hollies - *The road is long, with many a winding turn, that leads...* - I switch it over to some generic modern pop station. Get greeted with some standard issue female pop star. That'll do. The Hollies song is too raw. I wonder whether Shaun feels the same. As if some divine being has put that song on, right here and now, when we're driving home. A song Dad used to listen to all the time. One of his favourites. Him and Mam would dance to it when he'd had a few pints at weddings or work dos, requesting it especially. A song about brotherly love. I do love him. I love him. I reach over and squeeze his knee. A silent acknowledgement of his being, our bond. I love him. This road is long.

*

Shaun is the first I drop off, his street looking darker, grimmer, and more depressing today than on Wednesday. Maybe because of the glum weather. Maybe because there is now more furniture littering the pavement. Neighbours having a huge clear out. A bin now lying on its side.

'Cheers man,' he says at the car window, 'Nice to meet you, Jasmine,' he says.

'I'll see you soon. I'll message you,' I say. Jasmine smiling and gesturing with still hand at the window as I reverse. The sound of a bin being lifted and dragged towards his flat. The sound of a reverse gear whining.

There is little to no conversation as I head to Jasmine's house. She is still in the back of the car just looking out the window, it now takes on a bit of a taxi driver dynamic. I'm half expecting her to ask if I've been busy. But she looks too tired to muster any form of humour. The red brick of her street looks darker with moisture, the shops and businesses are full of people getting their hair cut, buying newspapers, chocolate bars, and vegetables. Doing life. It is like when you get back from a holiday and are surprised when nothing has changed except weeds and grass have grown longer. Life continues. As I pull up outside hers there's a long drawn out 'Thanks.' Repeated twice or thrice as she prematurely released her seatbelt and gets to work grabbing her rucksack.

'I'll see you at work.'

'Aye, when I'm back. Have fun this week,' I apply the handbrake, unlock the back doors, and crane my neck into the back, her door already opened, hand gripping the handle.

'Ha, I'll try, good job I'm working from home tomorrow. There is a god after all.'

'See you later.'

'Bye. Good luck with that job chat,' she says. That's it, door slams. No grand monologues or great goodbyes. We part. All just individuals suffering in their own ways, in their own minds. I set off once more, turning the radio up several notches to drown out the silence. - *To call for hands of ablaze, to lean on, wouldn't be good enough for me no* -

Leave No Trace

Monday
Shaun

The air is stale as fuck in here. Can tell there's been no windows open, and it's been hot. That's the first thing I do. Pushing open all the ones that actually work. The air outside is cold now, but this place needs some air. The sound of life flooding the bleak room. The odd car here and there using the street as a turning place. A baby in a pram crying on. That bastard dog down the road. The flat's just as I left it. A heap. Cans adorn the coffee table. The reds and blues are the only colour in this soulless void. I drop my bags by the door. Key onto the coffee table and stand for a moment. Allow myself to reacclimatise. I feel empty. Two things I know for sure will occur. In what order I am unsure. The laptop over on the sofa is still plugged in, blue LED is still illuminated. Wonder how much that's cost me. That machine will provide the stimuli for both to happen. A wank and a cry. Done enough festivals to know this is how it goes. Not ready to indulge in either, just yet. Plenty of time for that. I pace the room. Paralysed by inaction. Check the fridge for inspiration. Both disappointed and relieved there's no peeve in there. Calculate there's enough stuff to sustain me till Friday, just. Look at the kettle. Boil it and then fail to pour myself a drink. Look out of the window. Nothing. Go for a piss. Flush. Inspect for a moment, then chuck the pills from my jeans pocket into the bathroom pedal bin. Back into the living room. Pick up the Fender Jaguar that's propped up between the wall and the sofa, and strike a few chords. Needs tuning. Put it down again. Promise to play it more again going forward, and learn some new songs. More recent ones. Maybe even write some. Lie on the sofa, and close my eyes. Hear the faint voices of Seb and Jasmine, the sound of zippers, the crack of cans, the ripple of rain, the squeak of a guitar amp, the beep of a contactless card, the hiss of an airbed. Roll over and hope for it to fade, so I can sleep and move on.

Monday
Jasmine

A new confidence descends as I switch on my phone, knowing whatever messages are waiting for me have not hurt me so far, so can't hurt me now. I head to the bathroom whilst it loads up. Keeping a ringing ear out for the message tone as I wash my face in the sink. Amazed at the water running out of taps. Appreciative over such a revelation. The water feels warm and comforting. I slowly massage the dirt away with liberal amounts of face wash. It stings, I'd forgotten all about the sunburn. It's hard to picture the heat from a few days ago. The softness of the towels as I dab away the dampness. I'll have a bath later to steep away the dirt on the rest of my body. I head back into my bedroom and pensively lean over my phone on the bed. No new messages. That is surprising. Check the signal. Still have 3 bars and 4G. Log in to Facebook, and see the FestiFell page has posted some photos. 'That's a wrap, folks.' Then a tick emoji. Underneath is a collage of the fireworks, a couple crowd shots, and some action shots of the headliners. Flick through. Look closely, and reverse pinch my fingers to zoom in on the crowd shot. A sea of smiles and bedraggled looking expressions. Scan to see if I can see us. Spend a while, but don't manage. Then there I see the bloke, the one I had a to-do with. The fish and chip wanker. His arms around his daughter at the second from the front row, looking full of happiness and glee. Shake my head and scoff. See I have two notifications. Click on. One about someone from school's birthday, one a friend request. Click on. Aurora Naylor.

Monday
Seb

The softness of the carpet is the first thing I notice. The comb lines in the cream pile show Mia has hoovered recently. Bless her, she knows how I am. The house is immaculate, toys all placed in their wicker baskets and the sofa cushions arranged how I like them. Kitchen benches show no crumbs from the morning toast, no stray oats on the hob, and no coffee rings on the kitchen table. She must have subdued the kids with telly and had a frantic ten-minute clean-up for me.

    I've dropped the bags in the hallway, shoes kicked off leaving a triangle of dried mud on the laminate. I'll get to that soon enough. I'm pacing around my house, feeling like an intruder in someone else's home. Almost tiptoeing, so as to not disturb anything. It is deadly silent, my ears giving off high pitched rings and only the ticking timer for the hot water is audible. Underfoot, the cream carpet feels exotic, and the cream walls and glass reflections of the family photos in the dining room almost sterile. I reach for the DAB radio on the oak dining room dresser and switch it on to break from the uncomfortable silence. The pulsing of my brain needs drowning out. BBC 6 Music comes on. I haven't switched this radio on for an age, CBeebies and screaming provide enough sound for one household. I had long since lost my way with music until this last weekend. I pace into the kitchen and fold a tea towel over the radiator, peer into the fridge with no intention of eating. A decomposable bag with my post fest food parcel inside, a yellow post-it reads 'Dad's'. I glance at the fridge magnets, digest the meal plan for the week. 'Takeaway' is written in blue Biro with a smiley face beside it. The thought will no doubt be one of great anticipation later, but not now. My stomach craves nothing.

I walk back into the dining room. It's playing an old song I used to love, one I've heard on this station a hundred times over the years, but its name evades me. It sounds different, maybe a remix, or perhaps my ears and brain have been rearranged by the weekend, by the constant bombardment, the drink, and the drugs. It feels like the time when I was struck down with COVID-19, senses suppressed. Wondering whether they will ever return. Willing it back, impatient at the fact time is needed for things to happen. Time today however is going slow. It has barely gone midday, plenty of time for a sleep and to sort out my bags. The tent and whatnot will be easy enough, I'll stow that away in the garage for another day. The clothes in the bag can get whacked into the wash on a hot one. Blast away the mud and scum from the weekend. Hopefully blast away the stains from the white tops. Mia has some special stuff for that. I wander back to grab the bags into the hallway, stopping at a professional photo of us all and smiling, the bairns full of milk teeth smiles and sweetie bribes. Mia and me looking proud at our lot. The image betrays the reality of a stressful Sunday afternoon, book ended with kids' groups and a trip to the walk-in centre. A split-second image captured for eternity failing to tell the whole story. I smile, then head back to the washing machine. Pouring out the contents of the bag, it feels damp, foisty, and smells so too. An earthy smell mixed with smoke and vinegar emanates and just for a second, I'm back around the campfire, the voices of Shaun and Jasmine as clear as if they were in this room right now. A pang of sadness that they're not with me in this moment of space and time now. Amongst the soiled clothes falls the mullet wig I bought on the Wednesday, a laugh which seems an expensive and unnecessary one now. It moults into my hand as I separate it from the rest of the washing. That will not be getting washed. A few spent glow sticks, a scrunched packet of cigarettes I procured at some point, and the ticket stub are the last to fall from the bag. Washing machine door closed and hot wash started, I head to the pedal bin and dispose of them. Knowing fine well this is their eventual destination be it today or in a decade. The wig is then cast onto the sofa to raise one final chuckle later when Mia and the bairns return before being boxed and forgotten for a time in the loft. If I've got the energy, I'll whip it on when I hear the key in the door in a few hours. Might even wear it for the food delivery that's due in the next few hours. A stroke of genius from past Seb to order me that.

The memory of a time before the kids is a tough one to dredge through the fatigued mind, I try and picture a time when I would potter around this house on a day off alone. I picture what my routine would be like, what I would eat. I recall feeling comfortable in my own company then, nowadays I feel as though I'm clock watching, waiting for the violent return of life with a wife or offspring spilling through the door to colour my life. How on earth did I occupy myself when the only person I was responsible for was me? I'd presumably have had a box set of something I'd watch. But all of our viewing is a shared one now, a bonding experience that is sacred. I have little desire to watch something alone, the experience would feel empty. 6 Music news plays, but I tune out as I wander around the house full of anxiety. I know sleep is on the agenda, but I feel I should be doing something. What would me from six years ago do? What killed time in that distant memory. The presenter on the radio is different from the one I remember, but then I must reconcile myself with the fact that I too am different. Time has elapsed and the man has changed. Six year ago me is dead. But what was six year ago me about? I head back into the kitchen to grab the dustpan and brush for the mud that's strewn in the entrance. Crouched over it my knees ache, and the lower back of mine feels tight, sore. That's what I'll do, I'll have a bath. Erase the dirt and scum off myself. Then slink into some comfy clothes and retire to my bed. I'll use Mia's bubbles and then dress in the pyjamas I got for my birthday. A few hours kip and I'll be right as rain, I convince myself as I dispose of the Lochtdale earth in the pedal bin and head upstairs. I turn on the tap of the en-suite bathroom and stand staring at the stubbly, tanned face in front of me. Pale patches where the sunglasses had been. Ears ringing, water battering the plastic tub, eyes stinging with tiredness and dehydration I feel the pinch of emotion hit me. The post festival blues, that I thought I'd grown out of, are in the post. The voices of the weekend warping around my brain, the hum of guitars and constant beat will disappear in time, decaying into the past like everything ever.

Tuesday & Beyond

Tuesday
Jasmine

The dawn chorus. I stand by the sun-streaked kitchen window observing the trees stretch and yawn in front of a wall of red brick. The sun hits from the horizon between garages and a gable end. I am fatigued, absolutely. My sleep last night consisted mainly of sweating, of bpm thump of skewed blood pressure in my ears, of non-existent voices chattering in a thousand polyester homes, bass ripping through the moist soil. Zippers cocooning revellers, yet I slept alone in my own bed, in silence, save for the occasional scratch or lick of a cat and a distant car alarm. Too tired to think, brain too wired and abused to sleep. I clutch my coffee and just stare, waiting. Waiting for the deluge of emails and WhatsApps and 'Have-you-got-a-minutes' and 'Sorry-to-bother-you' phone calls. The salmon swimming upstream cycle of today. Everyday. Monday to Friday.

I haven't put the radio on as per my usual routine, I need as much silence as possible today. A takeaway Thai, a bubble bath, two orgasms and five episodes of Fleabag (none of which my brain really registered) were my self-help last night. Before the embrace of a 12.5 tog duvet and Egyptian cotton.

I creak open the PVC back door, hinges always sounding worn and at risk of failure. A glance at the loudly ticking kitchen clock says I have five minutes of freedom left until I have to clock on for work. Calves feel tender from a weekend of bouncing and rocking. I head down the steel steps softly, to not disturb my downstairs neighbour, the hospitable Doris who has always urged me to make use of her little yard garden. 'Yarden,' she calls it. At the bottom of the metal steps, it reveals itself as a beautiful haven of green leaves and dainty flower heads. I shuffle over the patio flags towards the grass, it's long and in need of a cut. I'll endeavour to help the old lady going forward. Perhaps her encouragement to use her space is a hint. Something to add to the ever-growing list of mundanities that fills up spare time. Slithers of sunshine begin to emerge from the gaps in the fence panels and trellises onto my face. I take a sip of my coffee. Bitter and strong. Not how I like my men. I kick off my moccasin slippers. Feet bare against the damp grass. Prickle tickles the soles. I crunch my toes into the turf. Deep breath and eyes close. Colour pallet of oranges and reds through my eyelids.

 I exhale.

 Inhale.

 For a few final minutes, I am grounded. Crows in the neighbour's bird feeder squabble over crusts from breakfast toast. The gentlest of breezes ruffles the bamboo behind me.

 Breathe in.

 And out.

 Awareness of my heartbeat slowing despite the rush of caffeine in my bloodstream.

 Breathe in.

 Feel the sun's glorious rays, the 'big ball of bastard' on my upturned palm, on my upcurved smile. Scrunch the earth under my toes, the dampness on the soles of my feet.

 Breathe out.

 Eyes open, coffee slurp, cup upturned as the bitterness descends into me. Now it's time.

Seb

The tail end of a late September heatwave. A last-minute booking of a campsite not too far from Lochtdale, got a bargain. Finished work early on Friday and headed straight up. Car packed up ready. Tetris style, just like I like it. The Green Goblin tent erect once more. Kids are running in and out of it shooting one another with Nerf gun foamy bullets and stopping only to reload on crisps, dips, and Diet Coke.

'Careful,' we keep saying when they get within point blank range of shooting out one another's eyes. Mia is enjoying the last rays of the sun, making satisfied noises. Like an appreciative solar panel absorbing what might well be the last of the year's sun.

'Cheers,' I clink her glass as I pour my own drink, cab sav. My reward after successfully getting the barbecue running after a few failed attempts. Scrabbling around inside the tent for tongs, I get that smell in my nose. The petrichor. The faint reek of mud and a trace of stale alcohol. For just a moment I'm back in the fields. Imagine Shaun and Jasmine holed up in their pods, the pods now serving as hiding holes and bases for my darling offspring. I look up at the sky and see the greyscale march of clouds accumulating around the peaks of the fells.

'Looks like the weather's on the turn.' And before long, it turns. The rains wash down, cleaning the slate and granite. Washing away the footprints of the summer's boots, the wrappers of flapjacks that fuelled scramblers to the top, the fluff and shite of lambs long since slaughtered, and the soil between the roots of the diseased trees. Water turns white, as it gushes and falls over tufts of grasses and piles of stones. Tumbling down slopes, ready to be skimmed into the pools of next year. The last of the season's climbers rush to bothies and light fires, or dive into the orange glow of a tavern, if they manage to get down in time. Tent pegs lie lost and oxidising in emptying fields. Lakes and ponds fill up, as pleasure boats are tied up neatly into rows. We dive into the tent and watch the rain stifle out the barbecue.

'Everyone alright with crisps for tea tonight?' we laugh, as Mia begins setting up Junior Monopoly and I put new batteries in the hanging lantern.

Shaun

I'm having a few quiet ones with wor lass. We've been to her flat for a fajita night, then fancied a wander. There's nowt on the telly, so we thought we'd go round the houses. The smell of burning birch wood in the air as wood burners spew smoke through chimneys. Inside people's windows, life occurs with a cosy orange glow. Looks comfortable, and appealing.

'Fancy a pint?' she asks, so I oblige. I was out last night with Seb in town to see H.P. Milton. Was good craic actually, he was telling me about his new job and whatnot whilst I told him about Lucy. We got on to talking about FestiFell for a while and ended up googling it, because we couldn't remember the name of that rapper on the Saturday. Saw the lineup poster on Google Images, but the top story on the main page was about that lad that died. The dealer was arrested and is awaiting sentencing. His mugshot image is terrifying in the fact that it takes me right back to that Friday night in the tent. How thinly veiled euphoria and despair were that night. Next story is about that William. His coffin was carried by his dad, his brother, and his football coach. Apparently, he was a decent prospect at footy, was on the radar for a couple of clubs. Adored Carlisle United. 'Such a shame,' we agreed on the tragedy, not the football allegiance. Later on, he showed me a Facebook post of Jasmine, a Just Giving page for her to do Bowman Crag for some cancer charity, makes me think of Mam that. She's doing it in memory of her grandmother or something. She looks really good too, the outstretched selfie arm shows her scars fading away, barely visible without zooming. Fair fucking play to her like. I'm pleased she's going ahead with it. Didn't bother reading the story on the page, the heartfelt outpouring, but I slid Seb a tenner to donate on my behalf.

He had the car and I only had one. Didn't change anything, just stood further at the back and took in the class music. Been cutting down a lot on the peeve like, made a conscious effort to look after myself a bit better. Been trying to address them demons a bit, early days like. Even dragged myself out and did a few short runs around the streets, before it got too dark and cold. I've been telling Lucy about the first time I saw H.P. back at FestiFell. Told her about the pyro and the feel good. Tried to find some pictures on my phone, but it doesn't do it justice, some grainy pictures taken behind some tall fucker's head. I scrolled a few back and forth.

'Who's that?' she asked. Stopping on a photo of Seb, Jasmine and me stood next to some big #Love sign. Seb had sent it after the festival and said, 'Thanks for the 40th birthday gift brother, it's been immense x.'

'My brother and his mate,' I say.

'She's pretty,' she says. I remain silent. Her statement doesn't require a response. Keep scrolling through various vignettes of the weekend back in summer. There's not many taken, but the ones that are there are evocative. The trees are bare outside the pub windows, the wind whistles between the lead of the glass and Christmas lights that still hang from the pub guttering. For just for a minute though, I'm back in the fields.

'We could maybe do something like that?' she says. I smile and nod.

She heads off to the toilet. Leaving her own phone face up on the sticky wood table. It lights up with a message. I've got no interest in checking it though. There's trust between us. It's nice. I don't want to challenge that. It's only been a few months since I swiped right on her, but I get a good feeling about her. Makes me want to better myself. Her flat is warm and bright. Plenty cushions and plants to give it life. We talk. I feel I can open up with her. Tell her about my past, all of it, and discuss where I can see a future. Dare to dream. Proper stuff. She wants me to paint a picture for her sitting room, bought the canvas and the paints. 'In your own time.' she says. I'm building myself up to it.

The bartender is wiping down the bar, it's quiet in here, but then again, it's a Tuesday in January. I finish off the dregs of my pint. It's nearly time to head back to hers, we're in the deep end of a Netflix series. Nothing special, but it's alright. It's nice having someone to share it with. Over the speakers, I hear the jangle of a familiar riff. I tune in to it, a song that Seb and me saw at our first festival together. The one that started it all. Proper indie championship stuff. Gurn at the sign. Remember us with our arms around one another, younger versions of us, swaying in happiness to - *I've figured it out. I can see again.*

Leave No Trace

Printed in Great Britain
by Amazon